Praise for the Novels of Gabrielle Donnelly:

HOLY MOTHER

"A raucously promising debut, full of intensity and high jinks, humor, warmth, crossness and crudity."

—*Financial Times*

"Donnelly's plotting is skillful, her dialogue lively, and her way of airing large themes of belief and transcendence through the medium of comedy is quite exemplary. A considerable debut."

—*The Evening Standard*

FAULTY GROUND

"Written in an effortlessly beautiful style, with wit, subtlety and outstanding skill, *Faulty Ground* is a novel of ideas conveyed through humor and incident rather than didacticism."

—*The Sunday Times*

"[. . . A] compelling read . . ."

—*Literary Review*

ALL DONE WITH MIRRORS

". . . Donnelly has something to say, and she says it very well indeed—with just a drop of vinegar on her tongue."

—*Los Angeles Daily News*

"A sharp, well-written yarn for our times."

—*Time Out*

The Girl

in the

Photograph

Gabrielle Donnelly

B

BERKLEY BOOKS, NEW YORK

THE GIRL IN THE PHOTOGRAPH

A Berkley Book / published by arrangement with
the author

PRINTING HISTORY
G. P. Putnam's Sons edition / September 1998
Berkley trade paperback edition / November 1999

The Penguin Putnam Inc. World Wide Web site address is
http://www.penguinputnam.com

ISBN: 0-425-17058-6

BERKLEY ®
Berkley Books are published by The Berkley Publishing Group,
a division of Penguin Putnam Inc.,
375 Hudson Street,
New York, New York 10014
BERKLEY and the "B" design are trademarks
belonging to Penguin Putnam Inc.

PRINTED IN THE UNITED STATES OF AMERICA

10 9 8 7 6 5 4 3 2 1

For Owen Bjørnstad,
my husband and my friend

The Girl
in the
Photograph

Gabrielle Donnelly

Chapter One

It was raining when they buried Ignatius O'Riordan, fat drops pelting off the church roof and bouncing on Lake Michigan, the mist on its farther shore so woolly and white that a fanciful mourner might almost imagine it hid not midwestern American plains but the purple Irish mountains the dead man's ancestors had left a bare century before. One less fanciful would remember that those same ancestors had done the leaving in such a hurry that they had neglected even to tell their children which part of that country they had come from, or just who it had been, whether tenant farmers or fishermen, rebels, poets, or bank clerks, that they had left behind them there. No matter; Ignatius was with them this morning.

It was a good funeral, as the man deserved. The church was packed, smelling of damp wool and, faintly and comfortably, of liquor; outside, in the church hall, cases of wine, more liquor, and the latest generation of Agnelli's Catering Service stood dry and alert to help give the worthy soul his send-off from honest prosperity in this world to what would unquestionably be, for him, a better place yet.

Ignatius had died in his sleep, quite unexpectedly, at the age of seventy-three. A painless way to go, the best indeed, except that he had missed out on the sacrament he had still referred to as Extreme Unction, which would have disappointed but not alarmed him, since he trusted his God, and could not believe that He would be so treacherous as to take a man without at least a second's grace for repentance. Besides, the night he had died being the second Saturday of the month, he had been to confession only a few hours before; old Mrs. Garvey, indeed, had happened to kneel behind him while he was saying his penance, he looking well and handsome, as she repeatedly described to anyone who would listen, and she thinking even then that when that fine man's hour came, he would surely go straight to heaven.

"He wouldn't have had much chance to sin after that," Allegra had commented, rather doubtfully, to her brother Bob, at some time during the last few days.

"Unless," Bob had suggested, "he looked on Mrs. Garvey with lust before he left the church."

They had amused themselves for some time with inventing occasions of sin for their father's final evening on this earth.

Allegra stood now at the front of the church, tall, even between her two tall brothers, and uncharacteristically elegant in black wool, eyes quietly cast down, tranquil hands clasped lightly and in ladylike fashion. They were all of them, she thought, on stage today. Not on stage as she was accustomed to be at the comedy club, where she faced the audience, stretched, smiled, and sneezed as the fancy took her, and told jokes to amuse the living and the irreverent. No, today was a different form of theater, a drama old as the ages, sedate and somber, for which she had donned a costume and (lightly) made up her face; one in which, outside the church, she had spoken the words of a script as formalized—although unwritten—as those of the Mass Father Forde was now saying. Yes, so good of you to come. Yes, it was the best way to go. Yes, he was a good man, yes, so they do say I look like him, yes, we'll miss him, yes, so good of you to come.

"Lift up your hearts," said Father Forde.

"We have raised them up to the Lord," they responded.

Allegra was a performer, and knew without needing to turn her head what was happening in the crowded church behind her. A good turnout; well, in his quiet way, Dad had been a popular man. Huddled toward the back were Mrs. Garvey, Mrs. Baederdecker, Mrs.—what was her name? oh yes—Mrs. Donoghue, now shockingly frail old ladies whom Allegra still thought of as the vigorous matrons of her childhood: fierce, churchgoing wives and mothers they had been then, who had shaken their heads mournfully over the three little motherless O'Riordans, and every so often attempted to press their father to accept from them a casserole, a pie, a spinster cousin. Mrs. Hegarty, whose task it had been to fend them off, stood, fittingly, much farther up the church, although she had refused to join the family pew: Colette Hegarty, Dad's housekeeper since Allegra could remember, head held high but clutching surreptitiously at the arm of a daughter, her eyes more painfully rimmed with red than Allegra's own. A host of others, some of whom Allegra might, or then again might not, have remembered from childhood, women clutching handkerchiefs or prayer books, men with earnest, righteous faces, a couple of nuns from the convent, although none that Allegra remembered from the school.

Ron, her boss, was perched, incongruously, between an iron-jawed matron with a rosary, and a statue of the Sacred Heart. He looked younger than any adult had a right to, and his eyes darted curiously from pew to pew. He was very possibly the only non-Catholic in the congregation, and it was nice of him to come, since he had met Dad just twice. Still, he had insisted, saying that she needed support—"someone from the real world," was how he had put it—and she had been, as it turned out, more pleased to see him than she could have predicted. Ron was not only her boss but her second-oldest friend, and it was good to have a friend today.

"Let us give thanks to the Lord, our God," said Father Forde, his eyes heavy on his old friend Ignatius's coffin.

"It is right and fitting," they said.

There were just four of them in the family pew. Ignatius had been an only child, and one of Mother's two brothers had died young in the War: unusually for Catholics, the O'Riordans had only one uncle, one cousin. The uncle stood now nearest to the aisle, John Higgins, flown in for the inside of a day from his home in Los Angeles: he and Dad had always been close. Bob stood at the other end of the pew, as far away from John as possible: he hated John, as he now hated the Catholic Church. Still, Allegra could not but notice that he too was joining with the service, was mumbling the words of the liturgy—since, whatever happened, it seemed, the Mass never quite left you—with each bit the same tired familiarity as was John, who had not failed his Sunday duty in his life. Which could be amusing; but was more probably sad. Between herself and John stood Allegra's older brother, Declan, like herself unmarried, his face without expression, his mind Allegra could not imagine where. Declan and Allegra looked startlingly alike and were eighteen months apart in age. They wished each other well, but were effectively strangers, having for the last twenty years communicated more or less exclusively through Dad. She supposed that that was sad too.

It was time for Communion. John left the aisle to approach the altar, followed by Declan; Bob stared directly ahead, his brows drawn together in a frown. Strictly speaking, Allegra should stay in the pew with him. She had not been to Mass for many weeks, which made her officially a mortal sinner, and therefore disqualified from the sacrament; but she went today, nevertheless, leaving Bob alone and picking her way around the solid oak coffin—which Declan had chosen, for which she had forgiven him much—that held her father's earthly remains, to the tune of "Holy Spirit, Lord of Light," Dad's favorite hymn, which she would never again hear him hum in his bathroom, half unaware, in his growling tuneful baritone. On the way back to her seat, she passed Mary Margaret, her oldest friend, the only one remaining from childhood, who gave her arm a gentle squeeze, and for the first time since she had entered the church, she started to cry. Bob, still sitting in the pew, glared at her: the O'Riordan men did not approve of crying. She glared back through her tears, and poked him, spitefully, in the ribs.

It was Bob and she, comfortable once more in blue jeans and sweatshirts, who cleared the house the next day, busy Declan having already left town. As it turned out, there was not a great deal to clear. Ignatius had lived sparely, and there was little left in his austere, widower's house of more interest than the sentimental to his children, who were, besides, no longer children at all but adults, verging on middle age, with lives, and fully furnished homes, of their own. Before he went, Declan had claimed two chairs and a bookcase; Bob and his family could always use china, and Allegra would take a few mementos; the bulk of the massive, old-fashioned furniture would go to St. Vincent's. And that, beyond too-fast-fading memories, would be it. The end of the house where they had grown up. The end of Dad.

Allegra, wrapping in newspaper the gold-banded dinner plates that had been deemed too good for common, or indeed any, use, felt her eyes prick and overflow again, and scrubbed at them with the heel of her hand.

"If Dad knew," she said to Bob, busy himself about the knives and forks, "that you were actually going to use his good cutlery for eating, he would rise from the grave to die again."

Bob grunted, as Dad had. " 'I buy the best damn meat in the state,' " he said. " 'I don't need a fancy knife to slice it with.' "

They had always been able to make each other laugh: Bob, indeed, had been her first audience, and a tough crowd he had been, she often reminded him, on which to cut her professional teeth. Lois had told Allegra over the telephone that the night after Dad died, Bob had cried until dawn; but since he had stepped, alone, off the plane from New York, his eyes had been dry. Of how, or with whom, Declan had mourned, Allegra had no idea. Probably, Bob did not know she knew that he had cried: he seemed to have forgotten it himself, as he had forgotten that he had once been her baby brother, who, never knowing his mother, had crawled into Allegra's bed at night for fairy tales or comfort. He seemed, as Declan did too, to have forgotten many things, and to expect that she would do likewise. It was how they were, or maybe, how the priests had taught them, deep in their dark-desked colleges, they should be. And because they were two, and she just the one, and because they were men, and Irish men moreover, however complete their emigration; and because men's expectations, and Irish men's most of all, must be fulfilled, she obliged them. They were good men, her brothers, as their father had been; they would without question have crossed the continent had they recognized in it benefit to Allegra. Allegra sighed.

"I'm taking the blender," she said. "I think Mrs. Hegarty might have used it twice."

"For what? Puree of porterhouse?"

He had a point: it had a virginal air. "Maybe she should have it, you know. Mrs. Hegarty. She could make cakes for her grandchildren."

"You keep it." He frowned. The blender had been a birthday gift from Declan, who would neither notice, nor think to ask, what had become of it. But it was a family present, and in spite of it all, Bob still valued the family. "Keep it," he repeated.

As they left the kitchen, Allegra stopped, and looked, for the last time, in the little mirror that hung beside the door. She was not a vain woman, but she spent much time looking into the mirror, practicing routines, or simply talking to her own reflection. Ron described it as her favorite audience. Mary Margaret worried about the habit, having read in a magazine that it was a sign of loneliness. Allegra looked now for the last time, at herself at this age, herself in this north-facing dark light, reflected into the plain wood-framed glass, now, for the last time in Dad's kitchen, seeing the woman she had become from the girl she had been. Although not vain, she liked what she saw: a long-faced woman with high cheekbones and a prominent nose, watchful hazel eyes under straight dark brows. Allegra had never been a pretty girl, as M.M. had; but she was aware, and despite herself, was not displeased with the knowledge, that she was turning into not a bad-looking woman either. She was, as they all agreed, her father's daughter: and Dad had aged well.

"Your dad's dead," she told her reflection, which stared back at her, blankly, having not understood the clumsy syllables, or maybe, simply not heard them. So she repeated herself.

"Your dad," she said, "is dead."

It continued to stare. Apparently, it had decided that it no longer spoke English.

Allegra and her father had not been close, as widowers and daughters were popularly supposed to be; rather, he had appeared a little alarmed by her. He had not been a jocular man, and occasionally, while she was laughing with Bob, she had caught him studying her, covertly, as if she were of some alien, and slightly frightening, species. When he realized that sitting on a stool in a club telling jokes to strangers was not a youthful aberration, but how she proposed to

make her living in this world, he had looked at her narrowly from under that familiar brow and said nothing. Once, after she joined Ron at
the Cheshire Cat Club, he had come to watch her perform. Allegra,
for that evening alone, had excised from her act all mention of the
Church; and Ignatius had decided to assume that that performance
was typical.

Still, he had loved her, she knew, and she him: and now she would
never see him or hear him or talk to him again, not in this life, nor,
she was more or less sure, in any other. She frowned at her reflection,
which frowned back at her, acknowledging the sheer unfeasibility of
the notion. She had no father, no mother, and now, as of four and a
half weeks ago, no lover either. But no, she would not think of Nick.
Not now.

She ran to catch Bob up, and together they moved on through the
living room, so long abandoned by them that none but the faintest
echoes still lurked of the squabbling, laughing children who once had
played there. The master bedroom upstairs was a shell, as it had always been, a bare chamber, with a wide, hard bed Allegra had never
seen unmade, a sturdy crucifix above, and by the window, the mahogany closet with the flecked mirror inside the door, and the rows
of well-made suits which would be Bob's task, thank God, to sort and
dispose of. It had been many years since Ignatius had in any sense
more than the strictly technical inhabited this, his own most private
of rooms.

It was in the study where the ghost was. Ignatius's body, tall and
thin like all of theirs, upright if lately a touch stiff, still sat there,
above the ground, erect at the desk, his back not touching the heavy,
uncomfortable chair; his long head, the thick hair silver, as both hers
and Declan's were early beginning to be, still tilted to focus his spec-
tacles as he sifted through his papers. The top of the desk was unclut-
tered—only an old-fashioned fountain pen, a blotter, an inkwell at
the corner. On the right was the black telephone and leather address

book; on the left, *The Confessions of Saint Augustine*, well thumbed, and beside it, the silver-framed photograph of Mother, her hands folded neatly on her lap, her hair, which legend and dim memory had it, had been a glorious red, drained by the camera and pinned severely behind her ears, her eyes inscrutable. Mother had hated to have her photograph taken. The drawers on the left of the desk held the accounts of the Knights of Columbus, which Allegra would drop off with Father Forde on her way home; on the right were the neatly separated folders of bills and investments which would fall to Declan, the eldest, to sort. There would be no surprises there: Ignatius had kept his business affairs, as he had kept his conscience, in meticulous order.

Allegra sniffed as she opened the long drawer at the top of the desk, and scrabbled in her pocket for a still-usable tissue.

"Oh, for God's sake," said Bob, running an irritated hand through his own ingloriously orange curls.

Allegra cast him a sour look: Mary Margaret said, often, that both of Allegra's brothers should be painlessly, but fatally, shot.

"Shut up," she said. Then, "Oh, Bob, look."

The drawer she had opened was the holy drawer. The drawer that every Catholic household had, or used to have, of religious things past their use that still could not be thrown away, a tangle of broken rosary beads, cheap medals, ragged holy pictures with childish writing on their backs, dead palms from Palm Sundays long forgotten. Memories of a childhood vanished, a childhood, and a way of faith, that once, in a time she now imagined rather than remembered, had seemed inevitable.

Bob looked, and his lip curled. "Terrific," he said.

"Don't be a jerk," said Allegra.

"I'm not a jerk," he said. "I'm a mortal sinner, living in a hollow mockery of a marriage."

Bob's wife, Lois, had been married and divorced before she met

Bob: the Church had refused either to recognize their union, or to baptize their children.

"You're a jerk too," said Allegra. Because Bob was alive, and loved Lois, and she him, which was more than many had, more than she had herself or, as far as she knew, Declan either; and the sad, broken things in the drawer could harm no one. She rummaged through: it was faintly shocking how much there was that was familiar. "Look, here's the Saint Joseph I gave you for your confirmation, left all alone and abandoned—some grateful brother you are."

"Did he have a head when you gave him?" But he took the statue from her, and sorted through the drawer until he found its piously smiling top.

"Give it back. You're a mortal sinner."

Bob tilted his head, and simpered. "And, children," he said, "that same simple statue, which his sister had given him for the holy sacrament of confirmation, led him at last back to the arms of Mother Church." He held the two pieces together, hesitated, and replaced them, firmly, in the drawer.

"Declan should have the missal," he added, abruptly.

"Damn you."

Allegra had been hoping he would not notice the thick black book of their childhood, red-ribboned, its thin pages printed small, on the one side in Latin, on the other in the vernacular that had once been new, that now appeared even more outdated than the old dead tongue. If Declan still went to Mass, he would find the book of little practical use today. But Bob was right: his was the prior claim.

"I'm keeping the rest, though," she said.

"Why?"

"You know, you really are a jerk."

He shrugged, and returned to loading folders into a box. She shrugged back, imitating him to his disapproving rear view, and began to sweep the drawer's contents into a sack, her hand grabbing coverless pamphlets, thinly greening chains, amputated stumps of blue plastic beads. Toward the back of the drawer a gleam of light turned into a shiny, white-covered book which she had not seen or thought of for two decades, but now recognized as intimately as the hand which held it. Her child's prayer book, Dad's First Communion gift; yes, there was his neat writing inside. "To Allegra with love from Daddy—God bless you." When she left home it had never occurred to her to take it with her; poor Dad, she thought, with a pain all the more piercing that there was nothing she could now do about it, nor had she ever considered that that might have hurt him.

She honked at her nose—it was growing sore—and Bob sighed, loudly, in disgust. So she set aside without showing him the pretty, mother-of-pearl crucifix she had not seen before, as well as the few secular pieces that had found their way among the religious, the exercise book full of Declan's unformed writing, the three or four letters in faded ink and an unknown hand. At the very back of the drawer, under the crucifix, half jammed into a corner, was a rectangle of cardboard, a photograph. She pulled it out curiously. Since Ignatius had been an only child and her mother had died so young, the three of them had been brought up, almost, without family photographs.

"Oh!" she said then, before she could stop herself.

There among the tattered prayer books and smirking saints was a girl. An old-fashioned girl, in yellowed black-and-white, posed on a beach under a palm tree, a bold girl, robust, flaunting her curves in a two-piece bathing suit, her lips dark against her white teeth, her eyes slanted at the camera in a way both knowing and sweet.

"What?" said Bob.

"You'll never know, jerk," she said. Then thrust it at him. "Look. Look, who the hell do you suppose this is?"

Bob looked at the picture, whistled in a way that was older than the ages. "Probably better not to know," he said.

The O'Riordan men were capable of not wondering. Allegra was not. She retrieved the picture, so shocking in that holy company; turned it over; then squinted in disbelief at round young handwriting that she knew, almost, better than she knew her own.

"It's Mother," she said.

"Yeah," he said. "Right." In the O'Riordan family, they owned five photographs of Bob and Allegra's long-dead mother, one alone, two with Dad, and one each with Allegra and Declan. In not one was she smiling. Dad had said that she had hated to have her photograph taken.

"It is so," she said. "Look at the writing here. 'To darling Ted, with my love always, Theresa. Los Angeles, September 1949.' " Theresa O'Riordan, born Theresa Higgins. Theresa, written with the familiar bold capital T; Los Angeles, the sunny city of beach and palm trees that had been Theresa's home, that still was John's. "You see, it *is* Mother."

"Can't be." Bob took the photograph, looked, and looked again. "Hey, it is, you know, see, there's that mole on her cheek. Well, I'll be. Old Ma. *You* don't favor her, do you?"

"Go to hell." She took the picture, smiled at the girl, then frowned in puzzlement.

"I don't remember her looking like that," she said.

Bob grinned, almost snickered. "I guess you don't remember her wearing the bikini."

"I guess not, smartass." Allegra had been three when Theresa O'Riordan was knocked down and killed by a cab on Michigan Avenue, and for all her efforts, she could remember nothing but a kindly presence, large-handed, smelling of milk and, occasionally, of musky flowers. Dad had refused to talk about his dead wife: Allegra had long resigned herself to knowing her mother unknowable.

"She looks sexy," she said.

"Maybe she was," said Bob. Bob remembered even less of his mother than did Allegra.

"She wasn't sexy."

"Like you'd have known."

"I'd have known." She took back the unfamiliar photograph, turned it over, read again the inscription in the handwriting that was younger now than her own. September 1949; just one month before her parents' wedding day. "To darling Ted, with my love always."

"Who's Ted?" she said. "Darling Ted. I don't know a Ted."

Bob smirked again. "That's probably *really* better not to know. Look, I'm taking these pens and papers for the kids. God knows, we'll find a use for them."

Shot. M.M. was right. Allegra narrowed her eyes at her brother's skull, calculating at precisely which point beneath his clownish curls the bullet should go. Abruptly, she yawned, a sudden wave overtaking her of the fatigue that in the last few days had never been far away. She dropped the familiar silver-framed photograph into the bag, along with the lovely, laughing girl and the religious relics that had so long been her companions, and glanced out of the window, where the still-weeping sky barely hinted at black. There would be time for a glass of wine before she faced Father Forde: the priest was both deaf and garrulous.

"I thought he'd never stop," she said later, oh, very much later, to M.M., basking at last in the inexpressible comfort of her own small apartment, with whiskey in her glass beside her warmly lit armchair, while outside behind the bright curtain the rain beat unabated against the black windowpane. "I really thought he'd never stop. We had the Bishop. We had the Altar Guild. We had the Liturgy Commission.

And then at last, when I'm standing up to go—standing *up*, that is, as in vertical, and putting on my coat—he starts in on the Bears. The Bears. Dad liked the Bears. Bob likes the Bears. Do I look like I like the Bears?"

"How're you doing?" said M.M. "I mean, really."

"Me? How the hell should I know?" Allegra snorted, inhaled the lovely, smoky smell of her whiskey. "Ask me how the Bishop is, I'm an authority. I don't know, M.M., I'm tired." She closed her eyes and, undistracted for the first time by the merciful busyness of the last few days, tried to imagine a world without Dad. She could not; any more than, just four and a half weeks ago, she could have imagined the world without Nick. "You know what I keep thinking?" she said. "This is terrible, but. He sure picked his time, old Dad, didn't he?"

M.M. nodded. Allegra did not need to explain to her about Nick, because M.M. had been there from the start. As she had been with Mark before Nick, and Bruce before Mark, and Allegra could barely remember who before Bruce. And, happily married herself for fifteen years, had never offered one syllable of advice, for which Allegra knew she would go to heaven.

"Am I a terrible person?" said Allegra. "My father's dead, for God's sake, and all I can say is, Nice act, Dad, but your timing's off, let's try it again and get it right. Is that really terrible of me?"

"You do look tired." M.M. ignored the question, which, good convent girls both, they had been nervously asking each other for now a quarter-century or more. "Why don't you take some time off? You could use a break."

She blinked her mild blue eyes at Allegra in concern. M.M. had always worried about Allegra. When first they met, she had worried about her motherlessness; as life had worn on, about her continuing lack of husband and, most pitiful of all to tender M.M., of children too. Now, Allegra realized with a sigh of affectionate irritation, M.M. would be able to worry about her orphanhood.

"Thanks a lot," she said. "You mean I look a hundred years old. No, I know you don't. And I *am* having a break. Ron's given me time off."

Take time. It was what he had said when the telephone call—was it really only five days ago?—had come, quite serious for once, his small, strong hand steady on hers, his voice echoing tinnily, as voices did when the club was empty. You'll think you're OK, but you won't be, he had said. Take care of yourself, and take time. The club will still be here when you're better, and face it, sweetheart, you *won't* be feeling real amusing right now. Then he had bundled her back to his apartment, where his lover Mike had fed them vegetable soup and creamy sauced pasta, where both had hugged her and talked to her about bereavement, and after the first bottle of wine, Ron had told her some jokes about corpses which, before, she would have found in impossibly bad taste. Ron's sort knew about death, these terrible days.

"He's being really nice," she said. "Ron. He told me to take as much time as I need."

M.M. sniffed. "Is he giving you vacation pay?" she returned.

M.M. did not in the least care for Ron. She did not care for most of Allegra's adult friends, the ones she had met since she had moved to the city, who were such different creatures from sober M.M.: they were performers, like Allegra, fellow comics, musicians, actors—ragtag folk who worked by night and slept by day, who were capable of going, at times, for weeks without working at all. M.M., on the whole, did not either approve of them or find them good influences on Allegra, which annoyed Allegra a little, amused her a little, and touched her a little too. Ron had once said that M.M. felt toward him like a workhorse frightened by a yapping terrier, which caused Allegra no little guilt for finding it quite as funny as she did. On the other hand, Ron had indeed left it vague as to whether or not Allegra would be paid for her missing nights.

"We made an arrangement," she said, more stiffly than she had intended.

"Yeah," said M.M. Then she got up, sat on the arm of Allegra's chair, and put an arm around her. Allegra sighed, and leaned against her comfortable side. Growing up, she had got most of her physical affection from the McConnell family: when M.M.'s plumply huggable mother had died, a few years before, she had grieved almost as deeply as had M.M. "You're turning into your mom," she said, sleepily.

"It's rough when they die," agreed M.M. "You poor old orphan. How was the house?"

"OK. There really wasn't much to do. You know Dad, everything in order. Knew him, I mean. Got to get used to saying that." She shook her head to dislodge the thought, and then remembered the holy drawer. "Oh! Oh, M.M.!" As suddenly as it had enveloped her, the fatigue she had been bearing pulled back. "Oh, M.M., you will not believe what I found in his office."

She leaped up. Yes, the fatigue was gone: she could not imagine how she had ever felt tired in her life. "You'll love it," she said. "You will love it."

M.M., tumbled to the seat of the chair, watched her, smiling.

"Buried treasure?" she said.

"Almost. Almost. Where is it? Ah." She found the sack, which she had tossed into a corner when she arrived, and waved it under M.M.'s face.

"Old rosary beads," said M.M. "Mm. *Interesting.*"

"Ah, but there's more. You will love this, look. Dad had a whole drawer full of stuff, you know? Here. My first prayer book, and here's Saint Jude—remember Sister Philomena and Catherine O'Dowd?—and somewhere in here . . . yes." At the bottom of the sack was the photograph. "Take a look."

M.M., looking, smiled again, in sympathy across the years.

"Who is it?" she said.

Allegra took it, and with showy care placed both it and the familiar, silver-framed photograph beside another on top of her bookshelves, a second framed image, of Allegra's mother holding Allegra's baby self, both faces crumpled against a long-set sun. "That," she said deliberately, pointing to the snapshot in the center, "is my mother."

"It is not!" M.M. shook her head in delighted disbelief, leaped up, and squinted at the picture. How in their adolescence, both Allegra and Mary Margaret had pored over the few stiff images they had of Allegra's mother, searching for some sign of who, or what manner of woman, she had been; how they had attributed to her first this quality, based on a fancied frown, then that, on an imagined grimace; how, as they grew older, they had sadly acknowledged—kindly, inquisitive M.M. with little less heartache than Allegra—that the woman who had borne Allegra must remain to them both a mystery. "It's not," she repeated.

"It is so. Look. Look there at the eyebrows, and Bob said, look at the mole. Anyway, she's signed it. You see, it is her."

"Yes, but . . ." M.M. looked from the one picture to the others.

"Yes," said Allegra. "But."

"Oh, Leggie!" said M.M. "Leggie, she was gorgeous."

"She was, wasn't she?" Allegra studied in wonder the picture of the girl long gone. She had never seen her mother smiling before. "Gorgeous," she repeated, softly. Her mother had been gorgeous.

"I had no idea she was so pretty. Your dad never said."

"Dad never said anything."

Poor Dad, they had pestered him so mercilessly for stories of Theresa, the redheaded girl he had met in a bookstore in Los Angeles, and brought back to Chicago as his bride; and he had never even told them that she had been pretty.

M.M. turned over the picture, and her blue eyes widened. "Who's Ted?"

"No idea." Allegra reviewed the scant information she had about her mother's life. "Maybe some cousin?"

"You don't smile like that at a cousin."

"Well, you might."

"No," said M.M. with authority: her family was extensive. "You don't."

"Well, we'll never know now, will we? Bob said it was best not to wonder."

M.M. formed her fingers into a gun. "Bang," she said.

"Bang," Allegra agreed, and suddenly found she was biting her lip: she knew so little, so painfully little. Often, as a child, she had pictured to herself the scene of her parents' meeting, her mother, framed by shiny-jacketed books, dressed in a white ball gown and lovely as a Disney princess, with bright hair curling loosely to her waist; as Allegra grew older, the picture had darkened to a smokier, faintly film noir effect, with Ray Milland for Dad, and for her mother, Lauren Bacall, or possibly, in deference to the hair, Rita Hayworth. Then she had grown up, and the pictures, unnourished by further memento or anecdote from Dad, had faded almost to nothingness.

"I know what you're thinking." M.M. reached over and tugged gently at a lock of Allegra's hair. "Imagine if you'd found this when we were fourteen."

Allegra smiled. "The stories we'd have made up."

"Darling Ted. He'd have been a studio magnate, or an orange grove owner, or Errol Flynn."

"God forbid."

"He'd have been a hideously spurned admirer, or a disguised European prince, or the secret love of her life. God, the questions we'd have bugged your poor dad with."

"He'd have found a way not to answer. He always did. 'Your mother would have rather you concentrated on schoolwork than silly stories.'"

" 'Your mother would *not* have laughed to hear you making fun of a nun like that . . .' Oh dear, Leggie, and now he's gone you'll never even be able to ask him. Don't you just want to box God's ears, sometimes?"

"I've always thought He had a weird sense of humor."

"It's a male sense of humor. They're different from us: at least Our Lady knew about labor pains." M.M. picked up the photograph again. "Do you realize this is the first time I've seen your mother looking like a real human being?"

"Thank you very much. I suppose she was one. If you don't look too closely at Declan."

"She always looked so sad and dull. But look at that pretty smile she has here. Darling Ted. I wonder who he really was? There must be a story there."

Allegra sighed. M.M., whose own life was ordered so sweetly and so well, had always adored a mystery in the lives of others.

"Maybe I should go to Los Angeles," she said. "Ask John. We know how he likes to gossip."

John Higgins, the Jesuit-educated, who was even more close-mouthed about his dead sister than Ignatius had been. Once, in the very heat of their adolescent curiosity, Allegra and M.M. had composed a letter to John, asking—begging, in their florid language of child-women—for memories of Theresa, for a description, for an anecdote, for something, for anything. Ten days later, on a Saturday afternoon, Allegra had received a package, which she had borne in triumph to M.M.'s house to unwrap. It had contained a child's rosary, and a note: "For Allegra, with love, Uncle John." The rosary, she still had.

"You know something?" said M.M., slowly. "That just might not be such a bad idea."

"Oh, M.M.!" Allegra retrieved the photograph, and replaced it on the shelf.

"Well, you're off work. And I know you could afford a trip. And you could stay with crazy Melissa, she's always asking you."

"You hate Melissa."

"I do not, I just think she's crazy. And *I* wouldn't be staying with her."

"You hate her."

"You could sit in the sun . . . think about your dad . . . get over Nick . . . You know, Leggie, I hate you not knowing about your mother."

"Well." Allegra yawned, fatigue fighting growing exasperation. "There really isn't too much I can do about that, is there?"

"It would be so great if you knew something, at least. You were a kid when you asked questions before, and you're an adult now."

"Yeah," said Allegra. "And John Higgins is still a Jesuit boy."

"Oh, he's older now too, he must have mellowed. And that's another thing. This might be your last chance, you know. He won't be around forever."

"Really? Do people die?"

"Oh, Leggie. Sorry. But there are still things I wish I'd asked my mom that now I'll never be able to."

"Well, M.M., that's one of the differences between us that makes people so interesting. If *you'd* asked a question, your mom would have answered. And speaking of differences, I heard you had a husband and three kids an hour's drive away."

"Not a problem," said M.M. quickly. "Paul said he'd look after them all night if you want." But she had been reminded of real life, and glanced surreptitiously at her watch, calculating, Allegra knew, bath times and the likelihood of tantrums.

"Go," she said. "Thanks for coming, but go. I'm fine." She was, or as close as could reasonably be expected. She was used to her own company, and in the last few days had held more conversations than she sometimes did in a month.

"OK." M.M. stood, and took one last look at the photograph. She blinked at Allegra, as she did when she was serious. "Think about Los Angeles," she said. "It really is time you found out this stuff."

"Yeah, right." Suddenly, the full fatigue of the last day crashed down upon Allegra; and with M.M., at least, she need not be enchanting. "Do you mind going now? I'll call you tomorrow."

"Think about it," she thought M.M. said, before she herself fell onto the couch, and into unwise, unavoidable early-evening sleep.

She woke a few hours later, sour-mouthed and cold. She had dreamed, not of her father, but of her other loss, of Nick. Nick the lawyer, tall and well educated, who had come into the club a year or so before, who had laughed at her jokes, and taken her out to supper afterwards. Allegra had been in love with Nick. He was good to be with, elegant, intelligent, good company, well over six feet tall with a sharp, patrician face, a receding hairline, and a boyishly golden wiry fuzz on his hands and arms. He had liked her too, had liked her sense of humor, her long legs—together they made a striking couple—and her thick dark hair. On the other hand, there were things he had not liked. He had not liked her taste for spicy food, or, as he had let her know, her breath after she ate it; he had not liked her mild untidiness, or the times when her jokes had gone farther than he found comfortable—crossing the line to bad taste, he called it—or some of her co-workers at the club. And most especially, he had not liked her Church. Nick the restrained WASP had disapproved of all organized religion, and most particularly of the Holy Roman Catholic and Apostolic Church, from so profound a depth of his being that he had not even considered it impolite to say so to that Church's members. Allegra's reaction to this had been to increase her Mass attendance from the all but nonexistent to the very nearly regular. (It was doubtless wicked to go to Mass with the chief purpose of annoying someone, but presumably less wicked than not to go at all. She would ask her father, if she felt like making trouble. Oh, but no. No, she would not.) It was after Sunday Mass that she and Nick had split up. She had arranged to meet him in a restaurant for brunch, he had arrived late, and she, fueled by an extra Bloody Mary (and now that she came to think of it, a particularly annoying sermon on forgiveness), had embarked on a description of a tiff between Ron and Mike, highly colored, designed, mischievously but not maliciously, to irritate. About a third of the way through her tale, he had looked at her, blue eyes into brown. "This is not real life," he had said. Then, he had got up and simply vanished, had walked out of the restaurant, leaving his eggs Benedict barely touched, two twenty-dollar bills on the table, and Allegra openmouthed with astonishment; he had melted back into his own so very real life, the firm on Michigan Avenue, the parents and married sister in Oak Park, the spotless apartment in the near north which she would never now clutter with her presence again. And she had known, when the week and the next weekend had passed, and still the telephone had not rung, that not only was their affair over, but with it, in some essential corner of her heart, a profound change had taken place. He had touched upon a truth, had Nick: Allegra, in the most profound depth of herself, simply did not understand real life, and her relationships with lovers had shown it.

M.M. fed her coffee and cookies, and assured her that she would love again; but then again, M.M. would. It was all so different for M.M., with her living sisters and brothers, her garrulous aunts and cousins, her father and memories of her mother, her steady, quiet husband and hopes for her son and daughters. M.M. had a context in the world, a family. The McConnells were real life, if any family was. Allegra smiled—more pleasant by far to think of M.M.'s family than of Nick. They were a solid family, matriarchal, their women both supporting and resembling each other. They were Irish with a touch of German, brown-haired and blue-eyed, pinkly pretty in youth but tending to coarsen with age. They gained weight, had difficult menstrual periods but easy pregnancies, and as they grew older, needed slightly to watch their blood pressure. They laughed easily, and all of them had an ear for music. They were good people.

Allegra sighed, and sat up, grudgingly. So much for the McConnells—but she herself, who was she? She had grown up close to M.M.'s family, and loved by them, but she was not of them. Her face was her father's; and in her womanhood—her body's swift metabolism, its small but still-firm breasts, its happy acceptance of the contraceptive pill that M.M.'s body had so raged against when she tried it—she had no way of knowing whom she resembled.

She stretched, rotated her stiff neck, and stumped like an old woman to her small bathroom to look at herself in the mirror there. Yes, definitely, it was her father's face. Her still-surprisingly dead father's face.

"He's gone," she reminded herself. "You'll never see him again. Not ever."

But at least she had known who her father was.

She shook her head at herself, went back to the living room, and picked up the black-and-white snapshot, for the first time alone with this new image of her mother. And oh, she thought with sudden, surprising tenderness, oh, but her mother had been just a girl, and such a pretty girl too, so pleased with her curving body and her high-piled curly hair, making shameless goo-goo eyes under the bright sun. At Ted. Whoever Ted was. Allegra smiled, thinking of M.M.—Errol Flynn indeed. But he might as well have been, for all the knowledge this so tantalizing clue to Allegra's mother would ever lead them to.

And now, the man who might explain it to her was dead, revealing by his death that he had throughout his life kept hidden a photograph of his wife inscribed to another man. Oh, when Allegra reached her judgment day, she would have questions to ask about the celestial sense of humor.

Allegra was not, she knew, on the whole an unfortunate person. She was healthy in mind and body, she made a living doing what she enjoyed, and people liked her. (A brief flash of panic: They did like her, didn't they? Yes: there were faces that turned, smiling, when she walked through the shabby backstage of the Cat; there had been Mrs. Garvey's daughter, Julia, waving excitedly one afternoon from a car; there was the old man at the corner flower stall who always gave her a carnation. Yes, people liked her.) It was just that in the place inside her labeled Mother, the place where most people found love, or comfort, or disappointment, or anger, she had simply a hole, a nothingness. It made her different from other women. And sometimes, she grew weary of difference.

Then, letters, she suddenly remembered. There had been letters in the drawer in the office, addressed to Dad, on yellowed paper, franked with ludicrous three-cent stamps from the time before she was born, letters that through the years he had not thrown away. Dad's letters: never in her life had she dreamed of reading uninvited her father's mail. But Dad was dead, now. And Dad, it appeared, had kept secrets.

"I'm going to read them," she told herself. "I'm going to pour another glass of whiskey, and then I'm going to read them." She stared at herself for a second in reproach; then stuck her tongue out at herself, and returned to the living room.

When she shook out the sack, the letters floated gently, like petals, to the top of the pile. They were—as, of course, she realized with a painful little pang, what else would they be?—business letters. Then, no, not simply business letters, but letters from the bookstore where her parents had met. Notes from a Helen Viner, of Peppercorn's Books, Los Angeles, informing Mr. O'Riordan that his copy of *The Question Box* by the Paulist Fathers was now in stock. Peppercorn's Books; what a ridiculous name. But it must be the store, or why would Dad have kept the letters? And how like, how very like him and only him to have kept as a memento of his love affair these driest of souvenirs. M.M. would laugh. Bob would disapprove: or would have done, had she the slightest intention of telling him. Allegra snuffled a little, smiled at the thin sheets of paper, and replaced them, tenderly, in their envelopes. Then she saw, stuck to the third envelope, a fourth, smaller and thinner, addressed in that looping young hand that in her teen years she had studied in its rare samples—her third-birthday card, a child's book of Declan's—until her eyes ached and wept. The hand of the photograph. Her mother's hand. Allegra closed her eyes, consciously breathed deeply, and gulped at her whiskey before she opened the envelope. She had never read a full letter from her mother before.

> *Darling Nate,*
>
> *Welcome back! It was simply marvelous to see you—oh, so briefly—today, and I can't believe I won't see you again before Monday! You looked so handsome walking into the store, I just wanted to rush and kiss you in front of everyone, but of course, Mr. White Would Not Have Approved. Darn him—I wish I had more courage.*
>
> *I'll try not to miss you too badly, but I'm not making myself any promises. I'm going dancing on the pier with Alice and Albert tonight—I'll certainly miss you then. They're sweet, but I do wish they wouldn't spend all their time making love. Still, they'll soon be an old married couple, and just ignore each other!*

*I was so glad that John and Ted hit it off so well the other day,
weren't you?*

*Come back safely from Bakersfield, and don't you dare fall in
love with any other girls there. Do you realize we won't see each
other again for fifty-six hours and a half!!?*

All my love, darling,

Your

Theresa

Allegra read, poured more whiskey, and read again, warm tears
flooding her eyes as the black-and-white girl of the photograph sprang
from the flimsy page to envelop her in old-fashioned, flowery perfume.
Such a girl her mother had been, such a baby, such a kid, joyous and
unwary, living in days now unimaginable, when making love meant
flirting, and people married the one they fell in love with. Allegra
thought of Nick, and of Mark before Nick, and of Bruce before Mark;
and, barely a dozen years older than the letter's writer, she felt herself
soiled and old.

She read it again, and then once more. Oh, yes, twenty years ago,
how she and M.M. would have devoured this, how extravagantly they
would have speculated on Alice and Albert, how incessantly—and
how without result—they would have begged her father for details
of the Bakersfield trip, and of Mr. White.

And of Ted.

Because Ted was mentioned in the letter too. Allegra read yet
again, more slowly this time, calculating. Ted and Ignatius, it seemed,
had known each other. Ted had met John, had, indeed, hit it off with
John, which Theresa was glad about, and expected Ignatius to be too.
So much for M.M.'s mystery: whoever Ted was, he had not been kept
a secret, at least. But why, then, had Theresa, not a month before her
wedding day, so lovingly inscribed so very alluring a picture of herself, not to Ignatius, her betrothed, but to Ted? Well, Allegra would

never now know, because Ignatius was dead, and so was Theresa, and probably Ted, and almost certainly Mr. White.

But John was alive.

But John did not discuss Theresa.

But John must have mellowed, M.M. repeated in her ear. Go to Los Angeles, she urged from her comfortable home an hour's drive away. Go to Los Angeles and ask him. Allegra sighed. Right, M.M., she replied to her friend. Right, I'll go to Los Angeles and ask him, remember how he loves a gossip, good old John?

But he was Theresa's brother, said M.M. He knew her at least, and he knew Ted too, and he won't be around forever. Look, said M.M., look at the photograph, look at that sweet, happy face, aren't you at least curious?

Allegra rolled her eyes in irritation; and in doing so, caught sight again of her mother, or rather, of the girl who was to become her, her mother so unlike either the other photographs or Allegra's brief memory, the girl who forty years ago, had posed barely clad on a sunbaked beach, making shameless eyes at someone called Ted. How happy she looked in the sun: Chicago had been winter-bound now for months. Winter-bound, and swarming with ghosts of Dad dead and Nick departed; while in Los Angeles, Allegra had a good friend to stay with, and—she laughed a little hysterically as the night wind hurled more drops at her windowpane—even some money put aside for just precisely such a day.

"This," she said aloud, "is dumb. Expensive. And dumb."

She found pen and paper, and sat down at her desk. "Buy Ticket," she wrote to herself, in a large and not altogether steady hand. Then, "Call Melissa." Then, "Buy Frango Mints for Melissa." Then she finished her whiskey, and went to bed.

Chapter Two

"You know what's weird?" she said, three days later, to Ron as they sped down the faceless freeway to the airport. "For days now, I've been living on nothing but whiskey and pepperoni pizza, and I really don't feel bad at all. I don't look bad either, do I?" She peered at herself, surreptitiously, in the side mirror: no, she did not look bad. "In fact, considering everything, I think I look quite good."

"It's called the Bereavement Diet," said Ron. "Never fails. You should market it in Los Angeles, get rich and famous, and forget all about us."

"Oh, I won't forget the little people, Robbie."

"That's funny, Allie. Did you ever think of going into comedy?" Tall as Allegra was, Ron was short, barely five feet, and still—or so he claimed—getting carded in bars. Years ago, before Ron bought the Cat, the two of them had had an act in which he sat on her lap as a ventriloquist's dummy: they still did it occasionally, at parties.

"It'll be nice," he added now, looking through his car window at the leaden sky ahead. "Getting away to the sun. I'm jealous."

"I'm looking forward to it." Allegra had not told Ron the other reason for her trip—fond as she was of him, she did not entirely trust him not to see the funny side. "It was M.M.'s idea, she said I needed a change of scene."

"Somewhere you could see past her hips?"

"Cut that out." Allegra frowned: she was feeling guilty about M.M., with whom she had not shared the letters from Peppercorn's, but had hoarded them, inexcusably, greedily, all to herself. "We should all have friends like M.M."

"Solid. Dependable. Solid."

"Cut it out, Ron."

"Ooh, don't be so *mean* about my *girlfriend*." But he drove in silence for a while.

"Nick's a jerk," he said, then.

"Thanks," said Allegra. So that was really why he thought she was going; nor was he entirely wrong. "I admire your taste too."

"Just wanted to put it on the record. And Mike didn't like him either."

"And that makes me feel a whole lot better." They had been talking about her love life, sharp little Ron and sweet Mike, who adored Ron for reasons even Ron claimed not to know. Well, she talked about Ron and Mike too. Everybody talked about everybody: everybody except for the family she was crossing the continent to try to find more about.

"You'll meet some great guy soon," he said, "and you'll agree with us. Maybe you'll meet someone in L.A."

"Right," she said. "I'll fall in love with a movie star."

She would not fall in love with a movie star; she would not fall in love with anybody. She was a person outside real life, and it was simplest, on the whole, to let her heart just die. It had been hurt too many times, and hearts could not, no more than could bodies, simply go on being battered and recovering. Had to kill the old mare, Bo. Kindest thing to do. She was sufferin' too bad.

"And I'll still remember the little people, Gertrude," she added.

"Really, Allie," he said. "A career in comedy. Think about it."

At the airport, he stood on tiptoe to kiss her.

"Get over things," he said. "Have fun. Love to Melissa, and hurry home with a gorgeous all-over tan, so we all hate you and stop talking to you."

Allegra checked her pockets. Ticket, chocolate, and the envelope with the photograph inside.

"Love to Mike," she said, which was generous of her, since Ron had Mike, and everyone agreed that Allegra was so much nicer than Ron.

When she arrived at Melissa's apartment, Allegra fell straight onto her sofa bed, and slept for days. Not, of course, uninterruptedly. Sometimes, she rose to gobble Chinese or Mexican food; at one point, Melissa, making what Allegra's fuddled brain recognized as passable, but not excellent, jokes about corpses in living rooms, led her from the sofa to the bedroom; a few times more, her friend woke her to say things which, apparently not being jokes, Allegra received with a benign smile. But mostly, she slept.

She dreamed about Dad. Dad alive, Dad dead, Dad back from the dead, Dad pulling her with him to the grave, Dad pushing her from him and over a parapet into the ocean, Dad sad, Dad angry, Dad kissing her, scolding her, betraying her in nameless, terrible ways that made her stomach sick as she surfaced briefly, only to plunge again into a deeper sleep and further dreams. And Mother was there too, of course, her hair shining garish against the sepia dreamscape, and Nick, and Mark before Nick, and Bruce before Mark, and M.M.'s mother, and Ron's friend Zane, everyone who had ever died or left her, tripping a spectral procession behind her closed eyelids, while outside the sun beat on the cars and swimming pools and palm trees of the strange city. If she had spent the week dancing, she could not have been more tired when she finally awoke.

As soon as she opened her eyes, Sister Philomena started talking to her. Sister Philomena had taught Allegra history in high school, and had never liked her. Allegra thought, when she left school, that she had left the nun behind; but as her life turned out, Sister Philomena still spoke to her most days. Today, her theme was gracious guestship, in which, it seemed, Allegra was sorely lacking. Here she had a good and kind friend, who had allowed her to invite herself to her apartment, who had welcomed her, who had fed her, who had even given up her own bedroom to her, and all Allegra could do was lie like a sack and sleep. The very least she could contribute would be to get up, and ask Melissa how she was.

She stumbled up, wrapped herself in a robe, and wandered through the apartment. It was tiny, but cheerful; white-walled, filled with theater posters, and the wood and ceramic birds Melissa had collected ever since the two of them had been drama students together. It was also very quiet: Melissa must have gone out. And with a stimulating guest like Allegra to talk to—picky, Melissa, picky. Allegra went from the small living room to the smaller, light-filled kitchen area, where a note awaited her, propped against a fruit bowl shaped like a puffin.

Allie honey—

If you're reading this, I guess you must be feeling better. Good.

Remember sometime in the distant past, me coming into the bedroom and raving at you about Iowa and a guy called Jake? No? Oh, well—so much for my dramatic impact. Anyway—today—oh, it's Monday, by the way—today, I'm off to shoot a film! I'm a prostitute, I get to fall in love, get betrayed, and die!

(Yeah!) With Jake, who's TERRIFIC! (Yeah! Yeah!) In Sioux City! (Yeah—well, oh well.) Zippidy-doo money, of course, and I'll freeze my little buns off, but it's WORK. (Yeah! Yeah! Yeah!) Make yourself at home—food in the refrigerator—I'll leave some telephone numbers, and the car keys should be on the table unless Peter has them—I asked him to look in sometimes, make sure you were still breathing. They say I'll be back in 3 weeks, but then they'll say anything.

LOOK AFTER YOURSELF, baby, call me, DON'T be alone, because all these people at telephone numbers really want to see you.

I gotta fly—let's talk soon.

M.

P.S. Yes, I do know my buns aren't really little.

Sister Philomena's estimation of her, then, was justified: on reading so kindly, friendly, and funny a letter, the most pressing emotion Allegra felt was of relief at her friend's absence. Melissa was a good friend, but exhausting. Had she been around, she would have asked Allegra again and again about her father's last days on this earth, and how it felt to be an orphan; she would have seen, and speculated on, the photograph of Theresa Higgins; she would have had an opinion about Nick. Allegra was glad that Melissa had found work, because she was a dedicated and good actor who deserved an interesting role; but she was gladder that the role had appeared in Sioux City.

Fuzzily, she opened the refrigerator door, and stared at the unfamiliar juices and cartons of salads. Melissa had left her well provided for. She poured a bowl of blueberry granola, and wondered whether it made her less ungrateful, or only more greedy, that she enjoyed it much more than she usually did her own dull cornflakes. She had another bowl while she tried to decide: Allegra never gained weight, which made her women friends grind their teeth and tell her—jokingly, she was sure, on the whole—that they hated her. Then she turned her attention to the telephone numbers. Peter, the boyfriend, she knew well. Nice guy, Peter, cheerful, and crazy about Melissa. As well he should be. (Ha, Sister!—if ungrateful, she was at least not ungenerous.) Some of the others she also knew, or thought she did; some she did not. Probably all actors. She would take a rain check on calling them—she was really not in the mood. (Smart move, Allegra. You want to avoid actors, so you get on a plane to Los Angeles.) Melissa's friends would be friendly, she was sure, and funny; they would take her to the local dives she would never otherwise find, drink a little too much cheap wine with her, recommend comedy acts, tell her good stories and enjoy her own, complain with her about the government and the state of American movies. They would be her sort of people, and fun; if her sort of people, and fun, had been what she was looking for.

She laid the granola bowl in the kitchen sink, and went into the bathroom to check out the mirror. It was smaller than hers at home, and she looked puffy-eyed in it, and sallow: maybe the pepperoni pizzas were catching up on her after all. Or maybe it was the too-bright Los Angeles sun. Allegra was not used to seeing herself in the sunshine. The light caught her white hairs, which surely had increased over the last few weeks, and made them sparkle, silvery as tinsel, against the black mass of the rest. She turned her head, watching the effect. It was subtle now, but in a very few years, she would be more white than black: Dad too had whitened early. She wondered how it had felt for him, his wife buried with her hair still bright, to watch his motherless children growing gray. She left the mirror, went into the bedroom, took from her coat, heavy now and drab in the sunshine, the photograph of Theresa Higgins, and placed it, carefully, on a shelf in the living room. She looked at it, feeling a sudden pang of nostalgia for the club.

So my mom comes to visit, she says, Sweetie, can I make you a cup of coffee? I say, Mom, you're my guest, I'll make you a cup of coffee. She says, Oh, sweetie, you work so hard, you just sit down, let me take care of you for once. I say, Mom, it's my kitchen, I'm making the coffee, OK? She says, OK, sweetie. Oh, and sweetie, as long as you're out there, could you also make me a roast beef on rye, medium rare, hold the onions, heavy on the mayonnaise, home fries on the side, and possibly just a small portion, only small, mind you, of spinach soufflé?

It was dark in the Cheshire Cat Club, and smoky. Allegra, perched high on her stool in the mild spotlight, was able to become there whatever manner of woman she wanted to be, with whatever distribution she chose to award herself of sisters, of boyfriends, of mother. She could present herself as worrying about her weight, as owning a cat, as liking the taste of ice cream; she could make of herself for that one hour an ordinary youngish middle-class woman, and it would be, not a lie, in no sense a lie, but only a part of her job as entertainer. She sat taller in the club, and bent to look the other women in the eye: and they, knowing and needing to know nothing of the real Allegra O'Riordan, looked back at her with what they truly believed was recognition. She fooled them, after all these years, without effort; at times, for a few moments as sweet as slipping into clean-smelling sheets, she was almost able to fool herself.

But she was not at the Cat now. She was in Los Angeles, her mother's city, which she had not visited since the Easter some twenty years before when the family had flown out to stay with John. In her mother's city with a new and most puzzling photograph of her mother as she had been when she lived there. Her mother smiling with radiant lusty joy, on the front of a photograph signed, not to Allegra's father, but to Ted. Who had met and hit it off with her mother's brother John. Who had been educated by the Jesuits.

What are the three things God doesn't know? How many orders of nuns there are; how much theology a Dominican knows; what a Jesuit is thinking.

Not Allegra's joke but her father's, a hoary Catholic chestnut, the only joke she had known him to tell. Older Catholics were still amused by it; the younger generation kindly pretended to be—they all liked Ignatius. What a non-Catholic would have made of it Allegra had no idea: now that she thought about it, she did not think Ignatius had known any. She sighed, and went to find her address book. Allegra was fond of John, although Bob turned pinched with rage at the mention of his name. He had always been gracious to her, polite in her childhood, and as she grew into womanhood, courtly. Still, John was a Jesuit boy, and had absorbed all the proud inscrutability of the Society. What he really thought of Allegra in his heart, whether he wondered why she wore faded blue jeans instead of skirts, and no makeup, why she did not try to hide the gray in her hair, or have a husband and children, or at least a regular job; whether he ever searched her humorous, long face—in vain, as she well knew—for traces of his dead, pretty sister, this she could no more begin to guess than leap over the moon. He was a walking embodiment of Dad's joke, was John, a memory of the past, now their last living relative of the older generation. He was, indeed, officially *in loco parentis*. She smiled, unkindly: she would remind Bob.

"Higgins residence."

John had inherited the family business, and he and his wife, Kathleen, were rich: she had forgotten their live-in help. Forgotten too how they subtly embarrassed her. Maria sounded younger than she.

"Hello, Maria," she said. "May I speak to . . . to John, please?"

She had made a point, when she turned twenty-one, of dropping the "Uncle," but all these years later, she still stumbled over his name. That was embarrassing too. He continued to call her sweetie, as he always had.

"You're up early," was his salutation.

"Am I?" Most embarrassing of all was that, with John, a professional comedian could never think of anything remotely funny to say.

"No, I guess you're not, over where you are. Early for you theatrical types, though. Don't you all stay in bed till noon?"

"Not always." On a ledge above the sink, she noticed a clock. "Oh God, is it only seven-thirty? I'm sorry, I didn't realize. I've been confused."

"Don't worry, I'm up. I have a meeting." His voice softened, for his education had not killed his kindness. "How're you doing, sweetie?"

"Oh, OK, you know, thank you. I'm getting there. Thank you for coming to the funeral, I know it's a busy time for you."

"I wouldn't have missed it. He packed the church, old Nate, didn't he?"

"Didn't he? Oh, John, I haven't told you. I'm in Los Angeles."

"Are you, by God." Surprise was not in John Higgins's repertoire. "Then you'll come to dinner tonight, around seven. Now, where are you, and how are you going to get here?"

"Not far, I think. It's called West L.A., so it can't be too far from the ocean, can it? I have a car, and I'm sure I can find a map."

"Good. Kathleen and I will look forward to it. Take care of yourself, and we'll see you at seven. Oh, and by the way, sweetie?"

"Yes?"

"Have you thought which Mass you're going to?"

Damn. Old Jesuit trick. Caught off guard, Allegra tried to parry, fumbled, failed.

"Mass," she said. "Uh, no. No, I hadn't."

"Well." His skillfully unchanging voice consolidated his victory. "So you'll come to the eleven-fifteen out here with us, and we'll go to brunch afterwards."

Allegra snarled, clutched at her throat, and looked for sympathy to a bright ceramic parrot hanging on the opposite wall. She did not receive it.

"Sounds great," she said.

She replaced the receiver, poured a cup of coffee, took it outside to the small courtyard, where she sat, curling her lip in disgust at the rich crimson and purple bougainvillea that hung on the white wall opposite.

It was not so much that she objected to going to Mass. In fact, she had found during those Nick-defying Sundays of the last year that in many ways, she actively approved of it: there was drama in the centuries-old readings, a chance in this busy world for an hour's quiet contemplation, and even, at the end, a magical trick, a weekly miracle, here in the pragmatic twentieth century, in the transubstantiation of the bread and wine into Christ's body and blood. All circumstances being equal, Allegra would very likely have attended Mass more often than she did; would even, quite probably, have enjoyed it. Unfortunately, circumstances were not equal. To go to Mass without the excuse of teasing Nick meant to confront, not only her own feelings about the Catholic Church, but also its feelings about her. And according to the Catholic Church, Allegra, and most of her friends, were, statedly and specifically, sinners.

Allegra could hardly remember a time when she had not been in the Church's eyes a sinner. She was not one as most of the world defined the word: outside the Church, in fact, she would be generally regarded as a good person. She was loyal to her friends, kind to children, and affable to strangers: she usually kept her word, had never — or not since Bob had grown too big to bully — advertently harmed any person, and had actively tried to do good to some. She was not without her faults; but as a human being, she thought without undue conceit, she could look herself in the eye, possibly better than many. As an irrevocably baptized member of the One Holy Catholic and Apostolic Church, she was as sinful as Lucifer.

She herself did not believe this, of course. She was not only a baptized Catholic but also a sensible woman, one who, like most other sensible women of her age, had chosen to follow her own conscience before the dictates of the white-robed, celibate men half the world away in Rome. Unlike those men, she could not think that God, having put her into this difficult world, would judge her too harshly if she chose to spend some of its Sunday mornings in bed instead of in church; and if she chanced to spend some of those mornings enjoying the body which He Himself had after all created with the body of another, she could not believe it part of His plan that she, and an overcrowded globe, should pay for it by her pregnancy in this world, and damnation in the next. But in that very assuredness—or so the men in Rome would tell her—was where her sin of arrogance lay, as much as in her actual transgressions; and each lazy Sunday which she spent peacefully in her apartment, lying alone or with another, each morning when, after her shower and before she brushed her teeth, she swallowed the contraceptive pill she could not clearly remember a life without, brought her, according to Holy Mother Church, further sins, darker stains on her liberally educated, Democrat-voting, twentieth-century postfeminist, immortal Catholic soul.

No. Thinking about it, Allegra shook her head, and shivered a little. Mother Church, for Allegra's sort, held small welcome. Mother Church, as through her masculine priests she had made it perfectly plain, did not approve of those who questioned and mocked and sinned; who cracked cheap jokes at the expense of holy sacraments, and poor, chaste, and obedient nuns, and made rooms full of other sinners snigger at them, besides. It was a bleak, dim view that Holy Mother Church took of such as Allegra, and the weight of her disapproval threatened sometimes, if she thought about it, to stifle her, as she had been stifled as a small child on car journeys, wedged small and female in the front seat between her father and Father Forde, two muscular upper arms obstructing her breathing space, two baritones rumbling above her of a world of altar boys and Knights of Columbus, to which she would never be admitted.

John, like her father, chose to know nothing of this. To set out from the assumption that she practiced her Catholic faith as punctiliously as did he; to allow her to fail to snatch swiftly at the hairbreadth opportunity he offered, when she was not expecting it, to contradict him; and thus to be able to continue to assume, now and forever more, that his niece was a devout Catholic. He was good, was John. He probably had no idea either—had chosen to have no idea—of the sorrow harsh Mother Church sometimes caused his niece, of the Sunday Masses she occasionally attended, when, from the very moment she crossed the door of the church and dipped her finger into the icy stone font, until the priest had left the altar, she felt wave after wave engulf her of sorrow too deep for thoughts, of desolation reaching, long and sad and unending, all the way from this world to the next.

"Hi."

Someone substantial had plopped onto the chair next to hers, and Allegra opened her eyes to the real world. Immediately, she stifled the urge to giggle. The look of Angelenos often made her want to laugh, and this one simply had to be kidding. He was young and blond and blue-eyed, he had broad shoulders, slim hips, long legs, even a cleft chin. He looked, not like a person at all, but like a line drawing of a handsome young man in the cartoon section of the newspaper.

"Hi," she said, resisting the temptation to rub him and see if he would smudge.

"You're Melissa's friend, right?" he said. "I'm Scott, she told me to look out for you. Gee, I hope the movie goes well, she could use a break. Melissa's a great lady. So—you finding everything OK?"

"Yes, thanks," she said. "I'm Allegra." For so she persisted, obstinately, in identifying herself.

"Good to meet you, Allie," he said, predictably appropriating the diminutive. "You out here on vacation?"

He was a good dozen years younger than she, the brown skin around his eyes taut, his hair in the sun betraying neither a thread of silver nor the pink of scalp. Had she met him fifteen years ago, when she was young, she would have been overcome by now with lust; today, she could examine him with no more feeling than the faintest of curiosity. She was growing middle-aged.

"Sort of vacation," she said. "My dad died." Those syllables again. She would have to practice them later, aloud.

"Gee," he said. "I'm sorry, Melissa didn't tell me. It's rough when people die—my grandma died a couple of years ago."

"Thanks," she said, and reached for a phrase she was used to. "Yes, my mom's dead too. So I'm an orphan."

But that was a new word, and terrible, one she must clearly be more careful before bandying. A crease appeared in Scott's perfect forehead.

"Wow," he said.

"Yes," she said. "So. What do you do, Scott?"

"I'm a novelist."

She smiled.

"Fitzgerald was twenty-five when he made it," he said. "And Bret Easton Ellis was twenty-one. Actually, I mostly work as a waiter. Leaves me my mornings to write."

"Yes, I've done that. You see so much of life in a restaurant, don't you?"

He looked at her for a moment, then smiled, becoming even less probable as he did so. "Melissa said you were a comedian. I guess you'll miss her, huh? Do you know other people in town?"

"I have family. My mother came from round here."

"Yeah?"

"Yeah." Her mother, she thought, with another new feeling, a most astonishing burst of pride at the sunny, sexy girl so lately freed from Dad's hiding place; yes, her mother would have belonged in this bright city with people who looked like Scott. Then she frowned: it was altogether possible that she and M.M. had exaggerated the photograph's effect. "D'you want to see my mother?" she asked.

Scott's brows raised. "Sure," he said.

Turning into a crazy lady, Allegra, she told herself, picking her way across the sun-warmed flagstones to the apartment. Showing family photographs to strangers. Cuckoo time. But as she handed the picture to Scott, she realized that she was watching him carefully and biting her thumbnail as she did so.

But Scott's eyes flashed appreciation, as had Bob's. "Wow," he said. "Lucky guy she was looking at." Then, turning his blue gaze to Allegra, "You don't look like her."

"Sorry about that." Allegra was older than the black-and-white girl: and she had loved Nick, and Mark before Nick, and Bruce before Mark, and, too clearly, it showed. Yet she and M.M. had not been imagining things, at least. "She grew up here in town. Mother did. Met my dad in a bookstore, Peppercorn's." The dusty place with the overly quaint name, as far-fetched as her childhood fantasies. "I guess it's long gone now."

"Peppercorn's?" he said. He stretched his ridiculous body, and yawned. "No, it's right near here, just up the hill. Walking distance, even."

"Is it?"

Allegra shivered, sharply, in the sun. Somehow, to discover that her mother's bookstore was an actual physical place was a not altogether pleasant sensation, as if a living woman had sauntered into the courtyard and introduced herself, casually, as Scarlett O'Hara.

"Is it any good?" she asked.

"Terrific." He nodded reassuringly, as one imparting useful information. "I go there all the time."

"Well, good." With the skill of Scarlett herself, she shelved further consideration. "That's great." More comfortable by far was the familiar part of the story, now safely forty years old. "She worked there after the war, Mother did, and my dad was out here on business—we're from Chicago, or he is, was—and he got bored in his hotel and went to buy a book, and there she was. Mother." And this really was turning into cuckoo time. "You'll be interested in this, you're a writer."

"No, I am interested," he said. "Go on."

"That's all I know."

He frowned. "All?" he said.

"Well, she married my dad, went to Chicago, and died when I was three. I barely remember her."

"Weird," he said. "But your dad must have told you all about her, right?"

"Not really. In fact, he almost never mentioned her. I'm going to see my uncle tonight, her brother. He doesn't talk about her either."

"Oh, you should just ask him. I'm always talking about my sister."

"Yes," she said. He was young and so absurdly handsome; and the sun was shining in the azure sky. "Yes, maybe I'll do that. What does your sister do?"

He did not reply: he was staring at her, meditatively, with a look, she now realized for the first time, she had been receiving for most of her life.

"I can't imagine that," he said. "Not knowing my mom."

Her indulgence evaporated.

"Work on it," she said. "You're a writer."

But he only smiled.

"That I am," he said. "So, I'd better go write." He unfolded himself from his chair, and walked to the door across the courtyard. "I live in here. Yell if you need anything, OK?"

Well, if Allegra looked like he did, maybe she too would be exceptionally good-humored. Or, Sister Philomena swiftly suggested, maybe she would not.

Left alone, Allegra shivered again. Her mother's bookstore, then, was real. Real, and even, absurdly, here in this city of long roads and endless freeways, within walking distance. Allegra had nothing to do until the evening, and could, if she so chose, walk through the concrete landscape which Theresa Higgins had called home, to the place where Theresa Higgins had spent her working days. She could, if she so chose, go in, and talk to the people who worked there now. She could ask if there was anyone there who might remember Theresa, or the woman Helen Viner, or the couple Alice and Albert, or even the mysterious Ted. If she so chose. Over the years, Allegra had grown more used than she realized to the sheer anonymity of the phantom who had been her mother. What, after all, was there to know about? Theresa's had been a worthy life, doubtless, but too short to have an impact on that of Allegra or her brothers. A sheltered Catholic girl, daughter of a well-to-do Los Angeles building contractor, who had married a good Catholic boy at twenty-five, and died before she was thirty, having lingered, one hoped painlessly, in a coma just long enough for Extreme Unction. And that was the end of the story. It had even become comfortable to have it so, her mother an accepted mystery, the questions of adolescence set at rest, like a once beloved toy, laid affectionately in a box, to be looked at only at times from the safe detachment of adulthood. Now, it seemed, she could open the box. She could, if she so decided, walk up the hill right now, to stand in the store where, not the biddable phantom of her childhood fantasies, but her real, plump-flesh-and-coursing-blood mother had stood, to see the bookshelves her real eyes had seen, touch those her living hands had touched. She could this very afternoon, if she wanted, set in motion the restructuring of her mother into a flesh-and-blood girl, who one black-and-white day had flaunted her curves on a beach, and smiled. She thought about it, then went indoors, and poured herself more coffee. She would wait until she had visited John: maybe she would learn something concrete from him.

Good one, Allegra. She really ought to consider a career in comedy.

She shook her head at herself, and resolutely turned her attention to Melissa's stack of film magazines.

Kathleen and John Higgins lived in a comfortable house shaded by magnolia trees, on a bluff overlooking Santa Monica Bay. They had lived there since before the area became fashionable, and the furnishings were of the triumphantly ugly sort Allegra and M.M. privately identified as Early Catholic. John himself came to the door to greet her, thrusting his close-shaven jaw, as usual, for a kiss, and following it up, less usually, with a clumsy embrace which was half a back pat. Kathleen's greeting never varied: a touch of sweet-smelling cheek against hers, a light clasp of manicured hands on her elbows.

"What pretty flowers," she said, accepting the calla lilies Allegra gave her.

"Thank you for inviting me," Allegra replied. She did not recall ever having had a full conversation with Kathleen in her life.

She followed them into the living room, and stood, awkward as an adolescent, while Kathleen arranged the flowers in a vase, and John attended to the liquor cabinet. There was that about herself when she was with her uncle and his wife that she did not altogether like; her voice became high, her wits dull. To affect ease at least, she examined the cluster of framed photographs which crowded the top of the dark wood piano in a tone-dulling depth that would turn Fred, the Cat's pianist, pale and pained. A number were of Kathleen's family; there was just the one of John, a solemn toddler, wedged between his fierce father, Joe, and elder brother Robert, who had died in the War: Theresa, presumably, had not been born by then. The rest were of Kathleen and John's son, Jimmy, whom Allegra had last seen as a boy on his way to college. He had been adolescent-plump then, and cherubic: now, he was leaner, but still broad-faced, unmistakably his father's son.

"Jimmy's a real Higgins, isn't he?" she said to Kathleen.

"I always think he has a look of my family," said Kathleen.

"That's a loving mother talking." John handed Allegra a large whiskey. "The Murphys were all good-looking. Jimmy's an ugly Higgins like the rest of us. Here you are, sweetie; let's drink to your dad."

As Allegra took the glass from him, she felt his big hand brush her smaller. They had stopped making men like Dad and John: she could not see any of her own contemporaries ever growing so certain or so large.

"He was a good man," she said. "Wasn't he?"

"The best." The two lifted their glasses, while Kathleen sat, smiling, with her hands crossed: she rarely drank.

"You grow more like him every year," said John. "Are you in town for an audition?" He would not, she knew, be above enjoying a niece who was seen on television.

"Just to get away." It was only half a lie. "It seemed a good idea to take a couple of weeks off."

"You can do that?"

"Oh, yes. It's quiet at the club, I think Ron's quite glad not to be paying me."

He looked at her, frowned, then shook his head. "Well, those brothers of yours will take care of you."

My boyfriend knows when it's tax time because all of a sudden, I turn into June Cleaver. Usually, he comes home, and I'm, Hi, buddy, fix y'self a brewski, how 'bout those Bears? But then, one evening, there I am, in my frilly apron and my pearls, and, Hello, dear, how was your day? I'm just ironing your shoelaces before I serve the stuffed peacock's tongue en croûte, and he says, Did the forms arrive already?

In reality, Allegra did not only her own tax returns, but Ron's and Mike's too. She felt now a stab of longing, sharp as a physical pain, to be back in the dank backstage of the club, playing desultory dog-eared rummy with Ron and Fred, with the heads outside just visible from an angle of the wings, bobbing in laughter in the dark.

"How are those brothers, anyway?" said John.

"Doing well," she said. "Bob's talking about moving house again, the boys are giants now."

"Mm." He never inquired about his unbaptized great-nephews. "Declan?"

"I think he's in Geneva. Or is it Washington?" Declan was a financial consultant and traveled extensively. Dad had always known where Declan was, Allegra never. She supposed that now they would have to learn to communicate directly. "How's Jimmy?"

"Who knows? Says he's a screenwriter, but I never see anything he's written."

"He has several projects," said Kathleen, carefully, "in development."

A look came across her face when she spoke of Jimmy that Allegra had seen on other mothers' faces. She wondered whether their own mother would have looked so for Declan and Bob; whether her two brothers knew what they had lacked, or how sorely they had missed it; and in wondering, she shocked herself with a stab of murderous jealousy on her brothers' behalf for the unknown screenwriter Jimmy.

"Development," said John. "What I want to know is when someone will develop his bank account."

"He's doing very well," said Kathleen.

John grunted, and sipped at his drink. He was standing beside the piano and directly, Allegra noticed, beneath the larger photograph on the wall of his father, Joe Higgins. As Jimmy was John's son, so John was Joe's, three scrappy Irishmen, with short noses and pugnacious jaws.

"You're a Higgins too," she said to him. "Aren't you?"

"So they say." Following her eyes, he turned to look at the photograph with grudging affection. "He was never the most handsome fellow, but didn't do so badly for himself." He winked at Kathleen. "The Murphys were the lookers around the parish."

Kathleen Murphy Higgins, like M.M., came from a conventionally large Catholic family. It was, Allegra supposed, given Kathleen's name and her delicate, small-mouthed face, a predominantly Irish family, and both large, and growing—she and John, it seemed, were forever attending this niece's wedding, or that nephew's baptism. It was growing out of its nationality too: the names the priests gave its children in baptism were as likely to be Spanish as Irish, its weddings like the McConnell weddings, riotous flower beds of freckled Celts, dark-eyed Hispano-Hungarians, and pale-skinned Poles. But if Kathleen did come from a family like the McConnells, she must have had less joy from it than M.M., because M.M. had married Paul, whose family was as large and as diversely fecund as her own; while Kathleen had married a Higgins.

"Oh, the Higginses weren't so bad." Allegra had always scorned machination: now, her private soul sneered at herself, while her body sipped demurely at its drink, crossed its legs like a good convent girl, and quietly sent up its first trial balloon. "I found a picture in Dad's study, of Mother. One I hadn't seen before. She was smiling, and looked so happy . . . She was really quite lovely, wasn't she?"

"Theresa?" John folded his brow in puzzlement. "Can't say that I remember that. Shall we go in to dinner now?"

Dinner, in the dark dining room, on the mahogany table, under the dim reproduction Madonna and Child with Saint Anne, was the food Dad had used to eat, a solid joint of meat, abundant, accompanied by the potatoes for whose lack their great-grandparents had nearly died, and which neither Dad nor John saw reason to replace with a different starch, since rice would not have occurred to them, and pasta was for Italians. Maria had probably had to take special lessons to cook in the Higgins house.

"This is delicious," Allegra said, politely: she knew her manners, at least.

"A good butcher." John nodded, pleased. "We've used the same guys for forty years now. The Di Novos, all Italian rogues, of course. But Kathleen works her Murphy charm on all of them, and I swear they fatten the pigs specially for her."

Kathleen smiled.

"Do you cook, dear?" she asked.

"Not really." Oh, good one, Allegra. Witty. But she did not, really.

"That's why you're so slim," said Kathleen, kindly.

"Probably," agreed Allegra.

"Can't understand it," said John. "All this nonsense about being slim. There's a sweet-looking little girl at the office who fainted the other day, of hunger. It's a sin to do that to yourself, and I told her so."

From Sioux City, Allegra heard Melissa cough into her ear: Melissa had both a slow metabolism and defined views about the messages the media gave to women.

"She'd probably been reading fashion magazines," she said, obligingly accepting the direction. "Some of them put out really quite irresponsible ideas of how we should look."

"Shouldn't read them, then," said John. "*Vanitas, vanitas, omnis vanitas*—never leads to any good. Pass the salt, sweetie."

Allegra did as she was bid. But Melissa had not done with her. "Some people might argue," she continued, "that young girls in offices shouldn't be expected to be more responsible for the magazines they read than the businessmen who publish them."

"*Vanitas, vanitas,*" said John. "Salt?"

"We tried to stay slim in our day too, dear," said Kathleen.

"And I still remember the fights," said John. "My sister and my father, dear God, over potatoes. Potatoes. Kathleen, is there something different about the pork?"

"I don't think so, dear. Allegra, how is yours?"

Allegra's ears pricked up. Fights over potatoes? They had never been mentioned before, and God knew, it was hardly a momentous revelation. But yes, the girl in the photograph would have fought.

"What do you mean," she said, "fights over potatoes?"

"Mm? Oh, they fought. Over potatoes, your mother said they made her fat. Kathleen, was it Anthony you bought this from, or old Lou?"

"Lou, dear, Anthony has college on Wednesdays. If it's not good, I'll have a talk with him."

"No, it's good." He chewed, thoughtfully. "Just tastes different. What's Anthony studying? New techniques in prison breaks?"

"Dear!" said Kathleen. "They're really very good friends," she added to Allegra.

"What did they say?" said Allegra.

They both looked at her.

"What did who say, dear?" said Kathleen.

"Mother and Grandfather," said Allegra. "When they fought. What did they say?"

"What did they say?" said John. He winked at Kathleen. "I suppose he said, 'Eat your potatoes.' And I guess she said, 'No.'"

And yet he had said, distinctly, that he remembered the fights. Allegra sighed, remembering, now, how it was to try to talk about her mother to her mother's brother, how little he had ever given her of how much she yearned to know. Then jumped as M.M. poked her, hard, in the ribs, reminding her why she was there, and that these people who had known her mother would not live forever.

"The photograph," she said. "The one I was telling you about. Mother really was lovely, wasn't she?"

"Mm." John sipped at his amber glass—he did not care for wine—and glanced at Kathleen.

"Oh, yes, dear." Kathleen smiled kindly at Allegra. "Your mother was very pretty."

"She seems to have been popular too. I found . . ." During the afternoon, Allegra had composed a version of what she had found, but still the lie to John did not come easy. "That is, I also found, in a drawer of Dad's, you know, a couple of old birthday cards. To her, to Mother. Let's see. There was one from, oh, Alice, I think it was, and Albert."

"Mm." Thoughtfully, John chewed at his pork.

"It was a sweet message on it, really warm, and funny. She seemed to have been fond of Mother." She paused; John said nothing. "Such an old-fashioned name, Alice, isn't it? I don't know anyone called that, these days. Do you remember them, by any chance?"

"I remember Kathleen's Aunt Alice," said John. "She kept a parrot. Most vicious brute I've ever known."

"She was very kind to us when we were first married," said Kathleen.

"That she was. Crazy as a coot, of course. Remember when the parrot died, and she wanted a Requiem Mass for it? Cosmas, that was its name. Patron saint of surgeons, and most people who met it needed one."

"Dear!" But Kathleen laughed. "She really was quite an eccentric old woman," she conceded.

"Ha!" John snorted. "My wife's definition of eccentric: a woman who ate bird seed and never bathed in Advent. What would you have to do to be a full-fledged madwoman?"

"Do you remember the other Alice?" said Allegra.

They looked at each other again, and she felt, suddenly, puny: how a couple could overwhelm you. Dad, for all his parts, had been just the one man.

"Sweetie," said John. "Why would we remember someone from forty years ago?"

"No," said Allegra. "No, of course you wouldn't. I just thought you might have. Stupid, really." Stupid, M.M., did you hear that? Stupid.

John smiled at her. "Eat your dinner, sweetie," he said. "Unless *you* think there's something strange about it too."

"Do you remember the dances on the pier?" said Kathleen, suddenly. "You never cared for dancing, dear, did you?"

"Dances?" said Allegra. The letter had mentioned dances, yes, on the pier, with Alice and Albert. "You remember them, then."

"There was a ballroom on the pier," said Kathleen. "They tore it down. I was always trying to get your uncle to take me, but he wouldn't."

"Two left feet," agreed John. "Good enough for my father, and good enough for me."

"She mentioned dancing in the letter," said Allegra. "In the card, I mean. Alice did. You do remember them, Kathleen."

John looked at neither Kathleen nor Allegra, but his plate.

"Oh, my dear, no," said Kathleen. "I can't think why I mentioned it, really. Why would I have thought of that, John, after all these years?"

"Ignatius was a good dancer, now," said John. "I never was. Of course, back then, dancing was a skill. Even I could do the stuff they do these days. What d'you say, Kathleen, shall we go to a disco tonight?"

"How about Mother?" said Allegra.

"Mm?"

"Was she good?" said Allegra. "At dancing? Mother?"

"Can't say I remember."

But he had remembered Ignatius's dancing. Yes, thought Allegra, remembering with a surge of irritation other, so many other, such conversations—that was why she had stopped trying to ask these questions of her father or of John. But this was not like those other times.

This time, she was an adult; this time, she had found a photograph. And Kathleen had remembered the dances on the pier.

"There was another card," she said. The card was a fabrication, but the truth—and a truth, moreover, that she had learned from her mother's own hand—was that John had met Ted, and that the two had—what was the phrase?—hit it off. Well. She took a breath. "It was a nice card too. It was from, well, I guess another friend. Do you remember a Ted?"

There was a pause. John sipped again at his whiskey. And frowned. "Ted," he said. Then, "Can't say that I do."

But they had met. And hit it off. And he had remembered Ignatius's dancing.

"I've got it," said Kathleen, suddenly.

Allegra turned to look at her.

"I know what it is," she said.

"What is it?" said John.

"Cilantro," said Kathleen. "The pork's the usual cut, but Maria put cilantro into the marinade." She smiled at Allegra. "She wanted to do something special for you."

"I preferred it the usual way," said John.

Chapter Three

Early the next morning, while Allegra was still in bed, M.M. called her.

"Sorry," she said. "Did I wake you?"

"Sunshine," said Allegra, immediately, and malevolently. "Gallons of sunshine, liquid gold, toasting my face and caressing my legs—my bare legs, remember the feel of bare legs?—and making everything sleepy and lazy and slow."

"You don't have to be like that," said M.M. "Listen, can I get your address? Elizabeth wants to write you a letter."

"Don't involve your daughter in your lies." Allegra yawned, swallowing her own guilt at the four letters she had not shared with her friend. "You want to know if I've found out any more about Mother."

"I'm not, she does." M.M. paused, and Allegra heard her sip at her coffee. "So. Have you?"

"Oh. Yes," said Allegra. "Oh, yes, M.M. Yes, I've met Ted,

and I've found out why she was smiling. It's down to his knees, M.M."

M.M. sighed. "Just so long as you don't make jokes like that around my children," she said. "Really, Leggie. Have you found anything?"

"God, M.M., what do you think? Actually, until yesterday, I more or less just slept."

"Good. You needed it."

"And I'm all alone, because Melissa's off filming somewhere, but I've met my neighbor, who's a beautiful blond California hunk."

"Oh yes?" M.M.'s voice perked up. As much as a mystery, she enjoyed a romance, and Allegra flirted briefly with the temptation to lead her down this falsely pretty path. But it would only mean more explanations, later on.

"Yes," she said. "And he looks around twelve years old, and says he's a novelist. Aren't we getting old?"

"Thanks for reminding me. So. When are you going to start looking?"

"Oh." M.M. could irritate: and she had, in fact, woken Allegra from sleep. "I'm looking, all right. Hubba, hubba. I told you, he's a hunk."

"Leggie!"

"OK." Deciding to punish her friend, Allegra lowered her voice confidentially. "OK, I'll tell you. I went to see John last night. And let me tell you what he told me."

"What?"

Allegra heard the sound of M.M.'s coffee mug set on the table, and smiled maliciously to herself.

"OK," she said. "I'll take it from the beginning, OK? So I arrive at the house, I take flowers, we have a drink, and we sit down to dinner. OK?"

"Yeah." In Chicago, M.M. nodded, her eyes intent.

"So," continued Allegra. "So we're all grouped around the table, and we're eating pork, OK? You know, pork? And I asked John about Mother, and . . ." She paused.

"Yes?"

"And. *Something about the pork was different from the usual!*"

"Leggie!"

"I'm serious." Allegra's smirk died. What was so terrible that she could only joke about it was that she was, indeed, telling no more nor less than the truth. "We had quite the talk about it. In fact, every time I asked a question, that old pig popped up. Was it the cut? No—same old loin. Was it Anthony at the meat counter? No—he was at college yesterday, so his dad served us, Lou, you know, he's very reliable. Undercooked, overcooked? No, and no. It was a mystery! But then, right toward the very end of the meal, just when all hope was dying, Kathleen comes up with the solution. Tarragon in the marinade. What a woman, I tell you. Or was it cilantro?"

"Oh, Leggie." M.M.'s sense of humor could fail her at times. "Didn't he tell you anything at all?"

"Well, let's see." For her own amusement, Allegra furrowed her brow, stroked thoughtfully at her chin. "You know, now that you mention it, he did. Let me think. I remember it was . . . yes, it was definitely halfway between the meat counter and the cooking time, when I was actually lying on the floor sobbing, and begging to be told one thing, anything, about the woman from whose womb I sprang . . . he did let slip that she didn't like potatoes, which puts it all in context, doesn't it? . . . Really, M.M., I don't know why I'm here. Except for the sunshine, M.M. Sweat pouring down my back and pooling between my breasts, the shock of a cool shower before I step back into the warmth—"

"But that's interesting," said M.M. "Did Theresa really not like potatoes? Neither do you, you must have gotten it from her."

"Yes, I do."

"No, you don't."

No, now that she came to think of it, she did not.

"This is too bad," said M.M. "But you know, Leggie, you are in Los Angeles, and if John's no good, there must be some other way. Isn't it too bad we never found the name of the bookstore?"

Allegra snarled at the telephone receiver. She had more than once told M.M. that there were times, and countries, in which she would have been burned as a witch.

"Leggie?" said M.M.

"What?"

"Leggie!"

"Didn't I tell you?" said Allegra. "I found an old invoice in among Dad's stuff."

"From the bookstore? I'll kill you! Allegra O'Riordan, I will kill you, you know you didn't tell me. So?"

"Well, it's called Peppercorn's, of all names, and it seems it's still open."

"I will kill you. What's it like?"

Allegra sighed.

"I haven't been," she said.

"Not been!"

"I thought I'd go today. I hear it's a good bookstore."

"Allegra, I will kill you and I will jump on your grave and I will not say prayers for your soul. Not been! You will go there today, and I will call you tomorrow."

"Yes, Sister."

"And cut that out. You need to know this stuff, Leggie."

"Do I?" said Allegra.

"Yes, you do. You need to know who your mother was. Go. Go there now. And say hi to Melissa."

"When I talk to her."

"Did she get rid of that creepy bird collection yet?"

"I think they've all nested and reproduced."

"The woman is crazy."

"How unlike ourselves. Bye, M.M."

Allegra replaced the receiver, went to the bathroom, and looked into the mirror, her reflection harsh in the morning light, its expression severe. The California light did not become Allegra; she was not sunny, but dark and thin, a daughter of dark skies. It was Theresa who belonged here in this city of brightness and sharp shadows and handsome people, Theresa the pretty, light-haired girl of the new photograph, full of figure, smiling that day with such sweet sensuality into the sunshine.

It was better not to wonder, Bob had said. (Bang, repeated M.M. from Chicago.) But then, thought Allegra, as the men in her family had a dreary way of being, or claiming to be, Bob was very probably right. Any number of reasons why her mother might have smiled thus on that day; any description of who her friend Ted might have been. And, if there indeed was—as M.M. would put it—a story there, well, God knew, if or when Allegra ever married, she herself would hardly be unsullied by experience. It was very likely not a happy story, anyway, for a girl to smile so at Ted just a few weeks before she married Ignatius.

Suppose there was, after all, someone at Peppercorn's who did remember Theresa? Helen Viner, maybe? No, Helen Viner would be dead by now, or at the very least retired; but just suppose there was someone there who could re-create for Allegra at last a person, who could show her the unknown, what she had grown accustomed to thinking the unknowable, the living mother who for all these long years had been dead and undiscussed? A worm wriggled in Allegra's stomach at the notion, and she looked longingly back at the rumpled clean sheets M.M.'s call had brought her from. But M.M. would never forgive her; and it was more than a little irritating to Allegra to know quite to what extent M.M.'s opinion of her mattered.

Allegra curled her lip at herself, went into the sitting room, and looked again at the photograph of her mother, so different from herself. All that Allegra and the girl had in common was a dislike for potatoes. Although, now that she troubled to remember it properly, it was not the potatoes themselves that Theresa had objected to, but the idea that they made her fat.

"Shit," said Allegra, because if she thought about it, it was really very sad. Well, she would go to see Scott, to ask for directions to the bookstore: with luck, if he worked nights, he would still be asleep now.

But he was sitting at an old-fashioned typewriter in the window of his even smaller apartment, surrounded by perfect balls of crumpled paper, that crease again in the center of his brow. A writer. She smiled.

He looked up, and smiled back at her in greeting, shaming her.

"Hi, neighbor," he said. "Come in, have some juice."

"I'm not disturbing you? You looked like you were concentrating."

"Concentrating myself into the nuthouse. Mango or carrot? I don't have orange, the acid upsets my stomach."

He looked as if he had not had a day's illness in his life; but this was, after all, Los Angeles. On the floor by the refrigerator were stacked bundles of newspaper, tied neatly for recycling, and the glass he handed her urged her to save the rainforests. He was one of the good guys, was Scott.

"How's the waiting?" she said.

"Good. A good night last night, good tips. Maybe next month I can go up to the mountains, breathe some air."

"That's good," she said. Idly, she scanned the newspaper headlines beside the refrigerator. War in Europe, famine in Africa, a bishop in Missouri caught in a sex scandal. Nothing had changed while she slept.

"So," he said. "What did you find out last night?"

"Find out?"

"About your mom. Your uncle was going to tell you."

"I don't think so," she said. "I told you, we don't tell each other things in my family."

He frowned at her, his clear eyes blank, as of course, she realized, they would be. Allegra's instinct was keen for other people's families. His, she would lay bets, was warm, and undemanding, neither large nor small; there were few subjects taboo among them, and the photographs that were not on display were labeled, tidily, in a family album. They would be Protestant, or at least, not Irish. It was the Irish families who had the secrets. The poor Irish families who had left their native land, who had huddled, dozens deep, into creaking boats barely seaworthy to escape the hunger of the fair, sad old country, who had taken to the new land, along with their songs and their religion, the shame of survival while so many had died—yes, they had all had their secrets. And they had kept them close too, had hidden them, first in the corners of their rough shanties, and later, behind their newly respectable, snowy white, twitching lace curtains, had locked them in the cellars and barricaded them in the closets of their prosperous homes; and how surprised they had been when the secrets, like mushrooms in the dark, had sprouted and grown. She shivered.

"Did you say Peppercorn's was nearby?" she said. "I thought I'd go there this morning."

"Oh, sure," he said. "It's real close. Just up the hill and two blocks east, you can even walk. I'd go with you, but . . ." He jerked his head toward his desk.

"Oh, too bad," she said. Yes, Sister, she could be a hypocrite.

"Have a good time, though. Allie?"

"Hmm?"

"Does your family really not talk?"

"Really," she told him.

"Wow," he said, returning to his typewriter.

Allegra was the only pedestrian that she could see on the street. The human faces were locked in their own worlds inside the cars: a bald man, arguing on a telephone, a plump youth haranguing his dog, a beautiful blond girl, muttering anxiously to herself. Of course her family talked, she thought, scowling a little in irritation at Scott as she climbed the mild hill of her mother's city: if sheer verbiage were to be measured, the Higginses talked certainly as much as most, and very probably more than did Scott's. It was, now that she came to assess it, not inferior talk either. The Higginses told stories, made jokes, they expressed opinions. It was good talk, good crack, as Mrs. Garvey would say, such as their people had always held dear. There were only certain subjects that were avoided; and it was only unfortunate for Allegra that one of those subjects happened to be her mother.

She reached the top of the hill, and walked the two blocks east along the traffic-busy street. Novelty shops, and Thai restaurants: it must have changed since her mother's day. A liquor store, a nail salon. And then, proudly prosperous, double-fronted, with racks of magazines outside, Peppercorn's. Yes, it did then exist, the place without which her parents would not have met, and Allegra O'Riordan would never have come into being. The place her mother had known. At the sight, the worm wriggled once again in Allegra's stomach, and the temptation was sweet to keep walking, walking past it, and back down the hill to the small park she had glimpsed at its foot where brown-skinned children played. But M.M. would be calling her the next morning. Allegra shook herself. She was making a fuss, she chided herself: the chances of there being someone there who knew of Theresa were really so small as to be beneath calculation. She would go in; she would ask for Helen Viner; and on asking in vain, she could then honorably return to her everyday life. She nodded firmly to herself, straightened her hair, and tucked her shirt more neatly into the waistband of her jeans.

Inside the store, she blinked in surprise. It was modern. (Right, Allegra. Forty years have passed, and they won't have bought any new stock.) Oh, but how it had changed since the days when Allegra was accustomed to imagine it. Theresa's and Helen Viner's wares had long gone, Dad's *The Question Box*, the fat rows of new Thomas Manns and Mazo de la Roches, gone who knew where, passed proudly through families, or swollen in baths, or crumbled in attics, sitting cosseted on the shelves of a collector, or huddled in fusty rows in a thrift store. Wherever they were, they were no longer in Peppercorn's. Peppercorn's, these days, stocked shiny-covered paperbacks as well as hardcovers. It offered books on cassette, a whole section of tapes and compact discs. Above, on its ceiling, it illuminated with bright strip lighting, making reading easy and thought difficult, and dazzling into hopeless exile the dusty ghosts of a tall young man and the bright-haired girl serving him. Allegra stood, and stared at the ruination of her adolescent fancies.

"Can I help you?" A skinny kid bobbed before her, no older, probably, than her mother had been when she worked there.

"No, thanks," she said. M.M. coughed; Allegra ignored her. "No, I'll just look, for the moment."

It was a good bookstore, as Scott had promised; Allegra could recognize that, although she was not a great reader. It was well frequented too, even at this early hour: a sprinkling of slim, bejeweled matrons, one or two rumpled men who might be college professors or film directors, a girl with a no-nonsense haircut in a T-shirt that read "I'm a Writer, This Is As Dressed Up As I Get." Sitting ignored on a stepladder, immersed in a book on the Beat Generation, was the current hottest heartthrob film star of Hollywood. God, thought Allegra, he looked even younger than Scott. In a corner in the Performing Arts section, she found a collection of essays on Lenny Bruce she was sure Ron did not have, and began to feel better. Better enough to ask about Helen Viner? said M.M. Allegra sighed: she had not even told M.M. about Helen Viner. No, she did not feel better enough for that, she would never feel better enough for that, it was a stupid question, and when she asked it, everyone in the store would think she was nuts. She pulled a face at her friend, and to shut her up, took the book to the cash register.

The woman behind the desk was plump, wearing a sensible blouse.

"That be all for you?" she asked.

"Yes, thanks," said Allegra, but M.M. poked her in the ribs. She sighed. "I mean, no, as a matter of fact. It's kind of a long story. Can I see the manager?"

"Sure. Don!"

"Yo."

The skinny kid stood before her. This was the manager? Getting old, Allegra. Time for Geritol cocktails and the wonderful world of Maalox. Hello, Mr.—what was your name again?—Alzheimer.

"Hi," she said. "Can I have a word with you? It's kind of a long story, do you have a minute?"

"Sure," he said. His nose was too big, and young as he was, she could see that his hair would soon be thinning. He could not have looked more different from either Scott or the heartthrob: without a question, it was his looks which she preferred.

"You see," she said, and as she spoke, she could hear the foolishness of her words, "I'm trying to trace someone who might have known someone who used to work here, really quite a long time ago. It was my mother, you see, who worked here, that's where she met my father, and I never really knew her, but there was another woman who used to take book orders for him. For my father." (He's looking at you strangely, Allegra. Come to the point, before he leads you away in a straitjacket. Come to the point, and then you can go and sit in the sun, and read Melissa's magazines, and never wonder about your mother, ever again.) "I don't suppose," she said, "that, by any chance, you've heard of a woman who worked here about forty years ago, called Helen Viner?"

"Sure," he said.

Now, this was not part of the plan.

"You have?" she said.

"Sure." He turned to the plump woman. "May, did Helen arrive yet?"

"She just got here." She pointed a capable hand, wristwatched, wedding ringed, to the corner where Allegra had just been. "She's over by the telephone."

Oh, no, this was not part of the plan at all. Helen Viner was supposed to be untraceable. Helen Viner was supposed to be retired, probably dead. Helen Viner was supposed, at the very least, to have married and changed her surname. What Helen Viner was not supposed to be was just arrived, and over there by the telephone.

Numbly, Allegra followed Don across the floor, to a desk where a small woman stood, a list in her hand.

"Lady to see you," he said to the woman. He winked at Allegra. "Helen's the most popular person in the store."

"Oh, you." The woman laughed at him, and then turned to Allegra the stranger's face which—and the worm rose again inside her and twisted and danced—had known her mother's.

"Are you Helen Viner?" said Allegra.

The woman nodded. She was probably past eighty, but had once been pretty: her hair was a shiny silver bob, and her eyes, large in her softly wrinkled face, were still blue.

"My name's Allegra O'Riordan," said Allegra. "I think you knew my mother, it's kind of a long story." She looked at Don, who winked again at Helen, and wandered off. "Don't you want to sit down?"

"I sit down all day," said Helen. "I'm a telephone operator now, I used to be the store manager. But everything changed when the computers came." She frowned, quickly. "I've been in the book business since 1935—do you know how many years that is?"

"A long time," said Allegra: the nuns had taught her to be agreeable. And then, because having found the woman, she must at least ask the question, "Listen, this may sound strange, but I think you might have known my mother. She worked in this store, oh, about forty years ago."

"Then I probably knew her," said Helen. "I've been in the book business since 1935: do you know how many years that is?"

It was only then that Allegra realized that the eyes in the still-mobile face were as blank as a child's. Helen Viner was senile. Well, it was doubtless just as well. The sun, by now, would be hitting Melissa's corner of the courtyard; and in an hour or so, she could pour a glass of wine.

"That really is a long time," she said, kindly. "You must have seen a lot of people come and go, you probably don't remember Theresa Higgins, with the red hair."

Helen tut-tutted in exasperation. "Are you telling me," she said "what Theresa Higgins looked like? Why, she was my good friend before you were even born! My, my, Theresa Higgins, the times we had!" The old empty eyes became suddenly cautious. "Why do you want to know about her?"

Oh. She did remember. A hope flickered in Allegra's breast. "I'm her daughter," she said.

"Of course you are." Helen nodded, triumphantly. "She had red hair, you know—you don't look a thing like her."

"So they all say. But I am her daughter."

"Whose daughter?"

Yes, Helen was definitely senile. Thanks, God. Amusing. If He wanted, maybe Allegra could get Him an audition at the Cat. Allegra sighed. She was on vacation, after all: she need not wait a full hour for the wine.

"Theresa Higgins," she said.

"Theresa Higgins," said Helen. "Such a terrible thing, just terrible. But of course, it's all in the past now."

"Yes," said Allegra. "It was a terrible thing."

"She married that boy, Nate, you know, and went to live in Chicago. Poor thing, how she dreaded the winters there. Her dad bought her a silver fur coat, she said it cost far too much, but he insisted."

A kingfisher flash of long-forgotten memory, which Allegra would examine later, of her mother shivering, somewhere, beside a fire. Well, that was something to take from the conversation, after all.

"She hated the cold, didn't she?" she said.

"Who?"

"Theresa Higgins."

"She went to live in Chicago, you know, poor thing. She dreaded the winters. Her dad bought her a silver fur coat, it cost far too much, she tried to take it back to the store, but he insisted. It was a terrible thing. How is she?"

"Well, she's dead."

"Dead!"

The eyes widened in shock.

"Didn't you know?"

But that was strange, because Helen had said it was a terrible thing.

"Oh, honey," she said. "I'm so sorry. When did she die?"

"Thirty some years ago. She was run over by a cab." But she had definitely said that it was a terrible thing. "Did you really not know about it?"

"No, I didn't." She stopped, seemed to check herself. "No, I'm sure I didn't. We lost touch, you know, afterwards. It was a terrible thing, terrible."

"What was it that was a terrible thing, then?"

"Well." Her eyes shifted again; she looked, suddenly, sly, as if she were aware of her own senility and for some reason playing on it. She glanced to the telephone, and back at Allegra. "That she died, you know. Thirty some years ago. . . . She *did* die, didn't she?"

"Oh, yes." But she had said it was terrible before she knew of the death. Inside Allegra, the worm melted, to be replaced by a feeling of sinking. This was unquestionably strange. She looked around, at the brightly lit store. The girl in the T-shirt had gone; the heartthrob appeared not to have moved. Across by the cash register, May was watching them with curiosity. "Listen," she said. "Would you like to go out for half an hour? Can I buy you a cup of coffee?"

"Oh, no." Helen shook her head, firmly, and waved her list. "No, I have telephone calls to make. I'm a telephone operator, you know. I used to be the store manager, but it's all on computers now."

"Someone trying to lead you astray, Helen?" Don had reappeared, and was hovering, a little protectively, over the older woman.

"Helen knew my mother," said Allegra. "I was wondering if I could take her out for coffee, to talk about her."

"I have calls to make," said Helen. "Don't I, Don?"

"Lunch, then?" said Allegra. "I could come back later."

"Lunch?" Helen suddenly looked lost, and Allegra was shot through with sadness, for her age, and her poor lost mind. But she had said that something was a terrible thing, and definitely, the two of them must talk.

"Would you like that?" Don asked her. He cast Allegra a look that was not altogether friendly. "To go to lunch?"

"Why, yes," said Helen. "Yes, I guess that would be fine. You want us to go to lunch, right?"

"Only if it's what *you* want, Helen," said Don.

Allegra could not afford to consult Helen's wishes.

"I'll pick you up at noon," she said.

"Not today," said Don. "She's going to the dentist. It'll have to be tomorrow."

"Tomorrow, then," said Allegra. "OK?"

"Why, that will be fine," said Helen. "We're going to go to lunch, right?"

"Lunch," said Allegra. She tried a smile at Don, but he did not respond.

She was scowling as she walked back down the hill to the apartment.

So I went into a bookstore in Los Angeles. You been to Los Angeles? Nice people, but . . . The assistant was a really nice woman. I said to her, Do you have Portnoy's Complaint? *She said, Medical Books, second floor. I said, OK. How about* Less Than Zero? *She said . . .*

No, not Less Than Zero, *it was a nasty book.*

I said, OK. How about Oliver Twist? *She said, Dance Instruction, over in the corner. I said, OK. Now think about this, because it's important. Do you have* The Bible? *Well, she'd heard of that one, at least. She said, Film Scripts downstairs in the basement.*

It was too broad, thought Allegra, but there was something to work with there: audiences liked Los Angeles jokes, especially in the winter. It could not, of course, aspire to the heights of God's joke. Yes, very funny of God to let her mother die so young and Helen live so old; to allow Allegra to spend all those years wondering, with no clue about who her mother had been, and only now to show her a photograph and lead her to a woman whose mind had died before her body. If ever the Almighty were indeed to audition at the Cat, Allegra would look forward to seeing Ron deal with Him.

And yet. Her scowl changed to a frown of concentration. Senile or not, Helen had remembered, or seemed to, some things, and some of them, yes, now that she considered their conversation, some of them had even been interesting. Allegra shook her head, and turned to the old woman's words which had raised in her own brain that flicker of a memory so long buried, she would have thought, by now, forgotten altogether. Helen had remembered, yes, that Theresa had dreaded the Chicago winters, and yes—yes, that she had hated the cold. Yes, yes. Allegra's steps slowed. The memory was indeed there now, still, after all these years. Yes, there had been a log fire, somewhere, sometime, with dancing sparks that Allegra had almost believed were goblins, and outside, a world made still and fairy tale by snow. And her mother had been there, with reddened hands stretched to the fire, and she had been talking, groaning, complaining. It's so cold, Nate, she had said. Nate, isn't it cold? Nate, how can you bear this weather? Yes, Helen was right, her mother had hated the winter. And there was a coat too, which Helen said Joe Higgins had bought her; yes, again, yes, there had been a fur coat hanging for years in a closet, luxuriously silvery and lined with silk, until it had disappeared. Her mother's, of course, although she had never thought to realize it, and where on earth, now, would it have gone to? But Helen had remembered it. She had remembered too that it had cost too much, that Theresa had—did she say she had tried to take it back to the store?—but that stern Joe Higgins had insisted. That was her word, insisted. Joe had been a businessman, and self-made: Allegra had never before this heard of him as a generous man. But it could not have been easy for him to see his only daughter go all those miles away, even if he did not then know he would never see her again; thousands of miles, to a city whose winters she dreaded.

But that was not all Helen had remembered. She had remembered Theresa Higgins's hair, and that she had married Nate O'Riordan, and she had known that Allegra did not resemble her. And she had remembered something else too. She had remembered, most plainly and specifically, a terrible thing. Well, Theresa's death had indeed been terrible, a woman not yet thirty, with three small children. But what was strange was that when Helen mentioned the terrible thing, she had not yet known that Theresa was dead. Or had she? She had seemed surprised to hear of it; but then, she had seemed surprised to be asked, for the third time, to lunch. But then again, old people often remembered the past better than the present, and if she had remembered Theresa's hair, she would surely have remembered her death. Would she not? Or would she? Well. Allegra would find out more tomorrow. Until then, there was wine in the refrigerator, Melissa's magazines for the courtyard, and she was on vacation. She really need not think about Theresa Higgins for another whole day.

But even as she walked through the door of the apartment, the telephone was ringing, and it was John.

"How you doing, sweetie?" he said. "You get home OK last night?"

"Fine, thanks. I was just about to call Kathleen to thank her." Sister Philomena coughed, sharply; but it had indeed been, somewhere, on Allegra's morning agenda. "It was good to see you both."

"Mm. Well." His voice became pleased. "We had a bad shock this morning. Got up, went downstairs, and there was a hobo sitting in the kitchen."

"I'm sorry?"

"Jimmy. Hadn't shaved in a week. Kathleen nearly passed out, thought he was one of the homeless."

Jimmy was, in his father's eyes as in his mother's, in every sense perfection.

"Where'd he been?" said Allegra.

"God knows. And Jimmy, I guess. Doesn't do you any good to ask either of them."

"They're both Higgins men, then."

"What's that? Oh. Mm. Well, I'm sure you have better things to do than spend another evening with your family."

Another evening with Kathleen and John. Or rather, Kathleen, John, and this new piece of information about her mother. Allegra's eyes narrowed. John was a businessman, and thrifty, as his father had been. John might or might not remember fights over food, or dances at the pier; he could surely not have forgotten a silver fur coat that had cost far too much money, purchased at his father's insistence for his only sister's leaving present. If Allegra saw John tonight, she could talk to him about this. She could put the question to him directly, and he would, surely, have to give her, as he had managed not to last night, a direct answer. Yes; an evening with her family might well be interesting. But she carefully kept her voice mild: she too was a Higgins, after all.

"I'd love to come," she said. "I haven't seen Jimmy for years."

And it was true that she had always enjoyed her cousin's company.

"No," he said. "Good. Well, seven, then. Kathleen's cooking."

"Oh, good," she said dutifully. And sowed a seed for later on. "By the way, I went to Peppercorn's this morning."

"Oh?"

Or maybe the interrogative was her wishful thinking.

"It's a good bookstore, isn't it?"

"Hmm." John was proudly nonintellectual. Although she herself, Sister Philomena reminded her, had not exactly been curling up with Dostoyevsky since she left college.

"In fact," she said, "I had a surprise myself there. I actually met a woman who used to work with Mother. Helen Viner."

"Oh," said John.

"Do you remember her?" she asked.

"Who?"

"Helen Viner. She said she used to know Mother quite well."

"Mm. Then she'd be as old as the hills by now."

"Well, she is, quite." Allegra paused, and decided to shock a little. "She said it was a terrible thing. About Mother."

"Well," said John. "It was. Well. Seven o'clock, then."

"I'll look forward to it."

Allegra replaced the receiver, and nodded to herself in surprised satisfaction. She would see John, this evening, face-to-face. And she would look him in the eye while she asked the question about the coat. And John would not lie to her and tell her he did not remember. John was far too good a Catholic for that.

I went to Catholic school. Anyone here go to Catholic school? Uh-huh. You too, huh? Great place, Catholic school, isn't it? No, really, it is. I'll tell you the greatest thing about Catholic school. Afterwards, anything that happens to you—anything—has to be an improvement.

Allegra used the Church in her act, of course she did: with the material it offered, she maintained, it would be wickedly wasteful not to. Laura McConnell, M.M.'s eldest sister, had, one Saturday afternoon at a children's party, told her gravely that she had attended one of Allegra's shows, and had been shocked by some of the Church references. Allegra, taken aback but still, after all these years, wanting Laura's approval all the same, had thought quickly, and replied that while she regretted any offense caused, the fact was that for her, making jokes was her God-given skill, and the Cat, not the Church, her place of worship; that it provided her with a community and a fellowship which the Church did not, and while she agreed with Laura that we all needed to pray, still, the catechism had defined prayer as a raising up of the mind and heart to God, Christ had told the parable of the talents, and in the old story, Our Lady had rewarded the humble juggler, and she, Allegra, found more edification—more spiritual exercise, if Laura liked—in thinking up jokes than she did in saying Hail Marys. She had said that she was sorry it was so; that she wished she could find in the Catholic Church what she found at her place of work, but the sad truth was that she did not, so she took what consolation she could where she did find it. Laura had been impressed: she had always found Allegra interesting. Truth to tell, Allegra had somewhat impressed herself, and that evening, her act had flown. But it was the next morning, now that she thought of it, that she had finally broken up with Nick.

Allegra groaned as she poured a glass of wine, then brightened as she identified the face of the heartthrob on the top of Melissa's magazine pile. I've *seen* him, she told herself, proudly rubelike. She would read for an hour, then make a sandwich, then take a nap. She would need to conserve her strength, she told herself, for this evening.

She had not seen her cousin Jimmy for ten years. He had stopped in Chicago on his way to a college interview, and the two of them had got roaring drunk, which, when she awoke the next morning, drymouthed and heavy of heart, had also left her burdened with the guilt of having exerted a bad influence. But they had laughed a lot together, and imitated both of their fathers. And by now, presumably, he could be expected to be responsible for his own temperance.

He was a tall young man, like Bob, and despite what Kathleen might say, unmistakably a Higgins; but his cheekbones were higher than Bob's, and his hair much darker, almost auburn. He was more handsome, of course: he was a Californian.

"I was sorry about Uncle Nate," he said.

"Yes. Thank you." She supposed that one day, she would have a conversation that would not include this exchange. "He was fond of you." Well, Sister, he never said that he was not. "Do I still call you Jimmy? Or are you James these days?"

"Jimmy's fine."

"Pass the nuts around, honey," said Kathleen. She was looking at Jimmy, as Allegra had seen mothers looking at their sons, with a love that bordered on greed. Again she felt, for her brothers, that sudden envy, shocking in its viciousness.

You know when I worry? When I meet a guy called Johnny. Or Bobby, you know the sort? Great hulking guy, six-foot-two, two hundred pounds, what's your name? Billy. 'Cause if he's thirty years old, and still calling himself by a little-boy name . . .

Allegra!

Guiltily, she returned to the conversation.

"I still call myself Allegra," she said. "But I obviously don't enunciate, because everyone I meet calls me Allie. Do you live here, or are you just visiting?"

"Came to see my agent. And my dear old mom." Passing Kathleen, he kissed her, and she blushed like a girl. "I live in Santa Barbara."

"Pretty town, Santa Barbara," said John, joining them with the drinks. "Worth seeing." He pointed to Jimmy's ankles, bare between jeans and scuffed loafers. "Pity they don't sell socks there."

Jimmy looked at her, rolled his eyes, and smiled, quickly and sweetly. He sat down, sitting, she noticed, exactly as Bob did, with legs splayed and feet turned a little inward: he held his glass too with just her brother's firmly clumsy grasp. And yet he and Bob, as far as she knew, had barely met: the Higgins genetic influence must be strong. She forgave him his name; forgave him, even, his living mother.

"Do you know, you're my only cousin?" she said.

"Am I? How weird. You aren't mine, is she, Mom? There are dozens of us. What sort of Catholic did Uncle Nate call himself, anyway?"

"A damn fine one," said John.

"Damn fine," said Jimmy, and the two of them giggled like children, while John pretended not to be pleased. He sent himself up slightly in the presence of his son, deepening his voice for Jimmy to imitate: he was growing old.

"Remember when you guys came to visit for Easter?" said Jimmy. "I was just a little kid, but I remember the Good Friday. Dad and Uncle Nate spent the whole morning debating whether it would tip their lunch from a—what was it called, that snack meal you were allowed on fast days?—a collation to a full meal if they had potato salad with their tuna sandwich."

"Did they?" said Allegra. She did not remember, but could well believe it: she had spent many Good Fridays with her father.

"One thing you must realize about my son," said John, "is that he makes his living by telling lies."

"Oh, this happened. I remember the conversations. 'Well, John, this is a dilemma I grapple with every year.' 'You see, Ignatius, my usual ruling is, three eighths of an inch of sandwich filling, and one medium scoop of potato salad, *if* the salad's made without eggs.' All morning."

"You got a medium scoop?" Yes, there was a reason why Allegra had liked Jimmy. "You spoiled brat, we only got small."

"Hey, this is California, we indulge ourselves. But no eggs in the salad, mind."

"Of course not. Eggs are protein."

"Exactly. Protein."

"An awe-inspiring thing, an imagination," said John. "A gift of God, really."

"So round and round they go, bread, tuna, mayonnaise, lettuce, and tomato, can you have celery in the salad, *if* you have salad, if you cut out the tomato, only it has to be the tomato, because lettuce doesn't count, and of course, no eggs."

"Protein."

"Protein. No eggs in the sandwich, no eggs in the salad, *if* they have salad. So off we all go to Stations of the Cross, it goes on forever, I'm four years old, and Jesus is falling for the ninth time under Simon of Southeast Jerusalem, and all of a sudden, Uncle Nate lets out this terrible groan, and he turns to Dad, he's in agony, truly, and he whispers, 'But John—*mayonnaise is made with egg!*' Swear to God."

John shook his head. "Self-discipline never hurt anyone," he said. "Let me freshen your drink, sweetie. Jimmy, don't you think your cousin's looking well?"

"Terrific." But Jimmy frowned at her, sympathetically. "I hope you're taking care of yourself now, it's rough when people die. I always thought Uncle Nate looked sad. I wonder if he ever really got over Aunt Theresa."

"Don't you think he did? I'd think you would, one day, wouldn't you?" Yet her father had never remarried.

"Are we ready to eat, dear?" said John. "I hope you two are hungry. Kathleen's cooked."

He beamed as he led them to the heavy table, and leaned back, waiting for Maria to bring the fruit of Kathleen's labor. He was meant, Allegra saw suddenly, to have not one child but many children. Jimmy had been born late to his parents: presumably, one or the other had had a problem in that area, although it would never be discussed. Another secret. Although, to be fair, Allegra would never consider discussing with Kathleen or John the methods she took to control her own still-untested fertility.

A plate, heavy with food, was set in front of her. Allegra knew her manners. She took one mouthful, frowned thoughtfully, took one more, nodded in confirmation.

"This is really delicious," she said, and fell to with enthusiasm. Afterwards, although she tried, she could remember not one element of the meal but the muzzling, inevitable texture of the mashed potatoes which accompanied it.

She might as well have spared herself the trouble. Kathleen smiled at her in acknowledgment, but her eyes were on Jimmy, and did not leave him until he had achieved a steady, silent progression across his plate. One child was well enough for Kathleen: Allegra would pity a second.

"You're like your father," John told her. "He appreciated a good cut of meat." He nodded at Jimmy. "This fellow lives on beans and seaweed."

"I was vegetarian," said Jimmy. "For six weeks when I was twenty-one."

"Filthy messes you wouldn't give to the dog; he nearly died of starvation. I have meat at least once a day, every day except Ash Wednesday and Good Friday, and my doctor says I have the cholesterol of a man of forty. And I don't look like a famine-relief poster either."

"You were thin too, dear," said Kathleen. "When you were his age."

"At least I had a job," said John. "I suppose there's no point in asking if you'll still be here at the weekend?"

"Depends on how my meetings go," said Jimmy. "Why?"

"I might want you to look at my computer again." He reached for mustard, and helped himself liberally. "Can't get the damn printer to work. Oh, and your cousin's coming to the eleven-fifteen on Sunday."

"Oh. Good."

Under her lashes, Allegra looked to see his reaction to the summons. But if he had one, it was well hidden: he was, indeed, a Higgins man. And speaking of Higgins men, it was probably time to raise the topic. She sighed a little to herself, and cast her own eyes to her plate.

"I went to Peppercorn's today," she said.

"Isn't it terrific?" said Jimmy: of course, he was a writer, and would know bookstores. "Take my advice, though, and don't open an account there. Instant bankruptcy. Did you meet Don?"

"The manager? The kid with the nose?"

"That's Don. He's a great guy, incredible. He just adores his job, it's wonderful—he can track down every book you have heard of and its sequel, and the biography of the writer's Aunt Mildred. I once asked him for *The Winnow* by J. D. Baines. He could not find it—drove him crazy. Crazy. There's no such book of course, I'd invented it. You should have seen him—he went crazy."

"I hope you made it up to him," said Kathleen.

"Yes, Mom, I made it up to him. Confessed all, groveled for forgiveness, and bought up all his John Fante stock. Have you read him, Allegra? Great writer, came here in the thirties, wrote wonderful stories about the place. Don's always trying to get people to read him. But he was still depressed about J. D. Baines."

Allegra laughed. What a funny thing was a family, which drew you so quickly so close to a more-or-less stranger; and how tempting it was to stay in this cozy corner of a conversation, how easy and how sweet it would be to make a joke about liars, or to ask more about John Fante, or to cap his anecdote with the one about Ron and the tax audit, while John and Kathleen exchanged glances of half-laughing, impotent disapproval, and let pass forever the occasion to wonder. But Helen Viner had spoken of a silver fur coat; and had spoken too of a terrible thing.

"Do you know the old woman who works there?" she asked him instead. "Helen Viner. She's very old, I think they keep her on as kind of a charity case."

"Helen?" He nodded. "She's terrific. I go in there sometimes just to talk to her about the old days."

"Do you? She seemed quite senile to me."

"No, if you can keep her focused, she's OK. She's really interesting, you know—she's had an incredible life. She knew everyone—Hemingway, Fitzgerald . . ."

"J. D. Baines?" said John.

"He broke her heart, Dad, it was the tragedy of her life."

"She knew my mother too," said Allegra.

"Who did?" said Jimmy.

"Helen Viner."

"Helen? How?"

"Well, they worked together." Allegra sneaked a glance at John, who was looking at Jimmy. "At Peppercorn's."

"Aunt Theresa worked at Peppercorn's?"

"Didn't you know?"

"No!" Jimmy dropped his fork, and turned to his father. "Dad, you never told me that!"

"Didn't I?" said John. "I suppose you didn't ask. Do your ankles simply not feel the cold, or are you too busy inventing authors to attend to them?"

"Dad! I've been going all my life to Peppercorn's, and you never told me Aunt Theresa worked there! Meet my father, Allegra, the only walking stone wall known to mankind."

"Don't shout, dear," said Kathleen. "We're all in the same room. And I think our guest would like some more wine."

"Sorry, Mom. Sorry, Allegra." Passing the wine to Allegra, he caught his mother's eye. "Great food," he said, and she pinkened again.

"My mother worked at Peppercorn's," said Allegra, "until she married my dad, and went to live in Chicago." She paused. Jimmy was looking at her with friendly interest: the eyes of his two parents were on their plates. "Didn't she, John?"

"Mm?" John looked up. "Yes, I guess she did." He nodded, and with neither haste nor hesitation returned to his food.

"Helen said," continued Allegra, "that Mother had dreaded the move. She said that she hated the cold. Was that true?"

"I don't know," said John. "I really don't remember one way or the other."

"She said something else," said Allegra. "She said that your father had bought her a silver fur coat that was far too expensive."

"Did he?" said John. "Not like the old man as far as I recall. He was quite the tightwad, wasn't he, Kathleen? Came up through the Depression, of course. Used to save pieces of string. Remember the time he tried to ration the toothpaste, said we were using too much? Nearest I ever saw my mother come to losing her temper with him. A fine man, mind."

"She said," said Allegra, "that it was a very expensive coat that Mother tried to take back to the store. But she said your father insisted. Do you remember that coat?"

"Coat?" said John. "Remember his suits, Kathleen? No stinting of money there. Of course, in those days, a professional man had to look his best."

"The coat he bought Mother," said Allegra. She looked at John, for the first time in her life, with calculation in her gaze. John was a Catholic and a Jesuit boy. He was also a businessman, who would remember a too-expensive fur coat. John would avoid telling the truth; but he would surely not sully his soul with an outright lie. "Before she left, he bought her a fur coat. Do you remember it?"

John's gaze, gray and bland, met her own. "I can't say I do," he said.

And the world shivered, and changed, and would never be the same again.

"Can't you?" said Allegra. "That's interesting. I'd have thought you would have, wouldn't you?"

"Are you enjoying yourself, dear?" said Kathleen. "Are you finding your way around town?"

They began to talk about Los Angeles.

Chapter Four

Allegra had been taught that there were lies and there were untruths; that there were ways and there were ways of telling the same truth that could turn it slightly or completely to a falsehood, without involving an actual lie. A lie was a sin. Sister Philomena had said that every time a Catholic told a lie, it drove the nails an inch deeper into Jesus' bleeding hands and feet. She had also said that all untruths were not lies. She had said that if a stranger approached you on the street and asked whether you had completed your history assignment and you gave him an untrue answer, that did not count as a lie because the stranger had no right to know. She had added that an untrue answer to Sister Philomena herself—who had every right to know—would be most certainly a lie. She had said that the reason the congregation at Mass bowed its head at the moment of transubstantiation was in order that, in countries where the Church was persecuted, the faithful could truthfully assure prying government officials that they had not seen the consecrated Host that day. She had said that if you lived in

America and were harboring a guilty criminal, yes, even if it was your own mother (nervous titters from the class as all but Allegra imagined their mothers swinging a bloody meat cleaver), and the police came knocking on your door, then your obligation was to tell the truth and hand the guilty party over. She had said that if you lived in one of the persecuted countries, were sheltering a priest in your house, and denied his presence, not to the American police, but to those inquisitive non-American government officials, while adding silently "at least, as far as *you're* concerned," that made it neither a lie nor an untruth, but a mental reservation, and in those circumstances, altogether acceptable in the eyes of God. What she had not said was how much of a lie it was to claim, quite specifically, not to remember a too-expensive fur coat, purchased by a tightwad, forty years ago. A substantial one, almost certainly; unless it had been a mental reservation (but Allegra was not trying to persecute the Church) or John had felt she did not have a right to know (but if she did not, then who did?). And he would not incur the sin of lying unless he saw good reason for it. Yet what reason for lying could there possibly be?

Allegra's own relationship with the truth had long been complicated. In her stage act, she told, unashamedly, fat lies. She told stories about her mother, her boyfriend, her boyfriend's mother. She perjured herself nightly to make of herself a normal woman, and felt no remorse for doing so: it was her job. But it was also her job to identify other truths, truths so self-evident that they passed most people by, yet so universal that when Allegra, in her guise of normal woman, presented them, they would cry out in delighted recognition. In many ways, the truth was more important to Allegra than to most: to a surprising degree she found the thought disturbing that John had lied to her.

She slept badly; and the next morning, she called Bob.

"What do you want?" he said.

"Checking if you'd found a full-time job," she said. "Seems not. Too bad."

Bob was an architect, and successful enough to work from home on Fridays, which not many were permitted to tease him about; but then, Allegra was his big sister. He grunted acknowledgment of her pleasantry: he had heard it from her before.

"How're you doing?" he said.

"Good. It's nice here, I'm getting a tan."

"Yeah, me too. Mosquitoes are a problem, though."

Oh. He did not know where she was. But of course he did not: it was her father who would have told him.

"I'm in Los Angeles," she said.

"Oh? Why?"

"Why not? I've seen John."

"Good."

"Oh, he's OK, really, Bob." Although he had not been OK to Bob, and less so to Lois. "Oh, and I saw Jimmy last night—you know, he's a really nice guy, believe it or not. He's funny."

"Very good."

"He's a screenwriter these days. Remember that little kid who used to run around? Well he's as tall as you now, and he—"

"Good! Look, Allegra, I really do have to work, you know. Did you want something?"

"Yes, yes, I did!" Bob was easily capable of hanging up on her. "Don't go away, Bob, I want to ask you something."

"What?"

"Well, not if you're going to take that tone."

"What tone?"

"That tone."

Bob paused, sighed.

"What," he said, then, "do you want to ask?"

What. She stopped, tried to arrange her thoughts, screwing up her mouth in confusion.

"You'll think I'm crazy," she said.

"Sound of man biting tongue."

"Shut up. OK. OK." She took a breath. "I don't suppose," she began, "that by any chance, you might remember a coat that used to hang in Dad's closet? A silver fur coat?"

"Oh," said Bob. "Very funny."

"What d'you mean?"

"Oh, yes. Amusing. My sister's a comedian, you know."

"What are you talking about?"

"She keeps us cracked up all the time, it's real fun, you know?" His voice changed. "Did John put you up to this? Witty dinner table anecdotes. 'Call that brother of yours, sweetie, and see if he remembers'?"

"Bob," she said. "You've lost me."

"Yeah," he said. "And you've forgotten the day I burned the fur coat."

He what?

"You *burned* it?"

"In the backyard, don't you remember? Public protest against the exploitation of endangered species for commercial gain? Dad was furious, I was grounded for a month. And it was summer."

Yes. Oh, yes, summer. A teenaged Bob, bushy-haired and scowling in a heavy metal T-shirt, kicking sullen heels around the airless August house. But for the life of her, Allegra could not remember the event that had led to his imprisonment.

"You burned it?" she said.

"In the backyard, after supper, in front of everyone. You were there, I can't believe you've forgotten. I've never known Dad so mad."

"He would be. Did you know it was Mother's?"

"Oh, yeah. He told me."

"He *told* you?" Her father, who had never mentioned her mother, had told Bob that.

"Yeah. He said it was about the only thing he'd had left of hers, that it had been a special leaving present from her father and from her brother John, that after she died he couldn't bear to part with it because he remembered how beautiful she'd looked in it, and that now, on a stupid schoolboy whim I'd grow out of, I'd destroyed his last memory of the only woman he'd loved. Then he grounded me. For a month. In the summer. And I didn't grow out of it, I still think it's disgusting."

Alone in Los Angeles, Allegra sat, openmouthed.

"He told you all that," she said. "And you never told me."

"Well," said Bob. "You've forgotten my public protest, haven't you? There's someone at the door, I've got to go. Take care, talk to you later, OK? Bye."

Allegra replaced the receiver, and aimed at it a careful finger.

"Bang," she said.

Then sat, staring at the mute telephone, turning the situation in her mind, twisting it this way and that, trying to find on its glassy surface a crevice where she might place a fingerhold. John had then told a lie after all; not only did he know about the coat, but he had been one of its donors. But why on earth would he lie? If he had indeed been so generous as to join in an extravagant gift, then why not simply say so? It was not as if there were something to hide there. Unless, she thought, feeling again the sinking she had felt in the bookstore, unless there was. A terrible thing, Helen had said, Helen whom she was going to see today, poor Helen with her overstuffed mishmash of a brain, half-thoughts and fragmented memories. Oh, but to Helen through her long, confused life, so many things must have been terrible. Still, she had said it was a terrible thing. And John had told her a lie.

Allegra shivered sharply, and jumped when Scott knocked on her door.

"I thought you could use a map of the city," he said. "It's difficult to get around until you know your way."

"Thank you," she said. "That's kind." Instinctively, Sister Philomena opened her mouth; but was forced to shut it again. It *was* kind of Scott: he was a kind young man, devoted to his work, and he cared about the environment. It was too easy to belittle the goodness of WASPs, simply because they came at it directly, not bouncing off obscure saintly anecdotes, or convoluted definitions of sin. It was refreshing, she decided, to be with non-Catholics. "Coffee?"

"Tea, please, I know where it is." He reached into a cupboard, the muscles of his shoulders and back shifting beneath his tattered cotton T-shirt. A magnificent piece of sculpture; but one she could no more humanly desire than Michelangelo's marble David. Looking at him, she was suddenly reminded of Nick, whose back view had been so much narrower, his movements so subtly, but so unmistakably, those of an older man. For a second, she turned away, as the memory of his lanky body awoke her own to sorrow. But that would lead nowhere; with swift, kind brutality, she killed the sensation.

"OK." The tea found, Scott turned and smiled at her. "How was Peppercorn's? Did you find out more about your mom?"

"Aren't you supposed to be writing?" she said.

"I got ten minutes," he said. "So talk to me. What happened yesterday?"

He straddled a chair, and looked at her expectantly, a child waiting for a story. And, beautiful as he was, she must find a story to tell him.

"Well," she said, "it's really quite funny." And yes, she discovered, if you held it to a particular light, it could be. "OK, so here's the cast of characters. You have my Uncle John, who was Mother's brother, who never says a word about her. You have his wife, Kathleen, who never says a word, period. You have my cousin Jimmy, who says quite a lot, but none of it is about Mother, because nobody ever told him anything about her. You have two old friends of hers, called Alice and Albert, who might talk about her, except we'll never know what they'd say, because no one will admit to knowing where to find them, even though I'm almost certain they and Kathleen, and yes, probably John too sometimes, used to go dancing together on the pier. *And,* ladies and gentlemen, proudly completing the lineup, you have an old lady who works at Peppercorn's, who did so know Mother, pretty well, it seems, and will talk about her too, which is great, except that none of what she says makes any sense because she's completely senile." Yes, if you looked at it like that, it could be funny. "Rewarding, huh?"

But Scott did not seem to see the humor at all. "I don't understand," he said. "What about this John? Doesn't he remember her?"

"You'd think he would." Allegra choked on a laugh. "You'd think that being someone's brother, being born just a few years apart from them, and being brought up in the same house as them, you might just have a memory or two. Not John. He's forgotten it all. Quite a feat, really."

"That's weird," he said. He looked at her, again, with that slanted look. "Must be strange to live with."

Did you ever go out with a guy, and halfway through the evening, you feel he's watching you? Not watching you, va-va-voom, but . . . watching you? Like he's thinking, Ohhh. So that's the way she butters her roll. So she does her laundry on Saturday, huh? Verrry interesting. After a bit, you're thinking, Hey, is he from the planet Zekon, or am I?

There were times when Allegra tired herself with telling herself jokes.

"You should get back to your writing," she said. "And I have things to do."

She had wondered whether Helen Viner would remember her. But the old woman was waiting in the front of the store, clutching her purse, her feet close together, her face bright and intent, like the little girl in the classroom who has studied hard for the test.

"You're Theresa Higgins's girl," she informed her. "You don't look a thing like her."

"That's right," Allegra agreed. "Are you still free for lunch? Where shall we go?"

"There's a place across the street," said Don, who was hovering: if Helen was the child, then he was beyond question the mother. "It's not too expensive and not too unhealthy."

"We go there all the time," said Helen. "It's right across the street, you know."

"We'll be about an hour," said Allegra to Don, adult to adult.

She almost, indeed, took Helen's hand as they crossed the street. How small the old were, and how frail: Helen was hardly bigger than M.M.'s Elizabeth. But Elizabeth was taut and juicy, and if you buried your nose in her stomach—as Allegra sometimes did, pretending to gag in disgust while her goddaughter squirmed and giggled gleefully—you were wrapped in all the loveliest of aromas, honey and milk, freshly baked muffins, and nameless, expectant childhood. While to smell Helen—at the thought, Allegra felt her nose wrinkle in genuine revulsion. It was unkind of life to bring you, at the end, to this unlovely parody of what you had once been. But at least Helen was seeing her natural end. Allegra looked down at the thin strands of hair that bobbed near her elbow, and tried to sort distaste from pity, pity from envy, for this woman alive, while her own young mother was dead. That would take more than Sister Philomena to untangle.

The restaurant was dark, and quiet, which boded better for the conversation than for the food. Helen slipped into a low booth and took the oversized menu into her tiny hands, an elderly Alice who had drunk the magic potion and become small.

"What shall I have?" she asked Allegra. "I have to watch my cholesterol, you know."

"What do you usually have?" said Allegra.

"I come here all the time," she said. "With Don, you know. He's a darling boy. They do marvelous French toast here, but I have to watch my cholesterol. What shall I have?"

"Chicken salad's healthy," said Allegra.

"Then that's what I'll have! Aren't you smart. They do marvelous French toast, but I have to watch my cholesterol. Don always has the French toast, and I always have the chicken salad, and we split. I shouldn't do it, but he says he won't tell anyone if I don't. We come here all the time, you know, he's a darling boy."

"Well," said Allegra. "We could do that. You could have the chicken salad, and I could have the French toast."

"Oh." She shook her head, doubtfully. "But I have to watch my cholesterol, you know."

"Oh, well," said Allegra, with whom not even Sister Philomena could currently find fault. "I won't tell anyone, if you don't."

"Then that's what we'll do! Aren't you smart. I come here all the time, you know. With Don." She frowned. "What is it we're ordering, again?"

When the food arrived, she took most of the French toast, and fell upon it with surprising appetite. Allegra watched her, a little anxiously: now of all times, she did not want to be responsible for a heart attack. Dad burn it, Corporal, the old-timer was right about to tell us where the mine shaft was when that pesky French toast got her.

"So," she said. "You remember my mother? Theresa Higgins. With red hair."

"Oh my, yes." Helen nodded. "Theresa Higgins, of course I remember her. I've been in the book business since 1935: do you know how many years that is?"

But Jimmy had said that if you could make her focus her mind, she could hold a conversation. Allegra sighed, silently.

"That's a long time," she said.

"I didn't have to work, you know, we had plenty of money. Mother was furious, but what was I going to do, sit around all day doing lady things? Mother came from Boston, and she didn't think I should have worked at all. My brother Alex didn't like it either, said it reflected on Mother, he was always her favorite. Malcolm was good about it, but of course he died."

"I'm sorry," said Allegra.

"Thirty-one, he was my baby brother. A lovely boy." She took a tissue from her sleeve, and blew her nose. "My, aren't those flowers pretty, what do you suppose they are?"

"I think they're made of silk," said Allegra. "But they are pretty, aren't they? Helen, how well did you know Theresa Higgins?"

"It was a terrible thing," said Helen. "Just terrible."

"Yes, it was. She was my mother, you know. What was she like?"

"Theresa? Irish as Paddy's pig, but we were very good friends. She had bright red hair, you know, and a temper to go with it. My, how we used to laugh. I used to call her Molly Malone, and she used to call me—what did she call me? Some silly name. She was years younger than me, and Irish as Paddy's pig, but we were very good friends."

A redheaded temper. Yes, that would square with fights over potatoes.

"Did you say," said Allegra, "that she had a temper?"

"Oh my, yes, she was Irish, you know. I remember one afternoon, she was angry with Mr. . . . what was his name, the son of a bitch who owned the store back then?"

Allegra smiled, remembering the letter.

"Mr. White," she said.

"Mr. White, well, she was angry with him, I don't know why, and she spent the whole afternoon walking behind him imitating him behind his back—she was a marvelous mimic—and every time he turned around, she'd pretend to be dusting the shelves, it was the funniest thing you've ever seen. Little pretty redheaded thing following this great bear around the store, mimicking him." Abruptly, she stopped. "Now what in the world brought that on?"

Allegra sat still for a moment, and bit her lip, as the black-and-white girl, hot-tempered and a marvelous mimic, flounced impudently past shelves of books long sold.

"She was my mother," she said.

"So she was." Wrapped in the self-centered tranquillity of the young and the very old, Helen nodded, oblivious to any emotion of Allegra's. "You don't look a thing like her. We worked together, although I never had to work, we had plenty of money. She married that boy Nate, you know, and went to live in Chicago. She and I lost touch, of course. It was a terrible thing, just terrible. Those flowers are so pretty. Are they carnations, do you suppose?"

The terrible thing, again.

"What was a terrible thing?" she asked.

"Excuse me?"

"You said something was a terrible thing. What was it?"

"Oh." Helen looked away, and then back at Allegra. "Well, that she died so young, you know. Such a pretty young thing, so full of life. My, my, Theresa Higgins, Irish as Paddy's pig, but we were very good friends, you know."

But Helen had not known that Theresa was dead.

"But you didn't know that," said Allegra. "You said it was a terrible thing yesterday too, and you didn't know then that she was dead."

"Oh yes, honey." A firm nod of confirmation. "Yes, she died thirty some years ago. Nate came to see me the night afterwards, dear God, the state he was in. I shouldn't say this to you because he was your father, but he was drunk. Now, Nate was a great tall Irishman, he could hold his liquor better than anyone, and I'd never seen him drunk before. But that night afterwards, I heard a knock on my door, and I went to answer it, and there he was swaying in the doorway. Do you suppose, if we asked very nicely, they'd let me take one of those flowers home? They're so pretty, aren't they?"

But that was impossible: her father had not visited Los Angeles for several years after her mother died. Allegra, looking blandly into the blank, blue eyes, forced herself to clarity.

"Are you sure it was when she died?" she said. "I don't think my father came to L.A. at that time."

"What time, honey?"

"The time my father came to see you, drunk. Nate O'Riordan, you know."

"Nate O'Riordan, drunk? Well, I don't remember that, I must say! He was a great, tall Irishman, you know, he could hold his liquor better than anyone."

So my grandma and my grandpa are lying in bed, and my grandpa says, I'm going downstairs for a bowl of ice cream, do you want some? She says, Yes, but only if you remember to add the chocolate sauce, stupid old fool. Sure, he says, vanilla or strawberry? Vanilla, she says, and chocolate sauce. Sure, he says, nut sprinkles? Yes, but just a few, and don't forget to add the chocolate sauce, stupid old fool. Sure, sure. So he goes downstairs, he's gone a long time, and at last, he comes back up, he's got a big plate of bacon and eggs, hash browns, toast on the side, big cup of fresh-ground coffee. She looks at it, and says, Stupid old fool! You forgot the mushrooms!

It happened! Swear to God!

Allegra set her teeth, fought a sudden, shocking compulsion to take Helen by her frail shoulders, and shake and shake until the top of her useless old head fell off and the jumbled pieces of her brain lay scattered on the solid restaurant floor for a sensible person to sort and make sense of. She clutched her napkin until it passed; there was that here which was more important than her anger. There had been a terrible thing. One night, her hardheaded father had appeared on Helen's doorstep, drunk; and last night, upright John had told her a lie. And there was a photograph signed to Ted.

Helen, Allegra accepted, frowning to herself as she swallowed the fury of acceptance, was too clearly no longer capable of real conversation. But on the other hand, maybe she might lead Allegra to those who would be. If Helen and Theresa had indeed been friends, then it could well be that Helen had known other friends of Theresa's. She looked at the old lady, who was toying, a little wearily, with a lettuce leaf; but if Allegra could not afford herself the indulgence of self-pity or frustration, then neither, at the moment, could she extend the luxury of compassion.

"My mother used to talk about some people from around here," she said. "I only know their names, I don't suppose you'd remember them?"

"Remember who?"

"These people. Friends of my mother's. Theresa Higgins, you know."

"Oh, honey." Helen straightened her fork on her plate. "Theresa had so many friends, she was such a pretty little thing. Oh, look! I don't think I've ever seen such pretty carnations. Do you suppose, if we asked very nicely, they'd let me take one home?"

But Allegra hardened her heart.

"There was a couple," she said, "called Alice and Albert. I think they all used to go dancing together, on the pier. And—there was a guy too. A man. Called Ted, or possibly Edward?"

"Honey, so many years ago. Theresa was a marvelous dancer, now that I do remember."

Another new image. Theresa, whirling and dancing in a blue fog of tobacco smoke and clean-jawed, admiring young men. Allegra filed it, along with the earlier image, for later inspection.

"Then that's who she'd have danced with," she said. "Alice and Albert. Helen, do you remember a man called Ted? Did she ever go dancing with him too?"

"There was a boy," said Helen.

She paused, took her napkin, patted her lips.

"My, that was good," she said.

Allegra waited; but she sat in silence.

"You said there was a boy," she said then.

"Oh my, yes. He used to come and visit her at the store, she led him a terrible chase. What was his name now?" She paused, furrowed her wrinkled brow. "Oh, yes," she said, at last. "Yes. Nate. Nate something. She married him, and went to Chicago, poor thing, she dreaded the winters there. It was a long time ago. I've been in the book business since 1935; do you know how many years that is?"

Yes, it was an unusual sense of humor, was the Almighty's.

"That's a long time," said Allegra. And it was a long time. The old woman, now, really had behaved herself for as long as might reasonably be expected: it was not compassion but cold practicality that made the younger sign for the check. But faint as the scent of her mother was, it was still the strongest she had yet found.

"Do you think," she asked, "that I might see you again? I've really enjoyed our talk, you know."

"I'd have to ask Don," said Helen. "He's a darling boy, but I mustn't take advantage. I have calls to make. I'm a telephone operator, you know, I used to be the store manager."

"Of course you must ask him. Or—how about this? Maybe I could come and visit you at home?"

"At home?" said Helen. "Well, I don't entertain very much, you know."

"You wouldn't need to entertain me." Allegra blinked at herself, shocked: she was normally regarded as being rather polite. "I'd just like to talk some more about Theresa. And you might"—an idea striking her, for old people were such pack rats—"you might even have a letter from her, or something. A photograph?"

"I don't think so," said Helen. "You know, Theresa hated to have her photograph taken."

The truth of which, rather than any impulse of kindliness, shocked Allegra back into her usual self.

"I'm sorry," she said. "I know I'm being terrible. It's just that she was my mother, you see, and I'd really like to find out about her, if I could."

"Of course you would," said Helen. Allegra looked up in surprise: without warning or expectation, she was talking to a brisk, intelligent woman. "It must be so difficult for you, with people keeping secrets."

"Secrets?"

"What secrets?" The woman who had once been Helen was gone. Allegra suspected she had been lucky to catch even so brief a glimpse of her.

"You said someone was keeping secrets."

"Oh, I never keep secrets. It's bad for the health."

Allegra replaced her napkin on the plate: it was crumpled almost to shreds.

"May I visit you?" she said. "At home?"

"At home? Well, I don't entertain very much, you know. My, those flowers are so pretty. Is it time to go back to the store yet?"

As Allegra sorted the change, her soul rose from her body to shake a furious fist at the deadpan heavens. But it was really none of it Helen's fault. She sought for some harmless conversation.

"Do you know," she said, "that I think you know my cousin Jimmy? He says he comes into the store."

"Oh?" Helen's eyes widened, nervously, at the introduction of a new topic. "A lot of people come into the store."

"He's a tall guy, with reddish hair. He says he talks to you, often, about the old days, says you're fascinating. In fact—oh, I hadn't thought of this—he's Theresa Higgins's nephew."

"Theresa Higgins's nephew." Helen nodded knowingly, above those panic-stricken eyes. "Of course I know him. He comes into the store. What's his name?"

"Jimmy."

"*Jimmy*. Yes, of course I know him. He's Theresa Higgins's nephew."

Allegra's heart, suddenly, hurt. But she had been trying to be kind, truly she had.

"You probably know a lot of people," she offered.

And that was the right thing to say. "Honey, so many. I've been in the book business since 1935. Do you know how many years that is?"

"God," said Allegra, "that's a long time."

It was, as Sister Philomena readily agreed, the very least that she could do.

When they reached the store, Helen made hastily off. Allegra cursed herself: she had not thought to suggest the bathroom in the restaurant. She nodded, hopefully friendly, toward Don.

"We had a good lunch," she said. "We split the French toast. I wasn't supposed to tell you, but it seems to be a tradition."

Don allowed a thin smile. "She really should watch her cholesterol," he said.

"Well." But Allegra continued to try. "She knew my mother," she said. "We tried to talk, but—it's difficult to get her to concentrate, isn't it?"

"She does OK," said Don.

"Oh, I'm sure she does. It's just that it's quite important to me, you see. My mother died when I was small, and I really don't remember her."

"Yes," said Don. "Well. She may be gone for a while, you know, but if you want to look at the books?"

"I might come back in tomorrow," said Allegra. "We'd sort of half arranged"—Sister Philomena coughed; but if Helen had not arranged, then Allegra had, which did indeed make it half, after all—"that I'd go to visit her, and I'd really like to sort that out, you know?"

"She doesn't work Saturdays," said Don.

"Then I'll come on Monday."

"Whatever."

"You see," said Allegra, "I really don't remember my mother at all."

But Don had turned his back; and if he heard her, he gave no sign.

There was, of course, she reminded herself, wandering from the quiet store to the wide street, no earthly reason why Don should like her. A complete stranger making her way into his store, accosting his elderly friend, and tiring her with questions about a mythical dead mother—no, seen through Don's eyes, she was not an attractive picture. But it was a pity, because she did like him; and she was used on the whole, when she liked, to being liked back. Well, but she had more on her mind at the moment than popularity.

As soon as she reached Melissa's apartment, she went into the bathroom, and stared at herself in the mirror, her brows drawn into a frowning line. Helen had said that people were keeping secrets. She had said, again, that something in Theresa's life—and Allegra was becoming sure that whatever it was, it was not her death—had been a terrible thing. She had said that after it—whatever it was—happened, Allegra's father had been drunk. But that was not what Allegra was thinking of, now. Somewhere during the course of the lunch, Helen had said something else too, something that had been, not very strange to Allegra, but just a little, just enough to register as such. Allegra frowned further, replaying the conversation in her mind. Theresa, it seemed, had been a good dancer, yes, and a marvelous mimic. Yes, and she had had a hot temper, and been Irish as Paddy's pig, as Helen with her unthinking, outdated racial snobbery, had phrased it. Yes, Helen had called her Molly Malone, and Theresa had not appeared to mind too much, because the two had laughed together. And that, of course, was it. They had laughed.

Allegra could not remember her mother's laugh. Absurd, she

told herself immediately: of course she could. But no, no, now that she thought of it, she could not. She could remember her mother speaking, comforting a banged knee, ordering groceries over the telephone, singing "All the Pretty Little Horses," and "When Irish Eyes Are Smiling," even, now, thanks to Helen, complaining to her father about the cold. She could not once remember her laughing. Her mother had not laughed, much. Allegra had assumed that she had been serious by nature, like her husband. But Allegra and Bob both laughed a lot; and so, it seemed, had the girl Helen had known. And a terrible thing had happened to the girl Helen had known. Yes: it had to have been a terrible thing indeed that had killed a woman's laughter. Allegra shivered, and jumped with relief when the telephone rang. It was M.M.

"I couldn't get to the telephone earlier," she said. "Ricky was bitten by the next door's dog, and Elizabeth came down with tonsillitis. Never have two children sick at the same time."

"I don't plan to," said Allegra. To tease M.M., she sometimes affected horror of motherhood. "Are they OK?"

"Fine. Ricky's all bandaged up, Elizabeth's wheezing and grumping, they're both about to kill each other, so I've locked them in the playroom with Paul's gun collection—just kidding, unfortunately. If anything happens to Lucy, she goes to school anyway, two at home's my absolute limit." The sound traveled across the continental landmass, of M.M. seating herself and sipping expectantly at her coffee. "So," she said.

Far away in Los Angeles, Allegra sighed in irritation, and smiled in affection. M.M. would be sitting on the wide wicker armchair she alone found so comfortable, and would be drinking from the mug with the poppies on. She would only just have taken the pot from the stove: she liked her coffee punishingly hot. "So?" she mimicked.

"So what do you have to tell me?"

"God, M.M., don't you have enough to think about?"

"I live through you. A life of glamour and intrigue and no cartoons on TV. Come on, did you get to go to the bookstore or what?"

"God!" So much had happened in the quiet day and a half since they had spoken. Allegra squeezed her temples, trying to remember at what point she had left the physical M.M. at home in Chicago for the all-seeing M.M. who traveled everywhere with her inside her head. "OK. Yes, I did go to Peppercorn's."

"Yes?"

"Yes." Allegra smiled, decided to torment. "It's a good bookstore," she said.

"Good. What else?"

"The people there are really nice."

"Leggie!"

"Let me finish." Unkindly, Allegra paused for dramatic effect. "One of them is an old lady called Helen . . ." She paused again: she could really be heartless. ". . . who used to know Mother quite well."

"Leggie!"

"Yes." Yet another pause, probably adding to Allegra's lot a few more years in purgatory. "And I had a long talk with her today, and I asked her all sorts of things, and it turns out that she's very—how shall I describe Helen? Hmm. Oh, yes, I know. If called on, I'd say I'd describe Helen as, well, senile, going on mad as a hatter."

And she snickered, waiting for M.M.'s exasperation. But it did not come.

"Oh, Leggie," said her friend instead, sadly. "Didn't you find out anything?"

"Oh, M.M." All at once, Allegra wanted nothing so much as to be sitting in M.M.'s kitchen, and sharing her coffee. She would have the dark mug with the elephants walking around it, and would have added milk as a cooler. Maybe M.M. would have made oatmeal cookies. "I had lunch with her, and it was like riding a carousel through a maze. I'd ask her things, and she'd say stuff like that Mother was a good mimic, or that she loved to dance . . . and then she'd be off on some lunatic tangent of her own so that half the time you didn't even know it was Mother she was talking about, and you just wanted to . . . Ricky has better concentration than she does. Your cat has better concentration. Drunk, your cat has better concentration."

"Oh, poor Leggie."

"Well." Even from M.M., Allegra had always felt, enough sympathy was enough. She decided, for the moment, not to share with M.M. the more disturbing things she had glimpsed. "So I saw how you and I are going to be in fifty years' time. Really, she seemed quite happy to be senile: I was the one driven crazy. And now I'm going out, M.M. Into the sunshine. To lie in it and get toasty brown."

"That is just too bad," said M.M. "Will you see her again, this Helen?"

"Maybe. I don't know that there's much point."

"Do try once more. You need to know this, Leggie. I'd hate it if my girls grew up not knowing about me."

Suddenly, the irritation she had squashed in the restaurant returned to pierce Allegra's brain.

"Why?" she said.

"What?" said M.M.

"Well," said Allegra, "you keep saying I need to know this stuff. But why?"

"Well," said M.M. "You just do, that's all."

"Oh, good one. Remind me to sign you up for my next debating team."

"You try being incisive when you've spent three hours watching the Road Runner."

"You see, that's why I'm not going to. Bye, M.M."

"Ah," said M.M. "But you see—"

But Allegra, grabbing the last word by the force of modern technology, had already replaced the receiver on her. Still, she stayed where she was, frowning at the gaudy parrot on the wall, wishing that M.M. could have come up with at least a slightly less feeble defense. In school, Sister Philomena had said—rather, she had shrieked across Allegra's incessant cracking of gum and rattling of ruler: there was a reason why the nun had disliked her—that without understanding the past, we had no hope of making sense of the present. Sister Philomena was particularly proud of her own family's past. Her father (or so the nun claimed) had been a hero of the IRA, during the time of the Black and Tans. He had (or so Allegra now claimed the nun had claimed) killed fifty-five Englishmen in two years, and never once missed Mass. But then, looked at in that context, Allegra was proud of her own past too. Her own father had fought in the Second World War, for which Allegra had been carelessly pleased with him; as, when she thought of it, she saluted her dimmer ancestors, who had bought or fought their way onto those terrible ships from their land stricken by hunger, and more impressively still, had survived the journey in them to the new land that was Allegra's home. It was only her mother she knew so little of. M.M. appeared to think this a terrible, a heartbreaking lack; but how deep, in practical terms, could the need for knowledge of her mother really be? Despite it all, Allegra was surely an acceptably whole and healthy individual. Was she? she thought then, a memory of Nick's parting words slicing her heart like a bitter wind from home. But yes, oh God, yes, when she thought of the world, yes, she must, surely, be healthy enough. Through her life, Allegra had known her share of life's victims. A college friend who had died of anorexia; a colleague, the funniest comic she had ever known, who for no reason had gradually withdrawn into melancholia and hostility; any number of sad people she saw too often, walking the streets, serving in stores or shuffling through offices, their eyes not quite meeting the eyes of others, life's flotsam, damaged who knew how, able to function in the world but little more; no, Allegra, with her life, her friends, her capacity for laughter, was surely not such as they.

But suppose, she thought then, just suppose that M.M. was right? Most people, even the saddest of the inadequates she knew, did indeed know who their mother had been. They had, however confused their view of the world, at least an idea of their heritage, a comparison to make, an expectation to attain or avoid. It was, for most people, a given. Suppose, along with that, they had in the core of their being a . . . what? A normality, a reality, yes, even the most deficient of them, that was denied to Allegra's self? And if they had, if the human need for a history was indeed as profound as M.M. appeared to think it, then how would she go about filling it if no one would tell her anything; and if she went through the rest of her life with so basic a need unfilled, then what manner of grotesque, what monstrous not-quite-person, in her most profound soul, would that leave her at the end?

"Hi."

Allegra jumped. A girl stood in the courtyard, dark, and rather pretty.

"Hi," she said.

"Is Scott around?"

"I think so. He's across the way there."

"Oh." The girl blushed. "He left a notebook at the restaurant. I was just passing, thought I'd leave it for him."

"Well, here he comes now."

Scott was indeed coming from his doorway, carrying a bundle of newspapers, the sun glinting gold on the hairs of his forearms. He smiled at them both.

"Hi, Linda," he said.

"Hi." The girl's blush deepened as she rummaged in her purse. "You left this at the restaurant last night. I was just passing, thought I'd leave it for you."

"Oh, terrific." He nodded at the top of the pile. "Put it here, would you? I was wondering where that was, thanks."

"I was just passing," she said.

"Good to see you. How's it going, Allie?"

"Oh," said Allegra. "Fine."

"Good. Well. Gotta dump these before they break my arms. Thanks again, Linda."

"I was just passing," she said.

Allegra smiled at her, but the girl did not see. There were advantages, thought Allegra, in being almost middle-aged, and dead of heart.

My boyfriend's really good-looking, you know. Anyone here ever date a really good-looking guy? Listen, take my advice, and don't. You want to be the pretty one in a relationship, believe me. I mean, I don't mind buying him dinner and fixing his drains, and hey, I even quite like running to the drugstore at one a.m. when he's out of aftershave, the security guard's usually on duty, and the time he wasn't, well, I hardly used that leg anyway. No, what's really sad is when I start to go bald before he does.

Far too broad: but it was worth working on. Allegra looked to her mother's photograph, propped against a pelican-shaped vase, and caught the eye of the black-and-white girl, who seemed to laugh back at her, the rounded face sparkling in female complicity. Then, her smile died. Yes, she thought, remembering Helen's stories, that girl had laughed. The girl who had worked with Helen in Los Angeles had laughed, but the woman who had been Allegra's mother in Chicago had not. Yet, usually, people who were lighthearted in one time or place in life were so, given usual circumstances, in any other. It was strange simply to stop laughing. It could, of course, have been Chicago which had sapped Theresa's spirit, the city of long cold winters and plain midwestern people; it could have been marriage to Ignatius O'Riordan. Or it could have been Helen Viner's terrible thing.

Allegra ratted her hair and groaned, most horribly, aloud. A terrible thing might indeed have happened, but how in the name of God was Allegra ever to find out what it was? John, it was sure, would never tell her; Helen Viner, by now, almost certainly could not; and the mysterious Ted, it seemed, had simply vanished, had danced off with Alice and Albert and all the other light-footed ghosts from the torn-down ballroom, waltzing and fox-trotting into the limpid Pacific air. Oh, but wait; slow down and wait a minute, there was something to consider here. Allegra checked herself, slowed, replayed her thoughts. Yes, they had danced, those vanished young people, but yes, the ball-room they had danced in had been torn down: now how in the world did Allegra know that it had been torn down? Oh, yes. Kathleen had said so, the other evening. Kathleen. Allegra wandered back to the bathroom, and twisted her lips consideringly into the mirror. Kathleen had said she had no memory at all of either Alice or Albert. But then again, Kathleen had mentioned the dances on the pier as soon as Allegra mentioned Alice and Albert, which surely could not be coincidence. Or could it? Allegra squinted at herself in calculation. Kathleen said so little. But Kathleen, after all, had known Theresa Higgins. And Kathleen, now, would be at home, and very probably alone; and, alone, would be forced, if only for the sake of politeness, to carry her share of the conversation.

Kathleen was pleased to receive Allegra's call, and interested to know how her trip was going. She was glad that Allegra was enjoying herself, but could well imagine that it must be a hot day inland: it was surprising what a difference those few miles inland made; down by the ocean, it was if anything a little windy. She agreed that that must sound good to Allegra, and could see that she might easily be tempted to jump into her car and come down, although John, of course, was still at the office, and Jimmy would be back Lord knew when. When at last she understood that it was herself Allegra intended to visit, she said that she would tell Maria to put the coffee on.

She came to the door herself, dressed that afternoon in a shirtwaist dress, panty hose, and medium-heeled pumps. Allegra, who in honor of the occasion had changed from blue jeans to cotton pants, wondered whether anyone could ever grow comfortable in such an attire, or whether comfort was simply not a concept Kathleen entertained. Kathleen proffered the usual lightly scented cheek, and led Allegra to the small patio, where coffee was waiting.

Allegra sat at the table, facing the yard.

"What a gorgeous yard," she said, politely. Then, for the first time, looked at it properly, and saw that it indeed was, glowing and vivid, like an illustration from a glossy magazine. Such lushness, so near to the ocean, must put the gardener through hell. "Really," she said. "It's beautiful. I hadn't noticed it before."

"Thank you, dear," said Kathleen. With brief, unconscious tenderness, she reached to stroke the sharp petal of a bird-of-paradise growing just below. "It's my hobby."

"*You* did this?" Cold Kathleen, to coax such pink from the stocks, such royal purples and golds from the pansies? She looked at her aunt's soft hands, and saw that, though small, they were strong; though manicured, their nails still bore the faintest rim of dirt.

"Yes, dear." If Kathleen had noticed the rudeness, she would be too well bred to let it show.

"It's wonderful," she said. "Really, it's incredible. You must have a marvelous thumb."

"Thank you, dear," said Kathleen.

As Kathleen poured coffee into delicate cups, Allegra, with a cold squirm, remembered the flowers, commercially produced, that she had bought with cash and given to her; remembered too the expressions of kind pleasure with which they had been received. She smiled a thanks, and sipped at the drink: it was a little weak, doubtless as Kathleen preferred it. Allegra looked at the coffeepot and wished with all her heart that a genie would pop from its lid to grant her whichever wish she chose; in all the world, she wanted nothing more than to be back in Melissa's apartment, sipping tea and reading magazines, with this visit unarranged.

"What do you hear from your brothers?" said Kathleen, just before the silence became pointed.

"They're OK," said Allegra. "I mean, I guess Declan is, I haven't spoken to him lately. I talked to Bob this morning." She lowered her lids, sipped at her coffee. "They'll both miss Dad a lot. They really loved him, although they'd never talk about it." She smiled, attempting conspiratorship. Kathleen, like Allegra, had a family of only men, and must yearn at times to gossip and be cozy. "Irish men, you know."

Kathleen smiled in return. "Would you like a cookie?" she said.

"Thank you. Delicious." Allegra took one. "Did you make them?"

"Maria did. They have pecans. Jimmy's favorite."

"He has good taste." So much for woman-to-woman. With a deliberateness that shocked her a little, Allegra looked down into the soft yellow crumbs on her plate. "But at least they knew him, you know," she said. "Dad, I mean—my brothers knew him. At least they'll have the memory. I hardly remember anything about Mother at all."

"Oh, my dear." Kathleen laid a hand over hers. Still deliberate, Allegra reminded herself not to move away.

"Your mother died just recently, didn't she?" Allegra said.

"Five years ago this April. She was a good age, of course, and went peacefully. But I still miss her. We all do."

A good age indeed. Five years ago, Kathleen herself could not have been much under sixty. Once again—but not, this time, on her brothers' behalf—Allegra experienced that blood-red surge of furious envy. Firmly, she calmed herself: this was not the time to indulge her own reactions.

"You said my mother used to go dancing," she said. "You see, I didn't even know that."

"So she did," said Kathleen. "She was full of life, you know. She and Ignatius were always off at this dance or the other, and I could never persuade John to take me along with them. Funny. I loved dancing so, and I always thought my boyfriends had to love dancing too. But when you fall in love, you find that all sorts of theories just fly out of the window. As you probably know."

To Allegra's surprise, she shot her a glance of unmistakably inviting curiosity. So Kathleen wondered about Allegra's love life. Still calculating, still cold, Allegra stored this as a possible future bargaining card.

"What was she like?" she asked. "Mother?"

But it was a mistake. Kathleen's hand was withdrawn. "Theresa was very pretty," she said. "Are you too much in the sun there? You must be careful, you know — in this wind, you can get burnt without knowing it."

"Really, Kathleen," said Allegra. "I can't picture her, I know nothing about her. Can you even imagine what it's like not to know about your mother?" It was a low blow, and she saw the older woman wince a little. "Please, Kathleen. Tell me something, at least."

"My dear," said Kathleen, "I hardly knew her."

"But you knew she used to go dancing. You knew she was full of life."

"Just barely. John and I had only just started courting when she left town. You really should be asking your uncle about her, not me."

"John says he doesn't remember, Kathleen. Isn't it strange that he doesn't remember his own sister?"

"If he says he doesn't remember, dear, then I'm sure he doesn't."

"Oh, of course, of course." Hastily, Allegra returned to her coffee. Then — for she too was a Higgins — she gave her aunt an open smile.

"Isn't the mind a funny thing?" she said. "I know you don't remember Alice and Albert, but as soon as I mentioned them the other evening, you started to talk about the dances on the pier. Aren't we all incredibly complicated?"

"Alice and Albert?" said Kathleen.

"Friends of Mother's. They used to go dancing together. I know you don't remember them, but you immediately associated them with dancing. Isn't that interesting, all these years later?"

Kathleen smiled over her coffee. "The mind *is* funny, dear," she agreed.

"Isn't it, though." Allegra delved into her own mind: it was with a faintly shocking absence of effort that she encountered, approved, and adopted for her own a suitable fiction. "My last boyfriend was funny: he used to say I could remember an insult from fifteen years ago, but not where I'd left my car keys." She smiled; then—as well as a Higgins, she was after all a professional performer—let her brow darken just a little. "That wasn't why we split up, of course."

But she had played the card too late: she should have known it was not so interesting after all. "A very funny thing, the mind," repeated Kathleen. She looked down, and then looked up again and straight at Allegra. "Do you know that, later that same night, after I'd talked to John, I suddenly did remember your Albert and Alice after all?"

Oh?

"Did you?" said Allegra.

"Yes, I did, strangely," said Kathleen. She paused, took a breath. "And do you know what I remembered about them?" she said. "I remembered that they were about to leave town."

Oh.

"*Were* they?" said Allegra.

"Yes, they were." Kathleen's eyes did not waver: she had been living with a Higgins man since before Allegra was born. "I think—now, I might be wrong, but I think the boy had been offered work somewhere else. Detroit, I believe it was, he was something to do with cars.

Or maybe it was Cincinnati. Somewhere midwestern. Anyway, they were definitely talking about going. So I'm afraid you may not have much luck in finding them around here after all. More coffee, dear?"

Oh. Oh.

"Yes, please, delicious." Carefully, Allegra proffered a steady cup, and carefully keeping her forehead smooth, concentrated her mind on what was happening. Something about her mother was being kept from her. Kept quite deliberately, and at the expense of the sin of lying. Yes, it was another lie, bare-faced and full-frontal: and Allegra was not a persecuting government official, or a stranger on the street asking after a homework assignment; she was Theresa Higgins's daughter, and had a right—M.M. said she had a need—to know about her. "Isn't that strange?" she said. "That you remember that about them and nothing else?"

For the first time, now that the untruth was told, Kathleen's gaze wavered and she flushed.

"Yes, isn't it," she said. "I hardly knew them at all, of course—they were Theresa's friends, not mine. I suppose they must have been talking about it at the wedding."

The wedding. Somehow, it had never occurred to Allegra to wonder about her parents' wedding. She knew—although if you asked her, she could not say how—that her father had buried with her mother their wedding photograph, as he had buried her Connemara marble rosary that had been blessed by the Pope. Neither of which, of course, she could remember. Allegra looked down into the pale liquid in her coffee cup, and knew, suddenly and with a conviction that stopped just short of ferocity, that if her mother was gay at her wedding, then it was simply Chicago that had drained her. If she was not gay, then the terrible thing—whatever that terrible thing was that made both John and, now, Kathleen lie to her—had already happened.

"Do you have a wedding photograph?" she asked.

Kathleen sighed. But she had not made provision for a second falsehood.

"I believe so," she said. "Somewhere."

"Can I see it?" said Allegra.

Kathleen would know that Allegra knew that she was not the sort of person not to know where her photographs were.

"Of course you can," she said. "I can't think why we haven't shown it to you before."

She led Allegra indoors to the chest where the photograph albums were kept. The album containing the Higgins pictures was slim, and even so, only half filled. Allegra turned the pages. Her grandfather, Joseph Higgins, made rich through contracting new homes to the expanding city; her faded grandmother, Mary; and a fierce old lady who might be the mother of either, Kathleen did not know, and the book did not say. Her dead Uncle Robert, the war hero, handsome and jaunty; a boyish John; and Allegra's toddler mother, over which her daughter's fingers itched. And her parents' wedding, flat in black and white. Allegra scanned the shot. The two grandparents—her father's parents, she thought, were already dead by then—a younger John, a Kathleen who did not look so much different from now. Her handsome father, a little awkward, with greased-back hair, her mother, in a white dress, smiling. Smiling. Not laughing, as Helen had said she often had, as she undoubtedly had been in the picture of just a few weeks before, but smiling, smiling dutifully and a little glassily, on this, the happiest day of a good Catholic girl's life, her body hidden in folds of billowing white, her eyes distant. It had happened, then: the terrible thing had happened.

"I'm sorry I can't tell you any more," said Kathleen. "I hardly knew your mother, you see."

"You've told me enough," said Allegra. "What a beautiful dress you were wearing, the styles in those days were so elegant, weren't they?"

Chapter Five

The next day was Saturday. Allegra rose late from a night that had brought little refreshment, poured orange juice, and wandered into the courtyard. There was a different feeling to Saturdays; even in this foreign city she recognized it, a faint smell in the air of bathrobes and midmorning coffee, a muted reverberation, pianissimo, of the frenetic marching melody of television cartoons. She yawned, lazily, into the still air, and vacationing herself briefly from thoughts of her family, turned her face up to the sun—like a flower, she thought sleepily, except that flowers did not need to add sunscreen—and lay, fuzzily, remembering other Saturdays. Saturday mornings were the times when she and Nick had got along the best. She had dozed in bed, tired after the late performance on Friday, while he pottered around her apartment, sleepy-eyed and the closest he could be to untidy in the robe she had stolen from Bob; around noon, he cooked waffles, which they ate together, sticky and hot, in her bed. Yes, the Saturdays they shared had been sweet: it was the Sundays, at last, which had torn them apart. Those and her jokes and silly tales. No. She stretched her limbs, declining to pursue that last thought. The moral, self-evidently, was that were she ever to attempt a love affair again, which she was not, she should never try it with a former Episcopalian.

No, again. Waking up a little, she shook her head at herself. That was unfair: she had broken up, over the years, with other than Episcopalians. Mark before Nick, for instance, had been an excommunicated Southern Baptist, and Bruce before Mark a semipracticing Jew. Before Bruce, had been the usual mixed bag of agnostics of her time and urban social circle, the more or less lapsed Protestants and Jews, the half-Buddhists and quasi-humanists, one Greek Orthodox, and one—brief—Hindu. Oddly enough, she could not recall a Catholic.

Allegra actually liked Catholics. M.M.'s Paul, of course, was one, and so, surprisingly, was Ron's Mike, although how he reconciled his personal life to his religion, God, presumably, knew better than either Allegra or Father Forde. It was easier for Allegra to be herself with other Catholics; with them, she felt a muscle relax that she was not, usually, even aware of keeping tense. With non-Catholics, there was so much to explain, or more usually, to choose not to explain, to remind herself, for the sake of simplicity, not to express. A Catholic man would be sweet. She stretched her legs, and, idly, conjured for herself a Catholic lover. Someone dark-haired, maybe partly Italian, and tall; someone funny like Jimmy, kind like Mike, reliable like Paul. He would get her best jokes, would her Catholic man, he would fit her shape; he would find and tickle in her the secret hiding places of the soul that Nick, and Mark before Nick, and Bruce before Mark, had never guessed at; he would love her and woo her and win her, and lead her, at last, down a good Catholic church aisle, pacing in a creamy dress, bridal but discreetly suitable for her uninnocence, past sorrowing virgins and Stations of the Cross, to decent marriage under the approving eyes of John and Kathleen here, and her father beyond the grave; over the years, maybe, he would even contrive to coax her back—not, like Nick, for irritation's sake, but for the sake of peace, and an example for the children which he would try hard, and quite possibly successfully, to persuade her to bear—to the full arms of Mother Church.

Mother Church. Allegra's smile faded at the two short words, remembering how Mother Church felt for her. No, and again, no. Were Allegra to open her heart again, it would not be for a Catholic man. But it was academic, anyway: Allegra was not again to open her heart. She could not. It had been struck too many times, had lost its elasticity, grown stiff and hard with scar tissue, until it was like an old beaten pugilist, a played-out boxer, whimpering in the corner of the ring. Allegra dropped the magazine she was holding, felt the corners of her mouth droop with sorrow. "Don't make me go back in there, coach." "Ya gotta do it, Lenny. Ya gotta." "Ah, coach . . ." But Lenny was too brain-damaged to argue. He shuffled to his feet, danced a few steps, and—bam! an iron fist, square to his three-times-broken jaw, as the crowd burst into tumultuous applause and—

"How's it going?" Scott, wandering through the courtyard again with more newspapers: he seemed to spend a lot of time in the courtyard.

"Going fine," she said. And awarded herself a diversion. "Linda seems nice."

"Linda?"

"Your friend. From the restaurant."

"Oh, Linda. Yeah, she's great. You're looking good, Allie."

"I am?" He was wearing the shorts again, and a green T-shirt; but it was really not kind to laugh at him.

"Really," he said. "You got a little tan."

She looked down at her legs: so she had. "Black Irish," she said. "We tan easily."

"You're fully Irish, aren't you?" He squatted on the edge of a chair.

"That must be great, I'm a mixture myself. I always think it must be so cool to have just the one nationality to relate to."

"Oh, yes," she said. "It's terrific."

He looked down at his pile of newspapers. The Bishop's scandal in Missouri seemed to be taking most of the front page: she really should find out what it was about.

"Your mom was Irish too," he said. "Wasn't she?"

"Well, yes," she said. "Fully means both parents, doesn't it?"

"But she wasn't Black Irish," he said. "She was fair."

"Redhead, actually."

"Your mom was a redhead?"

He looked up at her, and away again. She had, she now realized, heard his typewriter going for most of the morning.

"Scott," she said.

"What?" he said.

"Scott! Are you writing a story about me?"

"She's not you, Allie," he said. He leaned forward, grasped her wrist. "I swear she's not. My girl is . . . well, she's just a girl, and she's blond, and she works in an office, and OK, she never knew her mother either, but I can't talk about it right now, and she's really not you, I swear."

"My God," she said. "You *are* writing a story about me. And I thought comics stole people's lives."

"I'm not stealing your life," he said. "I tell you, she's not you. . . . Do you mind?"

"Me?" Allegra and her friends at the club plundered each other's experiences, and those of civilians too, without shame or restraint, in search of material. Occasionally Allegra, responsible only for her own soul, wondered whether this made Allegra O'Riordan a bad person: never once had it crossed her mind to ask somebody if they minded. "If she's not me, I suppose I can't, can I?"

"She's not, you see. She . . . Damn." From his apartment, the telephone rang. Fluid and fast, he abandoned his newspapers, and sprang for his door. "I'll be back," he said. "She's not you, Allie."

From her seat, Allegra craned her neck to peer into Melissa's kitchen. "She's not me," she assured the pottery owl, who looked skeptical. She drained the rest of her juice, bought fresh-squeezed from the market, the bottom of the glass thick with strands of real orange. If Scott was to be a writer, he would have to learn to overcome his polite Protestant respect for other people's separateness, he would have to learn to pry, and be rude. He was young, of course, and naturally decent: he would have a lot to learn.

Allegra had never knowingly been in a book before. Although of course it was not Allegra, Scott's girl who did not know her mother was a young blond office worker, with who knew what other differences besides. It could not be Allegra; good God, Scott barely knew her. She took the empty glass to the kitchen sink, and went to the bathroom to consult the mirror. Not Scott's girl. No, she was not young and she was not blond, was growing, indeed, increasingly less brunette. Not Scott's girl at all. She drew down her father's brow over her father's eyes. If not Scott's girl, then just who was she? Good question. To most of her friends, she rather thought, she was unremarkable, a kind, humorous Democrat, as were most of them, with only the unusualness of her bereavement to mark her out—and that only when they thought to remember it—from the rest of their crowd. To her family, she was pleasant, and more or less untroublesome, until, of course, she started to ask questions about her mother, which they simply ignored anyway, so untroublesome she remained. To Holy Mother Church, she was a daily and deliberate sinner, which, again, distinguished her not in the least from ninety percent of her entire generation. There must, though, be more to Allegra. Must there not? As a child, she had sometimes wondered not so much who she was as how she was who she was, and precisely what was this entity that was thinking her thoughts and sensing her sensations, and how did it come about that it was she, and not some other creature entirely. She had not done so for years; but now, sitting on the chill edge of her friend's bathtub, with the taste of oranges still in her throat, she could alarmingly quickly retreat to that place. It had, she now realized, an actual physical location, in the very back of her skull; it was a cold and puzzled spot, still bewildered after all these years, still asking in faintly querulous perplexity just who on earth was this person, this Allegra, and what in God's name was it doing being her? Allegra shivered: no wonder she had abandoned her visits there. When Melissa's cheap telephone's tone bleated, she thought she had never heard so sweet a sound.

"Hello?" she said.

"Oh. Hello."

It was Declan.

"Oh," she said. "How are you?"

"Fine. You?"

"Oh, I'm OK."

"Good."

She and Declan were always polite with each other.

"You're in Los Angeles," he said. "I called your machine."

"Yes. I thought you were in Geneva." Or was it Washington?

"I'm back."

"Oh."

"Weather good?"

"Great. I'm getting a tan."

"Oh. How's John?"

"Fine. Jimmy's in town too. He's a nice guy. Funny."

"Oh. I have to be in L.A. next week, so I'll probably see you."

"Oh. Good."

"Yes. I arrive on Monday evening. I don't know yet where I'll be staying, so I'll call you."

"OK. D'you want to have dinner?"

"I probably should go over some notes. Do you mind if we don't?"

"I'll try to live with the crushing disappointment."

"What? Oh. Ha. Why don't I call you on Tuesday morning then?"

"OK."

"Is that OK?"

"Yes, it's fine."

"OK. Well, I'll talk to you then, then."

"OK. Look forward to it."

"What? Oh. Bye, then."

"Bye," she said, and carefully replaced the receiver.

Declan had not always been as he now was, although for the sake of simplicity, she usually told herself that he had. But once, he had been not only her buddy but her first and best buddy in the world. Once, if she bothered to awake her memory, and follow it back through early adulthood and adolescence, back to the childhood days before the three young O'Riordans had become the people they were, she could recall that he had been a different Declan altogether, a boy now unrecognizable in the man, a wiry, bold boy with sparkling eyes and a rebel tongue, who had made her laugh until her tears blinded her and her stomach cramped, and then forced her to laugh the more by imitating her delicious anguish. What had happened to that earlier boy? Nothing, that she knew of. Nothing beyond acne, a failure to make a sports team, a rather pudgy blond girl who had not returned a telephone call. Nothing out of the way, or terrible, that she could recall. And he was a good and honorable man now, was the adult Declan, Dad had always said he was a decent fellow, and that must count for something. But sometimes, when she remembered the vanished, laughing boy, she felt so sad that if she once let loose the tears, she thought, they would never stop their flow.

Allegra shivered suddenly in the cool indoors, went back into the courtyard, and scanned the top newspaper of Scott's pile. The scandal was of the usual Catholic sort, a bishop, a group of accusing women, one of them pregnant, a hint of funds embezzled. It was really becoming almost commonplace: when she got home, she should probably include it in her act. She began to read with further attention for useful material.

"It was the women's fault," said a voice. "Leading him astray like that. Of course, I really blame television."

She looked up. It was Jimmy.

"Hello," she said.

"I was at Peppercorn's," he said. "Mistake. I'm broker than ever, if that's possible. Is this where you're staying? There are a lot of birds, aren't there?"

"My friend Melissa," she said. "She's atoning for being a cat in a former life. You want some juice?"

"Sure."

"I was just talking about you," she said. "To Declan, believe it or not." She failed to recall, and did not like Declan enough to invent, a cousinly greeting. "He's coming here on Tuesday. You probably can't wait."

"I haven't seen Declan for maybe twelve or thirteen years," said Jimmy. "My dad and I met him in New York for some reason, I was just a kid. I challenged him to a game of chess. He beat me in three moves."

"That's Declan," she said. "All charm." She handed him the juice, and they returned to the courtyard. He sat on a chair, sitting like Bob again, she noticed with a pang of surprised tenderness: it had not been accidental, then; it was his body's habit, handed, presumably, from an earlier kinsman neither cousin had known. She suddenly hoped that he would come with them to church the next day: she suspected that he was the same class of sinner as was she, and companionship in the cold church, she knew, could make all the difference.

"Looking forward to Mass?" she asked, fishing.

He smiled.

"It's the highlight of my week," he replied.

Yes; he was a Higgins man.

"I think Declan goes regularly," she said. "Of course, you're not allowed to ask. Bob doesn't at all, he's quite bitter because of the way they treated Lois. I don't blame him, she's great."

"My Sullivan cousins go every week," he said. "All six of them, you'll see them tomorrow. We will, I mean. They're all six-five and blond, and they're all—*all*—married to short Hispanics, and they file into the pew, and your eyes go up and down, up and down. It's quite a sight."

"Fuck," said a voice from across the courtyard. "Fuckin', shittin', pissin' fuck. Fuck."

"Friend of yours?" said Jimmy.

"My neighbor."

In the doorway, Scott appeared, blinking mildly. "Sorry about that," he said. "I went back to work, and then I realized I was writing crap. Oh, you have a visitor, I'm sorry."

"That's OK," said Allegra. "Jimmy's a writer too. Cousin Jimmy—neighbor Scott."

"Hi," said Jimmy. His eyes flickered over Scott's face and body in a way that Allegra recognized but his parents never would. Another secret; and a different sin. Poor Kathleen and John. Poor Jimmy.

"Hi," said Scott.

"Have some orange juice," said Jimmy. "You look like you could use a break."

"Not orange," he said. "You got any carrot indoors? I'll get it."

He prowled past them into the kitchen and, back with a glass in his hand, settled himself astraddle a stone bench, and smiled agreeably at them both.

"You must work a lot," said Jimmy. "I never see you at the Writers Guild."

"I'm not a screenwriter," said Scott. "I'm a novelist." He looked at Allegra. "Trying to be."

"Trying quite hard," she agreed, and he blushed. Then looked at Jimmy with interest.

"Did you say you were her cousin?" he said.

"Did you say you were getting back to work?" said Allegra.

"It's the hospitality," said Jimmy. "Been a family tradition since Saint Thaddeus Higgins of the Welcomes, who never passed a beggar on the street without bringing him home for a meal. He went broke, his wife blew herself up with a pressure cooker, and his children all died of malnutrition. He was a great saint."

"*He* talks," said Scott.

"They all talk," said Allegra. "They just don't say anything."

Jimmy looked from one to the other, then stretched long legs toward Scott, and raised a skilled straight man's eyebrow.

" 'They,' " he repeated.

"Your family," Scott told him.

Jimmy raised the other brow, looking more than ever like a handsomer version of Bob. Allegra glanced at him, for the first time now, with consideration. He had, after all, been brought up by John and Kathleen: it occurred to her to wonder whether he knew something about his Aunt Theresa that she did not, and if he did, whether John Higgins's son the professional storyteller would ever let her know that he knew.

"Scott's interested in our family," she said. "Jimmy, what do you know about my mother?"

"Your mother?" He frowned, seeming surprised: if he was hiding anything, he was good at it. "Very little, I'm afraid, now that you mention it. Why?"

"Just asking."

"Allie doesn't know anything about her," said Scott.

Allegra glanced at him in annoyance: if she was to talk to Jimmy about Theresa, she would really rather not be doing it with a stranger around. But he showed no signs of moving: maybe he was not so polite after all.

"I don't, as a matter of fact," she said to Jimmy. "My dad never talked about her, you see. And your dad never talks about her. And yet, she obviously did exist, because Declan and Bob and I are around."

"Oh, my dad never talks about anyone," said Jimmy. "Did you know that during the War, Uncle Robert got a Silver Star? I found an old newspaper clipping, all scrunched up, right at the bottom of some piles of paper. I said, 'God, Dad, why didn't you tell me?' He said, 'Jimmy, if people want to know, and God forbid, they'll find out somehow.' He's talking about his brother the war hero!" He smiled, charmingly, and shook his head at Scott. "You should meet my dad, Scott, he's the only man I know whose ultimate ambition is to be a mushroom."

Scott laughed; Jimmy tried not to join him.

"I'm serious," he said. "The man's a fanatic. He just stops short of wearing a brown paper bag over his head when he goes to pick up the newspaper."

"Really, Jimmy," said Allegra. "What *do* you know about my mother?"

"Aunt Theresa?" Jimmy thought for a moment. "She had red hair. And her middle name was Imelda, damned if I know how I know that. And she went to live in Chicago. And—was she kind of sickly? No, that's Aunt Mary who went to Europe. That's it for Theresa. My own aunt. Crazy, isn't it?" He smiled again at Scott. "What a weird family."

But this time, Scott did not smile back.

"I don't get it," he said. "If she was your dad's sister, why wouldn't he talk about her?"

Allegra and Jimmy looked at each other, and for one second, she was closer to him than to anyone in California or Illinois, closer than to Ron, closer even than to M.M. Then Scott raised his throat to drain his juice, and she saw in Jimmy's face the bond of blood superseded.

"Looks like my cousin has a problem," he said, addressing not her but Scott.

"It would," said Allegra, "be nice to know a little about her. Since she was my mother."

"Huh." He stretched his legs farther toward Scott. "We'll have to think what to do about it, won't we?"

We.

So the Lone Ranger and Tonto, his faithful Indian brave, are riding across the prairie, and suddenly, they're surrounded by Indians. The Lone Ranger turns to Tonto. I think we're in trouble, Tonto, he says. What do you mean, we, paleface? says Tonto.

"Yes," she said. "We will, won't we?"

Jimmy and Scott exchanged glances, age-old, and male.

"OK," said Jimmy, after a moment, kindly. "OK, let's really try to figure how to find out about Aunt Theresa, this is interesting. Let's think here. We know Dad doesn't talk, and I don't think Mom's family knew her at all. God, so many years ago, how would you go about finding who else knew her?"

"Helen Viner did," said Allegra. "And that is sad, when your best source of information is Helen Viner."

"Aha," said Jimmy. "You know Peppercorn's?" he added, to Scott. "You know that old lady who works there sometimes? Helen. She's fascinating."

"Really fascinating," said Allegra. "She told me Mother was a good dancer. Then she asked me seven times who I was, and twelve times why I was asking about Theresa Higgins."

"You can get Helen to talk sense," said Jimmy. "It has to be the right day, of course." He stretched, and looked not at Scott but into the sky. "And she has to like you. You should get to know her, Scott. She's been around books since the thirties, hung out with everyone, Wolfe, Mann, Saroyan—she's seriously fascinating."

"Really?" said Scott. "Saroyan?"

"I mentioned your name," said Allegra. "She didn't know who you were, and got panicked pretending she did."

"Like I said," said Jimmy. "It has to be the right day."

"Did she know Saroyan?" said Scott.

"On the right day," said Allegra.

"She talks to me about things," said Jimmy. "She likes me. We're buddies."

"She didn't actually throw stones at me," said Allegra.

"God," said Scott. "If I could write like Saroyan."

"I could get her to talk about Aunt Theresa," said Jimmy. "We could go to see her now. It'd help if Scott could come too." He glanced at Scott, then away. "He could lure her with writing talk—she'll like you, Scott, she likes writers—and then Allegra and I could move in and grill her on Aunt Theresa. It's the perfect plan."

"She doesn't work Saturdays," said Allegra.

"I know," said Jimmy. "I meant, we could go see her at home. She lives nearby."

"She doesn't entertain much," said Allegra.

"Sure she does, on a good day. I told you, she and I are buddies. Man, her apartment is the best place, books floor to ceiling, signed first editions of Hemingway, telegrams from Steinbeck . . . Scott, you have got to see it." He drained his drink, and set down the glass. "Let's go there now."

"Now?" said Allegra.

"Sure. *Vámanos*. Let's go."

No. Let's not.

"You know," she said, "I don't think that's such a good idea at all."

"Why not?"

Why not. Because the idea of three strangers—rather, two strangers, and one a buddy on the right day—crashing unexpectedly in on an old lady on a Saturday morning did not seem considerate or right. Because, whatever Jimmy said, Helen herself had told Allegra that she did not entertain much, and Allegra should respect that. Because, and above all because, the black-and-white girl who had smiled in the photograph before the terrible thing happened to her, was neither material for Scott's novel, nor a handy expedient for Jimmy to allure Scott, but, damnit, Allegra's mother.

"Just because," she said, as M.M. had said to her over the telephone.

Irritatingly, she could not therefore fault Jimmy for reacting to her as she had to M.M.

" 'Because.' Fine minds in the Higgins family, you'll notice, Scott. Come on, Allegra, don't you want to know about your own mother?"

He winked at Scott. To Allegra's surprise, it was Sister Philomena who pointed out to her that the expedition might just result in some information for her, and if it was not to be undertaken under the auspices that she would have chosen, still, beggars could not be choosers.

"Of course I do," she said.

"And Scott, you'd like to meet Helen, wouldn't you?"

Scott shrugged, casually: he was really very young. "Beats writing," he said.

"There you are, you see. Telephone's indoors, right? I'll call, and check it's a good day, and let her know we're coming." He leaped up, and skirted Scott's bare legs as he made for the house, singing. "O-oh, nothing could be finer than to be with Helen Viner, in the mo-o-orning . . ."

"Your cousin's great," said Scott.

"Great," Allegra agreed.

Helen Viner's apartment was a ten-minute drive away. It was small, and crammed with books, like an old-fashioned bookstore. Like Peppercorn's had been. As well as of books, it smelled of old age, and faintly, of liquor. In the kitchen, still-wet dishes stood in a rack by the sink, and on the dull walnut living room table were laid soft drinks, and a plate of stale-looking cookies. Allegra kicked herself: she had not thought to bring flowers.

Helen was wearing slacks and a Mexican top. She greeted Jimmy affectionately, standing on tiptoe to embrace him. It was, apparently, a good day.

"I think you've met my cousin Allegra," he said. "And this is our friend Scott. He's a writer."

"Oh, for heaven's sakes." She smiled briefly, sweetly, at Allegra as she passed her to greet Scott, and Allegra regretted less the lack of flowers. "You didn't tell me you had another writer in your family. You boys must have ink in your blood."

"No," said Allegra. "*I'm* Jimmy's cousin."

"Are you, honey?" She smiled again. "My, what a big family. Tell me, Scott, what are you working on?"

"Just working," said Scott.

"We're here to pay court," said Jimmy: of course, with all his Murphy aunts, he would be easy around an older woman. "We were talking about books, and then we started talking about you. And then I told these guys if they played their cards right, I just might be able to wangle an invitation to come visit you. And they were so impressed, I had to follow through."

"Oh, you." She swatted him playfully. She did, in fact, seem genuinely fond of him, and he of her. Allegra might just have stopped to pick a couple of the tall purple flowers that grew in such profusion outside Melissa's building. But then again, so might Jimmy or Scott.

"I've never seen so many books," she said. Too many for a home:

they were dark, and dimly threatening. But Helen smiled as at a compliment.

"I've made tea," she said. "I don't have milk, because I have to watch my cholesterol. Scott, how do you like my apartment?"

"It's incredible," he said. "Are these all first editions?"

"Of course," she said. "And mostly signed to me. There's Thomas Mann over there; Steinbeck's up here; and William Saroyan, he was a brilliant writer but a son of a bitch, if you'll excuse the expression, is back there. I've been in the book business since 1935: do you know how many years that is?"

"That's a long time," said Scott.

"I used to take the tram to work," she told him. "And I always wore a hat, very ladylike, you know. And when I was married to Hank Edwards, I used to sit on the tram and take off my wedding ring, because if anyone found out I was married, I'd be fired. I used to take it off as we passed C. C. Brown's, that was my landmark when I was going into work, and hide it in my purse. And on my way home, I'd put it back on again when we passed the Wells Fargo. Hank used to make me laugh. He'd say, 'Well, Mrs. Edwards, were we married at the bank or the ice cream parlor today?' He was a no-good bastard, if you'll excuse the expression, but he always made me laugh."

"You'd be fired?" said Allegra. "For being married? That's disgraceful."

But Helen, flanked by the two men, did not seem to hear her.

"I didn't have to work," she said. "We had plenty of money, but what was I going to do, sit around all day doing lady things? Mother was furious. My brother Malcolm was good about it, but of course, he died. Oh my, the times we used to have. Los Angeles was a great writers' town in those days. Saroyan, Pep West, that sweet little John Fante, they'd all meet in Musso's across the street, and then they'd come into the store afterwards—feeling no pain, as they say—and their wives would call me, and I'd have to pretend they weren't there.

'Cover for us, Helen,' they'd say. Of course, that was on Hollywood Boulevard, back when Hollywood was a place to be."

Wait. No. Wait.

"They sound like such interesting times," said Scott.

But the Peppercorn's Allegra had visited . . .

"Marvelous times," said Helen. "It's all changed now, of course, nobody reads anymore."

. . . the one she thought was the one where her mother had worked . . .

"*I* read," said Scott. "What was Fante like?"

. . . had not been on Hollywood Boulevard.

"Did you say Hollywood Boulevard?" she said.

"Honey?" Helen blinked, and the two men looked at Allegra in not-quite-irritation.

"Did you say," she repeated, "that Peppercorn's used to be on Hollywood Boulevard?"

"Oh . . ." Helen's voice, which had grown strong, faltered, and she looked to Jimmy. "I think it did."

"Until the sixties," said Jimmy. "I just about remember it. Poky little place, you couldn't find a thing. Helen, do you realize you're a living part of literary history? I have to get you on tape sometime. Tell Scott about Nathanael West."

You ever been out with your girlfriend when she's trying to get off with some guy? You say, Shall we get some coffee? She says, You know, it's a really weird thing, but I've always had this crazy fascination with Costa Rica. He says, God! But that's incredible—so have I! She says, No! Really? What did you say your star sign was? You're sitting there saying, Uh, excuse me? Could we just get my cup of coffee, please?

The Peppercorn's Allegra had visited was not even the one where her mother had worked. Allegra sat quietly, as she used to when her brothers and father planned to watch a ball game, feeling small, and sad, and not quite there. Unnoticed, she took a cookie. It was hard: a crumb lodged in her throat, and not wishing to seem to be drawing attention to herself, she tried not to cough. But when she finally could no longer resist, the men barely glanced at her, and Helen did not even break her phrase. Really, they might well have all been back on the shores of Lake Michigan, discussing the Bears.

"My, this is fun," said Helen. "I never have visitors these days. Do you think it might be time for a weensy something?"

Which explained at least the smell of liquor. Well, she was old and had earned her indulgence.

"Helen," said Jimmy. "What a question for two Irish. Scotch, Allegra?"

"Definitely," said Allegra.

"Good woman. Scott?"

"Isn't it a little early?" said Scott. He signaled a glance to the old woman, and Jimmy winked in reply. "No, nothing, thanks. Helen, you've had an incredible life."

"It hasn't been dull at least," said Helen. "Tell me, Scott, what do you write?"

"I'm trying to be a novelist," said Scott. "But it's hard work."

"I never knew a writer who said different," said Helen.

"Tell the story about Dorothy Parker," said Jimmy, when he returned with the drinks.

"Dorothy Parker," said Helen. "She used to come into the store a lot. That was in Hollywood, back when Hollywood was a place to be."

"Tell the story about her," said Jimmy. "Her and the lamp." He nodded at Scott. "It's priceless."

"Dorothy Parker and the lamp." Helen mused. "She used to come into the store a lot, back when it was in Hollywood."

Allegra glanced at her watch. They had been there for forty-five minutes, and even with two men to impress, the old woman's concentration could not last much longer.

"When was it that you worked with Theresa Higgins?" she asked.

"Theresa Higgins?" Helen paused in mid-anecdote. "Now, why would you ask me about her?"

"She was my mother," said Allegra.

"And my aunt," said Jimmy. He looked a little guilty, Allegra thought, as well he might.

"Theresa Higgins was your aunt?" said Helen. "Well, for heaven's sakes, Jimmy. Why didn't you tell me?"

"I didn't know you knew her."

"My, my, Theresa Higgins. Somebody was asking me about her just the other day." She frowned at Allegra. "I wonder who it could have been."

Allegra looked at Jimmy.

"What was she like?" he said. "Theresa."

"Oh, a pretty little thing. Irish as Paddy's pig, with bright red hair, and always laughing. She married that boy Nate, you know, it was a terrible tragedy. Such a pretty thing. I met her daughter just the other day, she doesn't look a thing like her."

"Theresa was pretty?" said Jimmy. Then caught himself, and looked to Allegra. "Sorry, of course she was."

"She was, believe it or not," said Allegra. "I found a photograph in my father's desk, where she looked completely different than in any of the others."

"I don't think you can have," said Helen. "Theresa hated to have her photograph taken. She used to laugh and say it took a piece of her soul, heaven knows where she got that from. She was Roman Catholic, of course, and that was the trouble. The only photograph I ever saw taken of her was that day at the beach."

The beach?

"The beach?" said Allegra.

"She used to laugh," said Helen, "and say photographs took a piece of her soul, she was Roman Catholic, of course. But so pretty she looked that day, we told her it would be a sin not to record it. I still have it, somewhere, if it hasn't been lost."

"Did you say you went to the beach?" said Allegra. "And took a photograph?"

"I had a viewfinder," said Helen. "You looked through instead of down into the camera, it was a new thing in those days, and mine came in a leather case that went with my purse. You should see the little thing Don has now, it would fit into a thimble. And the pictures come out immediately, what's it called, now?"

"Polaroid," said Scott.

"Polaroid, aren't you smart! You probably have one yourself, don't you?"

"My sister does," said Scott. "It's great for my nephews' birthdays."

"Do you still have the photograph?" said Allegra.

"Honey?"

"You said you had a photograph," said Jimmy. "Of Theresa Higgins. Do you still have it?"

"Oh my, yes," said Helen. "Somewhere, if it hasn't been lost. I wonder where it could be?" She held up her glass, flirtatiously. "Do you think, perhaps, just a little spot more?"

"Helen," said Jimmy. "You are a wicked, wicked woman. Allegra and I would love to. Scott? No again? Such virtue: you'll never turn into Fitzgerald, you know, if you keep a healthy liver."

"Scott Fitzgerald?" said Helen. "He was a handsome devil. He used to come into the store a lot. Drunk and sober, if I may say so."

"You knew Fitzgerald?" said Scott.

"I told you," said Jimmy. "Helen knows everyone. Helen, I really am going to bring that tape recorder around one day and get you on cassette."

Forgoing subtlety, Allegra coughed.

"Did you say you had photographs?" said Jimmy.

"My, yes," she said. "If I haven't lost them. I wonder where they could be? Thank you, dear." She took the glass—it was pale, Allegra noted relievedly—and sipped. "Scott Fitzgerald. I knew him drunk and sober, if I may say so."

"Just imagine," said Scott, "what he might have produced if he'd stayed sober." As he shook his head, a shaft of sunlight caught the gold in his thick straight hair, and cast a gilded pool in the hollow of his neck.

"Now, let's think." Jimmy turned virtuous eyes to Helen. "Where would you keep your photographs? Do you have an album? A box, maybe?"

"A box!" Helen clapped her hands. "Aren't you smart! Now, where could it be?" She rose, and trotted into the narrow passageway, murky behind the living room.

"Sorry," said Scott. "But Fitzgerald."

"We'll ask her about him another time," said Jimmy. For which, irritatingly, Allegra could not reasonably fault him.

"Here it is," came Helen's voice. "My, such a big box."

A big box, with, somewhere inside it, if it had not been lost, a picture of Allegra's mother, on the beach, on a day before the terrible thing when she had been so pretty, it would be a sin not to record it. While the two men hurried to help, Allegra forced herself to sit still, to nurse her whiskey in quiet, to make no noise or motion that might alarm or distract. Whether she did so for the benefit of Helen or for herself, she could not know.

It was indeed a big box, and packed full with photographs, pictures dull and shiny, crinkle-edged and straight, sepia, black-and-white, and colored in shocking shades of polychrome. Allegra looked at them in dismay: they might be there for hours and never find her mother. Happily, for her audience, Helen sorted through rectangle after rectangle of cardboard, memory after memory of a long, rich life, which had only glancingly included Theresa Higgins, Irish as Paddy's pig and a marvelous mimic. "There's me with Larry Edmunds, he was a sweet man, and a handsome devil too, look how much taller than me he is. There's me with Mr. Goldwyn, what on earth was I doing with that son of a bitch? Me at six, look what a pretty little thing, and so serious. There's Mother. She was a great beauty, you see, she was from Boston, and she never wanted me to work, although my poor brother Malcolm was good about it, but he died. He was a lovely boy. And now, who's this, do you know, I've forgotten, isn't that terrible, oh, yes, Hemingway, aren't you smart! There were a lot of handsome devils in the book business in those days, it's all changed now, of course. Oh, and look. Look here, did you ever see such a darling little face? That's my great-great-nephew Joshua. He's called after my father, and he's three years old."

Allegra saw the photograph before Helen did. It was the same beach, the same day. The same line of palm trees, her mother in the same swimsuit, smiling, a little less sunnily than in Allegra's shot, but with a little more mischief, looking faintly surprised.

"That's my mother," she said, picking it up. "Theresa Higgins."

"I don't think so," said Helen. "Theresa hated having her photo taken, she used to laugh and say it took a piece of her soul. There was only that one day when we told her it would be a sin not to record it. Why, so it is. Theresa Higgins. My, my, that day on the beach."

"That's Aunt Theresa?" said Jimmy.

"Theresa Higgins was your aunt? Well, for heaven's sakes, why didn't you tell me? She was a very good friend of mine."

"She sure wasn't sickly," said Jimmy.

"Theresa? No, she was a lovely, laughing thing." Helen took the photograph from him, and looked at it. "What a day that was, the summer of 1949, I'll never forget *that* year." She turned it over, and frowned. "Now, how do you suppose that happened? 'To dearest Molly with all love from Helen.' We must have taken each other's copies by mistake, I'd never noticed before. Look, you see, Molly, from Helen, of course we can't have been thinking too well that day. I used to call her Molly Malone, because she was as Irish as Paddy's pig, and she . . . now what was it she used to call me? Some silly name or other."

Allegra sipped at her drink, and nodded to herself, unsurprised, as the last clue in the search for Theresa Higgins turned in her hands to mist and floated into the musty, book-smelling air.

"She called you Ted," she said.

"Ted." Without question, Helen accepted the identification. "Teddy Roosevelt, because she said I attacked like one of his Rough Riders, I was so small, you see, I had to be fierce. Oh, but we used to laugh. There's another shot of us somewhere, the two of us together, that same day, it should be in the same pile there. Yes, here we are. Pretty young things, weren't we?"

Even forty years ago, Helen had hardly been young; but she was pretty, and slim, and held a parasol cocked at a jaunty angle. Still, it was not to her that the eye turned. It was to Theresa, hands on full hips, one shapely leg inturned, her eyes huge and fixed deep into the camera lens.

"That was Aunt Theresa," repeated Jimmy.

Allegra took and looked at the shot, at the girl's skin still dewy through the black-and-white light, at the promise, clear as the long-vanished daylight, in the wide, shining eyes.

"That was my mother," she said.

"So pretty she looked that day," said Helen. "We told her it would be a sin not to record it. She laughed, the way she always did, and let us."

"Us?" said Allegra. Because clearly, someone else had taken the shot of the two of them together, and clearly too, from Theresa's smile, the someone was not another woman. It must have been her father. Well, if the explanation was less dramatic than M.M. might have chosen, it was unquestionably better that the one she was smiling at should have been her future husband. Allegra, still looking at the photograph, found that she was smiling too.

"I still can't believe that's Aunt Theresa," said Jimmy. "We have some photographs at home, Scott, and she looks like a depressed chicken."

Scott laughed, and then stopped, looking at Allegra. "I'm sure she wasn't that bad," he said.

"Believe it," said Jimmy. "It's all in the expression of course — she must have been having a good time that day."

"You young people didn't invent good times, you know," said Helen. "I could tell some tales. I knew Fitzgerald, drunk and sober, if I may say so."

Yes, thought Allegra, Theresa was indeed having a good time. "My father was a good photographer," she said. "Wasn't he?"

"I could tell some tales," repeated Helen. She fluttered sparse eyelashes at Jimmy. "My, I can't remember drinking Scotch in the morning before, you boys will be getting me drunk."

The drink Jimmy brought her was paler even than before; she raised a discreet eyebrow at the color, and accepted it with a steady hand.

"Such tales," she said. "You kids should come around one day with a tape recorder before it's too late."

Casually, Jimmy nodded at Scott: he had done this before.

"It's a date," he said.

"Is there a shot with my father in?" said Allegra.

"Honey?"

"This photograph," she said. "Is there another one? One with Nate in it?"

"Nate?" said Helen. "Nate O'Riordan wouldn't come to the beach that day. He was a great, tall Irishman, you know, and when he set his jaw against something, that was it. No, it was my poor brother Malcolm who took those. He died, you know, thirty-one." She took a scrap of cambric in a wrinkled, delicate hand, and sniffed into it. "He was a lovely boy."

"Malcolm?" said Allegra.

Ignatius was not at the beach. Ted was at the beach, but Ted was Helen. Malcolm was at the beach, who was Helen's brother and had taken the photographs. Allegra sipped at her whiskey, feeling her head begin to swim.

"Theresa hated having her photograph taken, but poor Malcolm got around her, told her she looked so pretty, it would be a sin not to record it. She was Catholic, Irish. He never saw the pictures himself, of course; he died before they were developed. He was a lovely boy. Lovely." She sniffed again.

"And Malcolm was the one who took these photographs," said Allegra.

Jimmy frowned briefly at Allegra, then leaned over, and patted the hand that held the handkerchief.

"Thirty-one," said Helen. "It was a terrible tragedy, just terrible. Mother was never the same afterwards, of course. I never blamed her, but she never smiled much after that, such a lovely, laughing thing she'd been. It was a terrible thing, you know, just terrible."

"Helen," said Jimmy. "You've seen some stuff, haven't you?"

The old woman looked up and at the young man, her eyes watering like a child's. Allegra frowned. It was Helen's brother Malcolm at whom Theresa had smiled that day; Malcolm, who had died young, before the photographs of the day had been developed.

"How did Malcolm die?" she said.

"Allegra!" said Jimmy.

"I'm sorry," she said. But Sister Philomena had told her that she was only truly sorry for something if she never did it again; she could not therefore have been sorry, because she continued. "I mean, how come he died so soon after taking these pictures?"

"He was thirty-one," said Helen. "My baby brother. He had a

heart attack, he'd never been strong." Her handkerchief went to her nose again. Allegra, looking at her, was seized, not with compassion, but with that same red rage she had felt in the restaurant for the futility of the woman's continued existence, the wretched uselessness of her creaking, overcrowded coffin ship of a brain.

"You see," she said. "If he knew Theresa Higgins, it might be quite important to me."

"God, Allegra!" said Jimmy. Scott had looked away.

"She was my mother, you see," she said. "Helen, how did Malcolm die?"

"Isn't this silly," said Helen. "He's forty years dead, and here I am an old woman, and still crying for him." She sniffed once more, replaced the two photographs in the box, and glimmered waterily, first at Jimmy, then at Scott. "You wicked men, to get me all tipsy like this. Isn't this terrible, I've forgotten what we were talking about. My heavens, look at the time: would you kids like some lunch?"

"Yes, please," said Allegra.

"No, thank you," said Jimmy. "We've kept you long enough, you'll want to get on with your own day now." He packed all the photographs into the box, and replaced it in the cupboard; he inquired sternly what she intended to eat, and narrowly inspected the unappetizing meal she showed him of dry chicken, cherry tomatoes, and saltines; he swept them out on a flurry of injunctions to take it easy, and promises to return soon with a tape recorder, and yes, maybe if Scott was interested, with him too. Helen submitted to all docilely, and when at last they left, stood at the door, waving like a little girl.

"We could have stayed awhile longer," said Allegra from the back seat of the car.

"No," said Jimmy. "No we couldn't. You saw how she was getting, she'd had enough."

"She's terrific." In the front, Scott turned his unlikely profile to

Jimmy: he seemed, for the moment, to have forgotten his curiosity about Allegra. "I didn't know people like that were even around anymore. She's incredible, Jimmy."

"You have to know how to talk to her," said Jimmy. Carefully, he kept his eyes on the road. 'You hear a lot of the same stuff, but you always hear something new too. I'd never heard that story about Mann before, for instance. Jeezus!" He swerved to avoid a truck. "Go back to Oklahoma, asshole! Sorry, Scott, you're not from Oklahoma, are you?"

"No, he's not," said Allegra. The drinks that Jimmy had poured for her had been stronger than Helen's, and she was feeling truculent: sour and ignored. "I think something happened," she said. "To my mother."

"Goddamned asshole," said Jimmy. "Or as Scott would say, fuckin', shittin', pissin', fuck, I liked that. Sorry—what'd you say, Allegra?"

"I think," repeated Allegra, "that something happened. To my mother."

"What do you mean?"

"Well, you saw the photographs. You saw how happy she was looking that day, like you said, she was having a good time. And I know you have her wedding photograph at home, which was just a few weeks later, where she's looking like—yes, just like you said—like a depressed chicken. And she looked like that forever afterwards. I think something happened in between."

"Right." Man to man, Jimmy winked at Scott. "Something happened."

"I'm serious. Don't you think it's weird that this Malcolm took the pictures and then died just a few days later?"

"People do die young," said Jimmy. He wore a ring on his right ring finger, a plain silver band: when the car stopped for a traffic light, he twisted it with his thumb. You've seen some stuff, he had said, kindly, to Helen. Yes, and Jimmy too, of his kind and in his time, had seen more than his share of stuff. But she could not consider that right now.

"And afterwards," she said, "my mother blamed herself and never smiled again."

"No, it was Helen's mother who never smiled again. Or it could have been Dorothy Parker by that stage, you saw how she was losing it."

Scott stretched himself, and leaned back against the car door. "But wouldn't it be interesting," he said, "if she was right?" He turned to look at Allegra, slowly, through heavy-lidded, kingfisher eyes.

Jimmy, stopping at another light, took shameless advantage of the opportunity to give him a speculative stare.

"Think she might be?" he said.

"Yes," said Allegra. "Wouldn't a terrible tragedy in my family be interesting for you?"

"Sorry," said Scott.

"It's my family too," said Jimmy. "And . . . they do hide things, don't they?"

"Don't they," said Allegra.

Their eyes met in the driving mirror, and for just a few pulse beats they were kin, products of the same age-old bloodline, divided only recently by the separate children of Joseph and Mary Higgins.

"This is crazy," said Jimmy, suddenly. "It is seriously crazy that you don't know about this stuff. Listen, Allegra, here's what we'll do. We'll get them, Mom and Dad. We'll sit them down, we'll ask them about Aunt Theresa, and we won't stop asking till they give us some answers. OK?"

"Right," said Allegra. "We'll tackle Kathleen and John. We'll do it after we've both been to Mass, tomorrow. You are coming to Mass, aren't you?"

"We will," he said. "We'll do it tomorrow. We've made a pact.

Scott here can be our witness. Look, Scott, we're shaking hands on it. And you can check on me to make sure I keep my word."

He drew up at a stop sign; lightly brushing Scott's shoulder, he leaned into the back seat to pump her hand. She responded. Beggars, Sister Philomena repeated, could not be choosers.

Chapter Six

There was mail waiting when Allegra returned to the apartment—more magazines for Melissa, and for herself an envelope carefully addressed in a childish hand. Elizabeth's letter, making an honest woman of M.M.

> Dear Leggie,
> I hope you are well. I am sick, I have to eat plenty of ice cream. The dog next door bit Ricky's leg. She is a GOOD dog, Ricky is yucky. Daddy said he hopes Ricky didn't give her rabies, and Mommy got mad at him. I AGREE WITH DADDY.
> Which is your favorite ice cream? I like Rocky Road.
> With love,
> Elizabeth

Allegra read, smiled, and read the letter again. There were drawings enclosed, of a dog with teeth bared by Elizabeth, of a vastly fat child eating ice cream by Ricky. If Elizabeth's daughter were to find them in forty years, they would give her no clue of the hours Elizabeth and Ricky spent giggling together at their own indecipherable jokes, or how, when they were parted, they both grew dull and sad. Allegra looked at the telephone: it would be good to hear her goddaughter's voice. But no sooner had she picked up the receiver than she replaced it. She was not ready to talk to M.M.; not yet. Instead, she went to the bathroom, and stared at her own perplexed face, struggling to make a pattern of what Helen had told her.

Everything had shifted since the morning began, everything changed. Peppercorn's, it seemed, then, was not after all her mother's store, and Ted not Ted; he was Helen Viner herself, the name a private joke shared with the playful Theresa. But then, Ted had not taken the photographs. Malcolm had, Malcolm, the lovely boy, Helen's baby brother, who had told Theresa that she looked pretty—and oh, she had, she had—and almost immediately afterwards had died, mysteriously, of a heart attack at the age of thirty-one. That might yet be all there was to it: people did occasionally die young, and Theresa, after all, might reasonably be supposed to have smiled at young men before she met Ignatius. Allegra smiled herself, remembering how M.M.'s mom one day had mentioned an early boyfriend, how filled with shock both she and M.M. had been to think that she had had any romantic life, any sort of a life at all, before she met and married M.M.'s father.

No. She shook her head: no comfort lay there. This had not happened before Ignatius: Ignatius and Theresa, indeed, had been only weeks away from their wedding. Ignatius, Helen said, had refused to go to the beach that day; and yes, it must have been soon after that that he had appeared drunk at Helen's door, Nate O'Riordan, the tall, hardheaded Irishman, drunk because of the terrible thing.

Jesus! Allegra gaped, and watched herself turn pale in the mirror, as an idea flew into her head too awful to frame. But no. Her father had killed during the War, and the war being just, had been proud to do so. In peace, he had been no more capable of taking a life than of missing Mass. Jesus, Jesus. To think that, for even an instant, of your own father. It was not good for her, this wondering, it was making her imagine in the mist monsters more terrible than there could be, when in reality, there still might not even be a monster there at all.

Wearily, her mind sore as a too-often rubbed wound, she went once more over the situation. Helen Viner talked of a terrible thing; but so muddled was her mind with memories that it was beyond use. Ted was Helen; Alice and Albert had vanished, possibly, or possibly not, to Detroit, possibly, or possibly not, to Cincinnati; Malcolm Viner was dead. Kathleen and John knew what had happened that summer; but Kathleen was married to John, and John had been to a Jesuit school. Jimmy had promised to help her with Kathleen and John; but he had done so mostly to impress Scott, and besides, living among his family a larger lie than she herself ever had, was no match for John, the Jesuit boy. God, thought Allegra sullenly, was very probably a Jesuit boy Himself.

It was not M.M. she called after all, but Ron.

"Do you miss me?" she asked.

"I'm pining. We both are. We keep a picture of you under our pillows and commit unspeakable acts of depravity on it every night."

"Just so you don't forget me. How's everyone?"

"Same old same old. Roger's left Annie for Tom, she's furious because he's taken her best jockstrap. Silly bitch."

"Which one?"

"Who cares? You OK, sweetheart?"

"Yeah." She hesitated; almost confided; decided not to. "How's Mike?"

"Off praying." Of course; it was Saturday evening in Chicago. Mike's regular Mass time, which Ron teased him about, Allegra siding with Mike or Ron, depending on which she liked better at the time.

"Praying to Christ to forgive him for being a faggot. Or failing that, to send him someone prettier than me."

"Say hi. I'm going to Mass tomorrow. With my uncle and aunt."

"Yummy. Is Kevin Costner Catholic?"

"If I see him, I'll bring him back for you." She hesitated, again. "Ron?"

"Hmm?"

No.

"I'm getting a tan," she said.

"You bitch from hell," he said.

"Tanned bitch from hell. Bye."

"Kisses, bitch."

She was disappointed, but not especially surprised, when she arrived at John's house the following morning, to find Jimmy not there.

"His agent called," said John. "Wanted him to meet some people. Damn inconsiderate woman, calling on a Sunday morning; if she'd called last night, we could all have gone to the nine instead. I told him to tell her he had another engagement—which he has—but he says he's not in a position to. He'll join us later. Sunday morning. I've never worked a Sunday in my life."

"Well, but some people do have to," said Allegra, mildly enough. Bob would have pointed out that those people included the staff at the restaurant where John intended to take them for brunch, but Allegra, out of lassitude or affection, did not, of which Sister Philomena grudgingly approved. She approved of Allegra's clothes too, a skirt and prim blouse—Melissa's costume for when she took an office job—in a pale lemon shade which suited Melissa, but left Allegra feeling sallow and plain. Good-woman clothes; depressing clothes; clothes to go to Mass in.

"Never in my life," said John. "Remember that thou keep holy the Sabbath Day. I've never worked Sunday, or Good Friday, or Saint

Patrick's Day. You're looking well, sweetie—do you have money for the collection? Where the hell's my wife?"

The church they went to was prettier by far than the grim German-Irish barns of Allegra's home city: its walls were decorated with gold leaf taken from the Indians (shamelessly pillaged from the brutally exploited Indians, footnoted Bob from across the continent), its Madonnas and saints exotically dark-eyed. The people too seemed taller than in Chicago, their bodies were toned, they were colorfully clad, and many of them were blond. Several waved at Kathleen and John as they entered, and the Sullivan cousins—who, unexpectedly, exactly fit Jimmy's description—beamed an inquisitive welcome at Allegra. But as she sat down, John's left shoulder looming above her right as her father's had, Kathleen an alien being, small-boned on her left, her hands clasped neatly in her lap, Allegra felt, now that she did not have the thought of Nick to distract her, the sorrow settle into her every nook and cranny, felt it snuggle into the hollows of her neck and the cracks between her fingers and toes, as much hers here in her mother's sunny city as it had ever been in the gray Midwest.

She did not fight to conquer it; it did not occur to her to try. She sat as the rest of the congregation sat, eyes downcast, features relaxed, through a Mass that was neither longer nor shorter than usual, with readings of medium length and immediately forgettable, and a sermon of exquisite tedium. She sat, a cold-souled sinner, while the broad-faced priest murmured Spanish-accented words, and lifted the Host, and put it down, and lifted it again; and at last, while a fat young woman with frightened eyes sang hymns in the voice of an angel, they all, the bright young couples, the quiet-faced old people, the teen-agers, the bachelors, and John, and Kathleen, and yes, Allegra herself, filed to the gold-leafed altar to receive on their sinners' tongues the very body and the very blood of Jesus Christ the God and man, sacrificed two thousand years before for the forgiveness of their sins, and now, through the miracle of the transubstantiation, most fully and physically present in the wafers of bread, the drops of thin red wine.

She blinked in puzzlement as—Mass ended, Communion thanksgiving over, and a candle lit to the Sacred Heart for the repose of Dad's soul—they left the church: for a moment, she had thought she was back in Chicago. But immediately, they were surrounded by the Sullivan cousins, a pride of tall, tawny Californians with slender dark spouses and children of all sizes and complexions, who greeted all three of them with enthusiasm; they were fond of both Kathleen and John, and by unquestioning extension, of Allegra too.

"Come to a barbecue," said one of them, either Angela or Colleen. "Emily's eight next week, and we're celebrating early."

"Oh." Kathleen looked at John. "We were going to brunch. We don't know what time Jimmy will be home."

"So leave a message. God forbid he should have to fix his own meal." Angela or Colleen winked at Allegra, who stifled a sigh as she smiled back. Jimmy had left her to face Mass alone; but he would turn up later, she was sure; and feeble as the hope was that they might learn something that day, it was all she had, and how closely she clung to it she had not known until now, when it was being so firmly taken from her. Angela or Colleen had the unmistakable look of one who got her own way.

"I don't know," said Kathleen. "We don't have a gift."

"That child has more stuff than she knows what to do with." ("Do not," happily cried Emily, ramming her butterscotch head against her mother's stomach as she careened down the church steps.) "Do come, Kathleen. Allie would like to—wouldn't you, Allie?—and anyway, I need your help with my sunflowers."

"Well," said Kathleen. "Thank you. That would be very kind."

"Kind!" Angela or Colleen wound a strong arm around Kathleen's narrow shoulders, and squeezed. She was athletically built, with a handsome, kindly face, presumably taking after her father. Rose

Sullivan was Kathleen's sister, and the two resembled each other strongly. "I'm not kind at all, I just want to get your help in the garden. This woman's incredible," she added to Allegra. "She only has to look at plants and they grow, I swear she's a magician."

Allegra smiled again, and spoke politenesses over a heart suddenly sore with loneliness. They had each other, had the Sullivans, they did not need Kathleen and John too. Well, but they were kind people, and Sister Philomena had many words on the subject of self-pity.

Angela, as Allegra had established her to be, and her husband, Luis, lived in a low, comfortable house with a spreading yard, to a corner of which Angela immediately led Kathleen. Allegra sat with John in the shade of an avocado tree, watching Kathleen's body change as she touched the ailing blooms, her usually stiff movements become fluid, and tender as those of a Madonna. She had had no idea that her aunt could be thus.

"She really knows what she's doing, doesn't she?" she said to John.

"Kathleen? Yes, she's a good little gardener." He clinked the cubes in his glass, and Allegra felt for Kathleen a most unexpected pang of pity. She decided to allow herself a little mischief.

"Isn't it terrible?" she said. "About that bishop in Missouri."

She should have known better.

"Terrible," agreed John, immediately. "The way the media's leaped all over it. Vultures, all of them, it's sickening."

"Well," said Allegra, "but it does sound as if they have something to leap on."

"Charity," said John. "Charity and compassion. Those who look to the mote in the other man's eye, and ignore the beam in their own."

"It seems to have been more than a mote," said Allegra. "Apart from everything else, there was quite a lot of money missing that should have gone to help the poor."

"The mote in the other man's eye," said John. "A priest is a man of God, but we all know he's only a man. The people who print those stories should be examining their consciences most carefully."

Well, what the hell did you expect? demanded Bob. Allegra sighed, then raised her glass in salute to Luis, passing them to set up the barbecue. This was, almost certainly, the most private she would be with John for the rest of the day. She must, she decided, have an affection for battering her head against stone walls, because she proceeded to try to capitalize on it.

"Did Jimmy tell you he came to visit me yesterday?" she said.

"Mm. He said you lived in an aviary."

"I do, more or less." Yes, he would have been funny about Melissa's decor. And he would not have mentioned her more interesting neighbor. Allegra looked down into her own drink, keeping her cousin's secret. "Did he tell you we went to see Helen Viner?"

"Who?"

"Helen Viner. The old lady who used to work with Mother, you said you remembered her."

"Did I? Can't say I do or don't, really."

"Well, she remembers you." And who was to say what Helen Viner remembered or did not remember, what forks of lightning sometimes shot across the darkness of her worn-out mind, throwing into too-brief clarity what scenes from her too-long life? "You met her at the store, and got along well." That was not a lie: it was in her mother's letter. "A small, fair woman."

"Sweetie, a small, fair woman, forty years ago . . . You want a hand there, Luis?"

Luis had dropped a sack of coals: he picked it up, and turned to grin at John in respectful derision. "From you? You couldn't light a barbecue to save your soul."

John barked with laughter, and settled back into his seat. "Not doing too well yourself, pal."

"She had a brother," said Allegra.

"Who?" said John.

"Helen Viner. She had a brother, he knew Mother too, you might remember him. He died. His name was Malcolm."

"Malcolm!" John frowned, in theatrical befuddlement. "Who the hell's called Malcolm? Hey, Luis, you ever known anyone called Malcolm?"

Luis grinned again, foolishly this time, and shrugged, clowning. "No' me, 'mano. I don' know no reech folks."

"I do," said John. "I know you. Guy's as rich as Croesus," he added, to Allegra. "Look at this spread."

"John," said Allegra. "Did you know Malcolm Viner?"

"Malcolm Viner." John frowned again. "No," he said then, firmly and, Allegra would swear, with satisfaction. "I have never known anyone called Malcolm Viner. I'm quite sure of it."

Lies, falsehoods, and lies which were not sins. Allegra felt weary, and rather old.

"Declan called," she said. "He's coming to town next week."

"Mm?" By not one flicker did John's expression change. "Good. When does he arrive?"

"Tuesday, I think. I don't even know where he's staying. You know Declan, information is hard to come by."

"Mm. So you'll come to dinner Tuesday night."

"Oh. Thank you."

"Unless you two want to go off and talk?"

"I very much doubt it."

Quite unexpectedly, he reached over to pat her hand. He was a kind man, was John, and that was a part of the hell of it. "Your brothers love you, sweetie," he said. "Never forget that."

Before Allegra could reply, the yard was overrun with people. The rest of the Sullivans had gone to their various homes to change clothes; now, they all poured in together, long-legged and muscular in sloppy, Sunday clothes. Allegra, still dreary in Melissa's skirt, shifted stiffly in her chair.

"Are you really a comedian?" A dark-haired boy of nine or so was standing in front of her, watching her appraisingly.

"Yes," she said.

"You haven't said anything funny," said the boy.

"With a face like yours around," she said, "I don't need to."

He considered this, guffawed, and ran to whisper to a group of his cousins. Allegra sat sipping her wine, her face bland. She liked children. Before long, they all came over to watch her, nudging each other gigglingly.

"Are you really a comedian?" said a fair girl, one, Allegra thought, of Angela's, amid a rustle of hilarity.

"Yes," said Allegra.

More giggles.

"You haven't said anything funny," spluttered the girl.

Allegra inspected her for a moment, then turned suddenly to point to the dark boy. "With a face like *his* around, I don't need to."

All audiences, she thought, should be so appreciative.

"Are they bugging you? Scram, you monsters, go torture the cat." Someone who was not Angela, so presumably Colleen, sprawled beside her, proffering a bowl of chips.

"Which are yours?" said Allegra.

"Brendan." She indicated the dark boy. "And he has a sister somewhere, Kerry. They get along OK, but she can be a terror. He's a sweetheart. I was sorry to hear about your dad, ours died two years ago, we still miss him. Brendan, stop that! Did I say he was a sweetheart?"

Brendan had produced a water pistol and was squirting Angela, who, undismayed, continued to set dish after dish of salad on the table.

"She doesn't seem to mind," said Allegra.

"Oh, Angela's perfect. She's the shining example to us all, isn't she, baby? This is my baby sister." A woman as tall as Colleen sat next to her, the two linking their brown arms and rubbing their buttery heads together.

"Did you see to it?" said Colleen.

"Frogs are best," said the other. "But no hats."

"Unless Erica's around."

The one who was not Colleen sat up. "That depends . . ." she began.

". . . on the schedule!" finished Colleen, and both collapsed in laughter.

Allegra smiled, politely. This was sister talk, such as M.M. and the other McConnell women lapsed into. Quite without warning, an unremarkable conversation would shift to a different language altogether, whose words sounded like words Allegra knew, but whose sense was incomprehensible, impenetrable. It was sisters who did that: Allegra was sure she did not with Declan or Bob.

"Sorry," said Colleen. "We were just fixing up—Kerry, take your shoe out of your cousin's mouth this instant! . . . God, can you believe what I just said? Do you have kids, Allie?"

"No," said Allegra. One awkward, ugly syllable, marching the meandering conversation down a blind alley. Yet, what else was she to say? She had no children; no sisters; no mother. No—thank you, Nick—no real life. She looked across the yard, at the mass of family such as she herself could not dream of, and felt, for a sudden few seconds, a longing so powerful she could weep, to be back on stage right now, alone in the cool spotlight, with Ron backstage, and the laughing unknowable heads bobbing and dancing in the smoke-fogged dark room in front.

"You have time," said the one Allegra now remembered was called Siobhan. "Are you really John's niece? I didn't even know he had brothers or sisters."

"He had my mother. And my uncle, who died in the War."

"That's weird, he never, ever mentions them. But John doesn't mention things much, does he?"

Allegra raised her head, pulled back her jaw. "Mm," she said.

They looked at her, then at each other, and burst into laughter. "That's terrific," said Siobhan. "That's just what he does, isn't it? Do it again—no, wait, let me try. Mm. Mm. No, you're better than me, go on, do it again."

"She had the kids in stitches earlier," said Colleen.

"Mm," said Siobhan.

Allegra smiled again, this time a little thinly. She knew without testing that she would never be able to try out on these Sullivan sisters her even funnier imitation of their Aunt Kathleen. But quick as a flash, Sister Philomena reminded her that it was not kind to laugh at others, and unexpectedly, Dad was there to agree with her. Outnumbered, she reached for a chip.

"You should meet Father Carroll," said Siobhan.

"Is he here?" said Colleen.

"Course he is. He's at his devotions."

More laughter.

"He's this sweet old guy," explained Siobhan.

"Old," agreed Colleen.

"Real old. And he—His tummy doesn't work so well, and he goes straight to the kids' bathroom—*he* doesn't know the difference—and he leaves it, well, you know. Drives the kids crazy."

" 'Mom, is he in there *again?* ' "

" 'He makes it so-o-o . . .' "

" '. . . yuckeee . . .' Sorry, Allie, you see, you don't get to have any secrets around this family. But he is a sweet old guy. Baptized Mom, Kathleen, maybe even Grandma."

"Grandma? Right. That makes him a hundred and ten."

"Well."

"But he is a sweetie. Come on, let's go and meet him. There he is."

An old man with silky white hair was coming out of the house, leaning on the arm of a Sullivan brother. They waited until he had settled himself in a chair, and went to join him.

"Father, this is Allegra O'Riordan," said Siobhan. "She's John's niece, visiting us from Chicago."

"Hello, Father." Allegra had been brought up around priests, and was easy with them. She liked the sharp blue eyes of this one, and the fact that he held a martini, of which Nick would so have disapproved.

"Allegra O'Riordan," he said, an Irish intonation rather than accent still caressing his speech. "What a pretty name. And John's niece. He's a fine man, with a marvelous stock of whiskey, although I'm more for the gin myself. Back in Cork, my father used to make it from sloes."

"Did he?" Allegra sat, settled into the conversation. Sinner or not, this was more her conversational territory by far than talk of yucky bathrooms. "What was it like?"

"Terrible stuff, I wouldn't give you sixpence for it. I'm a Tanqueray man. And what do you do in Chicago, Allegra O'Riordan?"

"I'm a comic."

"Are you, now? Then you'll find plenty to laugh about in this fair city of ours. I knew a fellow from Chicago once, terrible crook, he was always giving us money. Joe Mazzutti, you wouldn't know him? Listen to me, I'm turning into my mother. Till the day she died, God rest her soul, she was writing to me, saying would y'ever look out for Corny Duff, he's moving near you to Pittsburgh. What part of Ireland are you from, Allegra O'Riordan?"

"I don't know. It's a long way back."

"And you haven't traced it? Shame on you, with the map of it on your face. Not like this bunch." He jerked his head affectionately toward the table, where Angela passed a plate heaped high with burgers. "Never seen so much yellow hair. But fine people, fine people. Would you look at how much food there is? In Ireland, that'd have kept us going for a month or more."

"Can I bring you something, Father?"

"Ah, no, thank you, Angela will look after me later. But you're a good girl to ask."

He sipped his martini, and they sat for a moment in companionable silence, the only unmarried adults in the gathering. Aging was a curious thing, thought Allegra: the priest must be Helen Viner's age, but could be a full decade younger for all it encumbered him. Priests did make good old men. A lifetime of prayer, her father had said; more likely, a lifetime of being waited on hand and foot, Bob had replied. Allegra's own views wavered. Here, on this sunny early afternoon, with a glass of wine to hand and the horrors of Mass now firmly behind her, she could almost agree with Dad. She stretched her legs in their ladylike skirt discreetly toward the sunlight, and felt it seep into her bones.

"Did you really baptize everyone here?" she asked.

"Baptized, confessed, married, and the ones that aren't here, I buried. There were just the two of us priests when I first came, myself and young Father O'Hara, who's seventy years old now, and bald as a billiard ball the last time I saw him. Dear God, the terrible children we've seen grow up and turn into decent, good Christians. Your Uncle John, for instance. A holy terror he was. Sent home from school once for setting fire to the boy in front of him, and look at him now. And they say there are no miracles. If you'd seen John Higgins fifty years ago and you saw him today, you'd believe in God's grace, no question."

Allegra looked up, quickly.

"Did you say," she said, "that you knew John as a boy?"

"Terrible child. And you can tell him I said so."

Oh.

"Then," she said, "you must have known my mother too. Theresa Higgins."

The priest, who had raised his glass, set it down. "Theresa Higgins?" he repeated.

"She was my mother. John's sister, Theresa. She died about thirty years ago, do you remember her?"

"Ah, yes," he said. He looked at her more closely. "You'd be Theresa Higgins's girl. It was Chicago she went to, yes."

"I don't look at all like her," said Allegra. "But you do remember her, then?"

"No one," said Father Carroll, "in the diocese of Los Angeles will forget Theresa Higgins."

His sharp old eyes, still staring into hers, had turned without warning as hard and cold as two blue stones. Not knowing quite why, Allegra felt herself begin to feel a little sick.

"What do you mean?" she asked.

"A sin," said the priest, "is a sin."

"I'm sorry?"

"A sin," he repeated, "is a sin. May God in His goodness have mercy on her soul."

"Can I freshen you, Vincent?" John stood over them, a green cool bottle of gin to hand.

"You cannot, John," he said. "But you can help me up." He turned to Allegra, kindly once more, and patted her arm. "Didn't I tell you he'd grown into a fine man? Will you excuse me, my dear, I have matters to attend to indoors."

As, assisted by John, he made his way to the patio door, Emily and Brendan looked at each other, held their noses, and made silent gagging sounds.

Allegra sat alone, shivering a little in the sunshine. It was not an unfamiliar sensation. Priests could do that to you, they could lull you to confidence with their kindly worldliness, and then, with one word, one look, could leave you staring, sick and giddy, into an abyss which stretched down into eternity. It had happened to her before with her father's priest friends; she had learned over her life to ignore it.

But dear God, what in this world or any other, could he have meant about Theresa Higgins? A sin was a sin, he had said. Allegra looked, surreptitiously, around her at the people in the broad yard, the kind, fair people with their dark families, who had been to Mass that morning; and all, it went without saying, of course, were sinners too; all sinners, all children of Eve, all daily fighting the stain of original sin, all failing daily, as a priest, a confessor, must know better than any. But he had said that no priest in the diocese would forget Theresa, and the more Allegra thought about it, smiling carefully, faintly, as she went to refill her glass of wine, the sicker she felt. To be singled out as a sinner, that laughing girl in black and white who had given Allegra birth, singled out by the men who heard the sins of the whole sinful city, what on earth or in heaven could it mean?

"Hi, cousin."

"Jimmy!" She leaped to greet him, Jimmy, who was the same mold, if not the same model, of sinner as was she.

"Sorry about today," he said. "I really had to meet with these people, I'm real sorry."

"It's OK," she said. And it was: she had other things, now, on her mind than Jimmy's shortcomings.

"I really want to do it," he said. "What we talked about. I just couldn't get out of this meeting." He looked down, guiltily: he knew where his real betrayal lay. "How was Mass?"

"I survived," she said.

"I'm sorry," he said. Then bent to his cousin, who ran to him. "Hi, Emily, how's my beautiful birthday girl?"

Yes, thought, Allegra, watching him swing her, squealing; when she was a child, she would have adored Jimmy too.

"Allie's a comedian," said the little fair girl, running to join them.

"I know she is," said Jimmy. "Tell her your joke about the man walking down the street."

The girl batted her eyelids, hung her head in flirtation. "Can't," she said.

"Sure you can, it's really funny. Go on. There was a man walking down the street . . ."

"Did you eat?" Kathleen materialized at his side.

"Yes, Mom, I ate. They feed you at the Polo Lounge, you know, they're weird that way. Have you heard Luisa's joke? It's really funny. Luisa? Oh well, she'll be back. How was Mass?"

From the corner of her eye, Allegra saw Father Carroll at last coming out of the house, helped this time by Angela, with three children making silent whoops of disgust behind his back. She waited as long as she properly could, and went over to join him.

"Well," he greeted her, "Allegra O'Riordan from God knows where, and how are you enjoying this fine feast?"

"Very well, thank you, Father," she said. Was it the gin working, or was his Irish accent just a little more pronounced than it had been? "Can I get you something?"

"You cannot, my dear, Angela's looking after me, she's a good girl. Have you eaten yourself, now?"

"I'm about to. Father, you said you knew my mother. Theresa Higgins?"

"I did." His eyes, now, were mild and impenetrably bland. "I baptized and confessed her, but it was young Father O'Hara who married her, I was on retreat at the time. Young Father O'Hara, who's as bald as a billiard ball, and went off to live in Hawaii."

Allegra looked at him, squarely, not as a woman is used to looking at a priest.

"Why do you remember her, Father?" she said. "You said you all remembered her. Why?"

As squarely, he returned her gaze.

"Ah," he said. "Who wouldn't remember little Theresa Higgins, with the finest red hair I've seen west of Bantry Bay? Now, which one are you, child? Luisa, is it?"

The fair girl was standing between them, impartially equidistant.

"There was a man walking down the street," she said, "with a pineapple in his ear. Another man came up to him, and said, 'Did you know you have a pineapple in your ear?' The man said, 'I'm afraid you'll have to speak up. I have a pineapple in my ear.'"

Father Carroll burst into laughter, and after a moment, Allegra joined him. Part of her laughter was even for the joke, which she had not heard for years: Jimmy was right, it was really funny.

There was no more thought or private conversation to be had that afternoon. Allegra filled her plate with portions as small as she dared of chicken and salads; she answered questions on Chicago and how it was to be a comedian and what she thought of Los Angeles; she showed a magic trick with a quarter which went down well with M.M.'s children, and was no less popular here on the West Coast; she applauded, laughing with the others, as a scarlet-faced Emily puffed mightily to blow out trick birthday-cake candles that lit themselves again for every blow. As the afternoon wore toward evening, she pleaded errands, and asked if someone might drive her to Melissa's car outside John's house. She looked at Jimmy as she spoke, but at that instant, Brendan placed a football trustingly into his hands, and Angela leaped to her feet.

"That was a good afternoon," Allegra told her, perched a little awkwardly in the family wagon between schoolbooks, sports shoes, and all the unmistakable, unidentifiable paraphernalia of family life. "You have a nice family." And she had, Sister; and for the most part, it was.

"We like each other," said Angela. "We like John too, he's a darling."

"He loves the children, doesn't he?" Through the afternoon, John had rarely been seen without one child or another clinging to his leg or shoulders.

"Oh, he's great with them." (Great with baptized kids, muttered

Bob, but Allegra brushed him aside.) "He should be a granddaddy. Have a word with Jimmy, would you, he doesn't listen to us."

Colleen was wrong: there was indeed privacy in the family. You had to create it yourself; but if you troubled to erect the wall, it would occur to not one of these good, sunny people to peer over it.

"He doesn't listen to me either," she said, and Angela laughed.

"It's been good to meet you," she said as they drew up to Melissa's car. "Hope to see you again."

"I'd like that," Allegra said, and meant it.

It was when she was alone in the car, driving undistracted the wide, quiet, Sunday evening boulevard back into town, that the terrible import of the old priest's words came crashing through her soul. Because of course, she understood immediately, of course, of course her mother had sinned. It was Helen Viner's terrible thing, the only thing that could make sense of her father's silence, and John's evasions, and the tightness that crept around Kathleen's close-shut convent girl mouth whenever her name was mentioned. It made sense too, as nothing else could, of the change from the bold girl in the photograph who had been a brilliant mimic and loved to dance, to the drained woman, not five years older, whom Allegra remembered. Had a virtuous sorrow befallen her mother, Allegra would surely have been told of it; and surely no outside tragedy—no bereavement, such as Ron had known, nor loss of health such as Ron's friend Bill's, or livelihood, such as M.M.'s brother Stephen's, nor any other disaster that she could imagine—could so extinguish a human light as would that of conscious wrongdoing. It was the only explanation: it must have been.

But whatever could she have done, thought Allegra then, what sin could she have committed that no priest in the diocese would forget, and when and where, and how? A Catholic girl of forty years ago, living with her parents, working in a bookstore, engaged to be married to Ignatius O'Riordan? Stopping at a light, Allegra giggled aloud, sharply and more than a touch hysterically, as possibilities occurred to her. Maybe she had eaten barbecue-beef-flavored chips on a Friday. Arrived at Sunday Mass after the priest had begun the Offertory prayers. Swallowed toothpaste during fasting time, and still received Communion. Maybe—and this would be a grave matter indeed— the mysterious Malcolm had told a joke against the Pope, and Theresa Higgins had laughed . . .

Allegra caught her own eye in the driving mirror, and, as abruptly, her own laughter stopped. This was not the way it should be. The Sullivans were not passing their time thus, nor was M.M., nor even Sister Philomena, if she was still alive. The Sullivans and McConnells were proper people, real-life people, as, in her own community, was or had been the old nun. They knew where they came from, knew what it was they needed to do to lead a life that was both rewarding and virtuous, and what was more—luxury unimaginable to Allegra herself—they possessed the wherewithal to do it. Happily married, or willingly celibate, they could satisfy their bodies and comfort their hearts while basking in the full sun's beam of the Church's approval; sure of meeting there family, friends, souls of their own kind, they could attend regular Mass, and probably even confession too. Morning after morning they woke, night after night they slept, safe in the knowledge that they were not only good people, but good Catholics too. How different from Allegra. Only Allegra was alone, not daughter, nor wife, nor member of a religious community, nor even welcomed member of the Church into which she had been baptized, driving deserted streets in a borrowed car, cheering herself up with jokes about a mother who had hated to be photographed and a terrible, sinful secret that no one was telling her.

"Yo!"

"Hey, my man!"

Human sounds. At an intersection of two lonely streets, she had come suddenly upon a Pentecostal church about to start its evening service: vivid people in groups, with skin the color of chocolate, or mahogany, or tawny yellow, the women in bright silks, the men, virtuously suited, calling to each other in cheerful fellowhood. It was an attractive picture. Almost she stopped; almost, she drew her car into the lot to join the group. But those people were not her people, their secrets and sorrows and puzzlements not hers; and if she really wanted religious company, she could always go back to Mass.

She did not see another walking soul until she reached Melissa's apartment.

As she pulled her car into the port, she met Scott coming out, dressed in his waiter's costume of clean jeans and a shirt.

"Good day?" he asked.

"Terrific," she said. Oh, she could pretend to be a normal person, even a family member. "I was kidnapped by hordes of second cousins and force-fed chicken and pasta salad."

"That sounds like fun," he said. It probably did; in many ways, it had been. "What are you doing tonight?"

"I don't know. Lying low, probably, and repeating on my garlic bread." Or standing in the bathroom, staring dark eyes into mirrored dark, the daughter of a sinner whose sin she would never know. She grimaced; she would call M.M. "I have to call a friend in Chicago."

"Come to the restaurant."

"Oh . . . I've been eating all day."

"You don't have to eat: it's probably better if you don't. Make your call and come over, why don't you? Bruno's, two blocks down and three traffic lights east. I won't bug you about your family, I promise."

He smiled at her: he was clearly not used to being refused.

"Will Linda be there?" she said.

"Who? Oh. Yeah, probably. Bruno's, OK? Two blocks down—"

"And three lights east. I'll see how my call goes."

She went indoors, and began to change her clothes. But before she had finished, she decided not, after all, to call M.M., who was as free from sin as the Sullivans. Instead, she remembered a fellow sinner who had also been to Mass that weekend. It would be good to talk to another sinner. Impulsively, still half dressed, she went into the living room and once again called Ron's number.

"Ron's at the club," said Mike. Allegra could hear Barbra Streisand playing in the background. She pictured Ron's lover, lying big and gentle on the wide brocade sofa, thick socks on his feet, a mug of herbal tea by his side. "Shall I have him call you?"

"Not really," she said. "I mean, yes, it'd be good to talk to him. But it was really you I called to talk to this time."

"Oh?" he said.

"Yes," she said.

There was a silence.

"Everything OK?" he said.

"Yes," she said. "Fine."

"Good," he said.

Another silence. Smart move, Allegra. Decide you need to talk to someone, and call him before you've decided what you need to say to him. Diplomatic. No wonder John runs circles around you.

"I called yesterday," she said. "You were at Mass."

"Ron told me. Said you had a tan."

"A small one."

"Still a tan."

"I went myself," she said. "To Mass, this morning."

"Good girl."

Good girl. Thinking back on the church, and wondering how she could broach the subject she had called for, Allegra remembered, and shamelessly adapted for her purpose, the almond-eyed young priest and his earnest, soporific sermon.

"There was a priest there," she said, "who really irritated me."

"Oh, yeah?" said Mike.

"Yeah," she said. "He got up for the sermon, you see, and he started this long thing about sin."

"Sin?"

"Yeah." In fact, he had preached, at length and in some culinary detail, about his mother's cooking. "Real hellfire-and-damnation stuff, you know? I was quite surprised. Out here and everything."

"Yeah," he said. "That's unusual these days."

"I thought so," she said. She paused, and in an unhappy inspiration, thought of Mike's own particular sin. "And then," she added, "he started in on gays." He had never once mentioned gays, had the young priest. He had loved his mother's cooking, although not as much as he loved the nourishment the sacrament of Communion gave him; and there had been several obviously gay couples sitting peacefully in the congregation. "Gays," she repeated. "Wicked people. Sinners. A sin was a sin, and may God have mercy on them. That sort of stuff. I couldn't believe it."

"Well," said Mike, after a pause, his voice gone cold, "that priest was a chump then, wasn't he?"

"God!" Allegra could scarcely believe what she had just said, or that she, kind and broad-minded Allegra, had just said it. But there was no unsaying it; and, close on her mortification, came indignation, hot and righteous, at the sermon of her invention. "Mike, he was King Chump, he was the Mayor of Chump City. I'd have walked out, except that I was with my uncle and aunt, you know?" And so she would have, had the situation actually arisen; John and Kathleen or not, she honestly would have. Then, "Does it bother you, Mike? Having a priest call you a sinner?"

"You see." Mike's voice had not warmed, for which Allegra could hardly blame him. "I don't go to Masses said by chumps."

"Well, neither do I, usually, you know that. . . . But really, Mike, the Church does say, quite specifically, that the way you and Ron live is a sin, doesn't it?"

Mike sighed, wearily. "Yes," he said. "If you want to look at it that way, it does."

"Well, but Mike? Doesn't that make you feel"—feel what?—"feel weird?" she ended, feebly enough.

"Not really," said Mike. "I've obviously gotten used to being a moral aberration and a theological freak."

"Oh, Mike!" What had she been thinking; what on earth had she been thinking? "I didn't mean—"

"Door's open!" called Mike. There was a rattling, in the distance a sound of rubber and steel. "Well, Mr. William!" His voice, with warmth now to spare, rose to flirtatiousness. "Honey, I have to go, Bill's just arrived, looking positively *yummy* in the *most* divine blue shirt, and I simply can*not* keep my hands off him!"

The noise was Bill's wheelchair. Bill weighed under a hundred pounds, and was not yet quite blind. He was thirty-four and had been a ballet dancer.

"Give him a big kiss from me," said Allegra, fishing for the paper handkerchief without which she could not think of Bill.

"With the *greatest* of pleasure! Bill, Allegra sends a kiss, which I am coming to deliver right . . . this . . . second!"

Unconsciously, Allegra caressed the receiver before she replaced it and wandered into the bathroom. Her eyes and nose were pink in the mirror, but her skin was clear and her back straight. While across the continent, Mike, whom the Church called a sinner, tenderly performed the corporal work of mercy of comforting a man dying hideously and far too young. Allegra did not need Sister Philomena to point out into what brutal perspective this put Allegra's own problems. Although M.M., bless her, did quickly step in to retort that this wasn't a competition of sorrows, and that the burden of not knowing about her mother was one that Allegra had carried for far too long. Declan commented that he didn't see what made any of it M.M.'s business—he had never been nice to M.M.—and John asked, in careful puzzlement, just what made Allegra quite so sure that there was anything to know at all. Behind the din, Sister Philomena waited patiently for a quiet moment to express her thoughts on people who made up lies about priests. Allegra crossed her eyes at her reflection, and went to finish changing from the church clothes into her jeans.

Bruno's was a small restaurant, run by a Japanese family, over whom Scott towered, a respectful Aryan giant. He poured her a whiskey, and sat down with her at the bar to talk.

"Can you do this?" she asked.

"Sure." The owner, passing, lifted a brusque, kindly head in greeting. "Well, until people start to come in."

"Good. Thanks for the drink. *Sláinte.*"

"What's that?"

"An Irish toast. Sorry, I've been around Catholics all day, it gets kind of ethnic."

He smiled his ridiculous smile. Curious, she lowered her eyes, and looked up at him, lying, through her lashes. "Jimmy says hi," she said.

But he only continued to smile. "Does he? Say hi back. Did you get your uncle to talk at all?"

"God, no, there were a hundred children running around." And no, she was certainly not going to repeat to Scott what smiling Father Carroll had said to her. "Anyway, I thought you weren't going to bug me about my family."

"Sorry, I won't anymore. She's really not you, you know. My girl."

"Girl?" The waitress Linda, appearing from nowhere, was standing between them, smiling interest under aching eyes. "You have a girl, Scott?"

"Only in his typewriter," said Allegra. "You want to sit down?"

"Oh. OK." She blushed, sat, then looked assessingly at Allegra. "Have we met before?"

"I'm Scott's neighbor. Temporarily."

"Oh, right." Looking, she saw with visible relief Allegra's nascent wrinkles, the sprinkling of silver in her hair. She turned to Scott. "Wish me luck tomorrow, I have an audition. I'm an actress," she added to Allegra.

"Break a leg," said Allegra.

Linda smiled. She was pretty, with rosy olive skin and, under her pinafore, a shapely young body; but Scott had caught the owner's eye, and stood up.

"You guys sit," he said. "One of us should really look busy."

"Your raw material would like another drink, please," said Allegra.

"OK," he said, and Linda glanced at her again, through narrowed eyes. By the time he brought it, she had gone.

"She's not you, Allie," he repeated.

She waved a hand. "She's not me," she agreed.

Left alone, she sipped at her drink, feeling melancholy. Of course she was not Allegra, was not Scott's blond girl who worked in an office and had never known her mother; she would be more like other people than Allegra could ever hope to be. She would have day-to-day colleagues, a lover, siblings she could talk to, an uncle or aunt who would talk to her, so that whatever she wondered about her unknown parent, it would be neatly revealed, its accuracy uncontested, its ramifications sorted and categorized, by the story's end. She was a lucky girl, was Scott's girl, she lived in an easier world by far than Allegra's. Sister Philomena, scenting again self-pity, reminded Allegra that if she was not herself blessed with a conventional family, she nevertheless had a solid and good family of friends back at home, and that if she had chosen to leave them to come three thousand miles in almost certainly futile search of her own blood, she had no one other than herself to blame for loneliness; and of course, Sister Philomena was right. Nevertheless, the second whiskey was soon gone.

"Can I get another?" she asked Scott. "I'll pay this time."

"Another?" he said. "You sure?"

"Yes, I'm sure." A failing of WASPs, she suddenly realized, was that they confused drinking with getting drunk. Linda did not look like a WASP; she probably would not have asked that really quite impolite question. Allegra decided she liked Linda. She bugged her eyes, exaggerating sobriety. "I'm OK, you know."

"Of course you are."

But soon after the whiskey arrived came a large plate of fried calamari.

"Compliments of the house," he said.

"Thank you," she said. She drained her glass. "I should have some Chardonnay with this."

He frowned, a little. "Mixing it, huh?"

"A meal without wine," she told him, quoting Mike, who was Italian, "is like a day without sunshine."

"Another Irish expression?"

"God, no." In the Ireland her forefathers had left, whole families had died together, huddled in windswept hovels for the lack of food. Sometimes, when she was tired, or sad, Allegra almost believed she could feel the rain falling on the failing bodies, slipping in their thousands from the uselessly beautiful land to no land, no being at all. "In Ireland, it's more like, a day with a meal is a red-letter day."

He smiled, not quite comprehending, but went off apparently satisfied that she was not slurring her speech. A man who had sat next to her grunted.

"The praties they are small," he said.

She looked over at him. He was about her age, with curly black hair and large brown eyes set deep into a plump face.

"Are you Irish?" she said.

"Francis Xavier Bernard Farrell. You?"

"Allegra Mary Theresa Catherine O'Riordan."

"Yeah." He nodded. "Buy you a drink?"

"I have one."

"Buy you another, then."

"Scott thinks I'm drunk."

"Scott's Protestant."

"So he is. OK, thanks." And it was good wine too, cool and tart after the sweet whiskey and greasy fish: Scott had not been unduly modest about the food. She pushed the plate across the counter to share.

"It wasn't a famine at all, you know," she said.

"Excuse me?"

"1847," she said. "The Great Famine. It wasn't a famine at all. A nun at school explained it, Sister Philomena. The potato crops had failed, was all. There was tons of food in Ireland—cattle, grain, dairy—but it was all being shipped back to England. Tons of food. People dying of hunger, and not a famine at all."

"I hadn't thought of that," he said. "Bastards. Excuse me."

"Really," she said. "Bastards. She was great, was Sister Philomena." Well, Sister, would you rather it be told what you were really like? "Her dad was in the IRA, during Black and Tan time. He was a hero, well, she used to say he was. He killed fifty-five Englishmen in two years, and never missed Mass. She was always telling us that—never saw anything strange in it."

"Nuns," he said. "They're curious creatures."

"Aren't they, though." For the first time in the whole day, she felt, someone had said something with which she could fully agree. "But they all are, the Irish, aren't they? Let's face it, they're weird."

He laughed, and she laughed with him; she even began to imagine she might enjoy herself.

"Well, look at them," she said. "All those centuries they spent rebelling against the English, and so proud of themselves for it, glory-oh, glory-oh to the bold Fenian men . . . and Holy Mother Church tells them *once* to jump, and boy, they get those jumping shoes on. Don't tell me that isn't weird."

He smiled. "Well, but the Church offers them eternal salvation. In the bosom of Our Lord, and the company of His holy saints."

"Right. What a bunch of party guys—I hope I'm on Saint Ignatius's table." Yes, she was most certainly beginning to enjoy herself. "Let me ask you something. You're Irish, right, Francis Xavier Bernard? And I bet, I just bet, that you lose your temper sometimes, and you don't put up with any crap, and you're proud of it because you're Irish, right?"

He blushed a little, and smiled, down into his drink and then up at her, lines wrinkling the abundant flesh around his eyes.

"Somewhat right," he said.

"Right. Now let me ask you something else. I also bet, I bet and I bet you double or nothing I'm right too, that every Sunday morning of your life—of your entire life—you wake up feeling guilty because you're not going to Mass. Right?"

"Wrong," he said. "But that's because I do go to Mass."

"Oh my God, you're a practicing Catholic! Every Sunday?"

"Every Sunday."

"God. Then you'd know better than anyone what a crazy religion it is, wouldn't you?"

"How so, exactly?" he said. He was still smiling, and watching her with interest.

"Oh, God, where do you start? The communion of saints, the forgiveness of sins, praying to Saint Anthony when you lose your car keys, oh, and by the way, it's a mortal sin to use birth control—that's crazy stuff, isn't it?"

"Many people think so," he said. "Although I believe birth control is only a venial sin these days."

"It's still crazy," she said. "And I'll tell you something else." She took a sip of her wine—it was quite delicious—and thought of a new idea. "You have it worse than I do, because you're a man, and men Catholics are much, much crazier than women Catholics."

"They're *what?*" he said.

"Much crazier. I have this theory." It did not, she decided, make it any less of a theory that she was formulating it as she spoke. "It's a crazy religion, the Catholic Church, we're all agreed on that, right? And men are, intrinsically, much crazier than women, right?"

"I don't know that most men would agree."

"Well, they wouldn't, because they're men, and crazy, so you've just proved my point. Anyway." Briefly, she had lost her thread. She took another sip of wine, and found it again. "Anyway. Women can deal with the Church's craziness up to a point, because they don't take it too seriously. But a lot of men who do stay Catholic just take it and go with it, and they get weirder and weirder. Not all men, of course." M.M.'s Paul, for instance, and Angela's Luis had seemed reasonably sane. "But some of them. Boy." Declan. And sweet as he was, if you looked harder at him, Mike. And of course, it all came clear. "I know what it is. It's the ones who haven't married a woman. Have you ever been married to a woman?"

Still smiling, he shook his head.

"Well, there you are, there's no hope for you. You're irretrievably weird. Well, not irretrievably weird, you might marry someone one day, and get deweirded. But until then, you're weird. And you know who the ones are who are the weirdest of all, and are never going to get better?"

"No," he said. "Who?"

And as his eyes, kind in his large broad face, met hers in laughter, her own laughter switched, as abruptly as it was inevitably, to rage.

"Transubstantiators," she said. She could not, then, be so drunk: she had got the word out; indeed, she had created it.

"Who?" he said.

"Goddamned priests," she said. "Turn bread and wine into the body and blood of Christ in the morning, and behave like demons from hell for all the rest of the day."

"Transubstantiators," he said. "That's a good word. Did you make it up?"

"I met one today," she said. "A transubstantiator. A sweet old guy out by the ocean, Father Carroll, d'you know him? Well, he's this snowy-haired Barry Fitzgerald type, toora loora loora, Father Chuck, he even has a brogue for God's sake." The fairy-tale Catholicism of old movies, where crusty priests had hearts of gold, and a church scandal meant Bing Crosby taking choir practice in a sweatshirt instead of a cassock. "And he'd been transubstantiating all morning, well, he'd been doing it every morning for it must have been sixty years, and baptizing people and burying them and everything. And he asked me how I was doing, and he told me that my Uncle John was a fine man, and that I had the map of Ireland on my face." She stopped, gulped at her drink. "And then," she said. "And then he said, this priest, this minister of God, this transubstantiator, he said that my mother was the worst sinner he'd ever known. My mother." Yes, he had said that; he had said it about Allegra's mother. Yes, her own mother. "And he's been hearing confessions all this time, confessions, sins, for sixty years, and I can't imagine all the terrible things he must have heard, and that was just from regular parishioners, you only have to open the newspaper these days and look at what the bishops and the priests are doing and always have been, and my *mother* is—" She bit her lip, swallowed the salt in her throat. "And then he went to the bathroom." She gulped again. "Bastard," she said. "Transubstantiating bastard."

"What does your mom say?" he said, after a pause.

"She's dead."

"I'm sorry."

"Yeah." It was surprisingly comfortable, was talking to this strange man who went regularly to Mass. "Oh, God," she said, suddenly. "Was that terrible of me? Calling you weird like that?"

"Did you?"

"Yes." Did she? Yes, she did, although he did not seem to have taken offense. But it had been offensive nevertheless. "Oh, God, I'm sorry," she said. "Was it terrible?"

"It's probably true."

"Not necessarily."

"It's true."

"Well, let me buy you a drink."

"Sure."

He did not look twice when she ordered another for herself: she must then be sober. Surreptitiously, she checked her hands, which were, indeed, rock steady. Not for nothing was she the daughter of the great tall Irishman whom Helen Viner had only once seen tipsy.

"Scott thinks I'm drunk," she said.

"We've been through that already. Scott's Protestant."

"Yes, isn't he." She looked across the restaurant, to the table where Scott was gravely distributing hamburgers, and thought of him knocking on her door with a map, or walking through the courtyard with piles of newspapers to recycle. "Scott's my neighbor," she said. "He's a nice guy. Protestants are often nicer than Catholics, aren't they?"

"Less weird?"

"No, really nicer. Scott's a really good guy. He's kind. And good. *Good.* Probably never been inside a church in his life." She looked into her glass, and sighed, for the sorrowful sinfulness that was her own lot.

He nodded, and they sat in silence for a while.

"I should go," she said. "It's been a long day, I even went to Mass."

"It's been good to meet you," he said. "Allegra Mary Theresa Catherine O'Riordan."

"You too, Francis Xavier Robert Emmet Martin de Porres Kelly."

"Drive carefully," he said. "And watch out for transubstantiators."

At the door of the restaurant, she met Scott.

"You OK to drive?" he asked.

"Transubstantiators," she told him, which almost certainly confirmed him in his suspicion.

Of course she was OK to drive, was Ignatius O'Riordan's daughter. She made her way smartly out of the parking lot, stopped punctiliously at stop signs, and kept her eyes extravagantly alert for a hypothetical pedestrian who might be wandering the deserted sidewalks. She parked at a perfect right angle to the wall of Melissa's carport, and opened and closed without a hint of a fumble Melissa's front door. It was only then that it happened. Despair, lurking with patient glee on the outskirts of her soul, saw its moment, and moved, swiftly and accurately, to seize her by her scruff, as a large dog would a kitten, and shook her, and snapped her, and would not let her go.

"Oh, shit," she said, wearily, in recognition: despair was not a stranger to her. She went to the kitchen and poured a large slug of Scotch; looked at, and rejected as inappropriately compliant, the chairs around the kitchen table; and at last sank, she and her uninvited guest, to the hardwood floor under the china parrot in the living room, her back against the wall.

It was not fair for her to be thus; other women were not sitting so, abandoned and alone. Other women knew about their mothers. They knew, from their stories, about their childhoods, their teen years, their young womanhoods; they saw what sort of marriages they had forged, and with how happy a result, what manner of old women they were, gracefully or not, growing into. They knew these things, did other women; and, knowing, were able also to know how they felt about them. Because Allegra knew that other women had feelings about their mothers of an intensity such as she herself could only imagine. They had boiling love, or the bitterest of resentment, they had anger, or admiration, or pride or envy, or, usually, all of them together, all stirred up and indistinguishable, simmered over years, and mixed into a spicy stew that, like it or not, was at least a presence, a nourishment in their lives. Only Allegra, starved for information as her ancestors had starved for food, had nothing. No sign of what manner of woman she might reasonably expect to be; no map of strengths to build toward, weaknesses or mistakes to avoid. No discernible blueprint, no legible guide. Nothing but three photographs and a handful of faint memories; and now, an old woman had spoken of a terrible thing, and a priest had remembered a sin, and no one would tell her what they meant. And that was worse than nothing at all. Shivering, suddenly, from loneliness and the cold of the hard floor, she looked at her watch. Damn. Too late to call M.M. Later still to call Bob, and besides, Lois had made it quite clear, and Allegra could not really blame her for it, that while she liked Allegra and suffered Declan, any more than superficial discussions of the O'Riordan family were to take place outside of her own home, and away from her blond, unbaptized sons.

But it was not, she thought, too late to call John.

Right, Allegra. Call him, drunk and slurring, and see what you find out about your mother that you haven't yet.

But she was not drunk—"I am not drunk," she said aloud—and you see, she was not slurring. And the fact of the matter—"The *fact* of the matter," she added, again aloud—was that John had got away with far too much for far too long. He had lied to her; or if not lied, had told untruths. Or if not told untruths, had most incontrovertibly prevaricated. "Prevaricated," she said. She was crystal clear. And yes, Jimmy had promised to help her, but Jimmy, Allegra saw now clearly, was a child of Los Angeles; to expect him to hold to his word was as unreasonable as expecting to discuss physics with M.M.'s Elizabeth. "Unreasonable," she said. It was time, it was really most high time, that Allegra faced John, said to him, straight out, Look, buddy, what the hell is going on?

Big mistake, Allegra.

No. It was not a mistake. The mistake she had made was in not doing this before, in waiting around, foolishly, imagining that someday, somebody might tell her, of their own volition. She poured more Scotch with a still-steady hand. "Prevaricated," she said. "Unreasonable." Crystal clear.

It was John who answered the telephone: Allegra could not have coped with Kathleen.

"Hi, sweetie," he said. "You get home OK?" He sounded a little surprised: it might be late, even for a local call. Allegra squinted again at her watch. Just after eleven. Well, too bad.

"Yes, thanks," she said, politely. Crystal clear. "It was a good afternoon."

"They're good folks," he said. "Luis is an old Knights of Columbus buddy of mine. Rich as Croesus, did you see the spread?"

"John," she said. "What happened to my mother?"

There was a silence while the kaleidoscope of the conversation turned, its molecules split, burst into chaos, rearranged themselves into a different formation altogether.

"What do you mean?" he said.

And all in a rush, together, the alcohol she had been drinking since midday, the wine at the Sullivans', the whiskey in the restaurant, the wine in the restaurant, the Scotch in the apartment, all of it caught up with her, and she felt her mind slip from her control like the rogue cars she sometimes drove in her nightmares, sliding, brakeless, down dark streets into nameless dangers, desolation, and destruction.

"I mean," she said carefully. Her stomach swooped, swerved, miraculously righted itself again. "I mean that I know something happened to her, because nobody ever talks about her. Dad didn't talk about her. And you don't talk about her. And Father, that priest this afternoon—who is a *prick*, John, a prick—he started to talk about her, and he said she was a sinner, and then you came and took him away, and he wouldn't talk anymore either. He said she was a sinner. He said that. And I think." Oh, God. What did she think? "I think that, as she was my mother, and I am her daughter, I have a right to know what it was that happened. I think that. I really do. And I think you should." She was right there; he should, he most definitely should. "You should," she repeated.

"Sweetie," said John. "It's late. Why don't you go to bed? We'll talk about this later."

"I'm not drunk, John."

"I didn't say you were. Now, just go to bed, OK? You'll feel better later."

"You see," she said. "You're not listening to me. I say I want to know something, and everyone's so busy trying not to tell it to me that they don't listen to me. You—you change the subject. And Kathleen says she doesn't know. And Jimmy pretends to listen but he doesn't really, he's too busy . . ." No, she was not quite so drunk. "Too busy being busy, and Bob and Declan don't even care, and . . ." The terrible tears tore at her throat. "And nobody listens to me. Because I want to know. That's all I'm saying. I want to know."

"What do you want to know?" His steady voice was kind.

"I want to know." She closed her eyes for a second, striving to balance her mind on the sea of drink that was tossing it, Star of Ocean, save us, knowing that to ask the question now would be the worst thing she could do, because she could never ask it again, knowing that she must not ask the question now, knowing that she had no choice but to ask the question now. "I want," she said, "to know what happened. To my mother."

At the other end of the telephone line, John sighed. "What happened to your mother, sweetie," he said, "was that she went to Chicago and had three terrific kids. And God's will is God's will, but it's a damned shame she didn't get the chance to see them grow up into adults she'd have been as proud of hell of."

"Oh, John!" But it was not his kindness that made her cry, and cry the harder that he now might choose to assume that it was. Feebly, she attempted to rally. "Why did he say that thing, then? Father . . ."

"Father Carroll?"

"Right. Why did he say she was a sinner? Why?"

"Sweetie, Father Carroll's an old man. And we're all sinners, you know that. Look, it's late, you're tired, and you just lost your dad a couple of weeks ago. Why don't you go to bed, and we'll talk later, OK?"

To her most complete mortification, Allegra could summon in response to this no other reaction than relief at the conversation's end. She replaced the receiver, and sat on the floor, sobbing until her tears ran dry. Then she went to the bathroom, optimistically swallowed three aspirins and a large glass of water, and staggered to bed, on her way knocking from its perch the china parrot, which lay broken on the floor, in cheerful, shattered shards of scarlet, yellow, and royal blue.

Chapter Seven

They were there in the morning, Allegra could see them from the bed, bright reminders of her shame, shining vivid in the strong sunlight on the polished wood floor. Groaning, she turned over, and lifted a corner of the cheap, light window shade. It was well into the day, the sky was deep blue, and all of the world, that was to say, all of the decent world, all the quiet of stomach and clear of head, all of the world but Allegra O'Riordan had been up and about its business for hours. She groaned again, and closed her eyes.

It was a mistake. Behind her closed eyelids lay demons, memories sparkling and malicious as imps, disjointed but too quickly flying together, of the terrible, the truly appalling person she had been the night before. She remembered breaking the parrot. She remembered insulting a guy in Scott's restaurant. She remembered thinking she was being rather witty while insulting the guy in Scott's restaurant. She remembered telling Scott, over and over, and with increasingly obvious inaccuracy, that she was not drunk. She decided that she had

had enough of remembering for the time being, and opened her eyes again.

She should, she supposed, get up. She should claim as her own this drink-poisoned body with its head full of half-memories, should lift it from its bed of anonymity, should wash it, please its parched palate and comfort its surging stomach with coffee and hot toast and honey. She should dress it, settle it into a chair, and maybe later, take it out into the kind sun. It was the way of a wise and righteous woman. But, of course, a wise and righteous woman did not get herself into the state that Allegra was in.

She rose, still groaning, picked her way over the mutilated corpse of the parrot, and scuttled, eyes averted from the living room which had witnessed her disgrace, to the bathroom, where her performance would have made Father Carroll himself proud. It was a surprise, afterwards, to see in the mirror a recognizable Allegra, one with blood in the eyes and puffiness in the cheeks, but Allegra nevertheless. For a long, accusing moment, she looked at herself; then she shook her head, and went into the kitchen.

It was surprising too just how complicated could be the task of making coffee and toast. But, once made, they undeniably worked their effect: Ignatius O'Riordan's daughter had recuperative powers. Lacing her hands around the coffee mug, and tenderly protecting from probing the more painfully self-wounded corners of her mind, she began to feel not unpleasantly frail and Victorian. When she had eaten and showered, she should probably go for a walk: they said that exercise was good for what ailed her. She might walk up the hill toward the Peppercorn's which, after all, was not the one her mother had known; or she might walk in the other direction, to the tiny park with the playing children. After her walk, it would be time for lunch; and after lunch, you could take a nap. You really could not, she sadly supposed, take a nap after breakfast.

She stared out of the window, deciding on her direction, and saw a short, springy male figure crossing the courtyard. It was not until he was nearly at her door that she recognized Melissa's boyfriend, Peter.

"Hi, Allie," he said. He was clear-eyed and alert: he was vegetarian, and hardly ever drank. "You're a busy lady, but I've tracked you down at last."

Bet you're glad you did, she thought, sparing him as much of her unbrushed breath as possible, while returning his kiss. A little curiously, she squinted past his cheek to watch his expression: but it showed nothing. He was a nice guy.

"Melissa told me to keep an eye on you. I was sorry about your dad." He frowned at her. "How're you holding up?"

"So-so." She shrugged, brazenly, for all the world as if it were her father's death that was her affliction. It was a pity about the breath, however. "You want some coffee?"

"Sure." More familiar with the apartment than she, he fetched a mug and spoon, seated himself at the table, and poured.

"How's Melissa?" she asked.

"Fine." He smiled, fondly. Peter and Melissa were so unaffectedly in love that their friends joked about them, touched them for luck when they embarked on a new affair. Allegra, beside them, often felt jaded and overly worldly-wise, a too-sophisticated survivor of one too many love affairs. "You know Melissa, she's always happy." Then his eyes traveled to the living room, and the pieces of the wrecked parrot. "Oh, you had an accident."

"It happened just this morning, I'm always in such a fog." Sister, it did not remotely concern him just when it had happened; besides, now that she thought about it, it may well have been, technically speaking at least, this morning after all. "I thought I should have some breakfast before I tried to clean it up. D'you know where Melissa keeps her broom?"

"That closet there. Finish your coffee first."

"OK. I feel bad about it, really, that poor parrot. Of course, I'll replace it: d'you know where it came from?"

"Oh." He had reached across her for the sugar, and busily stirred it into his mug. "You know Melissa, just get her any little thing, and she'll be happy."

Allegra's stomach had just begun to settle: now, fingers of a more material dread danced around its edges.

"I want to get one like that," she said. "Where did it come from?"

"Don't know. Shouldn't think she does either."

The fingers closed in.

"It wasn't valuable?" she said. "Was it?"

"Oh, no!" He laughed, and shook his head, reassuringly. "It was an old, cheap thing, she'd had it for years, they've probably stopped making them like that, good thing too. I wouldn't worry about it."

The fingers now squeezed, as a memory of Melissa surfaced.

"It wasn't the one her grandfather gave her?" she said.

"Someone like that. It had a good long life."

"On her twelfth birthday, just a week before he died? The one that started her off collecting in the first place? The one she once told me—oh God, Peter—always cheers her up, because she looks at it and knows her grandfather's there smiling at her from heaven?"

"Oh. You know Melissa and her stories."

"God, Peter! Shit!"

"Don't worry about it," he said. "Look, it was a thing, an object, OK? She'll remember her grandfather without it, and she'd be much more upset to know you were upset. So it's no big deal, OK?"

It must be a considerable deal to merit such a speech. No, Allegra was no sophisticate today, but only a bilious, destructive child, who had got herself drunk and, drunk, had wantonly wrecked an irreplaceable treasure. She tucked inside her heart the leaden pellet of self-hatred and let it sink, for the time, unexamined: since Peter had gone to the trouble of lying, the least she could do in return was to pretend to believe him.

"OK," she said. From somewhere, she found a smile. "Thanks. So she's OK, then? Melissa."

"Fine. She's freezing cold, she's staying in the world's tackiest apartment, but she's working her little buns off, so she's happy. You know Melissa."

Melissa, it was true, had the gift of joy.

"Give her my love," she said. "I'll write her about the parrot."

"You're on vacation. I'm talking to her today, I'll tell her then."

"No. I'll write."

"OK." He shrugged, carefully indifferent.

He stayed for what the kitchen clock later would have her believe was only half an hour, talking about Los Angeles and friends in common, sometimes out of focus, sometimes to a slightly alarming extent in it. When he left, he kissed her again, casually, arousing a faint spark of hope: after she heard his car start in the street outside, she spat into her hand. But Peter, it appeared, was a very nice guy indeed. She winced in embarrassment; then, thinking of a way to cheer herself up, went into the bathroom, and practiced being Peter kissing her. It was good. Then she practiced being herself being kissed, which was even better. Ron would like it. Probably so would Jimmy. She went from being herself to being Peter, from being Peter to being herself. It was definitely good.

Then she remembered the parrot, lying wrecked in primary colors on the living room floor.

Then she remembered the telephone call.

She did not go for a walk that morning; she did not do anything very much. She disposed of the china carrion, made another cup of coffee, and lay on the sofa in the shaded living room, trying to watch a soap opera on the television, trying not to think, or make jokes, or do anything that would remind her that she was, and would spend the rest of her life being, the person who had made the telephone call. She thought she could bear it all—the bar, the drive home, yes, even the parrot—if she did not have to bear the telephone call. The shocking, irretrievable, drunken telephone call.

For she had been drunk last night, had John Higgins's polite niece, his dead sister's daughter, drunk on a Sunday, too drunk to keep her condition to herself. Drunk not because she was celebrating, or even, by this stage, particularly grieving anymore, but drunk because the drink had been there, and she had had no pressing reason—no husband or children like normal women, no self-control even, like decent people—not to consume it. She was a drunkard, had shown herself to him to be one, and neither could ever forget that the other would always know it.

When the telephone rang, she did not consider answering it. But after Melissa's message, came the measured tones of Declan, and she picked up the receiver.

"Hello."

"Oh. You're there."

"Yes. Where are you?"

"In Los Angeles."

"Oh. Aren't you early?"

"Not really."

"Oh."

"How are you?"

"OK. You?"

"You see, I can't call you in the morning because my meeting's been put forward."

"Oh."

"So do you want to have dinner tomorrow night?"

"Yes, OK. Oh, hold on. John's"—oh God, oh Christ, oh, God in merciful holy heaven, no—"asked us both to dinner with him."

"Oh. OK."

"That OK?"

"Fine."

"OK. So I guess I'll"—no, God, oh please, God, for the love of God, *no*—"see you there then."

"I have a car. I'll pick you up."

"Well, only if it's on your way."

"I'll be around town. Give me your address."

She gave it.

"I'll see you soon after six, then."

"OK. Bye."

"Bye."

Carefully, she replaced the receiver on the first buddy she had had in her life, and set about not thinking about seeing John.

The soap opera helped. Allegra liked soap operas and watched them when she could, claiming, quite speciously, that they gave her material for her act; and it was undeniably comforting, here in this pleasant land of her disgracefulness, to turn to the same ordered interior sets which filled her own television at home in Chicago, and watch the same mild-mannered people dealing so matter-of-factly with the same ludicrous disasters. People in soaps did not go in for introspection. Probably, they were all Protestants.

Muted across the courtyard, under the tinkling music of the melodrama, came the busy clack of Scott's unhungover typewriter, and Allegra, turning off her own thought processes, fell asleep.

She awoke, Ignatius O'Riordan's daughter, feeling better in body, which was at least a foundation to build on. Food, she knew, would make her better still. Soup, there was a can of vegetable in the cupboard. And a tuna sandwich—tuna for the protein, and bread for the starch. Smart choice, Allegra. Wholesome. Yea for the woman with the rhinoceros breath. Nodding commendation, she warmed the soup, fixed the sandwich. After she had eaten, she even felt able to face the sunlight.

She had not, unfortunately, reckoned with facing Scott. Scott, she realized too late to retreat, was sitting in the courtyard, legs akimbo, with fresh-washed hair and blue-whited eyes.

"Hi," he said. "How're you doing?"

"Fine." Through red-rimmed puddles, under grease-lank bangs, she glared at him for his impertinence. "How're you?"

"Oh, I'm great. Hey, you know, the weirdest thing happened last night, just after you left. Your cousin showed up."

"Jimmy?"

"Yes, wasn't that weird? He said he was always passing the place and meaning to stop by, but just hadn't gotten around to it. And then, last night, he does—and he finds me there." He looked straight at her and smiled, his eyes as blue, and as unreadable, as the winter Los Angeles sky. "Coincidence, huh?"

"Weird," she agreed. She perched on a chair, and felt herself brighten a little; this was more fun at least than what had been taking place inside her head. "In fact," she added, "it's quite strange, really. I saw him just yesterday afternoon, and he never mentioned once that he was coming out here in the evening. I wonder why not?"

But Scott only shrugged. "Who knows? He's a great guy, isn't he? He thinks you're terrific too. Frank and he had quite the talk about you."

"Frank?"

"The guy you were talking to. Tall, dark hair."

"Oh." Francis Xavier Linus Cletus Clement Sextus Cornelius. "Frank." And the guilt and the shame rolled in upon her like the waves of the far-off Irish Sea. "I hope they were saying good things."

"Oh, great things. Frank was asking all kinds of questions about you: I think he likes you."

To be liked by a Catholic man. Allegra shivered instinctively, for just a second a small girl again, unheeded in the car between Dad and Father Forde. But Scott must be mistaken: what man in his right mind could have liked the person who had been Allegra last night? She distracted herself with making mild trouble.

"Speaking of liking," she said. "I wonder how Jimmy and Linda would get along?"

"D'you think they might? I shouldn't think they'd have much in common, would you?" He smiled again, and stood. "I have to get back to work. Oh—Frank has a message for you. He says you're to watch out for transistor radios."

"I'm to do what?"

"No, it wasn't transistor radios. It was that other word you guys were saying. I can't remember it now, he was saying it all night."

Oh, God. "Transubstantiators," she said. The wince-inducing word, which she had thought she was so clever to coin. Oh, God.

"That's it. What does it mean?"

"Be thankful you don't know," she told him.

The rest of the day passed slowly, as such days did. Languid, Allegra witnessed the television's cycle mature, saw it slip, as predictably as at home, from soap operas to talk shows to outdated cop shows, and at last, into prettily processed news of the real world. Sometimes, during the afternoon, she slept; at unusual times, she went to the bathroom. The mail brought a card from Melissa, which she put aside hastily to read tomorrow; the telephone rang twice, but neither caller left a message. In the evening, she fixed more soup, and followed it with a dish of granola; on the television, the news gave way to suitably inferior sitcoms, and Allegra saw no reason to stay up late.

She woke the next morning feeling altogether restored, and lay in bed luxuriating in a body free from poison, a mind clear of fog. If only, she thought—just the one dread wriggling in her otherwise placid stomach—if only she did not have to see John today. Not today, not next week. Not for several weeks, not even for a year or so, not until the seasons had come and gone, as to some extent they must even here in this city, until Lent had happened, and Easter, Ascension Day, the feast of the Assumption, Thanksgiving, Advent, Christmas. After Christmas, she felt, she might be able to face John again; but not today, please God, not today.

Unexpectedly, it was M.M.'s mother who spoke up, as she occasionally did, her flat Chicago vowels allowing neither extravagance nor unkindness. She reminded Allegra that what was done was done, that there was no use crying over spilt milk, that what could not be cured must be endured. She pointed out that if Allegra had embarrassed herself, at least she did not have to live with having hurt somebody else, that as far as John was concerned, blood was thicker than water, and if she was really still worried about facing him, she might just look at the size of the whiskeys he poured himself nightly and reflect that the apple did not fall far from the tree. She told Allegra that the best thing she could do would be to go on with herself and stop being such a worrywart; and, Sister Philomena having been shocked into silence by the entire episode, there was no one to contradict her.

Deliciously soothed, Allegra stretched herself in Melissa's soft sheets and began to think, idly, about going home. Then yes, she thought, more seriously, the plan taking slow, sweet shape in her mind. Home. God knew, she had found out little enough about her mother here in her mother's city, and if she was going to spend her time here sitting in bars insulting the sort of crazy Catholics who liked to be insulted, then maybe her mother's city was not a good place for her to be. Yes, she would stay until the end of the week, to work a little more on her tan; then she would return the keys to Peter, and go home. Yes, and she would have a week in the apartment before she returned to the club, puttering, possibly painting her kitchen. She would see her friends soon, so that she could show off her tan and shiver theatrically in the cold Chicago air, although it must surely have warmed a little by now, some daffodils might even be out along Lake Shore Drive. Yes, she would go out this morning to buy gifts: something kitsch for Ron and Mike, New Age for Fred, luxurious for Bill, and whatever she could see for M.M. and the children—maybe M.M. would bring Elizabeth to meet her at the airport, M.M. in her thick tan coat, yes, and Elizabeth in the green down jacket that made her look like a leprechaun.

Leggie, no! wailed M.M., and Allegra snorted and stirred in irritation. What more could she do? she demanded, and wearily, for her friend's benefit, prepared to run yet again through the list in her mind. If John had ever been going to tell her anything, he never would now. Kathleen was married to John. Jimmy knew nothing. The Sullivans knew nothing. Father Carroll was in cahoots with John. Alice and Albert had vanished, and Helen Viner was senile.

Helen Viner, said M.M., thoughtfully. Allegra groaned aloud, and rolled her eyes, but M.M. had never known when to shut up. Helen had once been an intelligent woman; Helen had mentioned a secret; Helen had been there on the beach when Malcolm took the photograph. If Allegra were to face Helen again, unaided and unencumbered by Jimmy or Scott, and knowing now as she did that there was something to know; if she were to take her out of the store, maybe for coffee or for some sweet treat the old woman was not usually allowed; if she were to be patient, and gentle, and firm, and ask her over and over and over again until she got an answer, just how Malcolm had died, and what was the sin Theresa had committed . . . If wishes were horses, Allegra told M.M., quoting M.M.'s own mother, we'd never have to buy fertilizer. But at the very least, M.M. replied, she would surely gain another anecdote about Theresa—and tried not to look triumphant when Allegra shrugged suddenly at the thought, and giggled to herself, like a little girl.

It was remarkable the difference a day could make, she thought, a few minutes later, peering into the mirror, and swallowing the small pill which was her daily Morning Offering to sin. (No, in fact, a check of her mental calendar told her that, this being the week when she was taking placebos, it was not such a sin after all. But then, she had not thought of that before she took the pill, so the intent to sin had been there. Tomorrow, she could be virtuous, and now that she thought of it, the next day too.) Really, today, with the puff in her face deflated and the murdered corpse of the parrot discreetly buried in the trash can, she could almost believe herself a decent member of society. Almost. She quickly turned her mind from that perilous path, and set to thinking about Helen Viner.

She could not see the old woman when she entered the store, but gangling over a box of books was Don, scowling in concentration as he transferred them to a shelf.

"Hi," she said. "How are you?"

He looked up, recognized her without pleasure. "OK," he said. He returned to his task. "You?"

"Oh, fine. Where's Helen?"

He stopped working.

"Hadn't you heard?" he said.

Oh, God. Oh, no. Oh, God.

"Heard what?" she said, but she knew she need not ask.

"She died," he said. He frowned fiercely into the box. "Over the weekend." His jaw was clamped shut, and his eyes were glassy. Allegra's throat closed for him: she too had lately lost someone she loved.

"Oh, Don," she said. "I am sorry."

He looked up, and just for a few seconds, his face softened.

"Yeah," he said.

"You'll miss her," she said. "What happened?"

"Her heart," he said. "It was weak, you know. We think she went sometime on Saturday. A neighbor." He stopped, swallowed, and continued. "A neighbor noticed she hadn't drawn the blinds on Sunday, and found her. Sitting on a chair quite peacefully, she hadn't even cleared up from lunch."

"Oh, Don," she said. Then, lunch, she thought. On Saturday.

"Yeah," he said, again. "I drove her home from work on Friday, and she seemed fine. I was probably the last person to see her alive."

He bit his lip, and allowed her a shrug and half-smile. If Allegra were kinder, maybe, she would let him continue to think that. But it was not true; and she could not bring herself, for the sake of the living, to rob dead Helen of her last morning in this world.

"You know," she said, "you weren't, in fact."

Don looked quickly at her, hardening.

"What?" he said.

"I'm sorry," she said. "But you weren't. God, this is weird. My cousin Jimmy—you know Jimmy Higgins? Well, he's my cousin, and he's quite friendly with Helen too. Was. Anyway. God. He and I and another friend, just for no special reason, just on an impulse really, we just—this is so weird—we decided to go to visit her on Saturday morning. And she seemed fine then too, about eleven o'clock it would have been. Flirted with both the guys, showed us some photographs, she even had a drink. And two hours later, she's dead. God. Sorry."

If ever there might have been sympathy between her and Don, there now would never be.

"She wasn't supposed to drink," he said.

"She wasn't," said Allegra, "supposed to eat sugar or fat either, and she had a plate of French toast at lunch that day, and finished it. And she said it was what *you* always ordered for her."

"Yes," he said, after a moment. "Yes, you're right. She'd have been eighty-five next birthday. Look, would you go now, please? You don't seem to buy any books while you're here, anyway."

"I'm sorry, Don," she said. But he had already returned to his work.

Allegra left the store, and wandered down the hill, past Melissa's apartment to the park, where she sat on a bench and stared unseeing at the plump young mothers playing with their babies.

Helen Viner had died. She had waved them off, the three tall young people, she had rinsed their glasses and put away the stale cookies they left behind; she had prepared and eaten the bleakly nourishing food she showed them. Then, she had sat back in her chair, and had ceased to be. Allegra wondered whether she had felt death coming, since by now, she must have long been aware of its approach; or whether it had caught her, after all, surprised. She wondered what her thoughts had been, whether she had wished the three of them had stayed on to bid her goodbye; or whether she had been relieved to be left at last to perform that most private of all acts alone.

It unquestionably made Allegra a person wicked beyond all redemption that while she grieved for Don's loss here, and, wherever Helen had gone to, wished well to her there, by far her uppermost emotion was of boiling fury that she would now never know what the old woman had known of her mother.

She sat for a while; then, reflexively, made a sign of the cross over the departed spirit, and returned to the apartment. Scott was in the courtyard: he looked up when she entered, and smiled.

"Hi," he said. "How's it going?"

"Hi." She looked at him, and for a moment, her soul seemed to separate itself from her body, to balk and recoil at the idea of bringing news of death to one such as Scott. "Something weird happened," she said.

"Yeah?" He raised an anticipatory eyebrow.

"Yeah." She sat on a chair beside him, and looked past his youth and his beauty to the wall where the bougainvillea flaunted its crimson. "Helen Viner died over the weekend."

Scott's language was not the language of death. He frowned at the sharp-shadowed flagstones, golden brows straight above blue eyes, that one line puckering his smooth brow.

"Shit," he said.

"Yes. Saturday afternoon. It seems we were the last to see her."

"Really?" He shivered a little. "Strange. What happened?"

"Her heart went. It was weak, and she was nearly eighty-five." A mouse of a worry was nibbling at the edges of her conscience, and cravenly, she showed it to him. "You don't think it was the Scotch, do you?"

"Oh, no." Obligingly sensible, he bludgeoned it to extinction. "That was mostly water. Wow. Dead. And it had seemed to be such a good day too."

But there would be no more good days for Helen, nor bad days either, no more excess of memories jumbled every which way into her brain, like the photographs in the overflowing box; she was beyond the pettinesses of this world, and now knew everything, or knew nothing.

"She was a good lady," he said. "I'm sorry I only got to talk to her the once." From the flicker of guilt that skipped across his face, Allegra knew that he was thinking of the stories of Fitzgerald he would now never hear, and felt a pang of pity for the poorly mourned old woman. Then he looked at her, aslant, as she had seen Jimmy look at him.

"I guess that means you'll never find out," he said. "About your mom."

But it was not admiration which his perfectly half-drooping eyelids concealed, but rude, writer's curiosity about her condition.

"No," she said. "I guess I won't."

He hesitated, trying to ask her how much she minded, how greatly she cared about the history of her own now closed to her forever, whether she was aware of being, let us face it, a freak; but the politeness of his upbringing won out. If he was to be a writer, she thought, he would really have to work on that.

Declan arrived at a minute past six. He stood at the doorway, tall and beaky, his thick hair almost completely gray, the eyes under them inspecting Allegra closely, as if in faint puzzlement at how she had come to be of his blood. She had forgotten how much he resembled Dad.

"Hello," she said.

"Hello." His glance left her and scanned the apartment. "What a lot of birds."

"She collects them," she said. "My friend Melissa."

"Does she."

It was not necessarily a criticism, Allegra reminded herself, remembering too what she always forgot, what it was like to be with Declan.

"Do you want a drink?" she said.

"No, thank you."

"Well, I'm going to have one." She went to the cupboard, and picked up the Scotch bottle. It was light in her hand, and for a moment, she felt sick with the shame of having forgotten finishing it. Well, but vodka was probably better anyway, it would not smell. She poured herself a glass, and followed him into the living room, where he was perched on a chair, gazing impassively ahead.

"How're you doing?" she said.

"OK. You?"

"OK."

"Good."

"Yes. Have you talked to Bob?"

"No. You?"

"A couple of days ago. He seems OK."

"Oh."

Yet they had shared the same father, had Declan and she, and within the last month had both suffered the loss of him.

"It was a good funeral," she said. "Wasn't it?"

"You thought so?"

"Lots of people said so," she said. "They said it was a really good party."

"In that case," he said, "maybe we should have done it sooner."

But it was Declan who had dealt with the caterers, who had insisted on the extra case of whiskey. Allegra started to stop herself from sighing; then, defiantly, allowed herself to continue.

"How was your meeting?" she asked.

Thinly, he smiled his success. "It went very well, in fact," he said. He relaxed a little, back into the chair. "It's an interesting time in finance. The new laws in Europe have changed everything."

"Really," she said.

"Yes, the repercussions have been quite unusual. And with the Asian situation to be considered, it's really all very unusual indeed."

He refrained from acknowledging that it need not concern him whether Allegra pretended interest or not. She sipped at her drink, neither hurried nor lingering, until it was gone.

"We should leave," she said, then.

"OK," he agreed.

In the car, they hardly spoke. Once, in the days when Declan was the earlier Declan, he and Allegra had done everything together. They had formed secret societies, had terrified each other with ghost stories, had played, it seemed, games without end, games of tag, of checkers, of donkey, of cops and robbers, cowboys and Indians, Martians and Venusians; earlier still, they had cuddled together on their mother's then-giant lap, played with and patted her red hair, been soothed to sleep by the same voice which Allegra could just remember, singing lullabies, sweetly and a little off-key. Now they sat, staring out of the separate windows of a rented car, with a wall between them that neither could remember erecting, neither knew, nor cared to learn, how to traverse. It occurred to Allegra that he had not asked her why she was in Los Angeles. It occurred to her that she would not tell him if he did.

But at least, she reflected, Declan did not know about her what John knew. And with every traffic light, every freeway on ramp and off that drew them closer to John's house, she remembered with more vivid shame the half-remembered telephone call, and terrible waves swept over her of prickly heat and sour chill at once, leaving her sad, and tired, and old. She leaned her forehead against the cold glass on the windowpane and groaned aloud, wishing, a little alarmingly, that she had had another vodka.

"What was the street number again?" said Declan.

They parked, walked up the flat driveway, now growing familiar to Allegra under the riotous magnolia trees, and were let in.

John's greeting of her was exactly as usual. The salutation, the thrust of the cheek, the relaxation today, faint but perceptible, as he moved to greet her sibling of the more familiar sex, all were for all the world as if Sunday night had been as any other. Humiliation such as even she had not lately experienced suffused Allegra to realize she was thanking God for the Jesuit education. She moved away quickly to greet first Kathleen and then Jimmy, lurking inquisitively in the doorway.

"I may not be able to stay," he said. "I'm kind of waiting for a call. But I did want to say hi to Declan. I won't ask you to a rematch, cousin." He turned to Kathleen. "We played chess the last time we met, and he beat me in nine moves."

"Hello," said Declan.

"A blind man could beat you," said John.

"He's very good, dear," said Kathleen.

"No, Mom," said Jimmy. "I'm more in the category of very bad."

"In fact," said Declan, "I know an excellent chess player who's blind. He says he's not distracted by vision."

"Well, there you are," said John. "I have a nephew who's a chess champion, and a son who can't find the socks department. Come and have some drinks."

"He can't have been born blind," said Allegra.

Declan looked at her in surprise.

"You couldn't picture a chessboard if you'd never been able to see." She tried to imagine born blindness, the darkness with no notion of light, no conception of the look of a square or a diagonal, a bishop's move or a knight's. "Could you?" she asked.

Declan shrugged.

"I had an aunt who was born blind," said Kathleen. "It was really quite marvelous the things she could do."

They sat in silence until John and Jimmy brought the drinks.

"Brother and sister," said John, inspecting them with oblivious approval. "Two real, handsome O'Riordans, aren't they, Kathleen? I always said my sister married well."

He handed Allegra her drink, and, as before, she felt his solidity, which she must indeed have been drunk to think she could ever have assailed. Well, she would never have the chance to try again. She thanked him, averting her eyes.

"Brendan thinks you're radical," Jimmy told her. He looked slender beside his father, insubstantial. "And when Emily grows up, she's going to move to Chicago and be a comedian. Angela's going to call you and invite you over. We had a barbecue," he added to Declan. "Your sister's big with the under-thirteen set."

"Really," said Declan. He did not look surprised.

"They're good kids," Allegra said, insipidly enough, and Declan stared quickly down into his glass as if mortified.

"So, Declan," said John. "How's business? When can I tell my friends my nephew's the financial adviser on Capitol Hill?"

"If you really want to," said Declan, "you already can."

John smiled his appreciation of the insult.

Allegra's and Jimmy's eyes met: Jimmy, she now recalled, had refused to go to the Jesuits.

"How's the yard, Kathleen?" she asked.

"Doing nicely, thank you, dear," Kathleen replied.

Dinner was a long time coming.

The dark dining room was growing familiar too, as was the food. Maria had learned her Higgins cooking well. Declan heaped his plate healthily, and fell to with an appetite. Mrs. Hegarty, who, to Bob and Allegra's bafflement, was fond of Declan, had always said that he did not get enough home cooking.

"This is good," he said.

"Your father liked a good cut of meat," said John. "Not like my son."

"Right, Dad," said Jimmy. "Beans and seaweed."

"Do you remember Bob and the avocado?" said Allegra. "That time we visited. He found it in the kitchen, he'd never seen one before, so he picked it up and tried to eat it like an apple." She thought of the bitter skin bound tight around the slippery soft meat, and shuddered. "Ugh."

John and Kathleen glanced at each other and laughed too, but in a different way.

"What?" she said.

"It was you, sweetie," said John. "You did that, not Bob."

"Me?" She looked at Kathleen, who nodded. Declan's gaze was fixed on his plate. "Did I?" But of course she had. How else would her mouth so recognize the taste, and her stomach revolt? Yes, it had been a rainy day, and the magnolia trees had dripped at the window, their green leaves as dark as the fruit's knobby skin. Yes, of course it had been her. "My God, that's terrible. I've been telling the story for years, and blaming Bob. But it was me all the time, isn't that strange?"

Declan finished one mouthful and, carefully, arranged another.

"Memory's a funny thing, dear," said Kathleen.

"Oh, my God," said Jimmy. "Speaking of memory, wasn't it sad about Helen?"

"You knew?" said Allegra. She had been waiting for a fitting moment to tell him.

"Everyone knows."

"A rather large claim," murmured Declan.

Jimmy looked at him, and smiled. It struck Allegra that Jimmy had not after all received his telephone call.

"Helen Viner," he said, politely, to Declan, "was an old lady I knew who Allegra got to know too. Several people in town did know her: she just died. In her eighties, went suddenly. Nice way to go."

Abruptly, he stopped smiling, and looked down at his plate.

"God rest her soul," said Kathleen.

"Did you know we were the last to see her alive?" said Allegra.

"Were we?" He looked up again, although there were shadows in his eyes. "No, I hadn't thought of that. How strange."

"She died on Saturday afternoon, hadn't cleared up her lunch, Don told me. I can't think she had any other visitors."

"That is strange. Mom, Allegra and I went to visit her that very morning, at her home. God, that is weird. And we were asking her about the old days and everything, weren't we?"

"So we were," said Allegra.

Their eyes met. Had they had this conversation, as planned, at the Sunday lunchtime; had Jimmy not been called from Mass to his nebulous meeting and Emily not celebrated her eighth year in this world; were Declan not casting his shadow this evening, and Jimmy not saddened by death that was not Helen's, and John not reinforced and she diminished by that disastrous, that irreversible telephone call; then who knew but they might just now be able profitably to ask a question. But they had not; and Declan was; and so were Jimmy, and John, and she. God, beyond question, was a Jesuit boy, and agreed with John that this knowledge was such that Allegra could do without. Well, but Jimmy was here now, and she would take what she could get. She steeled her compassion against her cousin, and held his gaze, deepening her own.

He nodded at her, twitched his mouth—he was really so much thinner than his father—and set down his glass, firmly.

"Dad," he said. "Allegra and I want to ask you something."

His father looked up.

"Mm?" he said.

"Did you know that Helen Viner knew Aunt Theresa?"

"Mm. Allegra told me. Can't say I remember her or I don't, really. Kathleen, this meat is quite excellent. Isn't it even better than usual?"

"I told Maria no more cilantro," said Kathleen. "I hope I didn't hurt her feelings, she wanted to do something special for Declan too."

"Mom," said Jimmy. "Please. Dad. Helen showed us some photographs of Aunt Theresa, and she looked so happy and—and gay. And in all the other photographs, well, both of the other photographs of her that I've seen, that were taken since, she just looks depressed. And we want to know why that is."

Frowning a little, John organized a forkful of food.

"My sister never photographed well," he said.

"But she did when she was around Helen. And she apparently never did after that. And we think that something happened to her to make her sad. And we want to know what that was."

He looked at Allegra, and nodded again.

"I remember my mother quite well," said Declan. "She always seemed perfectly cheerful to me."

"I don't remember her laughing once," said Allegra.

Declan gazed at her, chewing thoughtfully on a mouthful, and shrugged.

"John's right," he said to Kathleen. "This really doesn't need cilantro."

"Screw you, Declan," said Jimmy.

John coughed.

"Sorry, Declan. But we're serious here, you guys. We've thought about it, and we've come to the conclusion that there's something about Aunt Theresa that isn't being told to us. And we think we're old enough to know what it is. In fact, we think it's our right—it's certainly Allegra's right—to know what it is."

With wild, foolish hope, Allegra looked at John, who sighed, and put down his fork.

"I already know," he said, "that this has been on Allegra's mind. She told me so the other day, quite forcefully." Allegra looked down. "I told her at the time, if you remember, sweetie, that there is nothing to discuss here. I don't have a story to entertain you with about your mother, I'm afraid. If you want me to make something up about her, then maybe I should just do that. If that's what you want."

Declan barked a laugh.

"Oscar Wilde said," he said, "that there are only two tragedies in the world: not getting what you want, and getting it."

John laughed back. "Interesting fellow, Wilde," he said, he who boasted he had not opened a book but his Thomas Aquinas in ten years. "Died a Catholic, of course. And they say the Church is hard on sinners."

"I saw his grave," said Declan. "The last time I was in Paris. Interesting place, but unfortunately, full of Parisians."

"Such an interesting city, though," said Kathleen. "We loved Notre-Dame, didn't we, dear?"

Jimmy sneaked to Allegra's calf an apologetic kick.

"Scott says hi," she told him, churlishly.

"He said you had a good time the other night," Jimmy retorted.

Dinner was an even longer time ending.

Chapter Eight

So that was that, she reflected quite calmly the next morning, feeling distant and untouchable as a mermaid as she sipped her coffee and let her gaze idle across the courtyard to the shameless bright bougainvillea. Helen now could not tell; John would not; Declan did not care to ask. And, when it came to it, it would affect but little the life of Allegra O'Riordan to know just what had or had not happened to her bright-haired mother forty years ago. The sun would still rise in the morning if she knew, and set at night; Dad would still lie in his grave, and Declan snub her; the audiences at the club either laugh or not at the jokes she told them. It was better by far to leave it. To recognize it all as a mistake, a lie she had told herself, like the lie about the avocado, a product of her own imaginings encouraged by her irresponsible cousin who had eyes for her handsome neighbor. If enough people said that her mother's life had been so, then it was undoubtedly better that so it should have been.

When Jimmy crossed the courtyard, she was able to look at him as a stranger, and see the middle-aged man he would grow into over the years. Tall as he was, he was narrower than her brothers, slightly built, like Rose. He would not fill out as his father had: if he was not careful, he might grow scrawny.

"Funny," she said. "I heard a rumor you lived in Santa Barbara."

"I go back tonight, dear Saint Cousin of the Welcomes. Can I have some coffee?"

She pointed to the kitchen. He helped himself, came outdoors, and sat himself next to her, casually facing Scott's apartment.

"He's out," she said.

"Who?"

"Scott. He went running. In very short shorts."

"Treat for you."

She shrugged: since he did not want to discuss it, there was nothing to discuss. And she too was going home soon.

"We didn't do too well," he said. "Did we?"

"I didn't think we would," she said.

"Well, I'm sorry. It must be rough for you. Not knowing."

The men in Allegra's family did not often contemplate Allegra's emotions. She smiled at him at last.

"Thanks for trying, anyway," she said.

He smiled back, ruefully. "Didn't do you much good," he said.

"Well. I'm not staying here, you know."

"No?"

"There doesn't seem much point, does there?"

"I'll miss you."

He looked as if he meant it. Really, there was a great deal of Bob in him; and now that she came to think of it, she would miss him too.

"We can send each other love letters," she said. "Tie them up with red ribbon and confuse the hell out of Bob's children after we're gone."

"Well, don't leave till after Friday," he said. "I thought we could go to Helen's funeral together."

"Helen's funeral?"

"It's this Friday," he said. "That's what I came by to tell you. I thought we might go to it together, as we were the last ones to see her alive."

Oh. Right. So that, not concern for her, was why he was here. Well, it was only foolish of her to have thought for the moment differently.

"Us and Scott," she said.

She scratched, irritably, at her neck. It was too hot here in Los Angeles, too hot to move, too hot to think, too hot to look anymore at the hot red flowers on the cool stone wall. She would go back to Chicago as quickly as she could: she would telephone her goodbyes to Kathleen and John.

"What I thought," said Jimmy, after a pause, "was that after the funeral, you and I might introduce ourselves to Helen's niece, I think she's called Ruth, she lives back East, and I guess she inherits all the stuff. I thought that, if we asked her nicely, she might let us have the photographs of your mom. I thought that, since you don't have too many photographs yourself, and it's obvious no one's going to tell us a damn thing about her, then that might be good. For you."

"Oh," she said.

"Starting tomorrow," he said, "Scott goes onto the daytime shift."

"Oh," she said.

"Yes," he said. "Oh."

It was a pity: she had, really, not even begun to tease him about this.

"Could I really go to the funeral?" she said. "It seems pushy, as I hardly knew her."

"I think they'd be glad for the numbers. Most of her friends had died."

"Well, that figures. You know something strange? I've never been to a non-Catholic funeral."

"I have."

Yes.

"What are they like?" she said.

"Depends," he said. He stood up. "So I'll pick you up at ten-thirty. Unless you'd like to come to lunch at Bruno's now?"

"Why would you want to eat at Bruno's?"

"I'm meeting your buddy Frank. He's a good guy. Come on, I know he'd like to see you."

Francis Xavier Napper Tandy Desperate Dan McGee. Frank the Catholic man, who had bought her a drink, and had laughed with her, and liked her when she was insufferable. Dad, driving, on her left side; Father Forde on her right.

"I think I'll pass, thank you," she said. "But say hi, OK?"

After he had gone, she sat still staring at the wall. Another funeral, then, her second in a month. She would have to buy something to wear, since none of her clothes here were suitable, and Melissa's Sunday outfit, stained with her shame and indeed, she now rather thought, with some sauce from the calamari as well, she would never wear again. She needed something new. A new dress to wear for the funeral of a woman she had hardly known, and, truth to tell, not greatly liked, while her own elder brother was a stranger to her. She shook her head, wondering at the curious places to which her life's path sometimes led her.

The telephone rang: it was Angela Sullivan Mendoza, breathing normalcy.

"Thank God I've found you," she said. "I kept on getting that machine. Listen, my kids have ordered me to invite you over, Brian's spent all week collecting jokes to tell you. By any chance you're not free this afternoon?"

"That's nice," said Allegra. Of course, she would not go; then, why not? she thought. A few hours in the real world with just the one Sullivan sister would be pleasant; nor would a little juvenile appreciation hurt her. "I have to go shopping first. Where can I buy something to wear for . . ." How to explain to Angela the reason she needed a new dress? ". . . for a quite formal occasion?"

But Angela was too wholesomely occupied with her own life to pry into Allegra's. "There's a shopping mall right near us. Nothing too fancy, but it has most of the big chains. Good: come here after, then. The kids are at school, it'll kill them to find you waiting for them."

The mall was cheerful, and bustling with people this weekday afternoon. Allegra quickly found a plain dress in darkest blue, shirt-collared, falling just to the knee. She tried it on, and looked approvingly at her reflection in the dressing room, its skillfully pink light so much kinder than that in Melissa's bathroom. Yes, this would do. A respectful dress, a dress to be sincere in for niece Ruth from back East, with flesh-colored panty hose and low black pumps. Sister Philomena tut-tutted while Allegra practiced her sincerity in the mirror. Really so sorry. Hardly knew her but. Seemed so well, and then. Know this is hardly the time, but by any chance. Yes, this would do: especially with the panty hose.

She took the dress to the desk, and waited for the motherly assistant. The last time she had stood by just such a desk, waiting for just such an anonymous woman, pinafored with the name that no one would read pinned to her breast, had been in Chicago, a month ago, when she was buying the heavy black skirt and soft sweater for Dad's funeral. A month ago, when the grief was young, and the sorrow had still the power to surprise. A month ago, when his lifeless body was at least whole, which now lay, rotting alone in its sturdy oak box, under the unmoving ground that would cover him, as it covered all who died, summer and winter, lush green, hard brown, snowy white, forever. A month ago, when Allegra had not yet traveled to this sunny strange city, had not yet met or even heard of the woman whose funeral she was attending, who had known her mother.

"You OK, honey?" said the assistant.

"Yes, thank you." Allegra was always OK: she had had to be.

"You sure?"

"Yes, I'm sure," she said. "Thank you."

The Mendoza house looked bigger still when it was not filled with people, brightly lit against the shadows that were beginning to fall: it was, after all, in other cities which had seasons, not yet spring. Angela let her in hastily, and pointed her toward the kitchen refrigerator. She was on the telephone, arranging, as far as Allegra could make out, a shared trip to the zoo. Such busy lives mothers had, she thought idly, staring into the shelves crammed with foods she herself would not dream of buying—ground beef and Jell-O, Tater Tots, chocolate milk. From the corner, Angela's voice lifted and broke into the comradely chuckle that mothers share; and Allegra, older than she by two years, felt herself incomplete, a child still, who was able to do magic tricks with quarters, but had never in her life had to make meat loaf.

An opened jug of white wine winked at her a frosty overture. She ogled back, longingly; but took instead virtuous apple juice, and wandered into the living room. Proudly placed on a side table was a photograph in a silver frame, of Angela and a younger Emily, Angela's mother Rose, and an older woman who must have been Rose and Kathleen's mother. Four generations of women; many houses had them, M.M.'s sister Laura had one, although to M.M.'s own regret, her grandmother had died just before Elizabeth was born. She picked it up off the table, and looked at it. Four generations. Emily and Angela, big-boned and wide-jawed, Emily with her father's dark eyes; Rose and Rose's mother, delicate and Irish-refined. What must it have been like, she wondered, for strapping Angela to have Rose for a mother? Had Angela looked at her as an adolescent, and envied her small hands and naturally wavy hair? Had Rose tried to comfort her, pointing to long legs and broad shoulders, assets which she had promised Angela would appreciate one day?

Your mother do that? Mine's the queen. Dear, you're beautiful. But Mom, what about my extra head? Well, but dear, they're both such pretty heads . . .

And she, Allegra, if she had had a mother of her own, would she now be planning zoo trips for children, instead of standing in the living room of a stranger, with a suntan in February and a pill making her body sinful (yes, she had forgotten again that it was a placebo day), and trying, by telling herself jokes, to rise above the terrible longing that suddenly battered her poor, scarred heart for the likes of Nick?

"You like that photograph?" Angela had finished her call, and was standing beside her. "That's my grandma at the back there. She died five years ago, ninety-three years old, and all her teeth. So I can give Emily good genes at least."

"Emily's a great kid," said Allegra. "They both are."

"People do say that," said Angela, in pretended puzzlement. "It's good to see you, Allie—come in and watch me fix dinner. Is it Allie, by the way, or Allegra?"

"I've given up on Allegra," said Allegra, following her back to the kitchen. "I still use it to introduce myself, because I'm a stubborn cuss. But it's strange, you know. I say, Hi, I'm Allegra. And everyone—*everyone*—says, Good to meet you, Allie. It makes me wonder what they heard me say in the first place."

Angela laughed, distractedly, pulling meat from the refrigerator, spices from a shelf. "Then I shall call you Allegra," she said.

"Good," said Allegra. She helped herself to a cookie and sat at the scrubbed wood table, feeling herself a little girl again, in M.M.'s mother's kitchen.

Angela plopped pink beef into a pan, turned it with a spoon. "Say again," she said. "Are you here to work, or on vacation, or what?"

It was a good question, and one to which Allegra opted for the simplest answer.

"Just vacation," she said. "I'm going back to my own life pretty soon."

"That must be great," said Angela. "To pick up and go when you like. I haven't been able to do that for years."

Allegra knew that she lied. Angela would not have changed with Allegra, not for one second from an eternity. Angela tapped the side of the spoon against the heavy pan. "Kids," she said. "They take over your life." Then looked sideways at Allegra, a being altogether other to her, a childless woman, with diminishing time, and no husband in sight. "Do you ever think about them?"

"Sometimes." She did not, particularly; but almost without noticing it, Allegra had slipped into her own polite lie, which she trotted out for such occasions. Because she liked Angela, she even embellished it a little. "Depends on who I'm in love with."

"In love." Lying back, Angela smiled fondly. "That sounds great too. You forget that stuff when you're married."

Great. But then, briefly and cruelly, Nick took Allegra full in his arms, kissed her on the mouth, his tongue smelling of peppermint, and left her all over again.

"It's not so terrific," she said.

"Oh." Angela smiled encouragement. "I bet you have dozens of boyfriends. You're so funny."

Yes. Allegra was a funny woman. A funny woman who would always be alone.

And then there's the guy who thinks you're funny. You ever date one of those? Where shall we meet tonight? Whoo! Meet tonight! Ha ha ha! Hoo-boy! Whoo! OK. Right. Well, do you want to pick me up? Pick you up—that is good! Whoo! I tell you, I love this gal! At last, it's, Honey, I think I have leprosy. Leprosy—hee hee! Oh, I can't stand it! She has leprosy! . . .

"Guys don't always like it," she said. "Funny women."

Angela looked up for a moment from her pan to frown in puzzlement.

"Luis likes you," she said.

"Does he?" But like Allegra as Luis might, he had chosen for his wife, not one such as Allegra, but Angela. Someone from real life. "That's nice," she said, politely.

Outside, a car stopped, and in they ran, tawny Emily, little dark Brian, and a fair girl, followed after a moment by a tired-looking woman of Allegra's age. Their greeting of her was indeed rapturous, as why would it not be: they were great kids, warm, happy children from a warm, happy home.

"This is Zoe," said Emily, indicating the other girl. "And this is Zoe's mom. Allie's funny," she added to them.

"Allie funny," chanted Brian, hopping around her chair. "Allie funny, Allie funny. I know a joke, Allie."

"Do you?" said Allegra. "You'd better tell me, then."

"There was a man walking down the street," said Brian, "with a pineapple in his ear."

"That's Luisa's joke," said Emily. "She's already heard it."

"Well, I've heard Luisa's version," said Allegra. "But everyone tells a joke differently, you know. Go ahead, Brian."

"See?" said Brian to his sister. "OK. There was a man walking down the street with a pineapple in his ear. And another man came up to him and said, 'I'd better speak up. You have a pineapple in your ear.' "

He stopped, aghast.

"You spoiled it," said Emily. "You got it wrong."

"No he didn't," said Allegra. "You see, I told you, everyone tells jokes differently. Now, Luisa, she told it down the line, straightforward. That was fine. But Brian here has put a surreal little spin on it, and made it all his own."

They considered this. Then, since Allie was funny, they started to laugh. The more they laughed, the harder they laughed; and Zoe, after regarding them curiously for a moment, decided to join in the game.

"What sort of spin did he put?" said Emily.

"Surreal," said Allegra.

"Surreal!" It became a competition to see who was the most prostrated by mirth.

"Cool it, Zoe," said Zoe's mother. "You want another attack?"

Emily sobered for a second.

"Zoe has asthma," she explained.

"I'm sorry to hear it," said Allegra.

Allie was funny: there was nothing, now, that Allie could say that would fail to produce fresh merriment.

"I'm not kidding," said Zoe's mother. "You remember last time?"

She looked, not tired, but exhausted: even in the fading light, Allegra could see the dark circles under her eyes.

"OK, guys," she said. "You want to show me your rooms? I bet you can beat me at computer games, I'm the world's worst."

As, pushing, slapping, dancing, clinging, they herded her to the back of the house, Allegra exchanged a glance with Zoe's mother. It was of dislike, immediate, mutual, and deeper than the marrow of the bone.

She put in a good forty minutes at the computer, until the children were absorbed, their mothers would have had a respectable break, and she herself must surely have earned that glass of wine.

"Whatever happens to your hand-eye coordination?" she demanded, slumping a little dizzily into a friendly kitchen chair.

"Those kids were just dancing through. While I felt like I was trying to thread a needle, riding a bicycle along a tightrope."

Zoe's mother smiled, glancing at Allegra's wine with the faint disapproval of one who had to keep her wits about her.

"You should try doing it while you're nursing," she said, directing the pronoun at Allegra, but all the rest of her speech toward Angela, who laughed in fellow feeling. Allegra felt foolish, as if she had been caught pretending to a knowledge which she did not possess.

"I'm afraid I didn't catch your name," she said. "I'm sure you were called something before you were Zoe's mom."

"I'm Wendy," said the woman, whom Allegra then resolved to think of exclusively, and at every possible opportunity, as Zoe's mom.

Yet Angela seemed to like her, and they soon returned to a discussion of Emily and Zoe's homeroom teacher, to which Allegra could contribute nothing. She sat, sipping her wine, and feeling the kitchen just a little less warm.

You ever do that? You meet this person who is, quite openly, slime.
No, not slime.
This person who is, quite openly, mouse droppings.
Please!
Well, this person who is, quite openly, something. And then you find that other people, who seem quite sane, actually like them. And then you think . . .
What do you think?
You think, Am I missing something here?
Boring.
You think . . .

No, the joke was just not working.

"Sorry, Allegra," said Angela. "We're doing mother talk again, and it's not as if we didn't have enough time for it." She smiled at Allegra, kindly. "So, tell us about the big world. Did you buy your dress?"

"I did." Fighting the sensation of a little girl allowed at the adults' table, Allegra fell back on a trusty comic theme. "But everyone's so beautiful in California, I felt embarrassed to be in the same store as them. Don't mind me, please, I'll just shuffle through with this paper bag over my head."

"You bought a dress this afternoon?" said Zoe's mom.

"I wasn't aware there was legislation against it," said Allegra.

It was no sharper, surely, than the crack about nursing; but the other woman's face closed in.

"Comedians," said Angela, after the shivering, wincing pause. "You can't get a straight answer from them. More coffee, Wendy?"

"No thanks," she said. "I need to get home, the sitter has to leave early. I'll go find Zoe."

As she left, Angela got up and stirred tomato paste into the saucepan.

"Sorry," said Allegra.

"She's on her own, you know," said Angela. "Two kids, her husband left, and he's way behind on the child support."

"Oh, God," said Allegra. "Sorry."

"You weren't to know," said Angela. She returned to the table, forgiving her. "So. Is it a nice dress?"

"Very." She was a little girl after all, childless, and childish, describing her pretty frock. "It's blue. What are you cooking?"

"Spaghetti sauce. Exotic, huh? Oh, God." She grimaced, as a wail arose from the back of the house. "That's Zoe. She and Emily have trouble separating."

And even Sister Philomena need not forbid Allegra to think that if separation from Emily meant going home with Zoe's mom, then Allegra too would have had trouble separating. Still, she looked sympathetically at Zoe, whom she liked, as, tearstained and pouting, she dragged into the kitchen.

"That's a sad face," said Angela. "Cheer up, you'll see Emily tomorrow."

"She'll be all right," said Emily. "She's always like this when she leaves, but as soon as she gets home, she's fine."

"I don't want to go home," said Zoe.

"That's what you said last time," said Emily. "But don't you remember, as soon as you got to your house, you were as right as rain?"

"I don't want to go home," said Zoe. She sniffed, her pinched small face a sad contrast to Emily's bloom. Allegra looked at her with a little pang, remembering how she herself, at that age, had hated to leave the companionable McConnell home.

"If she wants to stay on for a while," she said, "I could always run her over after dinner."

The two little girls gasped. Their mothers exchanged glances, and Zoe's mom's hand went to her temple. Oh. Oh, God. Allegra was smaller than Emily, and sillier than Brian; Zoe's mom had been nothing but right in her opinion of her.

"But maybe you should go with your mom after all," she added, weakly.

Zoe started to cry again.

Zoe's mom looked at Angela, and raised her brows. Then she squatted, a little stiffly, beside her daughter, and smoothed her hair.

"I'll tell you something," she said. "If we leave now, but right now, mind, we just might be able to stop somewhere interesting on the way home."

Zoe's tears dried. "You mean . . . ?"

Zoe's mom lifted her eyebrows, mock-mysteriously. Her face changed when she looked at her daughter, her mouth became tender. "We have to leave now, though," she said.

"Oh boy," said Zoe. "See you tomorrow, Emily. Let's go."

"Looks like we're on our way," said Zoe's mom. "So much for trying not to bribe 'em. Bye, Angela. Enjoy Los Angeles, Allie."

"Oh, God," said Allegra, when they had left. "I'm sorry, I just didn't think. God, that's twice I've made her hate me. God."

"Wendy's OK," said Angela. "She just doesn't have time to be adorable right now. OK, kids. It's six o'clock and we have company. And what happens when it's six o'clock and we have company?"

The two children nodded, giggling.

"Adult time," they chorused.

"And what happens if an adult sees even half of one child during adult time?"

"The *whole sky* falls *in*."

"Then what are you waiting for? . . . If we're lucky, Allegra, we'll get fifteen minutes, so enjoy. Just let me do this . . ." She turned down the sauce. ". . . and this." She poured a glass of wine, led them into the living room, and smiled at Allegra. "Hello."

"I don't know how you manage," said Allegra.

"Oh, you learn." She waved question and children aside, to concentrate on her guest. "OK, the dress is blue, that's a good color for you. Going somewhere fancy?"

For a wild instant, Allegra searched her invention, and failed to find an occasion that Angela might find unremarkable.

"As a matter of fact," she said, "I'm going to a funeral."

"Oh, no." Angela set her glass down. "I'm so sorry, I didn't realize."

"Well, it was no one I knew very well."

"Oh." She frowned a question.

"It was an old woman who worked in Peppercorn's—you know the bookstore, up on Sunset?"

Still frowning, patiently, Angela nodded.

"Well, I got to know her a little. She worked with my mother, oh, forty years ago now. Mother died when I was little, you see, she was John's sister, and I've never known much about her, so I came out here, and I found this old lady, Helen she was called, Helen Viner, but of course she was quite senile by this time, and she could hardly remember anything about anything, except she did tell me Mother was a good mimic and a good dancer, I'm pretty sure it was Mother she was talking about, she used to get confused, as I said. And then she died. I think I was one of the last people to see her alive."

The eldest Sullivan daughter sat beside her family photograph, her eyes fixed kindly on Allegra, trying to discover any connection between this speech and a world that she herself either inhabited, or would recognize if she were to visit there. After a moment, Allegra took pity on her.

"Jimmy knew her too," she said, and rolled her eyes. "Our cousin has a *colorful* circle of acquaintance, doesn't he?"

She had succeeded there, at least: Angela chuckled her relief.

"I don't know where he finds half of them," she said. "Did you hear about the homeless poet he brought to Grandma's ninetieth-birthday party?"

In exactly the time she had predicted, the children burst in, and life at the Sullivan Mendoza house returned to normal.

Chapter Nine

For Dad's rainswept Requiem, St. Dominic's had been packed; here in Helen Viner's church, where the sun shone clear on naked walls, where no plaster saint lifted an admonishing finger, no painted Jesus greeted the weeping women of Jerusalem, there was no more than a sprinkling, either, of flesh-and-blood people. There was Don, of course, and one or two others Allegra recognized from the store; a tall woman in her fifties with good jewelry and bad ankles who must be the niece; someone who might be a neighbor, and a trio of old folk, their faces set in resigned and fearful comprehension. And Jimmy and Allegra herself, sitting together, good Catholic sinners, in a plain building which had seen neither an absolution nor a transubstantiation, which had created, surely, little majesty and inspired, almost certainly, no despair.

Jimmy was feeling the church's strangeness too. Allegra had seen his fingers reach for the holy water font which was not there, noticed his split second's hesitation in the aisle as he stopped himself from genuflecting. But Jimmy was more used to funerals than was she, more used by far than a man of his age should justly be; and there was little comfort for his sort in his own church, now in these days when he must need it so. God. Oh, God. A thought too terrible for words made her shoot a sidelong glance at him; but he looked healthy enough, only sad. In repose, very sad. Dear God, she found herself praying, look after Jimmy. Then, straightaway, good God, she was sounding like an Irish mother! Like Kathleen. (Kathleen, bending over her garden plot, knowing what she refused to know, or lying awake in the long dull hours of the early morning, praying with shameless simplicity to Our Lady, mother to mother, to be good to the son her Church condemned.) But dear God, look after him. Oh, any second now, she'd be throwing on a black shawl, and climbing the hill to Killarney. Look after him, dear God.

The service was simple. Two restrained readings—familiar words, here on this so alien ground—quiet organ music, and Don, scowling above the small coffin, giving a short eulogy about a good woman it had been his privilege to know. It was over almost before it had begun. Trying hard not to compare it with Dad's funeral ("They're good people," snapped Sister Philomena, unexpectedly ecumenical, "and show more true Christian charity than many Catholics"; "So do the Boy Scouts," returned Dad, which, Dad being a man, temporarily silenced the nun), she followed Jimmy out of the church.

"How're you doing?" she said to Don, outside.

"OK." He dragged a large-knuckled hand down the side of his bony face. "Hi, Jimmy. Good of you to come."

"She was a good lady," said Jimmy. "She had a good last day, you know. Talked about old times, didn't seem sick or anything. A nice way to go."

"Yes." Don's face opened when he talked to Jimmy; Allegra could have liked him a lot. "Yes, it was good that you saw her. Good that she wasn't alone all day." His glance fell on Allegra, and closed again. "Did you meet Ruth?"

Ruth was talking to the minister. She looked Allegra over, approving her blue dress and convent girl smile, but thinking her coloring too dark, and that she really should hide the gray in her hair.

"We're sorry for your loss," said Jimmy.

"Thank you." Ruth nodded briskly. "It was her time. And she didn't suffer."

"That's all anyone can ask," said Jimmy, and the minister nodded in approbation.

"We were the last to see her, you know," said Allegra. "We spent part of that morning with her, and she was really quite bright and happy."

"That's good to know." No questions asked; no interest shown. Every niece did not love every aunt. Allegra breathed a sigh of shameful relief that her next request was not to be the more difficult by being made of a family in grief.

"This," she began, and not, she was suddenly and wearily aware, for the first time since she arrived in Los Angeles, "is going to sound strange." Beside her, she felt Don tense. But Don disliked her anyway, and besides, it was really not his business. "You see, when we were with her, with Helen, that morning, she showed us some photographs of—of an old friend of hers. Who was my mother. Who died when I was little. I wondered if there was any chance I might just be able to get hold of them?"

She was right: it did sound strange. And Ruth did not care for the strange. Allegra realized she was growing tired of not being liked.

"I know this is a bad time to ask you," she said. "But I don't live around here, and I'm going home soon, and I would so very much love those photographs because I have hardly any of my own."

Faintly, Ruth frowned.

"No photographs?" she said. "Of your mother?"

"She died," said Allegra. "When I was little. That's why I'd really love your aunt's pictures. If it's not too much trouble."

"It sounds reasonable enough," said the minister, a small, bald-headed man, whom Allegra had to keep from hugging. "Don't you think so, Ruth?"

Ruth consulted her wristwatch, slender and gold on her substantial wrist.

"I'll be at the apartment," she said, "from about two o'clock onwards. You could come by then. I don't suppose you're coming to the crematorium."

"Ouch," she said, when she and Jimmy were safe in his car. "Shit. Ouch."

"You could use a drink," he said.

"Right." Oh, but he was right, she could. "She'll really love me if I turn up smelling like a distillery."

"That's why God created breath mints. Come on, I'll take you to lunch at Bruno's."

Which might yet provide some entertainment; which, God knew, she deserved. She smiled to her reflection, ghostly in the car's window, and winked at herself.

"You like Bruno's, don't you?" she said.

"I'm developing a sick addiction to the food," he said. "Actually, Tom's a really great guy."

"Tom."

"Tom Takanawa, the owner. He's had a weird life, Jesus, some of his stories. His family lost all their land in the War, he was sent to a camp. Can you imagine, a little kid in a camp? Jesus."

He shook his head. It would be too irritating if Allegra were to be obliged to take Jimmy seriously.

"How's Scott?" she said.

"Working, working. Waits tables all day, writes all night. We all should have such dedication."

"D'you think he's a good writer?"

Opening just a crack the door he had so firmly kept closed, Jimmy grinned over the steering wheel. "Who the hell cares?"

Jimmy was popular at Bruno's. Tom himself came from the kitchen with smiles and a handshake, and so bland a recognition of Allegra that, for a moment, she wondered whether she could have been so very terrible that night after all. But then she remembered the empty Scotch bottle, and the telephone call, and knew the worse shame of being unable to identify precisely at which point she had become shameful.

"How was the funeral?" said Scott. His shirt today was gray, and bagged decorously over his chest and biceps; but there was no hiding the gold-specked forearms and square hands, no making polite the jeans-clad lower half. Jimmy watched with a half-smile as the other moved loosely about the table, as free of vanity or self-consciousness, and as accustomed to being admired, as one of Kathleen's roses.

"It was short," said Jimmy. "It was OK, really."

"It was Protestant," said Allegra. She looked to Jimmy, veteran of funerals, Catholic and far from Catholic, to see what she could see. But Jimmy only continued to smile and to watch the smooth brown hands dealing cutlery: John Higgins's son had shut the door again.

"What can I bring you?" said Scott.

"Cheeseburger," said Allegra. It was not a day for a salad. "Medium rare, with plenty of fries. Oh, but you'd better hold the onion." Ruth would not care for interesting breath. "And a vodka."

Vodka would not smell; it arrived in a stout-bottomed glass, icy cold, and tasting of winter nights. She sipped, and straightaway felt sad.

"She doesn't like me," she said. "Ruth. Does she?"

Jimmy shrugged. "She's hardly researched the subject."

"She didn't need to. She doesn't like me." She looked down into her glass, and up again. "Nor does Don."

"Don's upset right now. He really loved Helen, you know."

"He didn't like me when she was alive."

"Don's a funny guy. He was born seventy years old, and he won't be happy till he catches up with himself."

"No, he's not that funny." Sad, and sadder, she shook her head. "He doesn't like me. It's weird, Jimmy. Back home in Chicago, people really like me." She stopped herself, to check again. "Well, I think they do. Yes, they do." Did they? Yes, yes they did. "Yes, people like me. But here. Don doesn't like me, Helen didn't much like me, I met a woman at your cousin Angela's two days ago who *really* didn't like me, and now here's this Ruth, and she doesn't like me either. How does that work out?"

"Angela likes you," said Jimmy.

"She thinks I'm crazier than a coot."

"I like you," he said. He smiled. "And—Frank likes you."

Frank. She shivered instinctively, at the masculine arms shuttering her vision, the rough specks of tweed flying into her impotent throat, superfluously silencing her voice, which even when sounded went anyway unheard.

"Frank can't like me," she said.

He looked at her under raised eyebrows.

"He can't," she repeated. "He mustn't."

"OK," he said. He nodded, and twisted his right hand to rub the ring, which must have a story, but what story she now need never ask him.

"I am going home," she said.

"I'll still miss you." Jimmy had a hundred other cousins: but they were Kathleen's family, Murphys, and the secrets they had were not Higgins secrets. They spoke the same language, did Jimmy and she.

"I'll miss you too," she said.

As the burgers arrived, steaming, the sunlight struck warm through the window onto her right side and his left. It was comfortable, being here, with Jimmy. White wine would be good in the sunshine, and to sit gossiping and growing sleepy until this absurd winter's afternoon turned to evening. But Ruth would be at the apartment soon, and Allegra must have the photograph.

"I guess I'd better go on to coffee," she said.

"I'll join you," he said.

"Thanks," she said, and most unexpectedly felt her eyes pricking: he did not have to do that. "You're a pal."

The door to what had been Helen Viner's apartment stood open. In the back bedroom, on a wide, hard bed that must have swamped the old woman, Ruth was sorting clothes with capable hands.

"Most of it's for the Goodwill," she said. "It's too bad she was so small, some of these things are handsome. But we're all so much bigger than she was."

In her day, Helen had been elegant. Fine silks, doll-sized, now discolored; jostled still-good tweed suits; delicate cashmeres, hopeless and redolent of age and mothballs, lay sad in a reeking abandoned pile.

"I always heard she was frivolous," said Ruth. She pulled from its hanger a satin caftan, swirling pinks and golds, that had flirted and laughed at parties now long forgotten, and inspected it, frowningly. "Pity my granddaughter's too old for dress-up, she'd have enjoyed this." She motioned it toward the charity pile, but even for Ruth, the gown would not lie dead. At the last moment, she laid it aside. "Maybe her daughter, one day."

"Helen had an interesting life," said Allegra.

"She didn't need to work," said Ruth. "Pops left her plenty of money. But she insisted on being a Bohemian."

Bohemian. The woman in the caftan glanced up briefly, and

laughed; behind her, a small-boned, determined girl rolled her eyes in exasperation. Allegra looked down at the discarded clothes on the bed. So might her own childless life too well end up: old clothes, and those not even old good clothes like Helen's, but a series of holed pants, worn sweaters, and just a couple of dresses, all set aside and sorted by one of Bob's sons—no, by one of Bob's sons' wives, that was women's work, and always would be—who would not know or care who poor, crazy old Aunt Allie had loved and laughed with, or what she had worn to do it, all those eternal decades ago. Any more than Ruth cared about Helen. Allegra looked calculatingly at Ruth. Ruth was an easterner, it was in her speech, in her clothes, in her carriage; and she could hardly have been more than a child when her Uncle Malcolm had died in California, of a heart attack, at thirty-one. But it was worth asking the question.

"Did you ever live in Los Angeles?" she said.

Ruth looked at her.

"If I may ask," she added.

Ruth failed to find a reason why she might not. "I was born here," she said. "My father moved us East when I was seven, so I hardly knew Aunt Helen. She used to mail us the most extraordinary books, until Dad told her to stop. But she was very good to my grandchildren, I will say that. Sent money every Christmas."

When Ruth was seven. Surely, before the trip to the beach. And Ruth was a WASP, and Allegra was a stranger. She grimaced before she spoke again.

"Do you remember Malcolm?" she said.

"Malcolm?"

"Your uncle? Helen's brother."

"Oh, yes. Malcolm." She sniffed at a blue silk shirt, and tossed it into a garbage bag. "He wasn't my uncle. Gran married again after Pops died, a Mr. Brewer. He was a judge. Malcolm Brewer was his son. We were two years gone by then."

So, smiling faintly, God the Jesuit boy had closed the final door on the terrible thing that had or had not happened to Theresa Higgins.

"I believe," said Ruth, "that that closet outside is where my aunt kept her photographs."

She watched while Allegra found and removed the large box, and waited for her to return to the bedroom. Watched too while Allegra sat herself on the other side of the bed, and tipped the box over, letting the long memories come tumbling for the last time over the faded counterpane.

Almost immediately, the corner of Allegra's eye caught her mother under the palm trees, but somehow, she found herself not ready to recognize her yet. Instead, she sifted through the pictures she had been too impatient to look at the last time; the shot after shot of Helen, smart and stylish in the clothes of five decades, talking and laughing with people unidentified, now mostly unidentifiable, who laughed back at her. Allegra had not realized what fun Helen had had.

"She had such an interesting time," she said. No, Helen's companions were not all anonymous: Hemingway was looking at her with unmistakable approval. "All those people she knew. Someone should really put these together and make a proper record."

"My grandson's bookish," said Ruth. "He'll be fascinated when the time comes."

Ruth knew Allegra knew she was lying. She watched with sharp, sidelong eyes as Allegra sorted old snaps from older: she would be none the wiser if Allegra claimed that Hemingway was her Uncle John, and took him home for Scott. But Scott would not enjoy gains gotten so ill: and then again, who knew but that the granddaughter's daughter might yet turn out Bohemian. Tenderly, Allegra touched the Helen who was the age she herself was now, slender in waspwaisted suit and snap-brim hat; and Ruth coughed, and rustled the yellowed silken underwear.

Embarrassed, Allegra had a happy inspiration. She searched for and picked up the baby photograph Helen had shown. "Isn't this your grandson?" she said. "Josiah? Helen showed us this particularly, she was very proud of him."

It was the right question.

"Joshua." Ruth leaned over, took—another woman would have snatched—the picture, and tut-tutted her disapproval. "That's an old photograph, he's three times the size by now. I'd have thought my daughter would have sent a more recent one." Then, despite herself, her face softened. "That was a darling outfit. Aunt Helen was interested in the children, I will say that."

"She talked about them a lot," agreed Allegra, probably truthfully.

"They were all she had." Absentmindedly, Ruth scanned the broad carpet of Helen's dead friends and lovers for more pictures of her family. "I hardly knew her myself. She and Dad never got along, she was Bohemian, as I said, and she would insist on working, as if we needed the money. Really, she was a selfish, irresponsible woman, as far as I could make out. But my daughter liked her when she visited her. That's when she became interested." She frowned. "I really think my daughter might have sent some more recent shots, we have plenty. Look there." From across the wide bed, she nodded to a brightly colored corner of cardboard. "That's another old one. My daughter with Hannah, it must be two years ago by now."

The daughter was smaller than Ruth, and softer, with her great-aunt's blue eyes, and a faintly alarmed expression—as well, thought Allegra, she might have.

Ruth's gaze swept the pile once more, and she let loose a sigh of impatience. "Those really are the most up-to-date pictures she had. Really, it was too bad of my daughter. Aunt Helen was so interested, and we were her only family left."

And who are you, Sister Philomena demanded of Allegra, to give yourself airs of virtue? She's thinking of her grandchildren, not of herself, and you too selfish with your sinful pills even to have children to think of.

Allegra shook her head to rid it of the nun, and idly turned a curling postcard of a white beach.

"Oh," she said, then, and did not even notice Ruth's stiffening. The writing on the back was in her mother's hand.

> *Darling Teddy,*
> *It's much prettier here than at the store—I might just not come back! The two about-to-be A. Andrews' send their love. Say Hello to Malcolm.*
> *Love, Theresa.*

Allegra read it, put it down, picked it up again, the letters jumping and scrambling before her eyes. "Prettier here." "Hello to Malcolm." "Two about-to-be A. Andrews.' " Two about to be—oh, God, it must be Alice and Albert. "Two about-to-be," yes, it must, it really must. Oh, God. She read it again to make sure she was not imagining, but the writing, though faded, was quite clear. Yes. Yes, this was it, and that was who they were. That was their name, then. Alice and Albert Andrews. Then, oh, God. Oh. God. Their name was Andrews. Oh, God, how many Andrewses must there be in Los Angeles, or Detroit, or possibly Cincinnati.

"Something interesting?" said Ruth.

"May I take this, please?" said Allegra. "My mother sent it."

Ruth held out her hand. As she inspected the card, Allegra sorted through the pile, with haste-clumsy fingers, for the two photographs. Ruth took those too, and scrutinized them carefully for possible value.

"Looks like a fine day," she commented, at last handing back to Allegra, satisfied of her insignificance, the black-and-white girl who, while sinning, had known the dead Malcolm and Helen, and Alice and Albert Andrews.

"Thank you," said Allegra. She had almost added "ma'am," feeling, as her narrow, ringless hand brushed the discreetly manicured one, an atavistic instinct to curtsy. She would try it, later, in front of the mirror. Much later. She must go; but before she must go, she must order her thoughts to finish her business with Helen Viner.

"May I please ask you one more favor before I go?" she said.

Ruth raised her eyebrows.

"You see," said Allegra, "I really don't have much stuff of my mother's at all, you probably don't know what that's like, but I'd just love to have anything I can get my hands on."

Ruth smiled, politely: she did not, it appeared, either know or feel the desire to know what that was like.

"Anyway," said Allegra, "she and Helen were friends, as I told you, so if you find any more postcards, or even, God, I'd so love it if you found a letter, could I ask you to send them to me please? I would be so very grateful."

"Give me your address," said Ruth.

"What? Oh, yes." She fumbled in her purse for pen and paper, then impatiently shook it out onto the wide bed, exposing to Ruth's cold eyes its seamy secrets of frayed tissues, crumbling breath mints, even, oh God, the bent and crumpled emergency tampon. But even women like Ruth must have purses too: they simply knew how to keep them closed.

"Look," she said. "Here's my address at home in Chicago. And this is the telephone number where I'll be for the next few days, don't worry if the answering machine message says Melissa, it's where I'm staying. And you'll know that anything is from my mother because she called Helen Teddy, and her own name was Theresa, oh, or sometimes Molly, it was a joke they had because she was Irish."

"I see," said Ruth.

"Yes, Molly Malone. So. To Teddy, or Helen of course, from Theresa or Molly. I'll write it down by my address. If you find anything at all, I would so very much appreciate having it."

"Of course," said Ruth.

"She was my mother, you see," said Allegra. But Ruth had already folded the paper, and laid it neatly away in the recesses of her own good brown leather purse. If Ruth found anything that Allegra would find of interest, Allegra knew, she would send it on. But even so, as she replaced the box of photographs in the closet, and there fell into her hand a shot of Helen and the short young man Scott had called John Fante, she pocketed it as swiftly as a practiced thief. She would give it to Jimmy: Don, she thought, would not be above receiving it.

How d'you like those people who get into the fastest lane, and then drive real, real slow?

Not funny.

No, but how d'you like them? You're in a hurry to get home 'cause . . . 'cause you forgot to set the tape for The Young and the Restless . . .

Boring.

. . . 'cause you just had to have that extra cup of coffee? . . .

Please.

Well, you're in a hurry to get home 'cause for whatever reason, and there's the guy in the slow lane driving slow, but that's OK, 'cause he's in the slow lane, get it? it's appropriate, but in the fast lane, now I want you to follow me closely here, in the fast lane, there's this little old guy in a shiny Mercedes going real, reee-al . . .

The joke's dead, Allegra, let it lie quietly in peace, and pray for the repose of its soul. Besides, it was not an old man in a new vehicle that was blocking her journey, but the reverse: four kids who should have been in school, bouncing in a jalopy that should not be on the road, laughing and singing to the radio. They stopped at a light, and

Allegra, despairing of speed, looked around her at the city where her mother had lived. Sharp-cornered buildings, under a diamond-white light. In the next car, a middle-aged couple stared glumly into the distance; on the street corner beneath a palm tree, a hopeful small boy waved maps to movie stars' homes; to her left, in full sun's glare on a blistered road island, an impassive Mexican woman of Allegra's age offered oranges. Theresa Higgins's city, where she had lived, and danced, and mimicked, and enjoyed the sun, and, so Father Carroll had said, sinned; the city where Allegra sinned now, each morning, after her shower and before she brushed her teeth. The city where Alice and Albert Andrews, if they had not after all gone to Detroit, or possibly Cincinnati, might live still, might yet be able, if Allegra could track them down, to explain to her the mystery.

Oh, God, thought Allegra, then. Oh, God, their name was Andrews. Oh, God, and Saint Ignatius, and Saint Jude, patron of hopeless cases, God the Almighty Jokester was at his merry japes again. Alice and Albert Andrews. Ron's last name was Kessling; Nick's was Westingay. Allegra had friends called Skouras, called Bjornsen, called Szymanski, called Purwin. Alice and Albert would have to be Andrews.

They could, Sister Philomena reminded her, have been called Smith.

When Allegra reached Melissa's apartment, she laid photographs and postcard carefully on a table painted with swans, sat on the sofa, and wept.

The legend on the front of the postcard read Santa Barbara, but she was not allowed to look at it properly, not until she had made a decent inroad into her work. She put it out of sight in the cupboard behind the new bottle of Scotch—yes, she had found time to replace that, although not yet to write to Melissa about the parrot, which did not surprise Sister Philomena in the slightest—found a ballpoint, and a legal pad, and sat herself down beside the telephone. There was a column and a half of Andrewses in the directory: she would start at the beginning.

"Hello?" A woman's voice, unaccented, neither old nor young. Allegra took a breath.

"Hello," she said. "May I speak to Alice Andrews, please?"

"I'm sorry," said the voice. "There's no one here of that name."

"Oh." Well, of course it would not come so easy: nothing, for Allegra, came so easy. "I wonder if you can help me, all the same," she said. "I'm trying to get in touch with either an Alice Andrews or an Albert Andrews. By any chance, do you know them?"

"Why do you want them?" The voice sounded wary, which might be a good sign. On the other hand, it might simply mean that the voice belonged to a wary person.

"They knew my mother," she said, "oh, around forty years ago. They were going to be married at the time, and I guess they did marry, but I don't know if they're still alive, they'd be at least in their sixties and they might even have moved to Detroit, or maybe Cincinnati, so I guess I'm looking either for them or for their family, and I just wondered if you could help me at all."

A pause.

"I'm sorry," said the voice, then. "There's no one here of that name."

The receiver clicked dead. Allegra sighed, shifted herself to a more comfortable position in the chair, and moved to the next name. After an hour and a quarter, she had reached the letter K. She had had twelve conversations, left eighteen messages, had a dozen no-replies, three busy signals, and two disconnect notices, all of which she had noted meticulously on her legal pad. She had been sympathized with, dismissed, and, once, hung up on; she had talked to Barbara, and Chris, and John. She still had the Michaels, the Stephens, and yes, more than a few Walters and Williams to come, before she went back to the beginning to try those she had not yet spoken to. It was time for a break.

"You can keep your Smiths," she told the pottery owl, who frowned at her from inside the bedroom. "They can't be worse than Andrewses."

The owl said nothing. It had not forgiven her for the parrot.

Santa Barbara, said the postcard, in white lettering against a gray background, a wide beach fringed by feathery palm trees, stone buildings with Spanish-style roof tiles. Prettier than at the store—yes, it did look pretty, although it had probably changed since then. Jimmy would know: he lived there, where the girl who had been her mother had once taken a vacation. Santa Barbara, named for the patron saint of foreigners, who now was a saint no longer, having been determined a fictitious personage during the Second Vatican Council. She turned over the card of the not-saint's city, and read again the three trite sentences on the back. "Much prettier." "About-to-be A. Andrews'." "Hello to Malcolm." Malcolm, again. She looked, closely, at the handwriting. Was there a reason why the "Hello" was capitalized, and was the "Malcolm" written with just a little more emphasis than the other words? In Theresa's letter to Ignatius, she had spoken of a Monday: Allegra pulled it from her suitcase and compared the two capital M's. But they were both the same size, both large and looping, by their nature broader than Nate's N, the same M as that on "Mommy" from Allegra's cherished third-birthday card. From Malcolm to Mommy: had Theresa ever thought of the one when she wrote the other? And if she had, then what would her thoughts have been? Allegra stared at the uncommunicative purplish ink that had come from her mother's hand, until the tears came again, whether of frustration or simple eye strain, she could not tell.

When it was not quite dark, she returned to the telephone. K. Keith, Kelly, and Kevin. Kevin was a potential, if Alice and Albert and Theresa had met through the Church, which they might, or

again, might not have; Keith, or Kelly, a possible grandchild, if they
had stayed in Los Angeles and had sons who had stayed; or more distant relations if Albert had had a brother in Los Angeles who had had
sons who had married, providing, somewhere in the endless column
and a half in the directory, great-nephews to the Alice and Albert
who had danced with Theresa Higgins and made love so scandalously,
so innocently, in public. She would go through the column and a half
to the end of the alphabet, and when she reached it, she would go
back to the beginning, and try those who had not answered. Then,
she would go back again and try the answering machines once more.
She sighed, and crossed her eyes at the directory.

Then she uncrossed them as she read its cover. West Los Angeles, it said, and portions of Hollywood. Of course. The book with the
column and a half of Andrewses did not cover the whole of the city,
but only a section of it.

"You OK?" Scott, on his virtuous way home from work.

"You have to come in," she told him. "And you have to have a
glass of wine. I'm not going to give you juice, so don't ask."

"Just a small one," he said. "I'm writing tonight."

She poured him a glass larger than her own.

"I saw Helen's niece," she said. "A card-carrying witch. But look,
look what I found."

He looked at her in interest.

"What makes her a witch?" he said.

So he had given up on the Higgins family for his material. To her
own annoyance, Allegra felt a pinprick of irritation.

"The pointy cap was a clue," she said. "Look! Sitting there among
Helen's photographs, it was there all the time and I never knew."

He took the photograph, and read it, politely.

"From your mom," he said. "Well, it's good that you got something, at least."

"No, but look!" Oh, but he did not know what for. Well, this would teach him to abandon the Higginses for a witch. "I didn't tell you about Alice and Albert, did I? A courting couple, friends of Mother's, whose last name no one knew? Well, look there—the two about-to-be A. Andrewses, it must be them! So I've spent the afternoon . . ." It began to dawn upon her precisely how she had spent her afternoon. "I—and I'm a college graduate, now, and a taxpayer, and a subscriber to public television, and a general, all-around good guy—I have spent the afternoon telephoning every single goddamned Andrews in the book, asking if they might just by any chance happen to know an Alice or an Albert who'd be somewhere in their sixties by now and had a friend called Theresa forty years ago. Strange to say, I haven't made any new friends along the way, except for Douglas Andrews, but I'd rather not get into that right now. I'm up to the letter K, and that's just in the local book, remember, my eyes are going, my voice went somewhere around the letter G, they might not still live in Los Angeles anyway, and I'm just wondering . . ." Wondering where in God's name was the funny side in this fantastical situation that left her three thousand miles from home, jabbering hysterically to a kindhearted boy from a normal family, whose beauty was too pure and young even to give her the joy of excitement. ". . . wondering why just one . . . iota of it, just somewhere along the way, can't manage to be even the least bit . . . easy. For me."

She stopped suddenly, and chewed her lower lip. Then gulped at her wine. She might as well not bother to stay clearheaded: God, the impassive Jesuit boy, had nevertheless made it all too plain that He was not on Allegra's side.

"It isn't Andrews," said Scott. "It's Andrew."

"I'm sorry?" she said.

"If there are two Andrews," he said, "that means there's only one Andrew."

She blinked at him.

"There's a thing," she said. Only she, only Allegra in the world, in only this circumstance in the world, would be required, at this point, to discuss punctuation. Oh yes, when her time came, she would have words about what was, and what was not, in celestial terms, a good joke. "There's an apostrophe."

"I don't think so," he said. "There's a smudge."

"A what?"

She took the card from him, and held it under the light, for the first time feeling herself squint to focus, the way they had laughed at M.M.'s mother for doing. That was the next stage, of course, reading glasses. Scott was right. There was a smudge.

"Two Andrews," she agreed, carefully. "One Andrew."

Between Andrews and Andrew was an ocean of difference. Allegra turned back to the book: there were five of the singular Andrews, including one A.

"That'll be them," she said to Scott. She took a gulp of his wine. "If it is, I don't know whether I'll kiss you or kill you."

He smiled, and folded his arms, watching her, the card-carrying witch already forgotten.

"Hello?" The woman's voice which answered the telephone was not young.

"Hello." Not a young woman. Allegra would have to go slowly through her ridiculous routine, slowly under Scott's intent eyes, Scott who had not heard it performed again and again through the afternoon. "Hello, may I speak to Alice Andrew, please?"

"Yes?" said the voice.

Oh.

"Are you by any chance the Alice Andrew who is the wife of Albert Andrew?"

"Who is this speaking?" said the voice.

Oh.

Allegra turned from Scott, who was looking hopeful: she had been lured into optimism before this.

"My name's Allegra O'Riordan," she said. "You don't know me, but if you're the Alice Andrew I'm looking for, you did know my mother, she used to live here about forty years ago. Her name was Theresa Higgins?"

"Theresa Higgins," said the voice. "Oh, my Lord."

Oh! *Oh!*

"Theresa Higgins," said the voice. "Oh, for heaven's sakes." Then, "Did you say you were her daughter?"

Oh! *Oh! Oh!*

"Yes, I am." Allegra suddenly needed very badly to sit down; but she could not, because she was sitting already. Sitting and talking to Alice, who had made love to Albert in public, and had sent her love to Helen Viner through Allegra's mother. "Yes, she moved to Chicago as you know, well, maybe you didn't know, but she did, and she married Ignatius O'Riordan and then she died, and she had two sons and—me. I'm Allegra, I'm visiting Los Angeles, my dad just died, Ignatius, he never married again, he had a heart attack, she was killed by a cab, it was in the newspaper, oh, more than thirty years ago now, and I found your name in a letter, yours and Albert's, Mr. Andrew's, that is. I'm Allegra. O'Riordan. Theresa's daughter."

"Theresa Higgins," said Alice's voice. "Albert, you'll never guess who's on the telephone!" For a brief, spousal moment, the receiver was covered. "Theresa Higgins. For heaven's sakes. My Lord."

"Yes," said Allegra. She was talking to Alice, who sounded still sane, and Albert was alive. "Yes."

"Well, well."

"Yes." Allegra breathed deeply. By finding Alice and Albert, she had reached the end of her script; from now on, it was improv. "I'm visiting Los Angeles, you see, and I wondered . . ."

"Well," said the voice, "Theresa Higgins's daughter, if you're visiting Los Angeles, you'll just stop right in this very evening, and visit with us. Won't she, Albert? I guess I should call her Theresa

O'Riordan, but after all these years. Yes, she had two boys and a little girl, my, how proud she was of the girl, poor little mites left alone like that, but you'll all be grown by now, won't you? Two darkies and one carrot-top, she said, now, which one are you?"

"Could I really come?" said Allegra. "This evening?"

"Well now, Theresa's daughter, I have five kids of my own, listen to me, kids I call them, the oldest is nearly forty, and I know that if I don't catch ahold of you right now, I won't see hide nor hair of you for another forty years. Will we, Albert? Now, what's your address? . . . Why, that's no more than five minutes from us, so you'll get here as soon as ever you can. What's that, Albert? . . . Oh. Albert says it's more like twenty minutes, and you're to make sure and drive safely, we have the whole evening. My Lord. Theresa Higgins."

"I'm not the carrot-top," said Allegra. "I don't look anything like her."

"Well, I think we'll be the judge of that, Lord knows, I knew her for enough years. Listen to us, gabbing away on the telephone, when you could be over here. Climb into that car right now, and we'll see you soon. . . . Yes, Albert. Safe. And soon."

"Well?" said Scott, as she replaced the receiver. "Do I get kissed or killed?"

"What?" She had forgotten that Scott was there. She had been speaking to Alice. Indirectly, she had been speaking to both Alice and Albert. "They're both alive," she said. "And they remember Mother. I'm going to visit them now, and Albert says I'm to drive safely."

"That's terrific," said Scott.

"I should have a shower," she said. "Or a drink, no, that's no good, do I smell of wine? I'll take them flowers, proper flowers from the florist, not those tragic daisies they sell at the market. Here's a token of my esteem, it's wrapped in crinkled paper and smells like it died two hours ago. How do you suppose they get the leaves to look so depressed? You can't take any flowers at all to Kathleen, she grows her own. Oh, God, suppose Alice does too? Well, I wasn't to know, and you shouldn't take candy, you don't know who's on a diet. Scott—I'm going to see Alice and Albert!"

"I'll make you some chamomile tea," he said.

"No time. Should I change my clothes? God, can you believe I can be so dumb? I'd have looked through all the Andrewses, West Side, East Side, I really thought that was an apostrophe. No, not dumb, blind, that's age, you know. I'll be a little old lady looking through her bifocals, knitting sweaters for her canary. OK. I'm going now."

"Let me know what happens," he said.

"I'm going to see Alice and Albert," she said. "I feel like I'm going to see the Little Women, or the Bobbsey Twins. Remember the Bobbsey Twins? Bert and Nan were thin and dark, Flossie and Freddie were fat and fair, and did you notice we were never quite told what Mr. Bobbsey looked like? He was a lumberman. Laura Lee Hope. God, when I found she was really a syndicate, it just about broke my heart. Alice and Albert. Do you suppose they'll still be making love? That's what Mother said they were doing, they were probably just holding hands."

Gently, he took her by the shoulders, and led her to Melissa's car.

"Good luck," he said.

He was a nice guy.

Allegra O'Riordan lacks concentration. Not Sister Philomena this time, but her sidekick, Sister Christine, a younger nun, mousy and short, who followed the other down polished corridors and parroted her views with an enthusiasm that made Allegra, in idle adult moments, occasionally wonder just what had constituted Mother Superior's definition of the forbidden special friendships. Sister Christine had disliked Allegra, not for the legitimate, and meticulously observed, reasons that Sister Philomena had, but simply because the other nun had, and to denounce her, would fling, as Allegra was early aware, the first reproach that came into her not imaginative head. Allegra had not lacked concentration, not especially.

Not as she lacked it this evening, paying far too much money for roses that Kathleen's would put to shame, turning left in the car where she should have turned right, cutting across lanes to rectify her mistake, to a chorus of indignant horns from more righteous drivers. To her side, an expensively coiffured woman leaned out of a shiny Mercedes. "Loser!" she shouted. The insult was justified, but the choice of wording curious: not a description that Allegra herself would particularly have considered insulting at all.

She was going to meet Alice and Albert, who had known her mother, and by the sound of Alice at least, would talk about her; she was going to find, not John's silences nor Helen's meanderings, but a sensible, informed, and informative conversation on the subject of Theresa Imelda Higgins. She, Allegra O'Riordan, verging on middle age, was on her way to be introduced, fully, to her mother.

"Yessss!" crowed M.M., punching a fist in the air.

"Shut up," Allegra told her, trying not to grin.

"One thing's for sure," was Alice's greeting. "You don't favor your ma. Does she, Albert?"

"I'm like my dad," agreed Allegra politely. She was stifling a terrible urge to giggle at the thought of the two making love in public, since Alice was as cheerfully fat and garrulous as Albert was silent and gaunt. But they seemed happy enough, and smiled when their eyes met; and their small house, spilling baby snapshots and garish child-bought souvenirs under reproduction Madonnas and a portrait of the Pope, was welcoming. The roses were exclaimed over and arranged in a vase; cold cuts were brought from a refrigerator covered in crayon drawings; and Allegra, seated on a sagging sofa with a generous glass of bourbon to hand, began to feel warm; almost, for the first time since she had arrived in Los Angeles, at peace. Then she remembered why she was there, and had to fight back the giggle again.

"Like your dad," repeated Alice. "I guess you must be, he was a handsome boy, I do remember that, although to tell you the truth, I can't recall his face real clearly. Now Theresa, I can see her now, well, after all these years. That was a terrible tragedy, her dying so young, it was a cab, wasn't it? I guess you don't remember her at all."

"Not really. I was only three."

"Three, poor mite. And just you alone with all those men, I tell my sons it's my daughters who keep me sane, don't I, Albert? The men'd sit there all day and stare at the wall as soon as talk to you. They're good for what they're good for, but if you want to talk something over, go to a woman, is what I say."

"I think I agree," said Allegra.

"Hmm." She flashed on Allegra's bare left hand. "You're not married?"

"No."

"Well." She took in Allegra's silver hairs, the beginning of the lines around her eyes. "You take your time these days. How about your brothers?"

"Bob is, he has two little boys. Declan isn't."

"Grandsons, eh? Theresa Higgins and me, grandparents, who'd have thought it? And how's that handsome wild young John Higgins?"

"He's very well. Still lives by the ocean. He married Kathleen Murphy, did you know her? They have a son, Jimmy, a few years younger than me. Nice guy."

"Any grandchildren yet?"

"Not . . . No."

"That's too bad, I always say grandchildren are God's thanks to us for raising children, don't I, Albert? Oh, listen to me, gabbing on about grandchildren, Albert says I can't talk about anything else.

So tell me about yourself, honey, if you're not married, what do you do?"

"I'm a comic. In a club in Chicago."

"A comic, is that so? We always said our Stevie should have been one of those, didn't we, Albert? He has us in stitches, doesn't he? Stevie's our baby, you know—baby! he just turned twenty-seven. There he is in his wedding picture, look, behind you. He's a handsome boy, don't you think?"

"He's like you," said Allegra to Albert.

"Don't tell him that! His head's swelled enough without beautiful young women making it worse. Not married." She pursed her lips, thoughtfully. "I don't know why you young people take so much time to settle down. Now, take Albert's nephew Michael, for instance. Tall, good-looking guy, has his own business, he must be in his forties now, mustn't he, Albert? He's with a different girl every time you see him, says he just hasn't found the right one yet. Have some salami, honey, Lord knows you don't have any weight to lose. Would you believe I used to be as skinny as you? That was before I had my babies, of course, they change you, you know, so you just make the most of your figure before you start having babies too. The Andrew men like a slim girl. Michael does, doesn't he, Albert?"

"That's nice," said Allegra. And it *was* nice of the older woman: a kindly compliment, its motives, after her dealings with John, so deliciously, so blessedly transparent. "Alice, when did you meet my mother?"

"When! Honey, we were in grade school together, we were best friends until she got the job at the fancy bookstore. Well, we were always best friends, really—your oldest friend is your oldest friend, isn't she?"

"Yes." Allegra smiled, thinking of M.M. And from the sound of it, Alice had approved of Theresa's career no more than did M.M. of Allegra's. "You remember the bookstore, then?"

"Remember!" Alice snorted. "I can't think we were ever left to forget, were we, Albert? It was all your mother talked about from the moment she started there. I used to say to you, didn't I, I used to say, you'd think she was going to the Sheik of Araby's tent, not some fusty old bookstore every day."

So her mother had loved her work. Allegra found she was glad to hear it.

"That's good," she said. "That she enjoyed her job, at least."

"Oh, your ma never did anything by halves, poor soul. I sometimes wonder if people who are going to die young know it somehow, and put the more into their lives. But then, Albert says I'm just being fanciful, don't you, Albert?"

"I met someone from the bookstore," said Allegra. "Helen. Strangely enough, talking of dying, she just died last week, I don't know if you remember her? Helen Viner."

At the name, Alice's head jerked up in surprise.

"Helen Viner!" she said. "You met Helen?"

"Yes," said Allegra. "We had lunch a couple of times. She was quite senile, but she kind of remembered you two, in flashes." Or did she? It was no matter, now.

"Well, well," said Alice. "Well, Helen Viner, did you hear that, Albert? Well, the past is the past, and we all move on. I'm glad you met her, and you must be too, after all's said and done."

Allegra frowned. After all was said and done?

"What do you mean?" she said.

Albert got up. He moved slowly; he was arthritic.

"Let me freshen your drink there," he said to Allegra.

"What do you mean?" said Allegra to Alice. "The past is the past?"

"Oh," said Alice, although she and Albert had not caught each other's eye. "Nothing really, just a silly quarrel Helen and Theresa had, I can't even remember what it was about, and it sounds like Helen couldn't either. Well, Albert, don't just stand there, go and fetch us all another drink, while I bore her to tears showing her all the grandchildren. Don't be shy, Allegra, Albert likes a gal who can take a drink, don't you?"

Albert winked, heavily, at Allegra. "All the men in our family do," he said, and limped toward the kitchen.

Albert was not a Jesuit boy: to leave the room now was a tactical error such as would not have occurred to John Higgins as a possible option. Absently, Allegra looked at Alice as the older woman hefted her bulk toward a baby photograph. She could so easily allow the moment to slide. It would be pleasant to be shown the baby photographs, pleasant to have another drink, and feel the world go fuzzy around the edges and benign. Pleasant even, perhaps, to allow herself to be fixed up with tall, good-looking Michael with the business of his own, who had not yet found the right girl: who knew but that she would end up one day making love in public with Albert's nephew.

"What did you mean?" she said again. "The past is the past."

Alice looked up from the picture in her hand, and at her, small eyes sharp in the shrewd expanse of her face.

"Yes," she said, then. "Yes, if you don't know already, you should. Wait till Albert comes back with the drinks, and we'll tell you everything."

Chapter Ten

What you have to understand is that the Higginses were a bad lot. Now, don't look like that, Albert, she's a grown woman, and everybody knew it then, if they don't want to talk about it now. There was something wrong with them, wild blood. Robert Higgins, my Lord. You didn't know about him? Everyone else in the parish did: "You'll end up like Robert Higgins," Ma used to say to my brother Bill, but not in front of Theresa, of course. He was no good, was that boy. Reeling round the bars, betting on the horses, getting girls into trouble, oh yes, your grandfather Joe Higgins was a grandfather many more times than he admitted to, and my guess is, you have more cousins in Los Angeles than just John's boy, though Lord knows how you'd find them. John was quieter—I always liked John, he was a good, kind fellow underneath it all. But, oh, could he kick up trouble in his day! I remember he was sent home from school once, for setting fire to the boy in front of him. Jim Mackey, nobody liked him. But to set fire to him. No normal boy would do that, you'd have to have a little bit of craziness, wouldn't you? But that was the Higginses for you.

Nobody even knew where they came from. You didn't know that either? Well, they'd keep it dark, wouldn't they? Well, I don't know what they told you—or didn't tell you more likely, oh yes, I remember how they could be—but the truth is that they just appeared, Joe Higgins and his ma, one morning, from nowhere. My mother was there when it happened, and she talked about it till the day she died. It was the children's First Communion day, and Ma and her classmates done up as cute as buttons, I've seen the photographs, the girls with little white dresses and bows in their hair, and all the boys in suits. Remember how special you felt on your First Communion day, honey? Ma had new boots, and her godmother had given her white gloves and a white rosary, and oh my, was she proud. Poor little angels they all were, I always say, if ever you're innocent, it's on your First Communion day. Well, so they had the Mass, they'd been fasting since midnight in those days, that was when fasting counted for something, and they were crossing the schoolyard to their breakfast, Ma's tummy was rumbling like old plumbing, she always said, when a gypsy woman appeared. Or that's what she seemed like. Tangled hair, bare feet, a scowl from here to San Francisco—poor soul mustn't have eaten in days—and a gimpy leg she'd never tell anyone how she got. And a little boy, filthy dirty, and skinny as a wolf. That would have been your great-grandma, Mary Higgins, and her son, Joe.

The nuns took them in. Imagine that happening today to a homeless person. They'd be tossed a dollar and sent to the shelter, and that's what we call progress. But in those days, people helped each other. They fed them, the nuns did, bathed them, found them new clothes, well, clean clothes at any rate, and then they gave Mary a job cleaning the school, and two rooms and a kitchen in back of the schoolhouse, and of course, they educated Joe. Mary worked hard for it, mind. Ma used to see her limping up and down the corridors at all hours, with a bucket and mop in her hand, and always scowling, scowling. I guess she had plenty to scowl about.

Nobody ever knew who Joe's father was, I don't think he knew it himself. My Lord, you're finding out a lot of new things this evening, aren't you? Nobody knew who they were, or where they came from either, although some said it was back East, some said Arizona. Some said too that Higgins was Mary's maiden name *and* her married name, if you know what I mean. But people will talk, and that's the way we sinful creatures are.

Mary wasn't talking, she was closemouthed as the grave, was that one. Oh, but there was a story there, if ever anyone got to know it. She went to Mass every Sunday, but never once to Communion. Never, not even to make her Easter duties. She made Joe go, mind. Confession, Communion, and the next time the Bishop came, he was confirmed, wearing my Uncle Petey's old suit that was too small for him and had to be let out with sacking. But Mary herself just stood at the back of the church, Sunday after Sunday, scowling. She mustn't have felt she was in a state of grace, although nobody ever knew why. Yes, there was a story there.

There was no scandal, though, while she was there. No man came courting her that I ever heard of—I don't suppose any man would dare! No, she led a quiet life, did Mary, so Ma said. She'd clean the school when the children had gone home, and then she'd take her newspaper—she was an educated woman, Lord knows where from—and she'd take a plug of tobacco for her pipe, and on Fridays she'd take a bucket of beer, and she and Joe would lock themselves in those two rooms, and no one would see hide nor hair of either until the next morning. And that was her life. But she can't have been more than a young woman. Probably younger then than you are now.

Joe, now, he was a case. Ma was always talking about him, and the stories she told! Although now I think of it, he had a few years on her, so she can't have remembered all of them just the way she said she did. Still, they must have come from somewhere, mustn't they? He was a smart kid, was Joe, so they all said. He took to reading like a duck to water, and when I went to school, years later, the nuns were still talking about the way he could do sums in his head. Couldn't trip him up, that's what they said. Couldn't trip him up. He was a proud boy, the way Ma told it, dressed in the parish castoffs, but with his head held so high, you'd never think of teasing him about it. Good-looking too, she used to say. Now I think of it, she probably had a bit of a fancy for him, poor old Ma. He was so smart and well-spoken and all, not like my poor dad, yes, she might have had a fancy. But at least I know who my granddaddy was.

Joe adored Mary. Adored her. Ma used to tell about the time he caught Chuck Robinson imitating her, limping down the corridor, miserable as sin, with that mop. Truth to tell, I think they all imitated Mary, Ma used to, anyway, and funny it was when we were little. But this boy, Chuck Robinson, who I never knew, was doing it one day in front of a whole crowd of them, when Joe came around the corner. Well, he fell on that kid, and they had to call Father Becerra in to pull him off, or he'd have killed him. Chuck drowned in the ocean, a few years later. No one ever imitated Mary in public again, Ma said.

The nuns always said Joe would go far, and for once, they were right. He left school when he was fourteen, of course—poor little fellow, just a baby, like Terri's Ben, Albert, can you imagine?—but by then everyone in the parish knew Joe Higgins was a hardworking boy with a head on his shoulders. Ma said that the very last day he left the school as a pupil, there were three local businessmen waiting at the school gate to offer him a job. There was Mr. Saldani, who owned Saldani's restaurant, Mr.—what was his name?—who ran the grocery store, and young Bob Matthews, who was just starting out as a building contractor. Now, Mr. Saldani, and Mr.—what *was* his name, now?—offered him decent hours, a steady wage, and a secure job, and remember, Joe had Mary to take care of. But Bob Matthews said to him, "Well, Joe," he said, "I can't promise you the money these two good men can, and if you come with me, you'll be working all the hours God sends, and who knows for what. But I can tell you this, that hundreds of houses are being built in Los Angeles right now, and there'll be thousands more before long, so what do you say to a slice of the future?" "I'll take it," said Joe. At least, that's what Ma said happened. And by the time I knew old Joe, he was a well-set-up man with his own contracting business, and he did call his eldest son Robert, so there must have been some truth to that story, at least.

I never knew Mary, she died quite young, I believe, worn out by all the work probably, poor soul. But she was buried in the Catholic cemetery like any good practicing Catholic, Easter duties or not, Joe'd gone respectable by then, and had some pull. It's a funny thing, but I was just about grown before I realized that that wild Joe Higgins Ma used to talk about was one and the same as Theresa's dad. You'd think I'd have caught on earlier, wouldn't you? But the two seemed so different—and *they* sure never talked about the old days—that I just never did. Joe was a big, tall man when I knew him, very strict—even Theresa was a little bit afraid of him, I think—married to a little mouse of a thing from San Diego or somewhere else, and quite the perfect parishioner, oh my. All the family together at Mass, Knights of Columbus, Father whatsit, Father Carroll, that's right, always in and out for coffee or cocktails. He made a pilgrimage to Rome, Joe did, back in the days when it really was a trip. He brought Theresa a rosary that had been blessed by the Pope, and an Italian doll with woolly black hair. I don't know which she loved more, the rosary or the doll. I wonder what happened to either of them. Yes, they were a fine Catholic family, the Higginses.

Except that there was always trouble around them. And not just the usual young kids' scrapes either, but real, bad trouble. I remember once when Theresa and I were just little girls, we were all sitting down to supper when there was a knock at the door, and there stood two policemen in uniforms, looking for Robert. Policemen. Never found out what that was about, Theresa begged me never to mention it, and give me credit, to this day I have not, have I, Albert? But it was soon after that, that Robert went to join the Navy. Funny thing was, the War broke out, and he died a hero, and I think in their hearts, they were relieved he'd gone. He was a bad one, was that boy. Say what you like about Theresa, she had her crosses to bear, and she bore them.

Theresa. Now, what shall I say about her? Well, she was a pretty girl, prettier than me, wasn't she, Albert? With all that hair, and the loveliest skin. She was a clever little girl, a reader, I can see her now with her nose buried in a book, you couldn't speak to her sometimes. But she was lively as well, you know, always laughing, with a joke to tell, or a bit of gossip, oh, and those cruel imitations she used to love to do, but they were so funny, you had to laugh, even if you knew you shouldn't. We were all afraid of her, to tell the truth, with her sharp tongue and her temper and all. She liked her own way, did Theresa. I guess with those brothers, she'd had to fight for anything she wanted, but it's my feeling she'd have come out that way no matter what family she had. Well, you have brothers yourself, honey, and I can tell you don't have her iron. Yes, iron is what she was. That was OK by her mother, because she knew better than to try to cross her. She was a nice lady, was Theresa's mom, if anyone ever bothered to notice, which nobody did, but she wouldn't dare take on Theresa. No, the only one who would say a word to her was her dad.

Dear God, the fights those two had! Not about anything you'd think anything of these days—what time to come home from the dance, whether to wear lipstick, silly things, nonsense, really. But to hear those two at it, you'd think it was the Battle of Bunker Hill. I suppose Joe'd seen his son go to the bad, and didn't want his daughter to go the same way, and looking back now, I can understand that.

But I do think he was overly strict with her too, far stricter than my dad was with me, not that that was difficult, and fierce too. Wouldn't laugh at her jokes, never had much time for laughing at anything, did Joe. And wouldn't stand her airs and graces either, and that was too bad, because to tell the truth, your mother was full of them. Miss High and Mighty, we used to call her at school, not to her face, of course. The fact of the matter, my dear, was that from the time she was a tiny girl, your mother was a regular little snob.

The tales she used to make up! All of them lies and she knew it, but they were good stories, I'll give her that. A lot of them were about her grandma. Not Mary Higgins, oh no, I never heard Theresa mention *her*, not once. Not once. No, it was her ma's ma she talked about, down in San Diego where nobody ever got to meet her, Kitty O'Shea. No, that was the girl in the movie. O'Driscoll. That was the name, Kitty O'Driscoll. Kitty O'Driscoll, the Irish princess, who danced with the leprechauns in Clonakilty, wherever that was, and had long golden hair, and wore a gold crown and a silk dress of deep shamrock green. That was when we were little kids, of course, and we all thought she sounded like the most gorgeous thing. Later on, after Theresa discovered the history books, the story changed, and Kitty wasn't a princess at all, she was a barefoot peasant girl, who fought her way onto a coffin ship—for the longest time, I thought that meant a ship with a sore throat—and sent money back every month to her twelve, or fifteen, or twenty-seven, or however many she'd decided it was, brothers and sisters, starving back at home, still in Clonakilty, mind. She'd tell us all this stuff, straight-faced. We just used to wait till she'd gone and then laugh at her. The funniest thing was that as we left Catholic school and went into the world, old Grandma became less and less Irish, remember that, Albert? Remember that fancy dance we went to, I can't for the life of me remember where, where we heard her spinning a tale to some boy about Grandmother Katherine and her beautiful, ruined estate in Georgia—burned in the war,

I guess Theresa'd been reading *Gone With the Wind*—called, guess what, Clonakilty! Remember how we laughed? Well, she made such a fool of herself, you couldn't help it. I wonder where Clonakilty really was, we never found out, did we?

Right around the time she left school, she decided she wanted to leave the Higgins family too, and I can't say I blame her, let's just say it wasn't the sort of family a little snob would have chosen for her own. She'd say as much, quite plain, after a couple of cocktails, Theresa never could hold her liquor as well as I could, but back in those days, she hadn't quite figured it out yet. I can see her now, sitting in my mother's parlor, in one of those pretty, flowery dresses she used to wear—remember how nicely she used to dress, Albert? Oh, I don't know why I bother asking—and telling me, straight out, she was looking for something better. "We have too many skeletons, Alice," she'd say, which was as close as she'd ever come to admitting anything of what the whole of the rest of the parish knew. "I need to find some people with empty closets." That's what she'd say. Empty closets. Well, good luck finding them, honey, I'd think, and if you do, good luck getting them to stick around a closet like yours. But I didn't say anything, not to Theresa. She was so determined to get out of her people, and in her way, she did. Now, in those days, a young girl wouldn't think of leaving her parents' home the way they do today, well, our sort of young girl wouldn't, anyway, it wasn't the way most of us did things, and maybe Theresa, poor kid, wasn't just quite as bold as she thought she was. What she could do, though, was to get herself a job.

Of course, the job had to be around her precious books. Lord knows where all that reading came from, I don't think I saw anyone open a single book in the Higgins house but her mother's cookbooks and her dad's Sunday missal. But Theresa was never without one, any sort of a one, stories, histories, poems, funny that, isn't it? Maybe she got it from old Mary Higgins—what a joke that would be! Anyway, when she's looking for this job, there's nothing for it but it must be in a bookstore. Joe went crazy, of course, said she'd be mixing with immoral people, and asked to sell books on the Index, but nothing was going to stop Theresa on this one. She found her bookstore job, and it wasn't just any bookstore, mind, not somewhere Albert and I might just walk into and pass the time with her, that wasn't good enough, oh no. She has to go to the fanciest bookstore in town, all the way up to Hollywood Boulevard, three tram rides from her home—she'd leave at dawn and come back all pooped out—with art galleries next door, and writers and actors in and out, and Lord knows what all else besides. And oh my, did little Theresa Higgins get above herself there!

We'd go out together at the weekends—she'd allow us that, wouldn't she, Albert? And she'd be using this long word and dropping the name of that author nobody knew or gave a good goddamn about. Interesting people, that's what she'd call them. She'd talk about this poet who'd admired her hair, and that artist who'd taken her out for coffee, until Albert and I could hardly look at each other for wanting to laugh, could we, Albert? Remember when she bought that cigarette holder, and started to talk like Bette Davis? Oh, we laughed. Nobody said anything to her, mind. She was still Theresa Higgins, and we were all still a little bit frightened of her.

As the years passed, though, we couldn't help but notice she never brought any of these interesting people home. No, she'd talk about them, but we never saw hide nor hair of one of them, not anywhere near the Higgins house. What she was ashamed of there I don't know, it was a nice house, and Robert was long gone by then. The no books, maybe, or that her ma sometimes still said ain't instead of isn't. I thought artistic folks weren't supposed to mind about those things. Maybe she didn't really know them at all, maybe to them, she was just a little red-haired girl who stood behind a counter. Poor Theresa, she might have gone through some heartache there. But she never told me a thing, she'd stopped the cocktails by then, said they made her fat. I think they made her tongue loose, and she was worried what she might say.

Quite soon, she found she wasn't quite so young and not quite so pretty either. You know those redheads and how short their bloom is—you're lucky to have your dad's coloring. I remember one day standing beside her in front of the mirror searching out wrinkles—wrinkles! We were twenty-four! And I remember her, suddenly, starting to ask me questions about Albert—were we in love, how did we know it was love, how could you work it out so the person you fell in love with would be the one to fall in love with you? And I was surprised, because she'd never shown any big interest in you before at all, had she, Albert? Not quite interesting enough for her, I guess. I asked her why she was asking, and her face just went as red as her hair, and she started making jokes instead. She never brought it up again, and soon after that, I did notice she went quiet for a while. Then she got back to her old self again, or seemed to. I guess we'll never know what all of that was about.

The only friend of hers we did ever meet was your friend Lady Helen. Helen was a good few years older than Theresa, and just so sophisticated—she'd just been divorced, which we all thought sounded glamorous, God, were we dumb in those days—and she lived close by. She was fond of Theresa, although she called her Molly Malone, which your mother hated, and they used to travel to work and back together, and pal around sometimes at the weekends. I think Theresa used to make her laugh. Or maybe Helen was just lonely. It must be rough to be alone when you've been used to being with someone.

Theresa thought Helen was just it. Well, she came from money, you could tell, and I'm sorry to tell you, that always impressed your mother. And she'd read even more books than Theresa had, *and* knew the authors personally too, so that made her even more the big shot in Theresa's eyes. God, she admired her! Used to dress like her, talk like her, when she wasn't being Bette Davis, and sometimes you could hardly tell the difference, I think she might even have got that damn cigarette holder idea from her too. Oh, and, Albert, remember that time when she tried to fix her up with her brother John? Now, John Higgins and Helen Viner together was one of the nuttiest ideas I'd ever heard, and believe me, the least nutty part of all was that John was fifteen years younger than Helen was. Didn't stop little Theresa. "You're as young as you feel," she'd tell me. "And Helen still feels like a girl at heart." I swear your mother had a crazy streak in her. Didn't work out, of course, are you kidding? But for a while there, she really thought it would. It was around then that she and Nate O'Riordan were getting together, and I thought at the time, she had some notion that if *she* wasn't to marry one of her artistic types, maybe her brother could instead. Crazy, like I said. But I might be wrong, by then she'd stopped talking.

It was her dad who brought Nate O'Riordan home. Oh, you didn't know that? Yes, he found him at Mass one day, lassoed him, and led him home like a prize bull. Nate was everything Joe Higgins could ask for in a son-in-law, decent, plainspoken, a good Catholic with a steady job. And looking back on all the fights Joe and Theresa were having around then, I used to think that maybe the fact he lived in Chicago didn't hurt any either. No, you're right, Albert, that's mean. Joe did love Theresa; just couldn't get along with her.

Anyway, he took to Nate like the son he wished he'd had. Asked him to dinner, took him out to drinks and back to the house when he knew Theresa'd be home, did everything short of locking them together in the broom closet. Now, Nate was a good-looking boy, but he was painfully shy, and Theresa was funny about him, oh my, she was wicked. Called him Dad's Disaster, and Nate, Nate, the Awful Fate. I can see her now. "Father"—very Bette Davis, you know—"Father, I am *not* going to talk to that man, I get better conversation from the table lamp!" Well, she was sore at him, and I can't say I blame her, you don't want your dad finding your beaux for you. But oh dear, how she used to make us laugh.

The trouble was, Nate took one look at Theresa, and fell, hook, line, and sinker, head over his dumb heels in love. Oh, it would have been funny if it wasn't so pitiful, to see this great tall gawk of a man just gazing at a girl who wouldn't give him the time of day. He tried everything, did Nate. Extended his business trip. Hung around the house—she'd make sure to be out. Went out dancing with our crowd—she'd ignore him. He even ordered some books from her store and drove all the way into Hollywood, just so he could pick them up from her. "Mr. O'Riordan," she said to him, "I believe there are an array of excellent bookstores on the West Side." Or that's what she said she said, but he went back there the next week anyway. Truth to tell, by this time, I think her resistance was wearing down a little. I always told my boys, nothing wins a woman like stick-to-itiveness, didn't I, Albert? And like I said, Theresa wasn't quite so young anymore, and no one had exactly snapped her off the shelf.

I remember when she decided to marry him. Yes, she made her mind up to do it, cool as a cucumber. The weekend previous, she'd had a big fight with her dad, well, that was nothing new, and the couple of times I'd seen her in the week, she'd been grinning like the cat that swallowed the canary. Well, but on the Friday night, she came to visit me. Now, she wasn't grinning at all that day, no, she looked terrible, white as a sheet, and all her freckles standing out, and waving that damn fool cigarette holder like it was a spear. And then she asked for a cocktail, so I *knew* something was wrong. But you could never ask Theresa Higgins what was going on unless she'd decided to tell you, so I fixed her a Manhattan, that's what we used to drink back then, funny, I haven't had one for years, and I made a couple of jokes, and then we just sat there like two sacks of flour. I never knew what that was about either. She kept her own counsel, did Theresa, and that was what did for her in the end. Then, all of a sudden, she laughed, Theresa did, and said to me, "Guess what, Alice," she said. "I've decided to fall in love with Nate O'Riordan." Well, I just about spilled my drink. "What?" I said. "Nate O'Riordan?" She looked at me, very la-di-da with those big green eyes, and she just said, "Well," she said, "don't you think it would be *terribly* original?" I can hear her now. *Terribly* original. Then we had another cocktail, or I did, and we talked about something else, and she left. I still wasn't sure if she'd been joking or not.

Well, we all soon found out she hadn't been joking. Truth to tell, I was a little bit shocked at how fast she moved in. That was the Friday: she saw Nate that Sunday at Mass, and gave him this shy little smile, pretty as could be; poor dumb fool can't believe his good luck, and he asks her to dinner on Monday; the next thing you know, they're everywhere together, she's hanging on to his arm looking up at him like she's caught herself Tyrone Power. No, it was William Holden she liked, wasn't it? William Holden, then. I guess she'd talked herself into being in love. Poor soul. Anyway, nobody dared mention this change of tune to her, not if we valued our lives, and pretty soon, it seemed as if she and Nate had always been together, just like Albert and me.

That was a happy summer we had, wasn't it, Albert? Theresa was always happy round about then, she loved the sun so much, and she never burned like most redheads do, and of course, with her on his arm, poor Nate just about thought he'd died and gone to heaven with no purgatory in between. Old Speedy Gonzales here finally got up the nerve to ask me to marry him, and we all knew it was only time till Nate did the same for Theresa. Oh, and even John had escaped Lady Viner, and was getting together with that Kathleen Murphy—nice enough little thing, but I can't say the men in your family go much for a girl with personality—so you can imagine the grin that was never off of Joe Higgins's face then. A good time, a good summer. Until Malcolm Brewer arrived.

You've heard the name, then. Not from your dad, I'll bet. Malcolm was Helen Viner's half brother—no, he was only her stepbrother, wasn't he? something like that, I don't remember, and I don't suppose it much matters now—and he'd come to stay with her, to recover from, I think it was pneumonia, or maybe tuberculosis, he'd never had good health, I believe. But what I do remember, as clear as if it were yesterday, was taking one look at him and your mother, and thinking, We have trouble here. I said it to Albert too, didn't I? We have trouble, I said. But of course, you wouldn't believe me, and who was right after all?

Malcolm couldn't have been more different from your dad if he'd tried. He was a small little guy, and fair, with a delicate look to him, I could never have taken to him in that way myself, not that I would have done, mind, but he was just that bit girlish for my liking. Oh, I can see his hands now, they were long and thin and too clean-looking somehow, if you know what I mean. But he and your mother just took one look at each other, and that was it. You could smell it. Or I could, anyway.

I remember the night we all met. We went out to dinner, the six of us—Helen and he were very close, for all they weren't really related—to one of those Italian rib houses, and it turned out Malcolm had just come back from Italy, so he knew all those fancy pasta dishes which everybody knows now, but back then it was a big deal, and he starts telling us all about them, and then after that, he gets into the art galleries in Florence, and the painted ceilings in Rome, and things he saw in Paris, and London, and I don't know where-all else. Poor Nate just sits there, the only place he's ever been is Iwo Jima, and you can bet there weren't too many painted ceilings there. Helen's smiling away like it's the sort of talk they talk every day in her family home, and it probably is, for all I know, and Albert, of course, can't hear a word when you put a plate of meat in front of him but pass the salt. But I'm sitting opposite Theresa, and I'm looking at her, and I'm thinking, Oh, my dear God, because she has a look on her face that I've never seen there before, and I've known Theresa Higgins pretty near all her life.

So they finish talking about Europe and they start in on Los Angeles. They talk about the galleries up in Hollywood, and of course, he knows all the artists. They talk about the bookstore, and he knows all the books. Then Theresa gets to telling him about the people who come into the store, and imitating them in that funny way she had—and oh, she could be funny—that she never did for Nate that I ever saw, and Nate's just sitting there—poor boy, I felt sorry for him—and pretty soon, I sneak a peek at this Malcolm, and, Oh, my dear, dear God, I think, because when he's not laughing, he's looking at her in just the way she looks at him. I thought, We have trouble here, I thought, and I was the only one there who could see it.

Well, it gets worse, because after that, Malcolm and Theresa became friends. Helen encouraged it, and I suppose you can't blame her. Theresa cheered Malcolm up—he suffered from depressions too, no, not my kind of man at all, but Theresa could make him laugh like nobody. Helen wasn't to know better. In fact, fond as she was of Theresa, who knew what she was trying to fix up there? As I said, she wasn't to know. But Theresa! She let the guy visit her at the store, she went to lunch with him, she lent him books, borrowed his, I don't know what-all else. Now, nobody else could see this but me, they all thought it was fine, but I knew Theresa, and I knew it was downright wrong. And I don't mind who I say it to.

It got so I had to have a word with her. Remember that weekend we all went up to Santa Barbara, Albert? Such a pretty little inn we stayed at, we almost went back there for our honeymoon, but we didn't, we went to Catalina instead, Avalon, where Albert's uncle had a hotel. That was a nice place too. Well, the first evening up at the inn, I sent Albert off somewhere, and sat Theresa down for a talk. I said to her, "Theresa," I said, "can't you see what it is you're doing?"

She said to me, "Alice," she said, oh, she'd had a cocktail by then, we both of us knew it wasn't a conversation we could have dry, and she wasn't being Bette Davis that day either. "Alice," she said, "I've never felt like this before. I didn't know it was possible to feel like this. God gave me this feeling," she said, "and all I know is, it would be wicked of me not to feel it." Wicked of me. I can see her now, in a yellow dress with daisies. I said to her, "Theresa Imelda Higgins, how can you sit there and talk to me about God and what's wicked?" I said, "What's wicked, Theresa," I said . . .

"Wait a minute," said Allegra. "I don't understand what's so terrible here. I mean, of course I'm glad she married my father in the end. But they weren't married then, were they? And it doesn't sound like Malcolm was married either. And you don't have to stay in love with the first person you fall in love with, do you?"

"Oh, my God," said Alice. "She doesn't know. Albert, the child doesn't know."

"Know what?" said Allegra.

"Father Brewer," said Albert, "was an ordained priest."

You were the only one who called him Father, Albert. He looked about sixteen years old, for one thing, and besides, he told us straight out, he wanted to be plain Malcolm. We didn't call them progressive priests in those days, but I guess that's what he was. Still, he was a priest, chosen and ordained, and I don't care what you read in the newspapers now, a priest is a priest, picked out and called by Almighty God, and it's to God he belongs, not to his mother nor to his father, nor to any woman. Theresa knew that. It would have been better if we'd all of us called him Father from the start.

No, of course the Brewers weren't Catholic. They were pure-bred WASP, and if you'd taken one look at Malcolm, you'd have known it. God knows what they thought of him going into the Church like that, although I can make a few guesses. Malcolm said he'd wanted to be a priest since he was a little kid. He'd spent a lot of time ill in bed, he said, and his Irish nurse had given him books about the great saints and priests, and he'd decided he wanted to be one too. He used to say he was converted through sickness, just the same as Saint Ignatius—Malcolm never had what these days they call a self-esteem problem. Joe Higgins used to laugh at that story. He couldn't believe his luck then—his daughter everything but engaged to a good Catholic boy, *and* palling around with a priest too. He didn't know, of course, and nobody ever knew what Theresa's mother knew or didn't know, because nobody ever asked her.

I don't think Malcolm knew either, not until it was too late. For all his books and his traveling, I don't think he'd been around too many women, and maybe he thought all friendships with them felt like that. Poor guy, he didn't have a clue, really. But Theresa knew. Oh, yes, she did. Now, I never quite knew how much your mother really knew, if you know what I mean—oh, Albert, for heaven's sake, she's an adult—but I knew it was enough. And I knew she knew what she was doing here.

After we came down from Santa Barbara, she never touched another cocktail in front of me. Oh no, much too dangerous. And she went on just the same as she had been with Malcolm, making her best jokes for him, watching him laugh and patting him ever so innocently on the sleeve, making plans for coffee, and concerts, and when I'd try to talk with her, she'd look at me, but not quite *at* me, if you know what I mean, and just say, "Why, Alice," she'd say, "I don't know what you're suggesting, the man's a priest, for heaven's sake." She knew what I was suggesting, all right.

Nate knew something was up, but he couldn't quite see what. Men are such idiots sometimes, and Malcolm was a priest after all, and in those days, we were all idiots about priests. Or most of us were. I don't think he ever confided in anyone, that wasn't his way, as you know, and besides, he'd sooner have cut off his right arm than go gossiping about his Theresa, poor boy. But I saw him watching her, and trying to think good Catholic thoughts, and not to see what was going on as plain as the nose on his face, and I saw him getting angrier and angrier, and I can't say I was surprised.

He blew up at last, the day they all went to the beach. Do I remember that day? Why, I can't think I'll ever forget it, will we, Albert? Now, how did it happen? Oh, yes. Helen was going East on a buying trip, and she wanted to get some sun before she left, it was almost fall by then. And Malcolm thought the fresh air would do him good. And little Theresa just happened to have a new swimsuit she wanted to try out—now, tell me, who goes shopping for swimsuits in September? It was a two-piece, which was racy in those days, believe it or not. She had a nice little figure, Theresa, not fat, but full, it was fashionable then. I was flatter, like you—that was five babies ago, of course. You make the most of your shape before you start to have babies too. Anyway, Theresa had a good shape—and the swimsuit showed every little inch of it.

Well, naturally, Nate was going to the beach with them, he was Theresa's young man, after all. And he knew Helen was going, and that was fine, and he found out Malcolm was going too, and that was OK. And then he saw the swimsuit, and, as I say, he blew up. Oh, Nate had his own temper, when you found it—but I guess you know that too. I can still remember the go-arounds, can't you, Albert? Quite improper to appear like that in front of a priest; he wouldn't be part of it; he wouldn't permit it. Of course, that sort of talk was like a red rag to a bull to Theresa. Who the hell did he think he was, permitting or not permitting, she'd do what she goddamn wanted, and wear what she goddamn pleased, it was like she was talking to her father, only worse, because it turned out that when Nate had his Irish up, he was even more stubborn than Joe Higgins himself.

We didn't go to the beach that day, Albert and I, we went to my cousin Ida's wedding instead—a nice wedding, but we didn't like her flowers, they weren't bright enough, I like a bit of color myself—and as you can imagine, we weren't sorry to have a good excuse for not going. But Theresa went, oh yes, and very pretty I'm sure, in her new swimsuit, and Nate went somewhere else, no one ever knew where. Maybe he went to church instead, he was always a religious guy. Or maybe he went off for a drink. I liked Nate, for all he was so dull sometimes.

The next day, Malcolm said the ten o'clock Mass at the church, and of course, we were all there. And I don't know what anyone else saw, but I guess the swimsuit had gotten the message to him at last, because I can say that I have never in my life seen a man look so terrible. Never in my life. White as a sheet, he was, and when he gave me Communion, his hand shook so bad, I swear I thought he was going to drop it, didn't I, Albert? I looked over to Theresa, pretty as I've ever seen her, in a white dress, sitting between Joe and John as if butter wouldn't melt in her mouth, and I thought, Theresa Higgins, what have you done? That's what I thought to myself. What have you done?

Well, outside the church, they're all there, Theresa and John and Kathleen and Mrs. Higgins, and old Joe with a brow like thunder. And no Nate. "Where's Nate?" I asked them. "I don't know," says Theresa, giving me that not-quite-look. "Maybe he has a bug." So we stood there, passing the time, very Sunday morning, and pretty soon, Malcolm came across and joined us. "Are you all right, Father?" said Mrs. Higgins, the older folk always did call him Father. "You look pale." "Oh, yes," he says, very quickly. "Yes, I'm fine." And then! Theresa looks me straight in the eye for once, and she says, straight out, she says, "Maybe he has what Nate has!" I swear! That is what she said. But when she said it, she smiled so prettily, and Albert says he never heard her say it anyway. But I did. Anyway. "I'm fine," says Malcolm, again. "I'm tired because I got up early to see Helen to the train station." Then, he looks at Theresa, and oh, she did look well that day, as I said, she didn't burn in the sun like some redheads, but she had a little golden glow to her—no, *she* didn't have a bug, whatever Malcolm and Nate were going through—and he says to her, he says, "It looks like I'm going to be living like a bachelor for a week." I did not know where to look. Now, Mrs. Higgins, who's a kind soul, and hospitable, she smiles and says, "Oh dear, Father," she says, "you'll have to come and share our food." Malcolm keeps right on looking at Theresa, and says, "Don't be so rash, Mrs. Higgins," he says. "I might just take more than you bargain for." And they all laugh, and Albert and I go away and have a big fight, because he swears they were all just joshing around. Except that he will keep on calling Malcolm Father, which shows he knew better than any of us all along.

Well, I thought about it, and I thought, and in the end, there was nothing for it, but I called Theresa and said to her, "For God's sake, Theresa, think about where you're headed." And she, now, I've never told you this before, Albert, but I don't see it makes much difference now, and Lord knows, the poor soul can use all our forgiveness, but she laughs at me, in that Bette Davis way, and she says, "Oh dear, Alice," she says, "I'm so sorry that *you* couldn't catch anything better than the mechanic at the corner garage." Because I don't mind telling you that that's what Albert was at the time, but as you can see, he hasn't done so badly for me since, and anyway, at least he . . . Well, I just slammed the receiver down so hard I hoped it broke her eardrum, and I swore I'd never speak to her ever again.

Well, but the week went on, I didn't see Theresa or Malcolm, and nobody saw Nate, and after a few days, I started to feel kindlier toward her. She was my oldest friend, after all, and she was to be my maid of honor; and besides, I wanted to ask her advice about my going-away outfit, your mother always had such good taste in clothes. So on the Thursday evening, it was, I called, and I said to her, kind of the way you do after a quarrel, "Do you want to go and see—what was the movie?—tonight?" What was it, now? It had William Holden, so I thought she'd want to go. And she said, all polite, the way you do, "Oh, Alice," she said, "it's so good of you to think of me, and thank you so much for calling." She was still being Bette Davis, but I think she was really glad to hear from me. But then she said, "I'm afraid I can't," she said. "I have to go out this evening to visit a friend." A friend, that was it. Now, I knew all of her friends on this side of town, and she didn't name a name, just "a friend." "Oh, really?" said I. "What friend?" She didn't say anything, for a while. And then, she kind of gulped, and then she just said, "Oh, Alice," and I swear she sounded more like a little girl than she had done even when she was one. Oh, Alice. I said, "Theresa," I said, "tell me what I can do to help you, and I'll do it." And just for a moment there, I thought she might have, poor silly girl. But no, she just put her Bette Davis voice back on, such pride she had, and, "Thank you so much for calling," she says, "but I'm afraid I simply have to run now." La-di-da. I knew where she was running, and she knew I knew.

There's so much work to do preparing for a wedding, and I had a job myself then—working for Mr. Lee, remember, Albert?—that for the next couple of days, I wasn't able to think too much about Theresa at all, God forgive me. I remember it was the Saturday afternoon, and Albert and I had been out to choose curtains—remember how we argued, trying to choose between the checks and the stripes? My Lord, how important it all seemed then—and when I got home, Ma said that Mrs. Higgins had called me. "Me?" I said, and you can imagine what my stomach was doing, because I couldn't think of any happy reason why Mrs. Higgins would want to talk to me. But yes, it was for me, and no, Ma didn't know what it was all about, but she'd made coffee, and thought I should call her back as soon as I could. I won't tell you the things I was thinking as I went to the telephone, but I'm sure you can think of some of them yourself, and who's to say what I heard wasn't the worst of all?

The call wasn't about Theresa, of course, not in that way. It was about Malcolm. It seemed that Helen Viner had come back from her buying trip, let herself into her apartment, and there was Malcolm, dead of a heart attack. Dead of a heart attack, that's what they said, and that's what they stuck to, although he can't have been much more than thirty. Of course, he was sickly, like I said. But he wasn't *that* sickly, and besides, it was his lungs he had problems with, not his heart. And the look on his face that Sunday at Mass . . . Well, we'll never know for sure, but I have my own thoughts, and thank you, but I'll keep them my own.

Well, as soon as I heard the news, I wanted to talk to Theresa. But she wasn't talking to me. I called and called. No, she was out, no, she had a headache, no, she was asleep. It wasn't just me either. Nobody saw her, nobody spoke to her, except for her family, and I guess, Nate. It was like she'd gone into hiding, and didn't come out until the funeral. Oh, yes, it was a good Catholic funeral, at the church, and all, but I've been to priests' funerals since, and I've never been to one as quiet as that. None of his priest buddies concelebrating, none in the congregation either, only Father Carroll, looking as grim as all hell, saying those terrible words, in Latin, in those days. Am I misremembering, or had the weather turned colder? And the coffin was closed.

Helen was there, of course, looking twenty years older, poor soul, she'd found the body. And Joe and Mary Higgins were there too. And Theresa. Dear God, Theresa. She'd changed completely. Completely. I shall never forget the sight of her; it was as if all the color had been drained out of her, as if that lovely, laughing, glowing girl in her pretty dresses had . . . Nate was sitting next to her: nobody had seen *him* lately either. His eyes were all baggy, and I won't say I couldn't smell the liquor on him, and I won't say I could blame him either. But he looked at Theresa in the old way, or almost, and when we got outside the church, he put his arm around her, and she seemed glad to lean on him.

They were married very quickly, not a month after that. The story was that Nate had to go back to Chicago: there were a lot of stories going round at that time. I do remember Joe running out to buy Theresa a fur coat for the Chicago winter, a lovely silver fur, it must have cost far too much, even for Joe. She hardly seemed to notice. Ah, the plans we'd made as little girls about our wedding days, the dresses we were going to wear, the flowers we'd carry, the way we were going to be in love. And I did get to do all those things, I loved our wedding, didn't I, Albert? But poor Theresa, I swear she went through all her own wedding preparations like a zombie, Mrs. Higgins and I did all the work, Theresa just said "Yes" or "No." It was like she'd hidden away inside herself, and nobody could reach her.

Except maybe I did, just once, on the morning of the wedding itself. I was alone with her for the moment, helping to fix her veil over all that gorgeous hair—*that* was still as pretty as ever—and suddenly, I don't know what came into me, except maybe I was thinking of all those plans we'd made for this very day, such a happy day we'd been certain it would be, of course, I found myself saying to her, "Will you be all right, Theresa?" And she looked at me, just for a moment, on her wedding day, and the look in those eyes sent a chill through my whole body. I still see it, sometimes, all these years later. And then she said, "I don't know, Alice." That was all she said. I don't know, Alice.

Then we went downstairs, and got her into the car to get her married. It was a quiet wedding, which they blamed on its being so sudden, but Helen Viner was there, still looking old, of course, and she gave Theresa a kiss goodbye. That was nice of her. Then Theresa went off with Nate. He was a good man, was your dad: Theresa was lucky.

She wrote me a few times, from Chicago. Never got used to the winters, but was as pleased as punch with her babies, and specially to have a daughter, women are, you know. "Let's hope she turns out better than her bad old ma," she wrote once, I probably still have the letter somewhere, Albert says I'm such a pack rat. But she never came back, I could tell, not really, not the way she used to be. It was a cab, wasn't it, that killed her? I sometimes wondered about that. But no. She thought the world of you three, and no mother would.

I never heard from Helen again either, not that we were ever close. It looks like it's just you and me left of all of them, Albert, who'd have imagined it?

Chapter Eleven

There were shreds of chicken caught in Allegra's teeth, and in her mouth was a tang of oversweet mayonnaise. She did not remember eating, but it seemed that Alice must have fed her at some time during the evening, which was like Alice: she was motherly, and not one to miss a meal. Allegra drove west now, through a black night studded with lights bright and cold as rhinestones. West, down boulevards thronged with cars and empty of people; west, going a little slowly, for safety's sake; west, until the blocks of offices gave way to residential streets, and through the window came the salt air of the ocean. She was, she supposed, going to visit Kathleen and John.

John was in his robe when he answered the door. He looked at Allegra a little narrowly, but whatever else, she was at least sober.

"Kathleen's already in bed, I'm afraid," he said. "Will you have a nightcap?"

"Yes, please," she said. She followed him into the living room, and watched his broad, assured back bending over the bottles. "I've found Alice and Albert."

"Have you, now?" He finished his pouring, and handed her a glass. "Still alive, are they?"

"You said," she said, "that you didn't remember them."

"I don't believe," he said, "that I actually said that."

"Well." Whether John had lied, or by how much, was small potatoes here. "They're living in West L.A., five children and twelve grandchildren. They told me about my mother."

"Mm." John sat down, and for the first time that she had ever seen, rubbed at his temples. "Empty-headed girl, Alice, I never knew what your mother saw in her. Good-humored, I guess. What did they tell you?"

"They told me." Allegra stopped, and looked at John through her lashes, a last hope suddenly springing. So many people had told Allegra so many things; and after all, she did not know Alice or Albert at all. "They told me," she said, "that my mother had what was more or less an affair, with an ordained priest. A priest, John. And they told me that because of what she led him into, the priest may well have killed himself. Which I seem to remember as being a mortal sin. Which—if she really did do what they said—would have been absolutely her fault."

"Mm," said John. "And are you happy now that you know?"

And the weight that she knew she would carry for the rest of her life dropped, settled, and made itself comfortable on Allegra's heart.

She sat down herself, on the chair opposite his, and both sipped for a while in silence at their whiskeys.

"Theresa was weak," he said, at last. "We all loved her—no, that's wrong. We didn't just love her, we adored her. I'm sure Alice told you our family had had a bad time back there—yes, I thought she would—and when Theresa came along, it was right when the business was getting off the ground, we had a bit of money to spare and life was looking brighter all around, and all of a sudden, there was this little, laughing girl, who just seemed to be sent from heaven to make us all happy. God, we loved her. I guess we spoiled her. Father loved to buy her gifts—I remember there was a black doll, with woolly hair, you don't see black dolls anymore for some reason. She loved that doll. Jemima, I wonder what happened to it? But it wasn't just Father, she had me wrapped around her finger, of course, and even Robert doted on her. Alice told you about Robert, I'm sure? Yes, so now you know about him too. But he worshiped your mother. We all did—you would have too. Such a sweet little thing she was, pretty, and happy, and funny too, she used to love to make us all laugh. I often wonder if she knows her daughter's a comic."

"She did a terrible thing," said Allegra. "The thing that she did was, truly, terrible."

"She paid for it," said John. "My poor sister paid."

"She led a man to suicide," said Allegra. "She was a bad woman."

"She was a weak woman," said John. "And yes, she was a spoiled woman, and that's a burden of guilt we all have to bear who helped to spoil her. And whatever sins she may or may not have committed, she paid the price for them."

"What price?" said Allegra. "Living in Chicago with a good man she happened not to love, and a silver fur coat to help her through the winters—that was the price for a man's soul?"

"You weren't supposed to grow up in Chicago, you know," said John. "You were supposed to live out here. Father was going to cut Ignatius into the family firm—he had a lot of time for Ignatius, we all did—and he was to move to California. Theresa didn't want to go to the Midwest, she hated the cold, and her job and all her friends were in Los Angeles; and Ignatius, well, he just wanted to be where Theresa was. They even had a house picked out, a nice place, just a few blocks from here. I drive past it every morning on my way to the office, it's divided into apartments now. But of course, after what happened, there was no question of their staying. Ignatius was to give in his notice the very same week Malcolm died. Lucky he hadn't already given it; if you can call it luck."

"I wouldn't," said Allegra. "Dad was a good man, he deserved a good woman. Not—that."

"He loved her very much," said John. "People did love your mother, she had some extraordinary qualities."

"Not decency," said Allegra. "Not integrity, not goodness. John, she was worse than a murderer."

"That's for God to say, not you or me. All I know is that Ignatius loved her."

"Then he was a fool."

"No," said John. "No, Ignatius was never a fool. He took his family responsibilities very seriously. I know he was always concerned not to spoil *you,* in particular . . . but I never saw he need worry about that. You have more of a head on your shoulders than poor Theresa ever did, the O'Riordan in you, I guess. It certainly doesn't seem to be the Higgins part. It was difficult for him, raising you three all alone like that. I wanted him to move back to Los Angeles, people's memories are short, and Kathleen could have helped with the children. You could have grown up beach bums like my boy. But he'd never move here. I guess it reminded him too much of Theresa."

"I forbade him," said Kathleen's voice. Allegra jumped, and turned. Her aunt was standing in the doorway, wearing a pink bathrobe, her face without makeup crumpled and blurred, a glass of water in her hand. She smiled, kindly, at Allegra. "My dear," she said, "your family were trouble. Everyone knew it then, if they've forgotten it now. I married the only good one, it took him a long, long time to convince me, and all the time I was carrying Jimmy, I prayed day and night that he would be like my family, not yours. Thank God, my prayers were answered: he's pure Murphy. Dear, every time your uncle suggested to your father that he move to Los Angeles, I would call him later, when I was alone, and forbid him to come. I was sorry for you three little ones left on your own, but you were all half Higgins, and I was not prepared to run the risk of another little Theresa, or God forbid, a little Robert, anywhere near my son. John's right, Allegra, there is a lot of the O'Riordan in you, and you must thank God for that. And as John's niece, and as your poor father's daughter, you're always welcome in my home. But your mother was a bad woman, as I think you're beginning to understand. She was a bad woman from a bad family, who caused trouble wherever she went. And by the way, I must ask you never, ever again to suggest to me that my Jimmy looks or acts in any way like any one of the Higgins family. John dear, don't forget to turn out the lights when you come up."

Allegra watched her go, blinking; then turned to John. But he turned away.

"She's tired," he said. "We go to bed early these days. I knew she used to call Ignatius—his number would show up on the telephone bill—but I figured if she ever wanted to tell me why, she would. I would have thought, maybe, a little more charity . . . Still, there's the mother's instinct too. Kathleen's a mother in a million. Well, I guess you'll want to be on your way, it's late. Are you OK to drive? . . . Yes, good girl. You'll call us tomorrow, and come to dinner soon. Jimmy's gone back to Santa Barbara, and we old folk get lonely. I'll see you to your car."

At the front door, he stopped.

"I tried not to tell you," he said. "But you had to know."

"Yes," Allegra agreed. "I had to know."

"And do you feel better for knowing?" he asked.

"No," said Allegra. "No, I don't."

"No," he said. "I shouldn't think you do. But the Church says we must forgive each other, seven times seven, times seven. And whatever her sin, I know that Theresa paid the price."

"What about Malcolm?" said Allegra. "Did she pay enough for him too?"

"You'd have to ask Father Carroll about that."

"Father Carroll . . ." began Allegra, reflexively. But he was not after all a bastard, nor a prick or a shit, or if he was, it was not for the reasons she had been calling him one.

"He's a fine priest," said John. "And has more compassion than you give him credit for. You just might try it sometime, talking to a priest of your own faith. You might get a pleasant surprise. Or maybe you already have a priest of your own to go to?"

"Not the way my mother did," said Allegra.

John sighed. "Seven times seven, times seven," he said. "You're going to have to forgive your mother."

"Did my mother ever forgive herself?" said Allegra.

"No," said John. "No, she didn't."

"Then who am I," said Allegra, "to presume to know better than she did?"

John started to speak, then stopped. "They were fond of each other," he said, at last. "Your mother and Malcolm. You might re-member that, sometimes." He presented his cheek, and gave her once again that clumsy half-pat on the back. "Very fond," he repeated.

Allegra walked away from the solid house, passed under the magnolia trees, climbed into her car, and drove off. When she came to the main road, she turned not left, in the direction of Melissa's apartment, but right, to the bottom of the shallow hill, where the streetlights at last ran out, and all there was was white sand and the whiter lacy foam of the ocean, the moon reflected a rippling round in its inky waters. She parked the car, got out, and sat alone on the pale, cold sand.

So that, then, was who Allegra was, and that, now that all her questions were answered, was her family. A bad lot, so bred-in-the-bone wrong, that Kathleen—yes, decorous bland Kathleen—had refused to have them grow up near her son. A fierce old gypsy woman and her bastard son made good; his mousy wife, his good-for-nothing, possibly felonious heir, whose death had come as a relief to all. And Theresa. And what, after all Allegra's hopes and her imaginings, what a disappointment, what a cruel joke on herself, this Theresa Higgins, this black-and-white girl, this mother of hers, had at last revealed herself to be. Poor soul, Alice had called her with careless patronage, remembering her pretensions and social climbing, her pretty frocks and her irritating cigarette holder, Alice safe among her family, her five children and twelve grandchildren, who all knew their place in this world and the next, Alice whose life was more than twice as long as Theresa's. But no: Allegra shook her head, resisting the temptation to let her mind roam toward envy for Alice. Theresa had been not simply a poor soul: she had been not only a spoiled child, weak and silly and pretentious, not merely a regular little snob who for all her posturings had come to no good in the end. Theresa had been a bad soul. Theresa had been a bad woman.

Because Father Carroll had been right after all: a sin was a sin, and may God indeed in His goodness have mercy on the soul of Theresa Higgins, who had sinned in a way Allegra, with her missed Masses and her unmarried unvirginity, could not conceive of sinning, had sinned in a way that was black, and knowing, and given who she had been and the time she had been in, unquestionably mortal. Allegra sat, alone, on the timeless beach, on the very grains of sand, it was possible, where all those years ago on that sunny summer's day the sin had started, and stared at the impassive ocean, trying to work her mind around the sheer scope of her mother's sinfulness.

Theresa had seduced a holy man. She had, first, paraded the charms of her companionship, had lured him with the easy laughter which, it seemed, was a part of her legacy to her daughter, and then, quite deliberately, had flaunted her curving young flesh, to arouse the lustful desires of one of God's chosen and consecrated; desires he had quite specifically forsworn, desires which, when they rose, as they must, to answer Theresa's call, he had no earthly notion of what to do with. She had sinned for herself by tempting him; and then—since it was altogether clear that, whether bodily consummated or not, the sin had been committed in the hearts of both—she had sinned for him by leading him into her own sin.

Nor—and Allegra, daughter of upright Ignatius, shook her head in wonderment at the curlicued intricacies of her other parent's disgrace—had that been the end of it. It was altogether possible—even John had not denied it—yes, it was more than possible, it was likely, it was probable, that through that first, terrible sin of the body, the black-and-white girl had led her fellow sinner to one still worse, to a sin of the soul, to the one act agreed by all to be contrary to God's will and the human condition both, the most terrible, least natural, most unforgivable of all. It may very well have been that Theresa had led her fellow human to ruin, not only in this world but in the next. Sin upon sin upon sin upon sin, dear God.

Theresa, thought Allegra, deserved to go to hell. She deserved, thought Allegra, the kindly modern Democrat whom the Church called a sinner and who did not herself believe in judgment, the worst and the harshest punishment of all. To be so thoughtlessly wicked, so wantonly destructive; to stumble so lightly into wickedness herself, and then to lure another to follow her, yes, hell, or whatever stood for it in that unknowable world beyond this, hell and for all eternity was what the black-and-white girl deserved, if any did. Allegra hoped she was there; she thought she must be there.

But no. Allegra, who did not accept the Church's ruling on sin, clicked her teeth in irritation at the Church's promise of salvation. The Church preached that if you sinned and repented, then no matter what you had done, by your repentance you would be saved. And Theresa had repented at least. Oh, she had repented, John had said she had, and the photographs had borne him out: she was repenting, quite probably, yes, silly, sinful soul that she was, for all the days and the hours of the few remaining years of her life. No, Theresa would not have gone to hell: the Church had her covered. Well done, Theresa.

But if Theresa was saved, what then about Malcolm? What about his soul, the poor, confused, too-human priest? Malcolm, sinning once, and then sinning again, the second sin a direct result of the first, and that second sin the very sin which, committed in this life, by its nature all too probably precluded redemption in the next—what after his death had become of Malcolm? Would he at the last have achieved repentance? Would he, before he died, however he died, have managed in his life's last glimmerings an Act of Contrition to save himself from hell? Or would he have gone, still in the state to which Theresa had led him, to enter his afterlife with all the weight of both their sins heavy on his soul? And if he had, if he was, alone, paying the price for them both, then where was the gleam of sense or the shred of justice in that? The pinpoint stars in the black sky seemed to look at each other, and raise their eyes, Declan-like, at the fatuity of her question.

Well. She must be congratulated. She had done what she set out to do. She had fought the mist until at last it had cleared, revealing the demons in all their clarity; she had asked the question, and asked and asked it again, until at last she had got an answer. And this was the answer she had got. Allegra shivered, and cast her eyes up from the unknowable ocean, to the inky black sky above. Where, at last, did that leave her? Furiously, she turned to M.M., who had insisted that she needed to find out these things; furiously, she demanded to know, now that she had at last acquired the knowledge, what on earth was she supposed to do with it, how could she hope ever to fit it in with her picture of the world, and herself, and what was right and what was wrong? But M.M., daughter of kindly Mrs. McConnell, had been silent all evening, baffled and shocked beyond words.

It was Nick who replied to her, across the continent and the weeks of their separation. Rather, it was Nick who was too polite to reply. He simply looked at her, as he had looked on that last Sunday, and, Well, she could hear him thinking, what a story! And then, Yes, that would be Allegra's mother, that would be who she gets her sense of humor from, and yes, Allegra always did enjoy telling a tale herself, it's in the genes, I guess, and I never said anything, but I always found it just a little disturbing how easily she was able to come up with all those lies she used in her act, yes, that would be the sort of person who produced Allegra, yes, that would explain much of it. It's just as well, he added to himself, that I got out when I did, because who knew when—and good Lord, in what form—those genes would really start to show themselves?

She sat on, alone with Nick, for what might have been ten minutes or an hour and ten, then got up, climbed into the car, and drove back to Melissa's apartment.

A light still shone in Scott's window, he was up late writing, or maybe even waiting for her, but Allegra did not stop there: her story was not for such as Scott. Instead, she drove past the building, down the hill, two blocks down, and three traffic lights east, and found herself, as she had known all along that she would, pulling into Bruno's.

As soon as she walked in, she knew too that she had known she would find him there. He was sitting alone at the bar, slumped a little, and looking gloomy. She had forgotten how plump he was: almost fat. Not like an Angeleno at all. She slid onto the stool beside him.

"Francis Xavier Bernard Farrell," she said.

He looked up at her, and his face lightened.

"Allegra Mary Catherine Theresa O'Riordan."

"Theresa Catherine."

He shot himself in the head with a finger.

"You remembered mine," he said.

"Yours is easier," she told him. "But you can buy me a drink. You spend a lot of time here, don't you?"

"Seems that way right now. You just missed your cousin."

"I thought he'd gone back to Santa Barbara." Santa Barbara. The pretty city up the coast, named for the saint who was a saint no longer, where once her mother, in a yellow dress with daisies on it, had demanded or pleaded of Alice whether those feelings that God had given her to feel could really be so terrible as they indeed proved themselves to be.

"He just left. Said you guys had been to a funeral today."

"Oh, did he." Jimmy, it seemed, was free with other people's business, at least. But the funeral—what endless aeons ago it did now seem—was no secret, after all. "It was an old lady who worked at Peppercorn's. Helen Viner, did you know her?"

He shook his head. "Not from around here."

"No?" But she had not the space in her mind just then to place the question of where, then, he was from, and why he sat alone, night after night, getting fat in Bruno's. "You know what?" she said. "They say it's always better to know something than not to know, don't they? Well, what if there's something you want to know, and you try every which way to find out, and then in the end you do find out, and what you find out is much, much worse than anything you'd ever imagined?"

"Huh." He considered, seeming not to find the question surprising. Another Jesuit boy, she noted, vaguely. "I guess," he offered, at last, "you could try to remember why you wanted to find out in the first place."

"I don't think I ever knew that either." She paused, waiting for someone in her mind to remind her. But no reminder came. "I guess I just wanted to know."

"You were like Eve, then."

"What? Oh." Eve, the first questioner, who had bitten so greedily into the forbidden fruit of the one tree of knowledge, and in doing so had caused the loss of the entire garden. "Thank you very much, I've just created original sin."

"And the occasion for greater virtue by overcoming it."

"Right. Thanks, Eve, we owe you one." She slurped at the whiskey that had appeared in front of her: she had forgotten how comfortable she felt with this Catholic man. "Listen, remember last time, I told you about that bastard of a priest who told me my mother was a sinner?"

"Uh-huh."

"Well." Well. If the story was not for Scott, it had Francis Xavier Bernard Farrell's name stamped all over it. "Well, at the funeral we went to—that is, through the funeral, it's a long story, and anyway, it's not important anymore—through the funeral, I met a couple this evening who were friends of my mother's when they were all young." So young, so long ago, so very far from innocent. "And they told me what she did, my mother, the sin she committed. And. And it was." She stopped, sipped again at the drink. "It was terrible. Yes. Terrible. What my mother did."

"Oh, God," he said. "I'm sorry."

"A big sin," she said. "A terrible sin. Yes."

"Oh, Jesus."

"Yes."

He did not ask her what the sin was, for which she was grateful.

"Is there anything you can do?" he asked. "To make anything less sinful?"

"I don't think so." She thought. No reparable harm had been done to anyone: Malcolm could not be brought back to life or his sin undone, and even supposing there existed, somewhere outside the universe, an ear that might hear Allegra's prayers, it was too late by forty years to affect the situations in the eternal afterworld of her mother or of Malcolm. "It'd make it much easier if there was, wouldn't it?"

He nodded. "I'm sorry," he said, again. "It must be rough."

"I suppose it must be. To tell you the truth, I haven't really taken it in yet."

He nodded again.

"Where's Clonakilty?" she asked.

"West Cork."

She had been to Ireland when she traveled around Europe the summer after she graduated from college, and probably had been to West Cork too, although she did not remember Clonakilty. Father Carroll was from somewhere in Cork: she would ask him about the place where her mother's mother's mother had come from. Be he bastard or not, she would ask him many things, now that she knew what she was asking about, away from the Sullivans and their bright barbecues. She would ask him about sinning and sinners; she would ask him about Joe Higgins; she might even ask him about those cousins, Robert's bastard offspring, at whose existence Alice had hinted. Oh, and Alice and Albert, she would see them again and again, and John too; since the secret was lifted, she would be able now to ask him questions, which he would now be able to answer. And maybe, one day, if she asked long enough and thought fiercely enough, she would be able to decide what to do with the sad and the terrible knowledge that now lay stifling on her soul and her heart. One day. Maybe.

"I'll have to stick around here for a while," she said.

"That's good," he said. "For me, I mean, I'd like to see you again. If you'd like."

Oh, yes? Those prickles of masculine cloth catching once more in her throat.

"Only for a while," she said. "Then I go back home. To Chicago. Where I live."

"I know that," he said. He looked down into his drink, and she could see his cheeks redden. "I don't know if that's what you were asking, but when I say I'd like to see you again, I really only mean as a friend."

"Oh." But he had not seemed (across the continent, Ron hooted, and clutched at Mike for support) to be gay.

"Yeah. Do you mind me saying that? You're not offended, are you?"

"No, of course not."

"I mean, you're very nice and everything, and pretty too, but . . ."

"You're digging yourself a hole, Francis Xavier."

"Am I?" He laughed, a little shyly. "You see, I'm a little out of the male-female thing, and I don't quite know the rules." He reddened further, and grimaced, looking suddenly young. "Until quite recently, you see, it didn't involve me."

"I thought you said you hadn't been married."

"I haven't. I was a transubstantiator."

"A what?"

"Transubstantiator. You made the word up, last time. A priest."

A priest.

"Oh, my God," she said.

A priest. One of God's consecrated; one who could work miracles; one such as Theresa Higgins had led to ruin.

"Oh, my God," she repeated.

"You didn't laugh," he said. "Some people laugh. Not when you're in it, they don't laugh then. But when you're out, well, it's a bit like being an undertaker, or a taxidermist. I'm glad you didn't laugh."

He was a priest. No, he was a former priest. And Allegra had more of a head on her shoulders than Theresa ever had; John had said so. But he had been a priest.

"Why did you leave?" she said.

"What was your mother's sin?" he retorted.

"Sorry."

"I'll tell you one day," he said. "Maybe. It wasn't for any of the reasons you might think. And I didn't leave either. I was asked to go."

"So you're a spoiled priest," she said. A spoiled priest, a term from the convent, if ever there was one. He had been spoiled, like Theresa Higgins. She laughed now, a little shrilly. "I always loved the sound of that when I was a kid. I used to think of overripe fruits, lying in the sun and crawling with flies."

"Thank you," he said.

"Sorry," she said again.

He smiled a little, forgiving her.

"I prefer to think of myself as a former transubstantiator," he said.

"I really like that word, you know."

A former transubstantiator. A man who had once held the highest power not man but God can confer; who had held it, and for whatever reason, had lost it, now, forever.

"That must be hard," she said.

"It is," he said. "Oh boy, yes. It is."

"Buy you a drink?" she said. "For the road?"

"OK."

When the drinks arrived, he lifted his glass to her.

"May the road rise before you," he said, "may the wind be at your back, and may God hold you in the hollow of His hand."

"Thank you," she said. "How many Irishmen does it take to change a lightbulb?"

"How many?"

"Twelve. One to put in the new bulb. And eleven to sing songs about the old."

They sat together, the son of Adam and the daughter of Eve, the spoiled priest and the mortal sinner's daughter, drinking their whiskey, their elbows touching in comradeship, looking into the ravaged, trodden wasteyards of their souls, and wondering how, through the stones, and the rubble, and the shards of broken pottery, they might coax the roses to grow.